A Shadow's Tale

A Shadow's Tale

Jennifer Hanlon

OUR STREET
BOOKS

Winchester, UK
Washington, USA

First published by Our Street Books, 2014
Our Street Books is an imprint of John Hunt Publishing Ltd., Laurel House, Station Approach,
Alresford, Hants, SO24 9JH, UK
office1@jhpbooks.net
www.johnhuntpublishing.com
www.ourstreet-books.com

For distributor details and how to order please visit the 'Ordering' section on our website.

Text copyright: Jennifer Hanlon 2013

ISBN: 978 1 78279 136 2

A CIP catalogue record for this book is available from the British Library.

Design: Stuart Davies

Printed and bound by CPI Group (UK) Ltd, Croydon, CR0 4YY

We operate a distinctive and ethical publishing philosophy in all
areas of our business, from our global network of authors to
production and worldwide distribution.

CONTENTS

To everyone who made this possible.
You know who you are.

Acknowledgements

To the people of MC: CopynPaste, Gabriel, Manticora, Gryffindorgal4ever and Gryffindor_Gal_Filly, Pickles. A lot of Shadow's life was played out on various role play forums with you guys. I'm sure you'll recognise several pieces! Putting this together wouldn't have been possible without you.

To my friends: Alba, Astrid, Joanna, Hannah, Lucy and Bart, for putting up with proofreading, having to tell me when things don't make sense and just generally accepting that I'm more than a little insane. You're all amazing.

To my family, for being supportive of many kinds of madness, and my especially my mother for correcting a lot of my grammar and reality issues.

And finally, to the staff of John Hunt Publishing for their patience and for taking a chance with a new author.

Watch out for more tales from the clan coming soon!

Prologue

Stones scattered under my feet as I scrambled up the mountain. They were getting closer now, closer than ever. The hooves of their mounts clattered on the rocky surface as they leapt after me. My skirt tangled around my legs, slowing me down. I tore the material with my claws, tossing it to the side, running in the leggings I wore underneath. My breath came in ragged pants. No matter how much magic I used to aid my race, no matter how fast I ran, the City Guards were gaining on me. I turned sharply, hoping to throw them off. No such luck.

I broke out of the forest onto the summit of the mountain itself, skidding to a halt on the edge of the cliff, looking down, my chest heaving. The edge of the dimension. The only thing down there was the void. An expanse of nothing that claimed the souls of the dead, isolating them for eternity. Arellan was down there somewhere. I could only hope that Karthragan was there as well. Glancing back over my shoulder, I could see the City Guard getting closer, their mounts slowing a little to negotiate the tricky terrain, stopping just on the edge of the trees.

'Halt there, Shadow! You are under arrest!' called out one of the guards.

'Not in your life,' I muttered, taking another step towards the edge of the cliff. They wouldn't come this far out to get me, no matter how much High Priestess Arias wanted me caught. The fragile ground beneath my feet began to crumble a little. I narrowed my eyes at the guards. If I decided to jump, would they try to catch me? If I let them catch me, what would my future hold? Either way, I lost. Either I died, or I died. Well, screw that! Closing my eyes, I took another step back, a step into nothingness, and started falling.

* * *

I wasn't always called Shadow. I was born as Alexai Roth, *Angel's Blood*, in the language of my home. And my home was Synairn, another dimension to this one. I remember everything.

PART 1

SYNAIRN

My mother held me close as she stood next to the picture windows of her room, looking out over the city, only a few hours after my birth, looking out over the city-dimension of Synairn. In my memories, I thought her beautiful, a delicate face, her kind, blue eyes full of love. Her name was Arellan. Later on, I would learn that she was also known as the Messenger Angel.

'My Alexai,' she murmured to me. I cuddled closer to her, chewing on the end of her plait. She smiled gently at me, pulling her hair from my grasp. She stepped closer to the window, close enough for me to see the child reflected back at me. A shock of black hair, mixed with a single streak of white, contrasted with a pale face as bright blue eyes stared back at me. I reached out a hand to touch this strange child. My fingers touched cool glass. Slightly disappointed, I looked at the city for the first time. Towers made of pale stone, seamless and elegant, seemed to go on forever before giving away to plains of silvery grass, then mountains that ringed the edge of the city-dimension. The Deas Mountains. Beyond these mountains, there was nothing. The dimension ended there.

'Look!' Arellan breathed, pointing to a black speck against the pale violet sky. It grew larger and larger before sweeping past the window, all wings, legs and equine majesty.

'It is called a pegasus,' Arellan told me, 'the most beautiful creatures I have ever seen.'

'Arellan!'

The door crashed open. A man strode in with thunder on his face and determination in his heart. White robes swirled around him. A thin blade glinted in his hand. He kept the weapon pointed towards the floor, present but unthreatening. He held out his other hand to Arellan, his face set in an unforgiving expression.

'Give me the child, Arellan!' he ordered. My mother didn't back down. Holding me close to her chest, she raised her own hand, summoning her magic. The white light flashed in her narrowed eyes, ready to fight. She looked like an avenging angel, prepared to defend her beliefs.

'No,' she said firmly. Everything in her tone dared the man to challenge her. He looked set to argue, the sword trembling in his hand, but sighed, relenting. He sheathed the sword in the scabbard at his hip with a heavy sigh. He rubbed his temples, as if he had a headache. I watched him, curiosity filling my mind. It was an odd sensation. I tilted my head to one side, my eyes following his agitated movements.

'I can't fight you, Arellan. You know that. But please, for your own sake, give up the child before it becomes too powerful!'

'We can control her, Armen! The Scriptures prove that! Half bloods are capable of being in control!

'Arellan, please! No matter how much training you give her, she will always be evil in her soul and there is nothing we can do about that. The Senate is already up in arms about her being allowed to live this long.' He sighed heavily, his shoulders falling. The look on Arellan's face meant that she wasn't going to back down from her decision. 'You will be called to stand before the Senate. Be aware of that. Be prepared.' He saluted formally to my mother, the three middle fingers of his right hand pressed between his eyebrows before he turned and left the room, his white robes billowing out behind him. Arellan looked down at me. Her heart felt love, but her mind was filled with worry. A little confused, I slipped into a peaceful slumber, unaware of what the rest of my life would bring.

Two weeks later, we stood in front of the Senate. I knew that Synari children grew quickly before slowing down around the age of twelve where they would be almost adult in physical form.

It had been a survival trait born long ago when the Synari died quickly and easily and the trait had never been discarded. Only those who grew up fast had been able to evade the predators until they learned how to fight and how to stay alive. I was growing too fast, even by their standards. I knew that. I was able to walk after only a few days. I could read the simple version of the Synari runite language not long after that. At only two weeks old, I looked closer to two years. It worried Arellan. I could sense it. I didn't know how or why, I simply knew.

The Synari, as a magical race, needs stability. Every Synari, even from the youngest age, can feel the emotions of others and have an advanced level of telepathy. The most powerful among the Synari wield a form of pure, physical magic that can be manipulated so as to be used as telekinesis, transport or even as a weapon. For this reason, the Synari has the Senate: one hundred Synari and one hundred of the winged humanoid race known as the Careen that cohabit the dimension with them. The Senate is headed by the High Priestess – High Priestess Arias. They enforce the notion of pacifism in the dimension and encourage the pursuit of knowledge. The closest thing they have to an army was the pegusi-mounted City Guard, who are the basic equivalent of the police. The Senate work and live in the extensive and elaborate towers connected by walkways, known as the Senate Towers. That was where I had been living for the last two weeks and where I now stood, staring up at the great doors that led into the Senate Chambers, the room where they all met, where all the biggest decisions were taken. I looked up at the great double doors in awe, looking at the intricate carvings in the wood. Arellan was fussing over me, smoothing my unruly hair and straightening my cloak. A foot guard stood in front of the door, waiting for a signal that only he would understand. He turned, opening the doors, gesturing to us to go through. As I passed him, I heard him murmur a few words.

'May Arias have mercy on you, little one. No one else will.'

The doors closed with a final thud. Trapped.

Sitting in the stands around us, two hundred and two sets of eyes stared at me. I shrank closer to Arellan, trying to hide from their unkind, unsympathetic gazes, wrapping myself in Arellan's white cloak. She tried to conceal her smile as she bent down, untangling me from my hiding place. Only then did she formally salute an old woman in silver robes who stood out against the sea of white.

'High Priestess,' she said respectfully. My mother's voice echoed eerily in the silent, circular chamber.

'Senator Arellan,' replied the High Priestess. I glanced up at my mother. *Senator* Arellan? My mother was a member of the Senate, one of the hundred most powerful Synari in the dimension? I desperately wanted to ask her about it, but then remembered that Arellan had warned me not to say a word unless asked a question in the Senate Chambers. But the question itched at the back of my mind. My mother was a Senator? I swallowed hard, doing my best to ignore it.

'Senator Arellan, it is not normal for us to be confronted with one of our own number, but nor could we consider this to even be an approximation of a normal case. We are here to discuss the fate of the creature you brought into this world. A dangerous half blood. What would you have us do, Arellan Roth?'

'I would have you let her live,' Arellan replied clearly. A collective gasp ran through the assembled Senators. I gripped her hand tighter, unnerved by the hostility in the room. It seemed as if every senator glared at me, cruelty in their gazes as they judged me. I stepped closer to Arellan, pressing myself against her side. The feelings I was sensing from the gathered Senators could only be defined as hostile, something I was not yet accustomed to. It was unnerving.

'Can you explain this, Arellan?' asked one Senator.

Arellan turned her impassive face to the Senator who had spoken. I couldn't see her face, but I could feel her struggle to maintain her composure, to refrain from losing her temper and insulting the Senate for being so blind. When she spoke, she spoke clearly, in a level voice that seemed at odds with what her heart was feeling.

'It is common knowledge that the half bloods died out a long time ago, a notion enforced by themselves in order to spare themselves and their children the cursed burden their blood brings. However, this and the Half Demon Scriptures prove to us that they were in control. They were lucid. Why should Alexai be any different? We need only use the Scriptures to educate her properly.'

'Is it not true that some half bloods did lose control?' asked another Senator.

'The half bloods policed their own,' Arellan corrected. 'Those who lost control were rehabilitated or, failing which, executed.' As the last word left her throat, her voice threatened to break. Her fear of such an event happening was all too apparent for a moment before she managed to stamp down on her feelings. I was confused by her emotions, but I did recognise the fear. I reached up a hand to take hers, gazing up at her. She smiled slightly in reassurance, squeezing my hand before she turned her gaze back to the High Priestess. Arias sat back, her cold silver eyes raking over my mother and I as she judged us and Arellan's words.

'If the decision of the Senate was to let her live, what would you do to facilitate her life and keep our city safe?'

'I would ask for access to the Half Demon Scriptures so as to educate myself before being capable of educating Alexai.'

'And if the decision of the Senate was to destroy her?'

'I would fight you every step of the way.' Arellan's hand gripped mine tightly as she realised that her act of defiance could have disastrous consequences. Fear began to grip her heart again as Arias simply watched us, contemplating Arellan's words. I could almost hear my mother's heart beating faster, waiting for Arias's decision.

'We shall cast a vote; all in favour of the destruction of the half blood should show their colours now.'

With every spark of magic that touched the air, I felt Arellan's heart sink. I swallowed hard. At that age, everything that had been said had passed over my head. I was too young to understand that it was my life that was at stake. It wouldn't be until a year or so later that I would be mature enough to fully realise everything that had happened in that Senate chamber. For now, all I could understand that something very big was happening and that it was something to do with me. Whatever it was, given how angry everyone seemed, it wasn't good.

The vote had been cast. The secretary for the Senate was interpreting the results of the show of magic, turning it into the result that would determine whether I lived or died, even though I didn't know it at the time. I sensed Arellan's dreading anticipation as a piece of paper was handed to Arias. Her grip on my hand tightened, drawing me closer to her.

'The vote lies at 100 to 100. In this event, it is required of us to obey the laws laid down by the Senates who have ruled this dimension before us, which state that the child had the right to live.'

I heard Arellan sigh with relief. Her soul rejoiced as a heavy burden was lifted from her shoulders.

'However, Arellan,' Arias continued, 'I must insist that you hand the half blood over to the care of the Senate.' Arellan opened her mouth to argue back, but the High Priestess simply raised a finger. Arellan bowed her head obediently, remaining silent. 'I am not removing you from her life, Senator Arellan. I say this in the child's best interest. You know that the streets will never be safe for her to walk.'

The foot guard took me away as the Senate had things to discuss with Arellan that were not for me to hear. He escorted me with such a rapid stride that I had to run to keep up with him, moving swiftly through the corridors of the residential tower, with its long halls and winding staircases, where the walls were lined with doors. I played at trying to read the little plates on each door, but my grasp of the written language of the dimension wasn't strong enough to read the elaborately decorated letters. The footman pushed open a door at the end of a long corridor of blank doors. Roughly, he pushed me inside. I spun around, just catching a glimpse of a deep scowl on his face as he left, slamming the door behind him. For a moment, I stood and looked at the closed door, my head tilted to one side. Had I done something to anger him? If I had, then I didn't know what it was that I had done. Confused by his actions, I let my curiosity take over and began to explore the room. It was a room on the edge of the tower. Two of the walls were in fact a single arc and had the same picture windows as were in Arellan's room, allowing light to infuse the room with a soft glow. Bookshelves stood against another wall, a few books already at home there. The only other pieces of furniture in the room were a bed, a desk and a washstand. I stood in the centre, not knowing what to think about it. I wanted to explore, but my eyelids began to droop. The events of the day were beginning to take their toll on me. With a wide yawn, I crawled under the bed, curled up and went to sleep.

I awoke to see Arellan's face peering under the bed with a slightly concerned expression. She smiled as soon as she realized that I was awake. Yawning again, I crawled back out, rubbing the sleep from my eyes.

'Welcome back to the world of the living, little one,' she said, warmly. 'I brought you some *lia.*'

I took the sweet, chewable stick. It was by far one of my

favourite treats. The closest equivalent I have been able to find on Earth is a very solid stick of caramel. I scrambled up onto the bed to snuggle up to Arellan, happily gnawing on the sugary piece. I paused in my attack on the sweet as a question occurred to me. I looked up at my mother.

'Why did everyone call me a half blood?' I asked. Arellan didn't answer me straight away, but then sighed, reaching under her robes. She pulled out a heavy looking grimoire, bound in ancient dark leather. She opened the book to a place marked by a ribbon. I looked at the picture. I wanted to scream, to run, to rip out the page and tear it up. But I sat quietly. Transfixed. Flames flickered in the background of the image, tricking the eye to believe that they were real and dancing on the coloured plate. From out of the flames rose a pillar of black stone and, leaping off the pillar, was a creature of midnight nightmares. Four red eyes, one pair set above the other, stared out of the inferno, glaring out of the face of a gigantic black wolf. Its claws, glinting in the red light, were more like talons taken from a fearsome bird of prey, silver against the red. Its teeth, bared in a snarl of hatred and rage, showed teeth more akin to a sabre-toothed tiger than a wolf. Just below the picture, a caption had been written in flowing Synari runes. I struggled to decipher the writing, which was also written in the old speech: 'Karthragan, thee greate Principe of thee Darkness'.

'Mother?' I murmured, still unable to tear my eyes from the picture. 'What is that?'

Her fingertips gently touched the picture. 'That is your father, Alexai.'

Shock and rage flashed through me. I flung the book across the room, glaring after it with my fists clenched, daring it to show me that image again. It lay on the wooden floor, splayed open, with an air of injured innocence. 'No! That is *not* my father!' Arellan said nothing She stood up and retrieved the book, brushing it off and carefully placing it on one of the shelves. The evil book. The one that lies.

'I am sorry, Alexai, but that is your father. I swear it by the goddess.' She had to pause to compose herself as she sat down on the bed again. 'There was a prophecy, that the Messenger Angel would bear children to the Prince of Darkness. All of the oracles interpreted the prophecy with the Messenger Angel being a part demon and therefore dead along with the rest of her race. The followers of Karthragan, the Demon Hunters, tricked me into the ritual.' Her pale blue eyes searched mine, seeking some element of forgiveness or belief. I sat emotionless, staring at the book, feeling dread creep into my soul, one icy drop at a time. What was I going to become?

'That's why they called me half blood. That's why I'm dangerous.'

Arellan said nothing, reaching her arms around me to hug me close. 'I don't care. I will never let you go.'

As the days passed by, Arellan was forced to spend less and less time with me. Senate duties kept piling up, meaning that she had little time for me. I never thought much of it. She always tried to put aside time to come and see me while being profuse in her apologies when she could not. The High Priestess had assigned a few Senators to educate me as it was deemed too dangerous for me to attend school with the other children. My studies kept me too busy to worry about my mother or to look out over the city and wish that I was allowed to leave the confines of the Senate Towers. Armen was my favourite teacher. He treated me like a normal child, without the fear disguised as hatred of the other Senators. I wasn't allowed to leave the Senate Towers, so they became my playground. Armen taught me how to play like a normal child, playing hide and seek with me through the many corridors. But there was one. One who hated every fibre of my being. Who resented my life with all his soul. Meran. For many years, I didn't understand why. It wasn't the same fear-hatred I sensed from everyone else. This was deep-rooted. I was three years old when the first incident came to pass, when his hatred of me took a new form.

Meran was one of my tutors who, no matter how hard I tried to do things right, always found fault. That day, I had worked hard, learning to read and write with Armen. It was early in the evening, the pale violet sky outside my window turning to deeper shades of purple. Meran's lesson was the last one of the day. I was tired and looking forward to some food and curling up under my blankets. I blinked, trying hard to focus on the antidote to the certain substances that would become poisonous to me. The letters in the old book blurred with my exhaustion. It was complex, requiring exact amounts of each ingredients and precise timing. I added a Careen feather, concentrating hard on not doing anything wrong, on not warranting Meran's harsh words. I heard the subtle shift in his stature, the soft rustle of this robes as he prepared to lash out. I must have made a mistake! I scrambled to my feet, darting for cover. I didn't want to hear his words. I wanted to get away! I needed to get away! Sharp pain exploded across my back. Black blood had splattered in an arc across the floor. I fell forwards, landing heavily on the floor. Something in my mind snapped. Raw heat flooded through my muscles. Like a puppet with no will of its own, I got to my feet. I wasn't in control of anything! Everything I saw was tinted red. I saw more than before, in more detail. My head bowed, looking at my hand as if I had never seen one before. Meran cursed under his breath, backing away. My head snapped up to look at him. Fire flooded through my limbs. Darkness clouded my mind.

Waking up was difficult, as if sleep was a warm, heavy blanket that beckoned me back into its dark depths. But there was something else there. A presence close to me. I forced my eyes to open. For a moment, the bright light seared my eyes. My back erupted in pain as I struggled to sit up. A hand touched my shoulder, gently pushing me back down. I stifled a squeak. The High Priestess Arias! She was sitting right beside me! I quickly made a formal salute, but she waved it away.

'We are not standing on ceremony here,' she said. 'The Healers have informed me that they have done the best they can to aid your recovery, although they have alerted me to the fact that wounds inflicted by magic are more difficult to heal than others.' She sat back for a moment, observing me with a critical silver eye. 'When were you going to tell us about Meran? The Healers have told me that, while unconscious, you talked of his words to you. You appeared to have been quite distressed.'

I refused to look at Arias, turning my head to look at the wall. I hadn't planned on ever telling anyone. What Meran said to me held no consequence for the Synari. They had no need to know. Instead of answering Arias's question, I asked one of my own: 'What happened to me?'

'You underwent your first demonic crisis. The other half of your blood manifested itself. It was to be expected. You are of the average age for this to happen. You will need to be careful of what you feel in terms of emotions. Demonic magic is fuelled by strong emotion, and strong emotion will always leave you open to Demonic Possession. You will begin magical training as soon as I find a senator willing to take on the task. He or she will be able to explain this phenomenon in greater detail.' Arias stood up, marking the conversation as over, but just before she walked out of the room, she paused, one hand on the door frame. 'In light of this occurrence, the Senate found it fit to rename you. The Synari child known as Alexai is dead. You are a new being. A true hybrid. You will now be known as 'Shadow'. Rest well.'

For the next few days, no one dared come near my room apart from the elderly Careen who brought me food, and even she left as quickly as she could. Instead, I read. I devoured books with my eyes. Spell books, storybooks, even extracts from the Half Demon Scriptures. There was one book, however, that I refused to touch, that sat on my bookshelves and gathered dust. *Demons*. The book that held the picture of the creature that was my father. The silver glass in the corner of my room had been shattered. I had broken it in a fit of rage. I had caught my reflection one day, a changing girl. Even now, I can clearly remember the image that had been reflected back at me. My skin had turned a pale grey, my hair a mess of black and purple, the white streak the only thing that didn't change. My eyes were a mottled bruise of violet and blue, my teeth and nails lengthening. My senses became more acute, I became stronger. With each passing day, I looked less and less like Arellan, and therefore more and more like my father. More like a monster. It was that thought that had made me smash the silver glass so that I couldn't see the horror I was becoming.

Five days after the incident, Armen came to see me. He let out a quiet 'oof' as I jumped on him, hugging the Senator tightly, delighted to see him after my isolation. He smiled down at me with affection in his eyes. He ruffled my hair in a gesture of fondness.

'Come, little one, I have a little treat for you.'

He took me out into the city for the first time in my life. He had instructed me to keep the hood on my cloak over my head to hide my identity, but I didn't care. I allowed myself a moment of awe as I looked at the city from an entirely new angle. After living all of my short life within the tall Senate Towers, I hadn't realised how big the other towers of the city were. They looked tiny from my window, but now it was I who was dwarfed by their stature. Armen, amused by the look on my face issued me with a challenge: I wasn't to step on the cracks between the cobblestones. Gleefully, I jumped from one cobblestone to another, playing the game that generations of children had done before me. We reached the main street, weaving our way through the crowd to the front. I held on tightly to Armen's hand, a little unnerved by the press of people around me, yet another completely new experience. Rope had been strung between the buildings to create a barrier that stopped anyone from going into the main street, leaving a wide, clear passage. I tried to ask Armen what was happening, but he smiled and shushed me.

There was a commotion further down the line. I craned my neck to see further. Then I saw them. They always featured in my favourite books! The pegusi! Elegant equine bodies with their noble heads and slender legs completed by their giant feathered wings. A whole herd of them were charging down the cleared lane, heads tossing, muscles rippling beneath their gleaming velvet coats, a spectrum of colours from brown to orange to black to white. These were war pegusi, the mounts of the city guard. Smarter, stronger and faster than their domestic counterparts, they chose a single rider and would only take orders from them. They even shared a simple mental connection, able to feel what the other was feeling. I watched as one faltered in its stride, ears swivelling and sniffing the air. Its eye surveyed the children eager to get a closer look leaning on the makeshift fence. It took one hesitant step forwards. Then another. And another. It calmly clopped towards a delighted looking boy on the other side of the aisle. I felt a pang of jealousy and longing as he stroked the pegasus's nose. My fingers itched to stroke it too, wanting to feel if it was as soft as it looked.

'This is the Choosing,' Armen explained. 'They hold one every so often to recruit new people to the city guard. Whoever is chosen by a pegasus is drafted. Uh oh!' He pulled me back a little as a lone black pegasus, a giant even amongst the tallest of its kind, charged along the passage, zigzagging in the form of a creature driven mad. It crashed into the barrier not far from where I stood. I watched it admiringly. It was beautiful despite its wildness, a black so dark that the light glinted blue on its coat and feathers, long wings flaring. A spark of lucidity cleared its rolling eyes.

'Is it possible?' I heard Armen murmur distantly. The black pegasus stalked along the passage, sniffing at the people. A child reached out to stroke it, but the aristocratic creature snapped at him, sending the boy stumbling back. I squashed the tiny spark of hope. There was no chance that a being so beautiful would choose a filthy blooded half demon.

'Please, take me away from here,' I pleaded to Armen. The Senator must have sensed my distress. He took my hand and started to lead me away. A loud, braying shriek shattered the air. I dared sneak a look back over my shoulder. The black giant was watching me. Me! With a movement of personified grace, the pegasus unfurled its giant wings and soared over the barrier. It trotted towards me and lowered its head to nuzzle my hands. I smiled, limiting my emotion so as not to spark off any magic, reaching up to stroke her nose. On the collar around the top of its neck was inscribed its name. Merlas. I sneaked a look between her hind legs. A doe, a female pegasus. Armen put a hand on my shoulder.

'Congratulations,' he said quietly. He lifted me up to perch on her broad back. I suddenly felt a long way from the ground. Even though I had the physical form and height of a human seven-year-old, I had to stand on my toes and reach up in order to touch her shoulder. I leant forwards, running a hand down her neck, feeling the fine, soft hair beneath my fingers. She twisted her head round to nudge my foot, snorting quietly. I giggled, winding my fingers into her long mane, feeling the contrast between the coarse hair and her soft coat. Armen laid a hand on her neck and walked with me back to the building on the outskirts of the city where the pegusi lived.

The pegusi stables were two L-shaped blocks on the outskirts of the city, surrounded by fields. One block was reserved for the domestic pegusi, owned and ridden by those who were not bonded to a pegasus, and a second block for the war pegusi. The main difference between them was that the war pegusi block had no doors. Each stall had the pegasus's name written on it, but the pegusi themselves were allowed to roam free. I leaned against Merlas's reclining form, snuggled against her warm belly, thinking through what I know of the pegusi. Now that I was face to face with them, I realised that I didn't know much about them at all. Armen had explained to me the two different breeds of pegasus: the slender, delicate-looking carnivorous pegusi with their long, sharp canine teeth and dished faces and the heavier, sturdier herbivorous pegusi with their long hair from their knees to their hooves and big, expressive eyes. I nestled closer to Merlas, breathing in her scent, listening to Armen arguing with one of the carers, the people who looked after the pegusi.

'Senator Armen, you have to understand that we cannot accept a half blood amongst us. There is no way. It is too dangerous. The doe could give us so much more if we could get her to choose a different rider.'

'How long have you been waiting for her to choose a rider?'

'Ten years.'

'How many Choosings?'

'Forty and three.'

'If we separate her from Shadow, she will go back to her uncontrollable state. Do you really wish to return to that?'

I could sense the defeat coming from the carer as he spoke.

'No.'

'I do not mean to say that she should join the City Guard. Goddess knows, Arias would not allow it, but do not separate them. Merlas will calm down and Shadow will have a reason to try to keep herself under control now that our beloved High Priestess has forbidden her mother to see the child. For us, it makes the situation easier. The child keeps calm with the doe, and the doe becomes controllable. It appears to be what is known as a 'win-win' situation, no?'

'But sir—'

'Yane,' Armen's voice held a hint of warning. 'Merlas belongs to me. I agreed to let my own doe be used for that experiment, and it failed. Now, the two half bloods have found solace in each other and *you will not separate them.*'

'Yes, sir.'

That evening, I was burrowing under the blankets of my bed just as Armen opened the door. He chuckled, shaking his head. It was common knowledge to him that I only went to bed when I sensed him coming down the corridor to make sure I was not staying up too late into the night. Peeking my head out from under the covers to look at him, I smiled playfully. He ruffled my hair gently, perching on the bed, gently chiding me in the way that had become a customary part of the routine.

'How is Merlas a half-blood?' I asked, clutching a lock of coarse hair taken from the doe's mane tightly in my hands.

Armen sat on the end of the bed. 'I should have known you were listening. Merlas was, as I said, an experiment. A crossing between the two main breeds of pegusi. Can you tell me what they are?'

'The carnivore and the herbivore.'

'Yes. Merlas was born of a herbivore doe and a carnivore stag. In a sense, the experiment was a success. She eats both meat and herbage as well as developing a mixture of their physical traits. But she was strong. Stronger and bigger than the other pegusi. Her mother wanted nothing more to do with her filly, so the carers raised her. She quickly became uncontrollable, obviously a battle pegusi. It took three carers to do anything with her. The rest of the flock rejected her because she was a half blood.'

'Like me.'

'Like you.'

Armen left, leaving me alone in the dark. I waited a few seconds to make sure that he was out of earshot before scrambling out of bed. I didn't have very long, not if I wanted to escape. If I had enough time, I could get away. I could sense another presence, even though there was no one else living in this part of the Senate Towers. A malevolent presence that was all too familiar to me. My fingers fumbled with the catch on the window. I heard the door slide open. I whipped around. Meran. Just because he wasn't one of my teachers any more wasn't reason enough for him to leave me alone. It had never been reason enough for him not to haunt my mind and dreams, enough for him to stay away in the dead of night when he would project visions of blood and violence into my mind. It was too late to hide now. His eyes gleamed red in the light of the tiny orb of magic Armen had cast for me as a night light. The thought of my father scared me, but not as much as Meran did now. Meran was here and now. And he was dangerous. I backed up against the window, trying to plan a strategy in my mind. I heard him utter a spell, locking the door. There was no way out now.

He walked towards me lazily, as if savouring the terror that was starting to take a hold of my soul. I had to calm down. I couldn't afford to have an outburst now. I had to stay in control. I waited a few more seconds, waiting until he was nearly within an arm's reach of me. I ducked. I scrambled away from him, darting to the other side of the room. He growled in anger.

'You can't escape me, demon,' he snarled. 'I have waited too long for this.'

I waited for him to approach me again. If I managed to keep this up long enough, he would run out of time and be forced to leave. Unfortunately, he wasn't going to wait that long. A net of dark blue magic ensnared my ankle, anchoring me to the floor. I pulled against his hold. My magic started to spark in the air, uncontrollable. I didn't have the experience to harness its potential. He grabbed my arm, snapping a cuff of grey metal onto my wrist. I yelped in pain, wrenching my arm from his grasp. It burned as if I had stuck my arm into the very heart of a fire. The magic I couldn't control vanished. I had nothing to fight with. No way to defend myself.

Meran sneered to himself as the full weight of the situation became clear to me. I doubled my efforts to break free from his magic, but I felt so much weaker with the strange metal. Tears were starting to gather in my eyes. He grabbed a fistful of my hair before pulling a slender vial from his belt. He pulled out the stopper with his teeth. I tried to twist out of his grasp as the smell hit me. It was acidic, sickly sweet. It promised pain. Every fibre of my being screamed at me to get away from it. Meran sniffed the clear liquid with an air of appreciation.

'Holy water, straight from the temple of the goddess. Perfectly harmless to most races, but deadly to creatures of the underworld. I am finished playing with you, spawn of evil. Arellan would have been bonded to me if it hadn't been for your untimely arrival, but I shall now do her a favour. It is time this world was cleansed from this darkness.' He pulled sharply on my hair. I gasped in pain. He emptied the vial into my open mouth before clamping it shut and pinching my nose closed. Desperation rose in my soul as I struggled to pull my head from his grasp. Swallow or breathe? I had to breathe. The poison burned like its acidic smell. It pooled in the pit of my stomach before spreading out through my muscles. My legs gave out beneath me. I curled up into the tightest ball I could manage. I wanted to scream, to alert someone that there was something wrong, but I didn't want to give him the satisfaction of hearing the culmination of the pain I felt. The burning shot up my spine, igniting a flame in the base of my skull. I couldn't hold it back any more. I opened my mouth and screamed, only to find my voice muffled by a bundle of cloth. Tears streamed down my face. I glanced at the door, praying for someone to come through it to save me. Meran's cruel laugh echoed through my mind

'No one is coming for you, half blood. No one cares. No one ever cared for a demon.'

Through the darkness of despair, pain and anguish, a wave of calm descended. A motherly warmth. My eyelids drooped, half closed. I exhaled a long sigh, my mind floating above my body. New sensations overruled the agony. The heat of the sun on my back. The rush of wind on my face. The sound of rain on the roof as I lay snug and warm indoors. Feather light caresses. I sighed softly, letting myself fall into the touch. It curled itself around me like a fuzzy blanket, reassuring and comforting. I surrendered myself to it.

Something started hammering on the door, breaking me out of my mental escape. Pain slammed back into my body with the force of a flock of enraged pegusi. Meran smirked, murmuring into my ear that no one could get past his spell. My stomach was twisting itself into knots. My chest burned with every breath I struggled to take. A bitter, metallic taste had gathered in my mouth, my vision tinted red as blood trickled in the place of tears.

Silver light flooded the room, almost blinding me in its intensity. Meran scrambled away. Someone shouted my name. I screamed for help but the cloth muffled the sound once more. I began to cough. More blood dripped from the corner of my mouth as the cloth was taken away. Panicked voices erupted around me. I screamed in agony as another wave of pain slammed into me. Something pinned my shoulders to the ground. Cool glass touched my lips. I tried to spit out this new liquid but to no avail. It froze its passage down my throat to pool in my stomach. Darkness descended like a thick blanket.

My gasp of pain echoed strangely as I awoke. My muscles pulsed, aching and burning with magic desperate to escape. The more I struggled to restrain it, the more it fought to escape. I had to let it go. I relinquished all semblance of control. It tore away from me, great talons ripping through me, white-hot claws raking through my skin. I don't know how long it lasted. The black energy poured from my body like a river bursts through the dam. Eventually it slowed to a trickle. Then it stopped. My throat was raw from screaming, my mind was burning and my body a song of aches. Someone laid a cloak over me, blanketing me in its warmth. My tired eyes closed and I soon dropped into a sleep so encompassing as to be the eternal sleep.

I awoke again slowly, trying to piece together what had happened. It remained elusive. Every muscle and joint throbbed. My head felt as if someone was using it as an anvil. Even my hair seemed to hurt. I tried to remember what had happened, why I wasn't in my room any more. Why I was lying on the earthen floor of a great cavern whose walls were blackened and burned. A solid looking door marked the only way out. I remembered reading about something like this, a cavern deep under the Senate Towers where they brought people who couldn't control their magic. I got to my feet, clutching the cloak around my shoulders.

'Hello?' I called out. 'Is there anyone there?'

The door opened to reveal Armen. He gathered me up in his arms, hugging me close, pressing his face into my hair as if he couldn't bring himself to believe that it was still me, that I had survived. I bit back tears again as I clung to him, unwilling to let go. I didn't want to leave the shelter and comfort if his arms where I knew I was safe. His voice was choked with unreleased desperation as he spoke.

'We thought we were going to lose you, between Meran's attack and the power surge... Thank the goddess that a carer came to find me. He said that Merlas was acting up again, that she seemed afraid of something. I came to see that you were all right.' Merlas had been the one to let them know that there was something wrong? It took me a moment to remember that the doe would always be aware, even subconsciously, of my emotions, of whether or not I was in danger. For the first time, but certainly not the last, I was glad of that connection. I looked up at Armen.

'Can I go see her?'

The first thing Merlas did was pin me down with one wing. Running a scrutinising eye over me, she started licking the layer of blood, sweat and grime from my face and arms. Armen leant against the wall of the stable, smiling at the sight. I giggled, squirming under the feel of her tongue that was both soft and rough at the same time. Only once Merlas deemed me to be clean enough did she let me up. I stayed lying down for a moment, enjoying the comfort of the feathers Merlas had moulted and that served as bedding. She lowered her head, letting me hang on around her neck as she helped me to my feet. I kept my arms around her, my face buried in her mane, breathing in her distinctive smell of grass and hunting, of dust and sunlight. She had saved me with her thoughts. She had taken me away from that situation and comforted me.

'You scared the feathers off me,' she snorted in a very grumpy manner once I had let her go. I stared at her. Behind me, Armen chuckled.

'I forgot to tell you that the stories are true. War pegusi do talk.' I turned back to Merlas, stroking her nose.

'Thank you for helping me,' I murmured to her. Merlas nickered gently in reply.

A young carer stopped outside the stable, a terrified look on his face and his arms full of the cushion-like saddle the war pegusi used. He trembled as he bowed to Armen, unable to free his hands to perform a formal salute. Armen thanked him, taking the saddle from him. The carer couldn't have left quicker as he tripped over his own feet in his haste to get away.

'Today, I will introduce you to flying. This will become a reward for you, for good behaviour or work. This afternoon we will begin working with magic. You need to be able to harness it in order to defend yourself.' He lifted the saddle up onto Merlas's back, showing me where all the different straps went: two around her belly, one across her chest and one around her hindquarters. A last, loose loop of leather around the base of her neck served as guidance. He led the pegasus out into the field adjoining the stable where a carer stood with a pretty, dainty looking brown doe. Armen lifted me up onto Merlas, tying the final straps around my calves and thighs, explaining that they would help me to stay on her back while flying. I fidgeted, unused to the position my legs were tied into, astride the doe, with my calves tucked under my thighs in a kneeling position so as not to get in the way of Merlas's wings. Swinging himself up onto his own mount, he imparted one last bit of advice as he tied himself onto the saddle.

'Let her take off. Do not worry about it. She knows what she is doing.'

He walked the pegasus to a long, fairly narrow strip of silvery grass. Merlas followed, prancing a little and tossing her head. She jumped forwards, barging Armen's doe out of the way, leaping into a gallop. I dropped the loop, terrified, grabbing onto the mane with both hands, the doe's gait pitching me back and forth. Then nothing. Her great wings stretched out on either side of me, beating gently as the ground dropped away beneath us. I sneaked a peek down past her feathers. Everything seemed to be so small. I took hold of the loop again, but simply held it. I let her steer. She flew out towards the city, the warmth of daylight on our backs. Armen caught up with me, smiling. His mouth moved, saying something, but I couldn't hear what he said. The wind was whistling over my face, stealing all other sound from my ears.

The flight ended much too soon in my opinion. Landing was even more uncomfortable than taking off, the sudden transition from smooth flight to rugged gallop. If it were not for the straps holding me to the saddle, I would surely have fallen off. I loosened the knots, but was then stuck. I couldn't get down. The ground was a long way off. I desperately looked around for something I could use as an intermediate step. The doe solved the dilemma herself. She suddenly pitched forwards, her front legs folding beneath her. I slid down her neck to land in a tangled heap on the grass. Merlas snickered behind me. A hand pulled me to my feet, supporting me until my legs realised that they were supposed to hold my weight again.

'Did you enjoy your flight?' Armen asked.

I couldn't find the words to express how amazing the flight had been, how good it had felt with the sun on my back and the wind in my hair. Looking at Merlas, I simply nodded in response to Armen's question.

Armen decided to hold my first ever magic lesson outside in the court yard of the Senate Towers. Having very rarely been outside the Towers, I took a moment to gaze upwards at them. They were huge, taller than any of the other tower homes in the city, eight of them arranged in a circle, linked on several levels by covered walkways. The marble seemed to glow in its brilliant whiteness, the roof tiles a deep grey. Many of the white-robed Senators passed by, more often than not glaring at us. Armen simply ignored them, and I soon began to follow his example and did the same.

'Now, Shadow, according the descriptions in the Scriptures, your magic, although far stronger than any wielded by a Synari, it is manipulated in much the same way.

'First, I would like you to try to imagine an orb of magic hovering over your hand.'

I looked down at my hand, blinking. How was I supposed to access my magic? I'd never done it on purpose before. High Priestess Arias had told me that it was controlled by strong emotion. The twice that I had used it, pain and fear had been the presiding factors. I raised my hand in front of me to chest level, palm facing upwards. It felt right to do it like this. Strong emotion. Did it have to be negative? I didn't want to use too much and lose control. I already knew that it hurt. I decided to focus on the feeling of joy as I soared through the air with Merlas. I closed my eyes to think more clearly. In my mind, the pegasus slowly morphed into a ball of black energy. Warmth coursed through my body as if I was standing in sunlight. I cracked open one eye. A sphere of magic hovered above my hand, light glinting off the crystalline surface. It was wobbly and not an exact round shape, but it was there. Armen inspected it carefully, nodding in approval. He then proceeded to make me practise forming and controlling the sphere until I was too exhausted to give it shape.

I stayed in my room without protest the next day, thoughts of Merlas and the flight still fresh in my mind as I lay back on my bed and daydreamed. Night was falling rapidly outside, the light gradually dimming, the shadows lengthening. A strange tingling sensation shot through my body, not unlike a shiver or the feeling of someone stepping on your grave. I ignored it, rolling over onto my side. My rebellious hair fell over my face. Huffing, I raised a hand to push it out of the way. I froze. Nails, not claws, tipped my fingers. Scrambling off my bed, I darted for the broken silver glass. My shattered, distorted image looked back at me through blue eyes. Black hair, blue eyes, fingernails... I let out a yelp of surprise. What had happened to me?

Armen burst into the room, his concern clear in his expression. He found me curled in a corner, shaking uncontrollably and tugging on my hair. I couldn't summon my magic. I couldn't even feel it, just ice where its warmth usually ran through my blood.

'Shadow?' he asked, crouching next to me. 'What happened?'

'I don't know, it just happened!' I wailed. 'I can't even feel my magic!'

Armen barely suppressed a chuckle as he pulled me in for a quick bear hug, ruffling my hair. 'My poor little one, how scared you must have been! Worry not, it is perfectly normal for half bloods of your breed to experience a short period of time every moon, known as a 'vulnerable' period, where they revert to their non demonic side. For three days and three nights, you will be unable to use magic, any wounds will heal much slower and you will be weaker than you are accustomed to being. You will be, as the name states, more vulnerable. However, in light of all that, worry not. We will keep you safe. '

As promised, three days later, a tremor passed over my skin as I sat at my desk with yet another scroll from the Part Demon Scriptures. A glance at my hand confirmed my thoughts. Thicker, harder, sharper claw had replaced the delicate fingernail. Heat suffused my muscles as magic coursed through my blood. I willed it into shape as Armen had begun teaching me to do. An orb of my black magic, glittering in the light of dusk, shimmered above my palm. A half-smile twisted one corner of my mouth. I released the magic, stretching my arms over my head. As much as I loathed being a half breed, being forced into a form where I was unable to defend myself was truly frightening. I wandered over to my window where, if I tried hard, I could catch a glimpse of the pegusi stables. I could feel Merlas's presence and her emotions, but I couldn't talk to her. It was hard when we were so far apart. I missed her greatly when we were separated. I peered around the towers, trying to see the red tile roof of the stable, but something else caught my eye. Out on the plains surrounding the city. Flickering blue light. In the streets below me, people began to throng, shouting to each other. The Senate Towers burst alive with activity. The door slammed open. Armen stood there, his expression serious and afraid.

'Synairn is under attack. Arias has commanded that you fight with us.'

I didn't understand what was going on. I didn't even know what was going on. Armen swept me down to the lowest levels of the Senate Towers, protecting me from being jostled or trodden on as what seemed to be the entire population of Synairn headed in the same direction. We emerged into a cavern that rang with the sound of metal on metal. I found myself face to face with a Senator who looked none too kindly at me.

'Demoness or not, I find it difficult to believe that our benevolent ruler has decided to send a child into battle. It seems wrong to lay such scars on a young mind.'

'We have our orders, Rai. Equip her as best you can. I will return for her soon.' Before I could utter so much as a word, Armen left me in the care of the scar-handed Synari. I swallowed hard as I looked up at him, wishing Armen hadn't left. Rai held my gaze for a moment before he shook his head, muttering under his breath as he searched through piles of metal plates. I stirred not one foot. More Synari swarmed around me, but I dared not move, not even as they glared at me with open hatred. I simply bowed my head and wished the ordeal, whatever it was, to be over. Rai returned moments later, metal piles high in his hands.

'I have nothing that will fit a soldier as small as you, but what I have will have to do. Time is of the essence.' He started to put together various pieces of mismatched metals. A plain helm sat upon my head, although it fell far too easily over my eyes, leaving me to repeatedly push it back up. A shirt of leather fell to my knees, smelling of sweat, terror and blood. My soft indoor shoes were replaced with heavy boots of a material I couldn't identify. Plates of mismatched, dented metal were then strapped over my forearms, shoulders, torso and legs. I felt so heavy that if a person should touch me on the shoulder, I would fall over and not be able to stand up again. Armen reappeared at my side, resplendent in his pieces of metal plate that fitted him like a glove.

'Armen, what of arms? Surely the High Priestess cannot expect her only to fight with magic?'

'Find her a long knife or a short sword. She has practised with neither, but they remain among the simplest weapons to wield with any degree of accuracy.'

Rai wrapped a belt twice around my waist, on which was a scarred leather sheath. I pulled out the blade it housed, a single edged knife common among the Synari who hunted the abundance of wildlife that teemed in the forests around the city. The blade itself was chipped and dented with use, but its edge still gleamed with a deadly air. At Armen's command, I hurried after him, trying to keep up as he strode out of the hall and out into the city.

The sight that met me as we stood on the brink onto the plains was not one I was prepared for, let alone the wall of sound, smell and emotion that assaulted me until my head reeled from it. The fear and pain and anguish. The clanging of metal and cries and howls. The blood and sweat and cloying smell of death. Dry sobs caught in the back of my throat. I started to back away, wanting to flee, run, just get away from this place. Armen's hand on my shoulder stopped me. I glanced up at him. With infinite sadness in his eyes, he drew a sword that was almost as long as I was tall.

'I'm sorry, Shadow, but today, you must fight, for the good of our dimension.'

I had no choice but to follow him as he and countless others rushed into the fray with metal in their hands. Jostled by their movements, I fell onto the battlefield, into the heart of the fray. I screamed aloud. A man with nothing but rage in his heart raised his sword. My fear took control. A blast of magic threw him far away from me. I pulled out the knife I had been given as I tried to make sense of the goings on. Not far above my head, metal clashed. Another creature tried to separate my head from my shoulders. I squeaked, slashing at him with my knife before running as fast as I could in the other direction. I tripped on something soft that I didn't want to think too closely about, falling to the very solid ground with a bone-jarring thud. I tried to scramble to my feet, but the metal plates were so heavy. They dragged me down, robbing me of the ability to run. A short sword stabbed through my calf as if it were no more than a damp scroll, impaling it to the ground. I screamed in pain.

'Now ah've gotcha, ya little bitch! Yer no' ge'in' away again!'

Panic gripped my heart in its ice cold talons. Fear numbed my mind. Then the burning started. The power surge. Oh goddess, the power surge! My hands dug into the blood-drenched ground. My heart beat so fast. The fire built within every fibre of me until it spiked in my head. A wave of black magic erupted from deep within me, knocking back my attacker and everyone around me. Darkness overtook my mind and I fell back onto the gore splattered ground.

The first thing I noticed was the smell. The smell of blood and death and burnt flesh. It almost choked me in its intensity. I could barely breathe. I opened my eyes. I saw the empty, glazed eyes of a dead man in front of me. With a shriek, I sat up. Pain lanced through my leg, still staked to the ground by the sword. Somewhere not far off, I heard the moans of a wounded soldier trying to get to his feet, the sobs of pain of the other wounded, wails of grief for the dead. Tears began to drip down my face as I stared at the violet sky. What had I done? I slumped back to the ground. My muscles protested against the sudden movement, but I ignored them. How many had I killed? With one wave of magic, how many had I killed? Maybe I was just like my father. Maybe I was just as the Senate thought, evil to the very core of my being. A ruthless and cold-blooded killer. Not fit to live. Maybe a demon's only use was for destruction. Somewhere far above my head, something screeched. I took no notice. Something thudded to the ground. I did not turn to look.

'Little one,' crooned a soft voice. Still, I did not acknowledge the presence of anyone else. Merlas lay next to me, harrumphing softly. 'Oh, my little one...' She murmured in deepest sorrow before shielding me from the world in a cocoon of black feathers.

I don't know how long I lay on the battlefield before I heard a flurry of robes. Light flooded my eyes as Merlas lifted her wings to allow Armen to crouch next to me, his arm in a strip of cloth that bound the limb to the opposite shoulder, stained by a little blood. I took no notice of his arrival, all but dead to the world as he softly called my name. His fingers touched my neck, seeking the pulse point. I pulled back my lip to snarl, baring a fang, a growl grating in my throat. Merlas nickered a warning. He quickly pulled back his hand.

'Shadow?' he asked in concern. I said nothing still, nor did I move. 'By the goddess, Shadow, please answer me!'

'There is nothing that needs to be said,' I answered dully.

'Oh, thank the merciful goddess. I feared I had lost you.' He moved to examine the sword keeping me pinned to the ground like a piece of paper to a desk. 'This will hurt, Shadow, brace yourself.'

I did not moan or gasp as he wrenched the sword from the earth and my flesh. Instead, my claws dug deep furrows into the ground. I got to my feet, only betraying my pain through my narrowed eyes. Hauling herself to her hooves, Merlas took a long look at me through one dark, critical eye. I stood, hunched over, swaying slightly under the weight of the metal plates, favouring my injured leg. She snorted slightly, muttering something to herself about silly two-leggeds and their silly battles, grabbing the back of the leather shirt I wore in her teeth. Lifting her head as high as possible, she deposited me onto her back. Out of habit, I wound my hands into her mane, my head still bowed low. Armen laid a hand on Merlas's neck and, slowly, we began the long walk back to the Senate Towers.

* * *

Another year passed with no great haste. With great caution, I came out of the stupor the battle had caused, coaxed softly by both Armen and Merlas. Arias had said nothing about it, although Armen had been excused from the greater part of his Senator duties in order to become my sole tutor. He taught me to control my magic directly from the scriptures left by the previously extinct part demons. He taught me strength by having me clear new fields of boulders, carrying them with only my magic over miles. He taught me restraint by having me weave cloth with magic or dam a small stream. He taught me focus with puzzles and control with impossible tasks. For every day that I worked with determination, Armen took me to fly with Merlas. Sometimes to study, he took me to a great hall filled with books called a 'library', and left me to browse on my own, to choose my own reading. I even started to learn more languages, recommended by Armen for reasons he refused to tell me. I was, however, forbidden to use magic except in Armen's presence.

As I was confined to my room for the duration of time that I did not spend with Armen, I read for hours on end. It was at one such time that I first heard the voice in my head. The scriptures had warned me about such things, about the voice of the demonic parent trying to trigger a switch of control from the 'normal' side to the demonic. Part demons were, effectively, two people in one. As such, I simply ignored the voice. I focused my eyes on the book I was reading, allowing its words to blot out the demon's. Something somewhere in my mind flipped. Pain shot through my limbs. I fell from my chair, desperately trying to work out what had happened. Thankfully, it ended quickly. I lay panting on the ground, something crashed into the window. Merlas! Never before had I been so glad of leaving a window open at all times. Unable to fit her broad shoulders through the window frame, she stretched her head out towards me. I yelped as she grabbed the back of my neck in her teeth before pushing off again.

Merlas flew up to the mountains, to a clearing with a small stream. Standing close to the edge of the water, she dropped her head a little to look at her reflection. Hanging from the doe's mouth, barely visible against her black coat was a black wolf cub. I looked down at my hand only to see a paw. I yelped out loud. I was a wolf! How did that happen? Merlas dropped me onto the grass of the clearing, looking at me expectantly. Realising I wasn't changing back, she huffed, rustled her wings and wandered off, obviously affronted. I tried to follow her, but realised that four legs were more complicated to operate than two. I ended up in a heap of legs and paws with another yelp. Merlas turned back to look at me. I looked back at her with what must have been a most pitiful expression. Sighing heavily, she wandered back over. Lifting me up to stand on my four paws again. She placed herself next to me and lifted a front hoof. When I didn't react, she pawed at the air. I lifted the same paw. We put our legs down a little way in front. Merlas lifted a hind leg. I copied her.

She taught me to walk in a matter of minutes, running not long after that, working by copying her movements. When we were tired out from chasing each other around the clearing, we drank from the stream before lying down comfortably in the shade of the branches of an overhanging willow. I set about trying to change back. Exploring the recesses of my mind, I searched for the trigger. It took me a while, but I managed to find it. This time, the pain of the transformation wasn't as great, although it still left me breathless, shaking and disorientated. My senses of smell and hearing seemed to be extra sensitive. I could smell everything from the grass to an antlered rabbit half way further down the mountain to us and hear the beating of Merlas's heart as if it were a drum. Merlas nuzzled my hair, drawing me closer to her side and tucking me under a wing.

For three days, Merlas taught me everything about surviving on my own: hunting, gathering, finding shelter. I could have stayed forever on that mountain with Merlas, just living, surviving, with no worries about my cursed half-blood status. No Senators, no Arias, nothing to prevent me from doing what I wanted to do when I wanted to do it. I could practise with my magic unsupervised without fear of being found and punished. True freedom after years of forced restraint. It felt glorious. Until we were found.

We were hiding under the dense branches of the willow tree. I had been practising changing myself from Synari to wolf. It was getting easier and easier with each transformation, less painful, less tiring. It had become just like flexing a muscle. It was still a little strange feeling at times, often taking me a few seconds to remember exactly how many legs I had and whether or not I had a tail. I rested against Merlas's warm belly, my eyes half shut as I dozed contentedly. Her head shot up, ears pricked. She had heard something. Even thought my demonic side gave me a more acute sense of hearing than the Synari, Merlas's was more sensitive than mine. I strained my ears to listen. I could hear something. I struggled to distinguish it. A voice. No, two voices, a little further down the mountain and getting closer.

'Why are we hunting this half-blood? I thought that the Senate would have been pleased to be rid of it.'

'The High Priestess fears it turning rogue. By keeping it in the Senate Towers, they could control what it learned. She fears what Senator Armen has already taught her.'

'Is it really that dangerous?'

'Imagine two beings combined into one with more power than the High Priestess.'

'Ah. And the doe?'

'The High Priestess is less bothered about her. Merlas does not pose the threat of being able to destroy the city if she is angered.'

I glanced at Merlas. If Arias was angry with me, I didn't want to go back. It didn't bode well at all. In fact going back while she was angry was the last thing I wanted to do. Especially since she would know I had been using magic.

We waited until Merlas could no longer hear their voices before trying to sneak out in the other direction. Merlas walked quickly but quietly with me perched on her back. For the few days we had been living together, she had helped me gain confidence in riding her without a saddle so that I could now balance, kneeling on her back without a problem. I wound my hands into her mane, still acutely aware of just how high up I was.

'There it is!'

I barely had time to register the cry before Merlas pitched forwards, going from a walk to a full gallop. I hung on grimly, trying to block out the sound of hooves chasing us as Merlas dodged through the trees. As we reached another clearing, she took off with a sudden absence of movement I don't think I will ever get used to. Her wings began beating with a determined tempo, desperate to put some distance between us and the City Guard. I dared glance back. They were too close for comfort. One launched a bolt of magic, then several. Merlas managed to dodge most of them, but it slowed her down. They pulled up alongside us. I screamed as one grabbed hold of me, pulling me from Merlas's back. I kicked and struggled, trying to bite my captor. Merlas brayed in alarm and fury. She rammed the pegasus. A loop of rope landed around her neck, the end held by the other guard. His pegasus dived, losing height rapidly, dragging Merlas down. She shrieked in fury. I cried out to her, reaching for her even as she fell. The guard holding me snapped at me to be silent as his mount's wings swept through the air, carrying us back towards the city.

To say that Arias was furious would be one of the worst understatements of my short life. To begin with, she would not even speak to me. When she eventually started talking, a torrent of anger poured forth. I felt so small and insignificant in the gigantic chamber from where Arias ruled, a tiny black speck in the bright light, where the figures carved into the pillars of white stone glared down me, as if I was a mote of dust in an obsessively tidy person's home.

'We let you live, Shadow, gave you everything you needed, healed your wounds and kept you safe. You repaid us by disobeying the rules put in place to keep you safe and then you ran away!'

'I was scared!' I protested weakly. 'I was alone and didn't know what to do!'

'That does not justify your actions. You have been trained to control your emotions. But that matters no longer. I wash my hands of you.' Dread mounted in my heart, freezing my breath. I waited to hear what she was going to do to me. She glared at me, her nails clicking against the arm of her throne as she thought of a suitable punishment.

'You will go to Aspheri, to the realm of your father. He may do with you as he pleases.'

A curious sensation engulfed me, not unlike that of jumping into a cold river. My surroundings disintegrated in a heartbeat before I had time to say anything.

* * *

It was hot, far hotter than Synairn. Demons of various sizes and shapes surrounded me. They spoke in a harsh, guttural language that was so different to the soft, lyrical Synari that it took me a moment to realise that I could understand them. And they were mainly discussing how best to kill me. I summoned magic into my hands, hoping to be able to fight my way out of the ring of demons that surrounded me. They parted like a knife parts soft butter, but not because of me or my magic. Two silver haired boys stood there. Identical in every way, they looked to be a couple of years older than me. One raised a hand, beckoning to me. I nervously followed. Now that the immediate danger was gone, I took in my surroundings. A scarlet sun stained the sky with crimson light. The ground had been baked and burned until it was black and cracking. Crude stone dwellings turned the dirt into haphazard streets. On a slight incline was the only vaguely civilized looking building. A palace made of some sort of black stone. The twins leading me were odd in their own right, with long shaggy silver hair and silver eyes with skin pale enough to rival mine. I observed them with curiosity, wondering who they were and why everyone was scared of them. They didn't look all that scary to me. Arias and Karthragan were more terrifying in my mind.

There was a rising feeling of dread the closer I got to the temple. Something in my blood recognised it. My magic hummed happily through my body, revelling in the heat. Inside the temple, the corridors were made with the same black stone as the outside, although torches lined the walls, casting flickering shadows, and gleaming red on the twins' silver hair. We passed several more demons, although they all shrank away at the sight of the two boys. I wondered who they were to be so feared. I kept close to the twins, afraid of this strange place, of the demons looking at me as if I was the next thing on the menu.

The further we went into the temple, the more I felt as if I was in a maze. The twins navigated easily, knowing exactly where they were going. I followed like a foal follows its mother, unable to do anything else. I was lost in this place. All the corridors looked the same! We eventually reached our final destination. The chamber was huge, as big as the Senate Chambers back home. Here, the black walls glittered in the torchlight and there, sitting on a throne carved of black wood, was Karthragan.

He looked nothing like the wolf in the demon book. He looked almost Synari, almost normal. Pale skin with black hair that fell over his brow, obscuring one pair of his eyes, the tips of horns protruding from the mass. Not how I imagined a demon to look. But I knew him. I could sense him. A dark presence the exact copy of the one in the back of my mind. He looked down at me, a girl in black lost against the black floor. In the blink of an eye, I found myself pinned to the wall, his hand around my throat, up more close and personal than I ever wanted him to be ever again. His four red eyes gleamed under black hair, narrowed as he sniffed at me.

'Wolf,' he growled. I struggled against his grasp. I couldn't focus enough to use magic and he was so much stronger than I was! He raised a finger, a finger tipped with a fearsome claw. With one quick swipe, he carved a deep gash around my right eye, from my eyebrow to my cheekbone. I screamed. The pain gave me the focus I needed. In a single blast, I managed to send him flying half way across the room. I fell to the ground but scrambled back up to my feet. Clamping a corner of my cloak to the wound, I glanced around, looking for a place to run and hide. From somewhere outside the chamber, chaos erupted, voices yelling about the prince being bested by a girl, about the girl being marked as his, about a winged horse. Merlas! They had to be talking about Merlas! Demons didn't breed pegusi and she would be the only one who would come and find me!

A furious bundle of fur, feathers and teeth burst into the room, her ears back, her long canine teeth stained black with demon blood. Merlas roared in fury, rearing up onto her hind legs, pawing at the air with her sharp hooves. Karthragan ducked, escaping her attack. Merlas's teeth snagged the back of my cloak, tossing my easily onto her back. Through the haze of blood in my eyes, I saw Karthragan jump forwards with a sword. Merlas bellowed a warning as she leapt into the air, delivering a strong kick to his chest as she took off. Once more, I felt the sensation of jumping into cold water as Merlas crossed dimensions in mid flight.

Merlas landed in the courtyard outside the war pegusi block, barely pausing before she trotted towards her stable. I clung to her mane with one hand, the other holding the edge of my cloak over the wound, tears and blood streaming down my face, my magic sparking in the air around me. Merlas folded her limbs beneath her, lying on the feathery ground of her stable. I slipped off her back, sobbing still, to rest against her side. She nickered gently, folding a wing around me as she nosed my hand away from the cut. Dust started to settle on the exposed flesh, irritating the wound. I scratched at it desperately, ignoring the pain as my claws tore into my skin. Pushing my hands away, Merlas set about licking the deep gash clean, taking care to be as comforting as possible. I relaxed into her touch. The touch of a mother to her child. Each gentle rasp of her tongue helped me to calm myself, to stop shaking. The sound of feet running down the aisle jolted us both from the moment of tenderness. Merlas quickly covered me with a wing, hiding me from sight. Armen appeared, breathless and wild-eyed

'Did you find her?' he asked Merlas. The doe cautiously lifted the wing. He breathed a sigh of relief. Reaching out a hand, he helped me to my feet, supporting me in his arms. I hugged him tightly, unwilling to let go. Armen held me, murmuring reassuring words to me. 'Come, Shadow, we'll keep you out of sight with your mother until we can send you to another dimension to hide.'

Armen took me through the outskirts of the city to a small house where a lamp burned with a silver flame. He knocked three times on the door. It opened immediately to show a pale-looking Arellan. She wrapped me in a bear hug so fierce I thought my bones would crack under the pressure. Ushering Armen and me into the house, she quickly shut and barred the door. Only then did I realise that there were tears streaking down my face once more and that my limbs were still quivering in shock. Arellan knelt down in front of me, rubbing my arms in reassurance.

'It is okay, Alexai, it is okay. It is over now. He cannot hurt you. You are safe.'

She took my hand, leading me up the stairs to a bathing room. She directed me to sit on the raised side of the bathing pool as she began running water into it. Taking out a small chest from one of the many storage holes in the walls, she knelt in front of me, gently taking my face in her hands and turning it so as to be able to see the wound better. I flinched as she touched it, instinctively pulling away. She softly shushed me, murmuring reassurances as she took a small jar from the chest, using a finger to gently use the cream to clean out the wound as I tried not to squirm.

After bathing and eating, Arellan took me to a small room close to hers. I nestled under the blankets, clean, warm and fed. She gently dropped a kiss on my forehead, smoothing my hair and checking the dressing she had put over my wound before straightening up, moving towards the door. I squeaked in fear, suddenly afraid of being left on my own again, jumping out of bed and racing to her side.

'Please don't leave me,' I begged, knotting my fists in her robes.

'It is okay, Alexai,' she said quietly, leading me back and tucking me under the blankets again. Instead of leaving, she sat on the edge of the bed, stroking my hair. 'I will not leave you.' I felt my eyelids droop as she began to hum softly, then to sing in a quiet voice. 'Sleep well, my little one.'

I stayed with my mother for almost a month. I had been away in Aspheri for nearly a week, according to Arellan. Time passed differently between the dimensions. Now that Arias knew I was no longer in Aspheri, regular patrols of the City Guard searched the streets and houses. Armen thought it better that I didn't go to see Merlas as he didn't know who he could trust in the stables. I missed her terribly. He and Arellan had found a dimension I could go to, and Armen taught me several languages I may have to speak to be understood. When the patrols came round to search Arellan's house, he took me to the Great Library. He said that it was in another dimension, the one I was going to be moving to, but I wasn't allowed to leave the Library to see what it was like outside. Armen was terrified of losing sight of me. I settled down into some semblance of a normal routine, learning with Arellan and Armen. She taught me about different cultures and helped me learn how to behave with other people, reversing my somewhat stinted education in that area. Armen taught me how to defend myself. I never wanted that time to end. But all good things must.

He came late one night. Arellan was just tucking me into bed when he knocked on the door. She ruffled my hair, saying that it was probably just Armen coming back without his keys. I giggled quietly, snuggling down under the blankets with the cuddly wolf toy Arellan had made for me. I listened to her start to walk down the stairs. It felt as if an icy hand had touched the base of my spine. Something was wrong. Something very wrong. I slipped out of bed, following Arellan. I paused at the top of the stairs, watching her cross the floor towards the door. I watched her open it. Her scream pierced the air. She slammed the door shut again.

'Arellan!' I yelled, running down the stairs to her.

'Alexai, you have to run. You have to get away. Far away from here, okay?' she said, bracing herself against the door as she slid the bolts home. I raced to her side, desperate for her reassurance. I could sense fear in her mind, hear the rapid beat of her heart, smell the cold sweat that had begun to break out over her skin.

'What is happening, Arellan? Who was that?'

Arellan looked down at me, kneeling down and hugging me tightly, burying her face in my hair for a brief moment. She straightened up, holding my arms tightly as she looked at me. Only one word, one name escaped her lips: 'Karthragan.'

Something thudded against the door again. He was losing patience fast. Black magic surrounded the wooden door, crushing it to charred splinters. Standing in the dark, red eyes gleaming, was the creature of my nightmares. Arellan took my face in her hands, resting her forehead briefly against mine before pushing me towards the back door, begging me to run, to hide, to get away from here. I crouched behind a dresser, terrified. Arellan turned to face him, preparing herself. I have never seen a sight so beautiful yet so terrifyingly lethal as Arellan readying herself for battle. Her magic created a whirlwind around her, lifting her black hair into a halo around her head, her robes twisting and writhing like some sort of living creature. I could feel the magic in the air, the dry and static feeling that put my hair on end. A fierce angel. A warrior angel. The Messenger Angel. But even her white magic wouldn't be a match for Karthragan's determination. I couldn't let her fight alone.

I raced back towards her, calling up my own black magic. I threw bolt after bolt at him. Nothing made any difference. Arellan begged me to flee. I couldn't. I couldn't leave her to face him alone. Not when I knew what he had done to her. What he had done so that he could continue the prophecy. I ducked a bolt of his magic, retaliating with one of my own. He then turned his attention fully to me, ignoring Arellan completely. I dodged another bolt. But I hadn't realised he had shot two. The second was so close. I couldn't move. My eyes were fixed with terror on a flash of light that could end my life. A blur of white masked my vision. A blur I recognised a heartbeat too late.

'Arellan, no!' I screamed. Too late. She fell to the ground with a thud. A black scorch marred the front of her robes. I knelt beside her, shaking her shoulder. 'Arellan? Arellan, please get up!' The room blurred as tears clouded my eyes. Why wouldn't she respond? Her blue eyes were staring at the ceiling, unseeing, uncaring. From somewhere far above me, Karthragan's cruel laughter echoed. Arellan's robes turned red. Anger boiled up within me, surging through the dam that held my emotions back. I didn't care. I didn't care about anything. I didn't care about keeping my magic under control or not being noticed by the Senate. I cared for vengeance. Vengeance for my mother's death. Arellan, who had done nothing wrong. I straightened up. A growl scraped the back of my throat. Karthragan raised a hand to strike.

'You are no match for me, Wolf. Tonight, the prophecy ends.'

Unleashing a feral snarl, I leapt at him. Black magic gathered behind him, forming a black disc in the air as I barrelled him backwards. The portal closed, sealing him on the other side. I blinked until my vision returned to normal, kneeling beside Arellan.

'Arellan? Please, Arellan, wake up!' I begged, shaking her shoulder. Her head rolled limply to the side. With my vision blurring again, I crawled under her arm, snuggling up to her body. Beneath my cheek, her robes grew wet as her icy hand cradled me to her.

Sometime later, Armen burst into the house. He scooped me up into his arms, running back out into the streets. I screamed, clawing at him to let me go back to Arellan's side. The shoulder of his robes tore beneath my claw-like nails, but it didn't deter him, not even as his blood began to drip down to stain the shredded cloth. He strode into the stables, not stopping until we reached Merlas's stall. The doe shot to her hooves, nuzzling my hair.

'What has happened, little one?' she asked in deep concern. I said nothing, clinging onto her mane as I tried to breathe through my sobs. Armen threw the saddle over Merlas's back, quickly doing up the straps. Disentangling my hand from her mane, he hoisted me up onto the doe, grabbing the guidance loop and running out into the field.

'Shadow, it's time for you to leave. To go to that other

dimension. Now that Arellan is gone, you will have no one to protect you from the Senate. You will be blamed for her death. So run. Run as fast as you can. Stay close to Merlas and she will protect you.' He slung a satchel across my torso, reaching up to hug me one last time as he whispered a quick blessing of good luck. Pulling back, he slapped Merlas on the rump, sending her forward in a full gallop before the jarring transition to flight. In a single flash of light, she flew through a different night's sky.

* * *

We hid in a cave for several days, the walls soon turning a charred black as I released wave after wave of magic in my grief. Merlas attempted to get me to eat during these times, bringing me her fresh kill and fruit she had found. I rejected each notion forcefully, throwing the food back at her. Often, she threatened to leave and not come back, but she never did. She would fly off in a huff before returning and tucking me under a wing while I cried myself to sleep.

A week passed before I opened the bag Armen had given me. I found a book of magic he had put together for me, Arellan's brooch and some sort of small booklet with a picture of me and details I didn't understand. A note in Armen's careful, spiked handwriting called it a 'passport'. It would allow me to start my life here, and it was time for me to start living again. Merlas agreed. Using a spell from the book, I cloaked Merlas's wings so that she could pass as one of the wingless 'horses' of this dimension. She dropped down onto her knees so that I could scramble up onto her back. Standing up again, she shook herself energetically, raising a cloud of dust from her coat. I grabbed onto her mane.

'Please don't do that,' I gasped. Merlas snickered quietly to herself, walking forwards at my command.

We found ourselves in a town not far away from where we had been hiding. People stopped to stare as we walked through the streets. I touched the pendant that had been in Armen's bag, a nugget of silver enveloped in bronze. It kept my magic in control without causing me pain while also casting an illusion to make me appear human, turning my purple hair black and my eyes blue. Hopefully, it would be enough to fool the humans. Strange metal things that I had read to be 'cars' rushed past. Merlas shied away from them, starting to prance, rearing slightly. I gripped the guidance loop tightly, trying to stay calm for her sake. I tugged on her mane twice, signalling to her to put our plan into action. There was no way I could just go up to the City Guard and present myself. Armen had suggested in the letter that we stage an accident. The City Guard would be more accommodating of any questions I couldn't answer if I appeared to be in a state of shock.

Merlas acted perfectly. A car roared past her at some speed. She squealed, rearing and pawing at the air. I screamed, clutching at her mane. People began to fuss around us. A couple of humans trying to grab hold of Merlas, but she danced out of her grasp. Her front hooves touched the ground only long enough for her to charge forwards, bucking madly. I screamed again, letting myself slide from her back.

The ground seemed infinitely softer from atop Merlas than landing on it. The black coating on it was as hard as a rock. I whimpered from my heap under my cloak where I had landed. Humans swarmed around me, asking if I was okay. Someone managed to catch Merlas, or rather she allowed someone to catch her. A man in a blue uniform crouched over me.

'Hey there, are you okay?' I looked up at the man, a human male, blinking a couple of times as I tried to refocus my mind. The fall had shaken me more than I had anticipated.

I didn't need to pretend to appear unfocused as I asked the question most likely to be the first to cross a person's mind.

'What happened?' I murmured.

'You fell off your horse. Don't worry, we've got her. Come on, let's get you checked out at the hospital.' A team of people with a stretcher moved all of the humans out of the way before helping me onto it. I had to admit that I hurt all over. My back was killing me. I made a mental note to remember to check the surface of any ground I was planning to landing on.

The healer shone a bright light into my eyes. I flinched away, squeezing my eyelids shut to stop the glare hurting, trying not to growl at him. Someone had taken away my cloak and clothes, replacing them with a flimsy, backwards robe sort of thing that was open at the back. It was highly uncomfortable as well as being undignified. I lay on a bed with railings around the edge, being examined by these people for injuries. I heard some muffled swearing as one of the healers ran a hand over the scars on my back, remnants of Meran's actions and my rigorous training. The healer withdrew from the small, curtained cubicle I was in to talk to someone else. I strained my ears to listen to their hushed conversation.

'Apart from a few bruises and a very minor concussion, there seems to be nothing wrong with the girl, she just won't, or can't, tell us who or where her parents are, nor where they live. Social services have done a check on her name, but they couldn't find much in the way of information. No school records, no medical records, just a birth certificate with both parents listed as 'unknown'.'

'What do you think caused those scars on her back?'

'We can only guess. The child isn't very forthcoming with information. Hardly surprising, she's still in shock. My guess is that she has been abused somehow. It would also explain how she came to be on a horse in the middle of Forfar.'

'Fear would certainly give a child enough confidence to get on a horse far too big for her in order to flee.'

'What do we do now?'

'I guess we hand her over to a children's home. Not much we can do for her.'

Arellan's Lullaby

Dreamweaver

Dreamweaver walks alone at night,
Travelling though his realm of dreams.
In his hands, he holds a world,
Shimmering softly at his touch.
He comes to you, softly stepping,
To weave his web of dreams.

The pegusi fly through the sky,
beating wings, the rhythm of the dream.
Dreamweaver comes to comfort you.
Chasing, running with the wolf,
Racing through his world of dreams,
Dreamweaver comes to set you free.

Dreamweaver walks alone at night,
Travelling though his realm of dreams.
In his hands, he holds a world,
Shimmering softly at his touch.
He comes to you, softly stepping,
To weave his web of dreams.

The raven's wings, gleaming bright,
Soaring through the warmth of sunlight.
Dreamweaver weaves his spells for you.
The panther stalks his prey at night,
Returns at dawn to his belov'd.
Dreamweaver weaves his world

Dreamweaver walks alone at night,
Travelling though his realm of dreams.

In his hands, he holds a world,
Shimmering softly at his touch.
He comes to you, softly stepping,
To weave his web of dreams.

PART 2

EARTH – THE ACADEMY YEARS

Eight years later

I hit the wooden floor of the children's home with a resounding thud. My cheek stung from the hit Stone had delivered. I glared up at him through the curtain of black hair that fell over my face. My skin burned under my fingers as I touched the reddening flesh. Eight years, I had put up with this. Eight whole years to the day since Arellan died. Eight years since my world was turned upside down by the dimension transfer. I ran my fingers over the pendant in the shape of an angel that I had never taken off since the day the police had found me. A last gift from the people who had cared for me even though I was not even worth the dirt on the bottom of their shoes. And though no one in this dimension knew who I really was, I was still no better than the lowest of the low. A child no one wanted. A nothing.

Stone stood over me, fists clenched, daring me to get up. Normally, I would have stayed down and accepted it. But not today. Today I fought. I scrambled to my feet, launching a punch of my own. My fist hit his nose, blood spurting onto my hand, the cartilage giving way easily under the impact. His eyes narrowed. The fight was on. His cronies backed off as we circled each other. Demoness against human. Son of Man against daughter of Evil. They didn't know that, but I did. That's all that mattered. I would not back down from this fight. Memories of sparring with Armen surged through my mind. The moves, the grace, the fluidity as each punch and kick flowed into another. The other children gathered in a wide circle, egging us on. More specifically, egging *Stone* on. They knew that whoever won, if they didn't support Stone, their lives were going to be miserable for a long time. My nails scraped his cheek, leaving three bloody scratches. His foot collided with my stomach, winding me. I launched myself at him with a renewed anger, screaming in Synari, not caring about the pain in my gut. All I cared about was winning this fight, proving myself to be just as good as they were. The housemothers broke through the circle of children, grabbing at Stone and me, dragging us off each other. I still screamed, fighting against their hold.

They hauled me away, throwing me through a door into a tiny room. The time-out closet. Didn't I know it well. There were two such closets in the home, for children who got a little out of hand and needed to cool down. I had managed to go a whole year without having to be shut in one, and with good reason. No one wanted to be stuck in there. The room was about a metre squared. The door only opened from the outside. The floor and walls were hard. There was no way out. I leant my back against the wall, letting myself slide down until I was sitting on the floor. Wiping my bloody nose on my sleeve, I hugged my knees to my chest and I rested my head against my arms, toying with a lock of black hair. I kind of missed having purple hair. It defined who I was, but I didn't dare take the necklace off in case my magic went haywire, or someone walked in. Sighing heavily, I started to use one of the breathing techniques Arellan had taught me. My anger began to drain away, leaving the strange feeling of heartache I always experienced when I thought of my mother. Curling up tighter on myself, I let my mind wander back to those few weeks I had spent with my mother, getting to know her, learning from her, imagining what it would be like to still be with her. Losing myself in this land of make believe, I waited until the housemothers came to let me out.

Time passes strangely in the closet. If I didn't know better, I would have thought it to be another dimension. When a house-mother finally let me out, I was sure I must have spent a day in there. It had only been two hours. She led me up to the top floor of the home, to the director's office. I caught sight of myself in a mirror as we walked up the stairs. What a sight. Although I was supposedly thirteen, I had the appearance of a girl in her late teens. An early developer. Thankfully, my growth was slowing down now. My hair was a mess of locks escaping from its plait, the sleeve of my shirt ripped. Half of my face was red from Stone's slaps, my nose had streaked blood down my jaw. I clenched my teeth as my eyes caught sight of the pale, prominent, half circle scar around my right eye. It sickened me as I remembered my father and all he had done. Of what he had taken from me. Raising my chin slightly, I promised myself that whatever happened, if he ever came for me again, I would be ready, and I would fight him. I would fight him to the death if necessary, to make him pay for taking Arellan's life.

I sat opposite the director. He watched me over his clasped hands. He wasn't saying anything yet, but I knew this tactic. If he waited long enough, the child would blurt out apologies and guilt. I knew the game so well. He had used it often enough on me in an attempt to make me rethink my attitude. I refused to back down, catching his eye and keeping it with a flat glare. He gave in with a deep sigh, pulling off his reading glasses and pinching the bridge of his nose. Another of his little tricks, an attempt to make the child in front of him feel sorry for him and hopefully apologise. The sigh conveyed everything I knew he thought of me. He had had enough of my attitude, of my fighting and of my 'strange ways'. Personally, I couldn't care less what he thought of me.

'What are we going to do with you, Alexai?' he asked in grave concern. I narrowed my eyes at his continued usage of a name I never wanted to hear again unless it was from Arellan's lips. For some reason, he insisted on using it. If it had been one of the other children in the home, I would have punched them, but I couldn't exactly do that to the director. 'You put every family interested in you off by your glaring and your attitude. I have had numerous reports from the school about you fighting. You even tried to attack the psychologist! This is not normal, Alexai. We've put up with a lot of behavioural difficulties from you since you came to this home. Your attacking everyone who didn't call you 'Shadow', your insults to the police force when they came to tell you that your horse was missing, your tantrums every time someone tries to talk to you about your mother, even your flippant attitude about your life. Now your fight with Stone. What is wrong with you?' His last sentence came with such force that I flinched. There was no way I could tell him the truth. If I did, I'd end up in a mental ward, for a start. The humans didn't really believe in demons or, indeed, much that didn't have anything to do with everyday life. They were perfectly content to live in their little world of things that made sense and not think about anything else. I was trying to come up with a decent answer when someone knocked on the door. Another house-mother poked her head round.

'Dr Chase? There's someone here to see Alexai.'

'If they're looking for adoption...'

'No, sir, they asked for her specifically. He says he's a teacher at the Academy and he wants to talk to her.'

I felt my mouth flop open in uncharacteristic shock. The director sucked his breath in sharply. The Academy? Every parent dreamed of the Academy. It was one of the most prestigious and select schools in Europe. They monitored every single child in the schooling system and only accepted the best. Why would they want to talk to me though? There was no way my school results or the comments from my teachers would warrant their attention. So what did they want with me?

I warily pushed open the door into the meeting room set aside for prospective parents to talk to their prospective adoptee in private. A young man sat at the table, the picture of a representative from a snobby school. Brown hair carefully combed, glasses perched on his nose, suit pressed until the deliberate creases down the side of the leg had been ironed into submission. I was glad I had taken a couple of minutes to change my shirt and wash my face. My hair, on the other hand, had refused to be tamed. I knocked on the door a little timidly before walking in. Uh oh. I recognised the thick yellowish file he was going through. My file. Everything that had happened since my admission to the home.

'Good afternoon, Shadow, as I believe you prefer to be called.'

'Yes, sir,' I replied quietly. I had to be on my best behaviour here. This was a chance to get out of the home, and I wasn't about to let it slip through my fingers, especially since this man seemed to accept the fact that I didn't use my Synari name any more.

'Sit down.'

I took a seat opposite him, trying not to look at the papers he had taken out of my file. They didn't look good. In fact, my psychological reports read like a nightmare, especially after I had attacked one of the psychiatrists. The sessions had pretty much gone downhill from there. The man set the file aside, looking at me over the tops of his glasses. For a moment, he simply surveyed me, then he started to speak: 'My name is Alexander Heath, professor of magical manipulation and recruiter for the Academy.'

'Pardon?' I asked, unable to believe my ears. A professor of magical manipulation? He had to be pulling my leg. There was no way anyone could know! Professor Heath chuckled to himself, obviously amused by my expression of disbelief.

'You heard me right, Shadow. We know what you are. That's why I have come to offer you a place at the Academy. We select our students very carefully, not for academic results, but because they are not quite human. We teach them to blend in with normal society while also giving them the academic tuition they need to go out into the human world and get a decent job. The spiel about being an elitist school is simply a cover story.' My hand automatically went to my pendant, making sure it was still there.

'Don't worry, the illusions work on humans. I have a gift called True Sight. I can see who you really are. That's why I'm a recruiter. Think about it, Shadow. Would you rather stay here and be shuttled around the children's home system until you turn sixteen, or would you rather have a formal education at the Academy, with other people like you?'

I didn't have to think about my answer. It was staring me in the face.

It didn't take me long to pack. Professor Heath was going to take me to the Academy right away. I hadn't gathered much in the way of possessions other than what I had to start with. My spell book, Armen's letter, the toy wolf Arellan had made for me and my clothes. It all fitted in one bag. I got into the car, looking out of the window to take in the home one last time. I felt no regret at leaving it, and the sorry beginnings of my life on Earth, far behind.

The drive to the Academy was long and uneventful. Professor Heath wasn't the most talkative of companions, but it didn't bother me. I was still trying to get over the shock that the Academy was actually a school for mythical creatures. As we neared the Academy, I perked up, wondering what the school would look like. How would the people there accept me? Would it be just like the haven I imagined when I needed to escape, a place of acceptance and joy, or would they shun me and keep me hidden like the Synari had done, scared of what I could do?

The gates were black iron and imposing, the walls high and thick, but the grounds inside were a boarding school director's wet dream. Ancient trees lined the long driveway, giving way to extensive grassland. On one side, the grass had been separated into paddocks where horses and ponies grazed. The other side was dotted with students in uniform. All the boys in their smart black trousers and blazers, the girls in perfect skirts and ties. I sank a little lower in my seat. Nerves were starting to kick in. What if the others rejected me? The driveway opened out into a circle with a huge pine tree in the centre. A sprawling mansion filled my vision as we pulled up. The main building itself was impressive, even without being flanked by two wings that were longer, but not as high as the house. I grabbed my bag, slipping out of the car and looking around nervously. The other kids were staring. They looked normal, until you looked a little closer. A hint of scale, strangely coloured eyes, and a woman with *wings* walking towards me. I bit my lip. Walking behind the woman was a sight I was delighted to see. Head bobbing as she walked, wings visible and tucked into her sides, Merlas paused long enough to whinny loudly.

'Merlas!' I yelled, running forwards to throw my arms around her neck. I had grown since I last saw her, now reaching halfway up her shoulder. Standing at one metre eighty, I wasn't likely to grow any more. She still bested me for height though, standing at an even two metres. I didn't mind. It meant I'd never outgrow her. The winged woman coughed politely. I felt my face turn red, turning to look at her, realising that I hadn't even acknowledged her presence. So much for trying to be polite.

'I'm sorry,' I said apologetically, 'I haven't seen her for years.'

She waved off my apology with a lazy flick of her hand. 'My name is Meredith Featherstone. I'm the headmistress of the school. Now, the tradition here is that you are assigned a student similar to your own age to explain the rules. We found that it gives the new students a better insight into how we work, so I'll let him give you the introductory speech. Follow me, let's go and save your guide from class. I'm sure he won't complain.'

I followed Miss Featherstone into the main building, into a place that looked as if it had been furnished from a couple of centuries before. I was surprised that they managed to keep so many antiques here and in impeccable condition with scores of teenage mythical creatures learning to control themselves. Miss

Featherstone swept up the central staircase up to the third floor, along corridors I was sure rivalled those in Aspheri. I would never learn my way around here! She knocked on a door, pushing it open. A classroom, with a nervous looking boy standing at the front holding a pile of notes, obviously about to give a presentation on something.

'Mr Carton's charge has arrived.' The boy at the front of the class looked relieved, racing to pack up his notes and shoot out of the classroom. I took a good look at him. Floppy brown hair fell into dark eyes as he grinned at me. He looked to be an energetic, playful kind of person, the kind that all the girls fawned after in school. In what was now my previous school, I might have been among those girls that adored the cute guy, but none of them had ever given me the time of day. No one had wanted to be associated with the weird girl from the home.

'Thanks for the great timing. You saved me from giving a presentation on the relations between unicorn herds,' he said, flashing a grateful grin at me. I found myself speechless, unable to formulate a reply. I opted to smile and nod. 'I'll take you to your room so you can dump your stuff.'

I turned around to speak to Miss Featherstone, only to find that she had disappeared, the only trace of her left being an open window. I frowned slightly in confusion. The boy laughed at me, shaking his head.

'You'll get used to that, trust me. I'm Jamie, by the way.'

Jamie escorted me to the dining room that evening, making sure I knew how everything worked. I never believed that Earthen food could taste so good! After the frozen, precooked stuff I was used to back at the home, my taste buds felt like they were in heaven. I tugged absent-mindedly at my pendant, feeling the need to take it off, but with eight years of pent up magic lingering under its protection, I was scared of what might happen. Jamie seemed to notice.

'Do you need to let it out?' he asked. I looked at him quizzically. 'I get fidgety when I need to cut loose on my magic. What kind are you? Demon or angel?' I blinked, trying to figure out how he knew. He sighed. 'The profs always pair newbies with someone who has similar powers or species. I'm half demon and half angel, so it makes sense that you're at least one of those.'

'Demon,' I murmured, looking down at my plate. 'Half demon.' Jamie must have sensed my discomfort at the admittance. He reached out and touched my hand, his expression soft and understanding.

'It's okay, you're not alone here.'

At his kind words, a wave of unfamiliar emotion washed over me, leaving me feeling weak and a little confused. For the first time in years, I felt accepted for who I was. Here, I was no longer an outsider. Here, there were people here who were just like me.

The next morning, I looked in the mirror in the tiny bathroom attached to my room in the girl's wing of the school, the angel pendant lying next to the sink. For the first time in eight years, I was looking into my own purple eyes instead of the blue irises projected by the illusion charm. They seemed a little weird and alien on me now. A second white streak had grown in my hair alongside the first, contrasting with the deep violet. My appearance seemed strange to me now, as if I was staring at a familiar stranger. I had once more donned a cloak like I used to in Synairn, hoping that it wouldn't be sneered at here. I touched the brooch holding the garment around my neck. An intricate spiral of white metal holding in place a purple gem, upon which was etched the likeness of a dove. It had been Arellan's. She had used it to hold up her own cloak. Now it was mine. Swallowing hard, I tore my eyes from the strange reflection in the silver glass and grabbed my books, heading for Miss Feather's office. I was supposed to report to her secretary to get my timetable.

I was a little put off by the secretary to be honest. She was a sort of humanoid dragon and more than a little scary. I cast an eye over the timetable. At the top, my class and species had been written, but it was the species that caught my eye. Demon/Angel. I took out the note that had been attached to the timetable.

Angel is the closest thing we have to your 'Synari'. Enjoy!

I was the same as Jamie! That thought made my heart swell up in joy. A passing girl raised an eyebrow at me. I quickly quietened down my emotions. I had to remember that I wasn't the only empath here any more. And an even more sobering thought: I couldn't let anyone get close to me. Not with Karthragan still out to get me. I could sense him searching, seeking, hunting me. Putting someone else in the line of fire between him and me was not going to happen. Not ever. I was going to have to live a solitary life until I was sure I could defeat him on my own. I wouldn't put anyone else in that kind of danger ever again.

The Academy encompassed both junior and senior school, all seven years. I had been put into the third year. Classes started at nine o'clock and finished at five to give us plenty of time to relax and eat before the night students came out to play. According to the rules, day students are allowed to mix with the night, but for our own safety, it was better not to. Student knowledge was that some of the vampires in the night class weren't really in control of their blood lust. I didn't care. I spent most evenings in the library, researching every single thing I could for my school work. I desperately wanted to succeed here. I also wanted to avoid Jamie, and the library was one of the rare places he wouldn't venture into unless he had no other choice.

I managed to keep this up for a month before Jamie started to follow me even in the library. He and an orange haired girl about the same age. She was the reason I knew Jamie was following me. She just couldn't keep her mouth shut. I soon learned that her name was Holly, a hurricane on a sugar-high in human form. In the silence of the library, I could hear her comments all too loudly, and it seemed to annoy the other half demon.

She came to me once, in the canteen, sitting next to me as if we were friends. I edged away as she attacked her food like a starved bear. She started to speak, a never-ending stream of questions while shovelling rice into her mouth. I gaped at her, trying to keep up as she asked me about every single personal detail under the sun, from name to favourite colour to species to family. Strangely enough, despite rocky beginnings and personalities that were so far apart they were polar opposites, she became one of my best friends. A friend I will always hold dearly in my heart.

Holly introduced me to Natalie, who she affectionately referred to as her 'smarter' half. Both were sorceresses who used wands to channel their energy. They were blissfully unaware of exactly what I was. I, for my part, was perfectly happy to let them continue on in their delusion that I was completely human, like them, just a sorceress on a different level. Only Jamie knew, but he kept it as a secret. He regularly hung out with us, getting up to the same shenanigans. I was glad he did. It saved several awkward questions, but ultimately, it would lead to their downfall four years later, but, for now, they were my best friends.

Holly was a prankster. Thankfully, Natalie warned me about this early on, so I was always on the lookout for her tricks. Of course, this doesn't mean I didn't get caught out from time to time, but hey, she could have done a lot worse to me than adding Tabasco to my food. To her credit through, it was hard to keep a straight face around her. We stuck together like glue, the three of us. Even though she was deathly terrified of horses, she came to watch Natalie and me in our weekly pegasus class. Natalie stood next to Merlas and I on a pretty brown pegasus she had fallen for as we waited for the teacher to arrive. Holly leant on the fence, waving at us. Nat and I grinned, waving back. The teacher arrived, and the class groaned. We had two teachers for pegasus flying: Mrs Fletch, who was nice enough, although she could be a little absent-minded, and Mrs Steel, who was pretty much a drill sergeant and was unable to believe that her 'baby', a really nasty piece of work for a pegasus called Snowdrop, could do any wrong. Merlas had already told me about a run in she had with the white pegasus. Thankfully they had both escaped unscathed, although I was sure that Merlas would have won any fight she got into with Snowdrop. After all, pegusi like her hadn't been chosen as war mounts for nothing.

Mrs Steel strode out of the barn with Snowdrop prancing on the end of his reins, which she thrust at Holly. I had to bite the inside of my cheek to keep from giggling at the sight of Holly holding the pegasus' reins. She looked absolutely terrified and pissed off at the same time. But that expression evolved slowly into one I had grown to know and fear. She was plotting something. I glanced at Nat. She looked slightly scared as well. She must have seen the subtle glint in Holly's eye as the prankster started fiddling with Snowdrop's saddle. I schooled my face back into an appropriate expression when Mrs Steel reappeared, looking down at my hands in an attempt not to burst out laughing. Mrs Steel cast a disapproving eye over the whole class. I was waiting for a scathing remark from her, and she didn't disappoint me.

'I expected the lot of you to be turned out better than that. Sarah, your horse is filthy. Ira, you could at least have made an attempt to tame your hair. Natalie, I despair whenever I see you sitting on that poor creature. Shadow, I don't care if you own your steed, I expect you to sit properly!' I gritted my teeth, winding my fingers into Merlas's mane. For a start, I didn't 'own' Merlas. She owned herself. Secondly, I had never got the hang of the strange saddles they used here. For me, the proper leg position was the heel tucked under the rider's backside, not dangling down, getting in the way of the pegasus' wing. Mrs Steel sniffed, grabbing her reins back from Holly without as much as a thank you. She started to swing herself up into the saddle. The saddle slipped, sending her into the mud. The entire class and Holly fell about laughing. I gripped Merlas's mane hard as I tried not to fall off her back. It was such a typical Holly thing to do.

I passed many a happy year at the Academy. Going to classes a lot stranger and more exciting than regular classes, avoiding doors that weren't really there, (courtesy of Holly), trying not to get too involved in the many food fights that broke out in the school canteen. I managed to get to my seventh year without too much of an incident, if you didn't count the run in with the dragon in the forest. And the possession of a couple of the students by Karthragan's demons, and…well, let's just say they were eventful and leave it at that. But we had fun, Holly, Natalie and I, always embroiled in danger. Of course, things started to go wrong in my seventh year. Very wrong indeed. And it started with Arias.

I was walking with Holly and Natalie, heading back to the dorms after a long day. I had gone through Magical Manipulation and combat practise that day. I can tell you, having those two subjects in one day is not a fun thing. I was sore all over and exhausted to boot. I paused. That feeling, like jumping into cold water. I realised a split second before I found myself face down on a marble floor. Oh, my head! It felt as if Merlas had seen fit to dance the fandango on it. I pushed myself to my knees.

'Welcome back, Shadow.' Oh goddess, I knew that voice. I looked up to see Arias sitting on her throne, an old book in her hands. My eyes narrowed into slits as anger boiled up in my mind. I jumped to my feet, struggling to control my demonic side. How dare she? How dare she! She no longer had any control over my life!

'Why did you bring me back? And did you have to poof me out right in front of my friends? It's hard enough to keep a low profile!'

'Shadow!' Arias snapped, slamming the book shut. 'You will not answer back. You will not ask reasoning. You will not take that indignant tone with me. I do not care where you have been for the last number of years! I remain your superior, as does every being in this dimension! You will show nothing but grateful and gracious respect to us!'

I bit my tongue to keep from making another comment. Instead, I got to my feet and bowed low. 'Why have you seen fit to rip me from a life I was actually starting to enjoy?' Okay, so I couldn't stop myself from making a remark. I must have been hanging around Holly too much. She was starting to rub off on me. Arias narrowed her eyes at me, but didn't tell me off.

'Synairn is at war again. We need you on our front lines.'

'Oh no!' I clenched my fists, battling down my magic. 'I battled for you once. I'm not doing it again! I'm not going to war!'

'You will do as you are told!' I swear the white pillars shook with the force of her voice. I flinched. 'You will report to the armoury immediately.'

I had no choice really but to obey. I turned tail, stalking out of her receiving room, my cloak billowing out behind me. One day, I was going to punch her. My superior indeed. She didn't command me anymore!

Synari scattered as I walked through the halls, heading down into the underground floors of the Senate Towers where all the weapons and armour were stored. I felt the genuine streaks of fear as they remembered who I was. Shadow Roth, daughter of the late Senator Arellan and Karthragan the Demon. No longer was I the frightened girl who hid in her room for fear of being the target of people's hatred. Years on Earth had taught me that you shouldn't cower. I was as strong as, if not stronger, than the Synari. I had nothing to fear from them. I could hold my head high and let them challenge me if they dared. Then I felt a familiar presence. I smiled slightly. One of the many Synari stepped out from the horde and held out his arms.

'Armen!' I called, running forwards and hugging him tightly.

'My, my, Shadow, how you have grown tall. I take it our beneficent ruler has brought you back for the battle?'

I pulled away from him, my smile fading into a scowl. 'Yes, she did.'

Armen accompanied me to the armoury, where Rai still stood chief over all he surveyed. He greeted Armen as an old friend before he cast an eye over me, nodding in approval.

'At least this time, the armour I give you will actually fit!' he said with a smile. I tried to smile back, but I think all I managed was a pained grimace. My stomach was starting to tie itself into knots as I thought of the coming battle. He said nothing more, digging into his piles of metal plate. I found myself, much to my dismay, outfitted in much the same manner as before. The leather shirt, although this time with a matching pair of trousers, with the plates covering shoulders, arms, torso, back and legs, although this time, he handed me a long scabbard attached to a belt, which I wrapped around my waist. I drew the blade, a heavy, unwieldy thing made for two-handed swordplay. With another grimace, I sheathed it again. I clipped my cloak over my shoulders once again to keep away the cold as Rai handed me a helm. I ran my hands over it, feeling the slightly dented metal of the helmet, which looked a little like the Roman helmets I had seen in my human history book. I jammed it on my head before nodding once in thanks to Rai and heading out of the armoury.

I had never been out on the streets of Synairn on my own before. It was a curious feeling, as if I was a child doing something forbidden. I followed the rest of the armoured Synari out towards the plain, the same plain I had fought on before. I had to fight down the fear that threatened to overwhelm me. Why had she brought me back for this? I didn't want to fight! I just wanted to get though the end of year exams and finish my school years without getting myself killed!

'Demoness!' someone called. I turned in the direction of the sound, ready to snap a retort. A troop of Synari mounted on pegusi watched me critically and, standing next to the captain of what I guessed was a unit stood Merlas, decked out in plate armour, wearing a proper Synari pegasus saddle and guidance loop. I rushed to her side, hugging her tightly. The unit felt faintly amused, if my empathy was anything to go by. I felt my face burn in embarrassment as I realised how stupid I must look to the seasoned City Guards. Just another silly little girl hugging her favourite pony. I pulled myself up into the saddle, strapping myself in, enjoying the feeling of being back with her, even if it wasn't in the best of circumstances. The Synari I guessed to be the leader of the unit moved his pegasus to stand lengthways in front of Merlas, blocking any forwards movement. Merlas laid her ears flat along her neck, making a low growling sound more akin to a dog than a pegasus. I laid a hand on her neck, shushing her quietly.

'Listen up, Demoness. Here are the rules. Obey my command to the letter, and you'll do fine.'

I nodded once. The captain passed me a bow and quiver of arrows, saying that the 'pointy metal stick' was only going to be of use to me if Merlas went down. I didn't like the sound of that. The unit moved out, heading for the plains where the battle would be held. For the moment, the Synari were alone, arranged in ranks. Several pegusi units, including mine, stood on a small hillock, waiting for the signal from a commander standing with the foot soldiers. I have to admit, I couldn't see the Synari as foot soldiers. I couldn't even see them as soldiers. Never before in the history of Synairn had there been so many battles in such a short space of time. It made me wonder what Arias was up to, because this was not normal. I swallowed hard. Merlas shifted nervously beneath me. The captain glanced at me, feeling indecisive, sympathy battling with fear.

'Hey, Demoness, just try to keep calm. There is no need to work yourself up.' He paused for a moment, as if trying to find his words. 'Try to see it this way, would you rather be battling a horde of bloodthirsty monsters, or facing an angry Arias?'

'Monsters every time,' I said before I realised that I had spoken aloud, not just thought about it. The pegusi mounted soldiers within earshot chuckled quietly. I bit my lip, looking at the captain. He was watching me with a critical eye that made my heart hit rock bottom. I had gone too far. It had been a test. It—

One corner of the captain's mouth twisted upwards in a smile.

'You are not the creature we thought you to be, are you?'

I didn't know how to answer that one, so I didn't. He probably meant it as a rhetorical question anyway. Instead, I looked down at Merlas's mane, hoping that the shape of my helm prevented too much of a blush showing.

'To coin a phrase I believe you use in your current dimension of residence, 'you're all right', Shadow,' spoke one of the soldiers, giving me a light, friendly shove. There was an emotion there, echoed by all the other soldiers. I couldn't figure out what it was. It felt alien yet comforting, a familiar stranger. I realised I had sensed this before, from Holly and Natalie. Acceptance. They accepted me for who I was. For the first time in Synairn, I felt relaxed. At peace. We chatted idly for a few moments, most of which I spent committing their names to memory. Why had Arias locked me away all those years ago when all it took was for the people to see that I was still like them? She had said that the streets would not be safe for me, yet here I was, sitting on the back of a pegasus, making light of the coming battle with a group of soldiers.

From the plains of the upcoming battle, a great rip in the air spilled light onto the silver grass about to be stained with blood. Creatures began to spill from out of the gap, onto our plains. I chewed the inside of my cheek, trying to keep the anger from boiling over. Next to me, Captain Kildren swore in a steady stream under his breath. He glanced at me.

'Shadow?' he asked, his nervousness not quite hidden in his tone. 'We, uh, could probably use a distraction when we charge on them. Normally, any one of us could do it, but, uh, being a demoness, you could perhaps, uh, be a little…'

'Scarier?' suggested one of the soldiers.

'Yes, scarier.' The captain watched my reaction carefully, looking a little afraid himself. I bit my lip nervously. I could appear to be in the throes of a demonic possession, but such an exercise was highly volatile, requiring me to only let a little of the demonic influence escape through the barriers in my mind. I had experimented with it a little back at the Academy, but I had always been supervised by teachers who knew how to deal with an experiment gone wrong. Here, I was alone. If I went too far, all I would get is an arrow through my head. Everyone watched me nervously. The beginning clashes of the battle sounded below us. Merlas twisted her head around to nose at my boot. I let a half smile twist one corner of my mouth. Why learn things if you couldn't use them without being watched all the time?

'Yes. Yes, I can, and yes, I will.'

Our unit took to the skies. I let Merlas fly as she saw fit while I tried to tap into the demon. It was difficult, forcing myself to take down the defences I had spent years constructing. Piece by piece, I dismantled them. It surged forwards, able to taste the freedom it was on the verge of gaining. I clenched my fists, panting, trying to slow the advance. It was terrifying. It felt as if I was truly breathing the air. As if I was really in my body for the first time ever. My vision tinted red, doubling in focus. My teeth lengthened slightly. My claws grew. The soldiers watched me with fear in their hearts. I was acutely aware of the magic coursing through my blood. It would be so easy to obliterate the lot of them, to end the battle before it could even properly begin. I gritted my teeth. No. I wouldn't. I'd kill every single person in my unit before I even touched the enemy.

'Shadow?' the captain yelled over the winds, trying to make himself heard. I could still hear the wariness in his tone.

'It's okay. I'm still in control,' I called back.

'Take point and scare the living daylights out of them!'

I grinned, drawing my sword. Merlas brayed to the open skies as we began our dive towards the heart of the enemy's ranks. Black magic streamed from the two-handed sword. My hair and cloak billowed out behind me. My eyes glowed. Everyone looked up. Fear shot through the crowd. Then we joined them in battle.

I don't remember much of the battle. I don't want to remember much of it. I fought as best I could. I was pulled off Merlas early on, leaving me to stand on my own, fighting with a sword I didn't know how to use. A blade too long, unwieldy and heavy for me to use properly. I swung it wildly, ignoring the cacophony of pain building up in my muscles. My wrists ached. My shoulders shook. Exhaustion sapped at my mind. And they just kept on coming. Blood spurted beneath the sword, bone crunching. I swiped furiously at my eyes, clearing the haze of sweat and blood. My helmet kept slipping over my forehead, blocking my sight. I pushed it back angrily, stabbing at another enemy. The sword lodged in his chest. I couldn't free it! Panicking, I tugged at it, widening the wound in the corpse's side. Another enemy tried to decapitate me. I screamed, raising my arms in defence. The blade snagged on the plates of armour on my forearms, dragging a deep gash through the metal. He jabbed the sword sharply at my exposed stomach. The blade sank into flesh. My jaw fell open in silent agony as I dropped to the ground. Black blood gushed from the wound. I fell onto my side, trying to breathe through the throbbing pain.

'Oh bloody hell, Shadow. Can't you do anything right?' came an irritated voice from above. All I saw was a flash of purple hair before liquid cold engulfed me.

I found myself face down on a fairly soft surface for once, the icy fingers of the abrupt teleportation lingering for a moment along my spine. My head hurt like hell. I could barely breathe through the pain of the sword still stuck in my stomach. Whoever it was that sent me away was going to get a good punch right in the face if I ever found them.

'Ohmygod, Shad! What happened?'

'And can you get off me please? Seriously, Roth, you're heavier than I thought!'

'Holl? Nat?' I asked groggily. That would explain the soft landing, if I happened to land on Holly. I groaned as I rolled off her. I managed to get to my knees, bent double over the blade. Natalie looked horrified. Holly, as usual, started her rapid fire twenty questions routine.

'What happened? Why are you wearing armour? Why are you covered in blood? Why—'

'Holly! Shut up, we have to get her to the medical wing!' Natalie insisted.

'Oh bugger!' I muttered under my breath.

The medical wing of the Academy is somewhere no one ever wants to get sent to. It was a converted church, complete with altar that the head medic used as a desk. It still exuded the feeling of religion and strict punishment if you didn't adhere to the status quo. Angels with faces contorted in pain and anguish looked down from the eaves, not helping an already gloomy atmosphere. The head medic, Mr Greene, looked human, but he wasn't a medic for nothing. He was what was known as a Converter. He takes pain and converts it into heat. Other than that, he scared the crap out of everyone in the entire school. I guess that was also kind of a preventative measure. If you didn't want to face the medic, you didn't want to get hurt, so you were more careful. It also pretty much meant that I was *not* happy about going there. Unfortunately, I was in no position to stop a determined Nat. Nothing short of a herd of wild pegusi can stop a determined Nat.

'Holly, if you've hexed your eyebrows off again, I'm not fixing them for you.'

All three of us jumped when the head medic spoke from behind us. He swept an eye over what must have looked like a pathetic trio. He raised one eyebrow before seizing my arm, guiding me with ease towards one of the alcoves hidden by a curtain, dismissing Holly and Natalie.

'Well, Miss Roth, if you would be so kind as to remove the armour, we can set about getting the sword out of you.'

My fingers fumbled with the buckles, trying to pull off the rusted plates while Mr Greene left for a moment. Once they were finally in a messy heap on the floor, Mr Greene started to look at the damage done. I snarled at him as he touched the sword. He grunted in apology. I shot him a glare, daring him to do something like that again. He sighed, sitting back and matching my glare.

'I don't ask how you managed to get yourself skewered like a demon kebab, you try not to kill me when I try to unskewer you. Deal?' I nodded, looking down at my lap. He was trying to help me, which was more than I could have bargained for in Synairn. 'Okay, brace yourself. I'm going to have to pull this out of you. It's going to hurt for a bit before I start converting. Just try to keep still.' For the first time, I noticed that he had brought in a bar of metal and a bucket of water. I glanced down at them and then back up at the medic.

'You didn't think I was going to put the heat into you, did you?'

I smiled tightly and braced myself.

Swathed in bandages, I made my way to the canteen. Thankfully, Mr Greene had taken away most of the soreness, for now at least. I knew that it would be back later with a vengeance, but, or now,

I couldn't feel any pain. It was a fascinating process he used, taking the pain from a person and sending it down from his hand through his body to his other hand which grasped the metal bar and into the water. With the boiling water, he had told me with a wink, the best thing he had found to do was make a decent cup of tea. I shook myself from those thoughts as I picked up a tray, looking at the food. Unfortunately, due to the diverse number of species, everyone's diet was watched really carefully. If you didn't have a good reason for skipping a meal, you landed yourself in the medic's office. The food on the 'human and humanoid' menu didn't really inspire me, but having just come from the medical wing, I wasn't about to turn tail and walk myself back there. I wasn't that stupid. So I took a serving of shepherd's pie and dithered over a dessert. I wanted an apple, but I couldn't really eat them. Stupid fangs always got in the way. The only other options were a rather pathetic looking banana or a piece of chocolate cake. To be honest, chocolate cake was more Holly's thing. I took it. Holly was likely to be here somewhere and would gladly take it off my hands. I carried my tray over to where Natalie and Holly were finishing off their dinner.

'Hey guys,' I said, sitting down and poking my food, handing the chocolate cake to Holly.

'Heya kid, you all done with the pain vampire?' Holly, being her usual exuberant self, had found it funny in her first year to nickname Mr Greene as the 'pain vampire', since no one really knew what species he was and he sucked out your pain. It makes sense in my mind, but no one had, thankfully, ever used the name in front of him.

'Got more bandages than an Egyptian mummy, but yeah, I'm okay. He patched me up pretty well, considering what I looked like going in.'

'Shadow…' Uh oh, I knew that tone in Natalie's voice. I opened my mouth to interrupt her, but she asked her first question, and now she was not going to stop asking until she understood everything. This is a girl who spent her weekends in the library for fun. 'Where did you go? I mean, you poofed out on us in mid-conversation. I didn't even know you *could* poof!'

'I don't know if I can poof. My dad can. I'm not sure about my mum. But no, big lady in chief of my mum's people decided that she needed me for a bit.'

'Er, 'needed you for a bit'? Right. Shad, you came back looking like someone was about to put you on a barbecue!'

I gritted my teeth, jabbing my fork at the suddenly rather holey potato. 'Nat, Arias doesn't give two hoots about whether I live or die. I'm just a particularly useful tool to her, one she likes to think she can control. If I die, it's another annoyance out of her hair.'

'But why?'

'Because I'm stronger than the rest of them. Scarier, because of that power. It's the reason I wasn't allowed to stay with Arellan.' I kept my voice low, only audible to Nat and Holl, but that didn't stop the irritation in my in my voice from leaking out. I knew they wouldn't betray my trust by telling other people this kind of thing.

'Arellan?'

'She's...was my mother.' Natalie nodded silently, and didn't ask any more questions. That, unfortunately, didn't mean that Holly was placated.

'Hey, Roth!'

I would have thought that the reflexes and highly-strung nerves I still had left over from the battle were in my favour. My opinion changed afterwards though. After all, if I had taken the faceful of potato, I wouldn't have ended up standing in the shower, trying to get various pieces of dried, raw meat out of my hair. Mainly because, when Holly threw that potato, I ducked. It hit the alpha of the Academy's teenage werewolf pack. And it was two days before full moon. Let's just say that it riled them up. And the thing about the werewolves was that, although they can't change forms at will for most of the month, for two or three days before and after the full moon, their forms were unpredictable and they could change at will. Or not, if their emotions get in the way. And the alpha was seriously pissed off.

'Oops?' Holly said. The alpha growled deep in his throat. This was not going to end well. The pack stood up. They rolled their muscles, loosening up. They were preparing to shift. I gripped the back of my chair tightly. Natalie and Holly had their hands around their wands. Neither side moved for the length of a heartbeat. A lump of raw meat collided with Holly's forehead.

'Oh, game on!' Holly was revelling in the soon-to-be chaos. I couldn't help but crack a smile. The alpha had no idea what he was letting himself in for. Before long, potato and meat were being slung liberally across the tables. Some hit the pixies, who are a really nasty species when it comes to revenge. Their strange drink that they had for each and every meal entered the fray. I dived under a table, already covered in various foodstuffs. This was only the beginning. Holly, the werewolves and the pixies. I really didn't want to be around when the rest of the Academy joined in: the sorcerers, the sorceresses, the succubi, the incubi, the elves, the angels, the demons, the banshees and the harpies. There was going to be certain chaos. As usual, Holly was in the thick of it. Nat crawled under the table to join me.

'Wotcher, Shad. Mind if I hang out here for a while? At least until it stops being bedlam out there?'

'Be my guest. I'm not budging.'

'Cool, thanks. And Shad?'

'Yeah?'

'I think the werewolves managed to get you. You've got meat in your hair.'

Needless to say, I had to spend a long time in the shower before I managed to feel clean again.

Thankfully, Miss Feather didn't punish us since we hadn't

actually destroyed anything. It was an uncommon occurrence, being let off with a simple warning. Then again, I suppose when you get that many teenage mythical creatures with supernatural powers together, the best you can hope for is that no one gets hurt. And we managed to work out a little of the tension between the species in the school. I wish I could say all of my tension was gone though.

To say that the Academy is full of surprises was the under-statement of the century. For example, you never knew who you were going to meet next. Case in point: I was hanging out in the library, looking for a book I needed for a mythical creatures assignment on vampires. The point of the exercise was to foster an interspecies understanding, although it had been noted that only the strongest of the day students had been assigned a creature of the night. After all, the main body of the interview was to talk to a member of the species you were supposed to be working on, and no one wanted to get on the wrong side of a not-quite-in-control vampire. In any case, demon blood would smell wrong to the majority of them. I was looking for a book on vampire etiquette so as not to make an enormous *faux-pas* and end up on the menu anyway. That might just put a bit of a crimp on my project. I pulled a book from the shelves, flicking through to the index. Someone coughed politely behind me. I turned my head to glance over my shoulder. A boy about the same age as me stood there, looking very nervous. He looked somewhat familiar, but I couldn't place his slightly feminine, delicate features. He moved with grace and stood with poise. This was a boy that every girl in the school would be following, but for the moment, there was not a girl to be seen. He gripped the strap on his bag nervously. Automatically, I began trying to class his species. Incubi? Unlikely. They don't tend to go for slender bodies. Elf? Possibly. His voice broke through my inner mullings.

'Are you Shadow Roth?' he asked in a lilting accent I tried hard to place. I closed the book in my hands, turning to face him fully.

'Yes, I am. Can I help you?'

'My name's Ilrune. I was told you came from Synairn…'

I watched him warily. How did he know about Synairn? 'Yeah, I was born there.'

A weight seemed to have been lifted from his shoulders. 'You were the demoness under High Priestess Arias's care.'

'That's right.'

'Well, as I said, I'm Ilrune. I'm Careen, more specifically—'

'You're a Wingless.' This raised the question of 'why the hell was he here?'. The Wingless were Careen children born without wings. Extremely rare, they were revered as a good omen and were the nobility of the race. Unfortunately, there was no way of telling if a child was going to be born wingless or not, not even if both the parents were wingless. It was a very uncommon and unpredictable phenomenon.

Ilrune looked at the floor, embarrassed. 'Yeah, they thought I'd be better off here, away from all the fighting.'

I placed the book back on its shelf, smiling reassuringly at Ilrune. He looked very much like a lost puppy. At least the Careen were well renowned for their ability to pick up languages in a few days of immersion. 'Well, welcome to Earth and welcome to the Academy, Ilrune. Don't worry too much, you'll get used to it. Come on, I'll show you around.'

It was coming into the end of the year, summer was in full flight. I revelled in the heat. I can survive in cold, but the heat makes me feel alive! Not to mention that I always came down with a cold in the winter, and that was not a pretty sight. Every time I sneezed, I either changed forms or something exploded. People had taken to diving for cover because they never knew exactly what was going to happen. But in summer, there was no threat of that. I made the most of it. After class, most of the students took advantage of being allowed out into a nearby town, leaving the grounds mostly deserted. Holly, Nat and I usually decided to spend some time down by the lake. It was a place where we could relax and be ourselves without frustrating each other. Nat would sit under our favourite willow tree with her book, I would do my homework, and Holly would use her magic to push people into the lake. Everything was as it should be. I stretched out lazily under the tree. No more essay assignments to do, no tests coming up and Merlas had returned from Synairn, safe and sound. It felt good to have nothing to worry about. I closed my eyes briefly. A half smile twitched one corner of my mouth. Unclipping my cloak, I focused my mind. I hadn't willingly morphed for a long time. I was afraid I'd forgotten how. Thankfully not. Like a reliable old car, I slipped into the motions with relative ease. In wolf form, no longer a cub, but a sleek, fully grown she-wolf, I winked at Natalie before bounding to the water, jumping in with an enormous splash.

After paddling around a little, I hauled myself out. The urge to shake all the water from my coat was overwhelming, but I needed to get back at Holly for attempting to splatter me in the canteen again. I waited until I was right next to her and Natalie. Then I shook, and took a fiendish delight in the task before I morphed back into human form.

'You're a stinker, Shadow Roth!' Holly spluttered. I grinned back, wringing out my hair.

'Hey, what's up?' Jamie appeared from behind the tree, grinning down at us.

'Nothing much,' we answered. Jamie was a part of our little band as well, but he occasionally took off. I tried not to let that get to me. I know I had already kind of defeated the whole 'don't-get-close-to-anyone' thing, but I wasn't ready to face what I felt for Jamie. He was another part demon in a universe I thought they no longer existed in. I was glad to know that he was there, but I couldn't afford to let myself get attached. It would only mean that either I would get hurt, or he would. Or if things went far enough, we'd bring children into the world, children cursed with being part demon. Not something I would ever inflict on a kid. Not after what I had gone through. He nodded to me.

'Miss Roth, if you will?' he asked formally. I frowned slightly, getting to my feet. I couldn't fathom his game. He smiled at me, his brilliant blue gaze locked on mine. He raised his hands, palms towards me, to chest height. Oh goddess. Oh goddess. Oh goddess! I knew what he was up to. He was asking for a courting ritual native to his species of demon. And it was highly dishonourable for both parties if one refused. I stared at his hands.

'I...I...I don't know how...'

'You'll pick it up, trust me.'

I bit my lip, but raised my hands and placed them palm to palm. He smiled slightly. My demon side raised its ugly head. For a moment, I tensed, ready to battle it down. But it wasn't trying to take over. It wanted to dance. Tentatively, I let go of my control. The demon stretched, her influence spreading through my limbs, curling herself in my fingers. I became more aware of our beating hearts. Beating in time, our rhythm. I took a deep breath, and began to dance.

This kind of demonic courting ritual is a little difficult to describe. It really has to be seen. The closest thing I can find to describe it is a tango crossed with a fight and ballet. It's supposed to be the two demons moving in time with each other's heartbeat, the demoness proving herself able to hold her own against a demon, and the demon's determination to have the demoness. At least, that's how it is in the more 'civilised' of the demonic species and cultures, including both mine and Jamie's even though, like humans, demonic cultures can vary enormously between different groups and clans. Jamie and I moved faster and faster, as is custom. It becomes a spectacle for those standing close by, but for the dancers, they don't even notice. At least, they don't notice until they find themselves back in the beginning position. I was breathing heavily, staring at

Jamie. He panted, grinning at me. He leant his head forwards, dipping lower to kiss me. I'll admit it freely. The dance, the kiss. I was head over heels in love.

We were laughing, heading for the dining hall after classes when I felt the telltale burning in the back of my mind. With a jarring shock, I realised I hadn't released the pent up magic recently, the build up that occurred roughly once a month and had to be released. I gasped, leaning against the wall, one hand on my chest, trying to breathe evenly, force it back a little, enough to excuse myself and run for the forest. Holly and Natalie looked back at me, their carefree expressions immediately turning to concern.

'Shad, what's wrong?' Holly asked. Natalie rushed to my side, wand at the ready. I shook my head, swallowing hard. They couldn't follow me, it was too dangerous. Summoning up every scrap of energy and concentration I could muster, I turned tail and sprinted out into the grounds.

I reached an unnatural clearing deep inside the forest. The trees had been stripped of their leaves, their branches broken and splintered, the trunks and ground blackened by the force of my magic. Once a month, I came here. Once a month, every month. I collapsed in the centre of the clearing, trying to stay lucid enough to control the direction of the magical flow.

'Shadow, tell us what's happening!' Natalie's voice made it to my ears through the rushing sound of magic.

'Stay back!' I yelled out in warning. The fire in my muscles was starting to blaze. I couldn't keep it in much longer.

'Just tell us, you silly little person or I will bug you for eternity!' Holly shouted.

I didn't have time to say anything more. Magic poured out of my entire body, blasting the clearing with another wave of magic. I could avoid having to do this, but I didn't want to. By being at school, in such a social environment, I exposed myself, my power of empathy, to high levels of teenage emotions. I had also allowed my own emotional levels to become uncontrollable as well. This, as always, led to dangerous build ups of magic. Magic that had to escape somehow.

I don't know how long it lasted. I never do. I tried to time it once, but my magic fried the stopwatch. All I can say is, at least I didn't scream this time. Instead, I realised a little too late that this time, I was going to be hit by what some humans termed as 'a double whammy'. Night had fallen, and the moon was nowhere to be seen. I felt the shivers run through my body. Glancing down at my hand confirmed my suspicions. No claws. I was human again for three days and three nights. Whoopee. I slowly got to my feet, staggering, grabbing onto a tree to steady myself. Of course, human meant a lot weaker. Even in demonic form, a power surge left me tired and out of action for a day or two. Human form meant that I was going to be in pain for the next day at least, whether I managed to crawl out of bed or not. Holl and Nat had never seen me human. Not once. Normally, I planned the month with a moon phase chart, casting an illusion charm on a ring or something to give myself the appearance of my half-demon form. This month, I had completely forgotten about it. I felt a hand touch my shoulder.

'What was that?' Natalie asked quietly, locking gazes with me, trying to find an answer in my eyes.

'Yo, Shad, dude! What happened to you?!' exclaimed Holly, barging in on Natalie's quiet concern in true Holly fashion. I shook my head at her. Natalie, thankfully more subtle than the other third of our trio, shushed the girl with a silencing charm. Taking a deep breath, I focused on putting one foot in front of the other in order to get back to my room. Natalie let me go on ahead for a few moments before following. I silently thanked her. I was going to get grilled for this later, but in the immediate aftermath, Natalie was willing to let it go. It would hurt so much to have to lose her when I eventually moved on from here.

When I opened the door to my room, I found Jamie waiting for me. I sighed heavily at the sight of his confused expression. Yeah, I know, I looked human for the moment, but he didn't have to stare. I headed for the tiny en-suite attached to my room, intending to melt into a puddle at the bottom of the shower for a while.

'Go away, Jamie, I'm really not in the mood,' I grunted irritably, knowing how scratchy my voice probably sounded. It certainly felt raw. Jamie let out a long humph of frustration.

'Well, I've got a letter here for you. Come and find me tomorrow to talk about it.'

'You read my post?' I said, narrowing my eyes. 'Isn't that some sort of big human no-no?'

'We're not human, Shad. Good night,' Jamie said, winking as he left the room.

I sat with my back against the wall, scalding hot water cascading down on my head, trying to wash away the residual ache. With a deep sigh, I stood up, turning my face to the spray and washing the last remnants of shampoo from my hair before shutting off the water. Dressed in the baggy trousers and tank top that constituted my pyjamas, I wandered towards my bed, sleepily plaiting my hair. Grabbing the envelope Jamie had left, I curled up on my bed under my favourite purple blanket. I cursed the absent moon for my current inability to catch a scent off the envelope to determine who it might be from. I pulled out two pieces of paper, one a page that looked to have been ripped out of a fairly old book, the other, a scrap torn from the bottom of a notepad. The scrap read:

You are in danger. He's coming. Watch your back.
–A

I sat back, trying to think about who 'A' could be, and why they would want to warn me about being in danger. I didn't recognise the spiky script from any of my classmates, nor Jamie, Holly or Natalie. I picked up the other piece of paper to see some sort of poem written there:

On the twelfth moon of the Aquarius Summon
The demon will be strong
He shall be summoned by the Messenger angel
Three beating hearts become many
The demon may be vanquished
Through the beating of a lover's heart
And He shall lose his power to their cores
On the sixteenth moon of the Aquarius summon
Two infants shall be born
One a Halfling wolf, one a Halfling Lycorn
By the third moon of their birth
The magic shall rise
And so the prophecy shall begin.
On the night of her 360th moon
Wolf and Demon shall lock in mortal fight
Only the victor shall prove to lead the darkness
Neither heart will continue to beat
Through the mourning tears

One line of the poem had been heavily scribbled out. I didn't have to wrack my brains too hard to discover the culprit. I sighed heavily, rolling over on my side. I was tired, exhausted, but the poem had stirred something in my mind, reminded me of something from so long ago. I just couldn't remember what. Little did I know that this was the beginning of the end. I slumped back against the pillow, too tired to think any more. I closed my eyes, praying that my vulnerable period would pass faster than it sounded.

Jamie was waiting for me at breakfast the next morning. I silently glared at him, grabbing some food and sitting far away from him. Unfortunately, he followed me. I bit into my apple, a fruit I could only really enjoy during my non demonic time since my fangs usually got in the way.

'Is there some part of being a jerk that means you ignore perfectly clear body language?' I asked icily, still annoyed that he had opened, read and scribbled on my post before I had even read it.

'Hey, hate the game, not the player,' Jamie retorted. 'I'm just trying to protect you, Shad.'

'Funny way of doing it,' I muttered. Holly ran over to us in her usual hurricane mode, sitting next to me and immediately tearing into a bowl of cereal that was so full of sugar it made my teeth ache in sympathy. Natalie followed in a somewhat more sedate style with a plate of toast. Jamie cast me a look that clearly stated that we would talk later. I glared back.

Three days and three nights later, I sat up a tree on the edge of the forest, waiting impatiently for night to fall again. I hated being trapped as a human, and this one had definitely outlasted its novelty period. At least I had evaded Natalie's questions. Holly had teased me for the first two days, but I think she was as confused as Natalie. I leant my head back against the tree trunk, watching the sky. Something crashed further in the trees. I squinted, trying to see through the dark shadows of the trees, muttering a curse under my breath about human eyes and how useless they were for seeing in the gloom. Something was moving in there. Something not human that made my hair stand on end and my head hurt.

'Hey, Shadster! Whatcha doin' all the way up there?' Holly's voice echoed up through the branches.

'Shad, we really need to talk, you've been avoiding me for three days!' Natalie's plaintive call wasn't far behind. I gritted my teeth, trying to listen, but all I could hear was Holly and Natalie below me.

'Shush,' I hissed, glaring down at the pair.

'Hello you lot, what're you all up to now?' Jamie said, sauntering casually across the grounds towards us. I rolled my eyes. Just what I needed. Another nosy part demon. I didn't know if he had made the name connections, but I sure didn't want him to meet 'dearest Daddy'. Then again, he said that his father was the anthropomorphic personification of War. Maybe he knew what it was like to have the evil paternal figure.

'Trying to get a couple of answers off Shad. You know how hard that is when she doesn't want to talk.'

'Maybe I can help you, then,' Jamie smirked.

'Don't you dare!' I threatened.

'Really? Okay, why has she been all weird for the last few days?'

'Vulnerable period, her breed of part demon has them. Turns their physical over to their primary half.'

'Earth speak, please, Jameson?' Holly interrupted.

I could almost see the evil grin growing on Jamie's face. 'She hasn't told you? She's a half demon.'

There was silence for a moment before Holly broke it. 'Whadda ya mean, she's a half demon? OHMYGOD! That means she's just like you! When's the wedding?! When are the children gonna come?!'

'Shut it, Holly,' I growled, dropping down from the tree. A bolt of magic slammed into my back, sending me to the ground. I glanced behind me. What I saw made my blood run cold. The black hair, the ragged cut-off trousers, the red eyes. Karthragan! How did he track me here? He wasn't supposed to be able to track me here! Frozen by panic, I couldn't move. All I could do was pray that I smelled different in human form. There was no way I'd be able to take him on in this state. I yelled at the others to run, scrambling to my feet, trying to get to the school. I had to get to a teacher, to warn everyone. Another blast of magic caught me off balance. I hit the ground once again with a painful thud. Karthragan grabbed me by the hair, wrenching me backwards. I thought my spine would crack under the pressure. Somewhere to the side came the sound of a battle cry. The pressure on my spine vanished. Flipping over, I spotted a violet-haired girl with a huge sword dodging bolts of magic.

'Get the humans inside, Shadow!' she yelled. I remembered that voice. She had sent me back from Synairn!

'But who—' I started to ask before she repeated her orders. Deciding that this was one woman I shouldn't mess with, I grabbed Holly, sprinting towards the main building of the Academy. Natalie came running out of the front door, wand at the ready. The sun finally set. The shivers ran through my body as the warmth of magic coursed through my blood once more. Thrusting Holly to Natalie, I ran back out to where the fight between Karthragan and the strange girl had reached magical levels. The girl moved unevenly, as if her leg hurt. Karthragan must have managed to land a blow on her! Yelling a few choice words of my own, I joined the fray.

'Get out of here, Shadow!'

'I can help!' The momentary distraction allowed Karthragan to land a punch on me. I gasped, frozen to the spot. His hand had gone through me, lodged in my stomach without leaving a mark. I could feel it. A brief flash of surprise flitted across his face before a smirk twisted his cruel features. He pulled his hand away, letting me crumple to the ground. He raised his sword, preparing to deal the final blow. The blade sliced through the air. It clanged as it hit something solid. Natalie stood not far off, wand raised, holding a shield in place above me. Gratitude flowed through my mind as I scrambled out of the way, summoning my magic, ready to fight. Holly and Natalie joined us, preparing themselves to kick some serious butt. Karthragan laughed. I didn't like the sound of that. He had something up his sleeve. I just didn't know what it was. Something slammed into my back, pinning me to the ground. I rolled, trying to throw whatever it was off. I froze. Jamie.

'What the hell are you doing?' I snarled, trying to shove him off. He smirked.

'What do you think I'm doing?'

I employed a technique I had only ever seen used once, and that was by Holly on a boyfriend she had caught with another girl. I kicked up backwards as hard as I could. Jamie yelped in a surprisingly satisfying high-pitched voice I shot out from underneath him, running to Holly and Natalie, starting to herd them towards the school.

'You've got to go!' I urged them.

'Nat, have you ever realised that whenever Shadow says that and we obey, she always ends up beaten to a pulp?' Holly asked airily.

'Please, don't argue,' I begged them, 'you have no idea what he's capable of!'

'No, Shadow, we're staying. You might have lied to us all these years, but we're still your friends.' Natalie replied firmly. She opened her mouth to say something else, but Karthragan launched his next strike. A wave of magic, not unlike one I unleashed during a power surge, knocked us all off our feet. For a moment, I couldn't breathe, the wind knocked out of my lungs. I coughed as I pushed myself up, wrapping an arm around my ribs.

'Shadow?' came a quiet voice. A hand touched my shoulder. The strange girl was there. I finally got a good look at her. Her violet hair was cut in a severe bob although it was messy from fighting. Her eyes were equally purple. She looked so familiar. 'Come on, Shadow,' she said, helping me get up. 'I've taken care of Dad. Let's get you seen to.'

'Holly… Natalie…' I murmured, looking around for them. My eyes fell on two limp forms still lying in the grass. I froze. They weren't breathing.

I vaguely remember the girl dragging me off to the dorms, back to my room as I stared blankly ahead in silent shock. I sat in the shower again, the way I had done three days ago. Silent tears streamed down my cheeks, mixed with the scalding water. Oh goddess, they were dead. Holly and Natalie were dead! I had lost yet more people to Karthragan. When would it end? When would I be able to make friends with people without fear of Karthragan coming and taking it all away from me once more? Would he always be two steps behind me, just waiting? An hour later, the girl had to pull me out of the shower. She sat me on the bed, wrapped in a blanket, staring blankly at the wall.

'Look, Shadow, you can't afford to do this to yourself. It's too dangerous. You know that.'

'Who are you?' I murmured dully, not even looking at her, continuing to glare flatly ahead of me. My eyes were dry of tears, but I still felt the need to cry.

'I thought you would have recognised me, Shadow. I'm Amarath, Amarath Roth. Your twin.' I tore my gaze away from the wall to look at her. Her hair, her eyes, her whole face. Everywhere in the scriptures, it had said that demons come in pairs. I had never actually realised the implications of that. Every demon had a twin. Amarath was mine. I let out a harsh, bark-like laugh. I had lost both my best friends, another friend betrayed me and I had found a long-lost sister. Ignoring her as best I could, I stood up and got dressed. I put on the clothes that would be almost a uniform for me for the next few years. All black, a long-sleeved top, jeans with a belt that could hold potion vials, ankle boots, and my cloak. I glanced around the room. Everything in it reminded me of Holly and Natalie. The books Natalie wanted me to read, the whoopee cushion I had taken off Holly for overuse. Photos of the three of us laughing. Every memory I had gathered at the Academy, Holly and Natalie were a part of. How could I put it all behind me, knowing that I was the cause of their demise? How could I move on, knowing that their death was my fault? Amarath touched my shoulder gently.

'Shadow, we need to go. I'm really sorry about your friends, but we need to get out of here before Karthragan turns up with reinforcements. Stop acting like you're dead or you *will* end up as a corpse! Pack up your stuff, we're leaving. I've got someone I want you to meet.'

PART 3

EARTH – THE CLAN YEARS

We left the Academy. I packed everything, got Merlas and we left. Amarath teleported us to a clearing somewhere, a power she assured me I was capable of wielding, just not trained to do. I wasn't really listening to her. My mind was too focused on Holly and Natalie, the things we'd done together, the teachers we'd pranked, the trouble we had gotten ourselves into. Amarath snapped her fingers in front of my face. I jumped, glaring at her.

'What did you do that for?'

'You weren't listening. I told you, this is Shaeman.' I hadn't noticed a tall man standing next to us. Another part demon. I could sense it. His face appeared open and friendly, despite the scars I could see, although they were mainly hidden beneath his clothes. His shaggy, silver hair had once been cut short, but now left to grow out, reaching down to his shoulders. One lock of hair, messily plaited, reached down to his waist. His clothes were a deep red, covering as much skin as possible, with some sort of half cloak covering his right side. Despite his hair colour, he appeared to be only a couple of years older than I was, in his early twenties. His silver eyes stirred something in my memory, but I couldn't place it.

'Shadow,' he said, nodding at me. 'We have met before, although not introduced.' I racked my brains for any memory of a silver haired man when it struck me. This has to be one of the twins who took me to Karthragan when Arias banished me to Aspheri!

'You, you were one of the boys who led me to Karthragan, weren't you!' I snarled. I clenched my fists, riling myself up for a fight, eyes narrowed and temper flaring. If Amarath thought we could trust this moronic, backstabbing...

Shaeman put up his hands in a surrendering gesture. 'To be

fair, I was eight at the time. At that point, if I didn't obey Dad, then the consequences were severe. We didn't tend to question his authority.'

'Long story short, Shad, Shaeman's our half brother, him and his twin Vrael. Kar's been breeding like a rabbit on Speed. Vrael managed to get himself chucked into another dimension. We've got to pull together as a family if we're going to get through the prophecy.'

'Prophecy?'

'Oh, in the name of Arias! What did they teach you in the Senate Towers?'

'Obviously not what you think…'

Amarath and Shaeman sighed, exchanging long suffering glances before beginning to explain. In the rules of demons and part demons, they were born in pairs. That much I had finally understood. It also seemed, in the case of powerful demons and all part demons, one of the twin's lives was subject to prophecy. In the most part, they weren't an important factor. However, the more powerful the demon parent, the more the prophecy took control of their life. This time, it fell on me. Karthragan happened to be the Prince of Darkness, the big cheese of the demon world. The poem that Amarath had sent me was the prophecy. In short, I was going to die at his hands and him at mine to determine who would rule over the demons.

'But before we start working on that, we have to find Vrael. Between the four of us, we should be able to deal with Karthragan should he decide to try to start the prophecy early. Which doesn't work, by the way, so don't get any ideas.'

'So, where is this brother?'

'DOTD.'

DOTD, or the Dimension of the Dead, was aptly named. No one who has ventured there for any length of time has returned whole, or indeed, returned at all. I'd only ever heard of one person, an explorer from Synairn, who once made the journey there. He came back as a changed man. He locked himself in his home for months, refusing to speak to anyone, refusing to leave. One day, he stepped out of his front door, and disintegrated into dust. He never spoke to anyone of his journey. When the City Guard searched his house after his death, they found nothing about his travel to the dimension. Not a single word or drawing. And now we were heading to the exact same place. Amarath, Shaeman and I. I did vaguely wonder about our sanity. Why were we going to a place that had such a cursed reputation? Even if we did find Shaeman's twin, there was no guarantee that they would even recognise each other. However, I did have to respect the fact that I had no idea what I was doing, and they did. Maybe demons weren't affected by the curse or something. Following their lead, I pulled the hood of my cloak low over my face. Shaeman's hand gripped my shoulder tightly in order to teleport me, neither of my siblings willing to let me try on my own. Squeezing my eyes shut, I prepared myself for the unpleasant freezing sensation that I had come to associate with interdimensional teleportation.

The dimension of the dead was cold. Very cold. I drew my cloak tighter around me to try to stave off the bitter, icy wind, tucking my fingers into folds in the material. The landscape itself was hostile, with jagged mountains clawing at a grey sky, sharp stones littering the plains. Even the trees were dead, bark blackened by some long-dead fire, their twisted branches broken and crumbling. It looked as if someone had taken all the colour from this world, leaving it with nothing more than shades of grey. The only spot of colour I could see was the dying sun, a patch of red struggling to maintain its place in the sky as gravity tried to drag it down behind the mountains. Before us lay fields of tangled briars and brambles, with sharp thorns inviting us to spill our blood on them. Shaeman sniffed the air then tilted his head to one side slightly, listening out for something. Amarath drew her sword, her eyes scanning the landscape for anything resembling danger. They glanced at each other. Shaeman gestured towards a tiny column of smoke. Amarath nodded. I felt as if I had missed out on something. Amarath and Shaeman seemed perfectly capable of dealing with the retrieval of Shaeman's twin without my help. Why had they brought me along? It's not even as if I knew very much about demons, nor about what we could do. Amarath began to hack a path through the thick net of thorns with a ferocity I sincerely hoped she would never turn against me. Pulling my hood a little further down over my face, I followed her, with Shaeman close behind.

The column of smoke came from a village, the only thing in the barren landscape that actually seemed to have some degree of life. We crept closer, trying to be as discreet as possible. Amarath and Shaeman had mastered a sort of predatory lope that was silent and unnoticeable, even if Amarath's was slightly more awkward as she favoured one leg. I, on the other hand, was about as discreet as a bull with diarrhoea. We paused at a thicket of dry, brittle bushes to observe the little village. Pale, flickering light illuminated the windows of the blackened timber structures. A larger source of light came from what I guessed was the heart of the village. Amarath gestured for us to advance. I shivered as we passed through the empty streets, wondering what sort of creatures could live here. It was as if nothing could live here. Everything was so dead. The sound of clashing metal and cheering voices filled my ears. Amarath peeked round one of the dilapidated houses before pulling back and gesturing to Shaeman to look. I looked around as well. In what appeared to be the central square of the tiny village, people were gathered in a circle around a grey, flickering fire and two fighting men. My gaze was locked on the two clashing swords. The light danced on their bare torsos, flashing across the planes of their toned muscles. The firelight played in the silver hair of one of the combatants, tied back in a loose ponytail. His movements were fluid and graceful as his slender, lithe body, turning the battle into a dance, the ultimate predator. I hadn't realised how closely I must have been watching him, not to mention the fact that my mouth was hanging open in awe at their display of combat skills. Amarath elbowed me in the ribs, a smile playing on her lips.

'I wouldn't get too many ideas, Shad, since that's your brother.' I rolled my eyes at her, shaking my head. Yeah, he was good-looking, but after the fiasco with Jamie, I was definitely not looking for a man in my life. I swear, even though I'd only just met her, Amarath was going to be the death of me. I turned my gaze back to the fight as the fighter I now knew to be Vrael thrust his sword through the chest of his opponent. I felt my eyes widen. It had been a duel to the death?! My astonishment at that, however, was nothing compared to the shock as I watched the defeated man look down at the blade protruding grotesquely from his ribs and *laugh*. He laughed and pulled the weapon out, handing it back to Vrael, saying something to his in a strange, harsh language that I couldn't understand, a language so feral and growling as to be intimidating. The language of the dead. It made my fangs ache just to hear it. Shaeman, his eyes fixed on his twin, whistled low under his breath. In the middle of the crowd complimenting him on his fight, Vrael stiffened, alert. His eyes scanned the streets, looking for the source of the noise.

Someone grabbed me from behind, yelling out in that language. I scrabbled at the arm around my neck as my hood was yanked down. My claws cut deep gashes in my captor's flesh, but they didn't seem to even notice. A hand grabbed my hair, pulling my head to one side to expose my neck. I heard yells of surprise and indignation as Amarath and Shaeman were given the same treatment. Vrael spoke, his voice commanding and authoritarian as he strode towards us, displaying the same graceful, dangerous lope as his brother had, sheathing the sword in a scabbard on his hip, a shirt hanging over his shoulder. He was pale, paler than his twin, but shared the same silver hair and eyes, although his hair, instead of being cropped short like Shaeman, had been left to grow long to his shoulder blades and swept into an elegant queue. The villagers were restless, that much was obvious. The man holding Amarath snarled at Vrael before raking his teeth down Amarath's neck. Black blood immediately welled in the two grooves left by his fangs. Shaeman roared in fury, tearing himself out of his captor's grasp, lunging towards me. Amarath dealt her own captor a nasty head-butt, probably breaking his nose, before she leapt for Vrael. Shaeman's fingers dug into my arm a split second before he teleported.

I found myself face down in a pile of dirt. Why was it that the norm for being teleported by someone else seemed to invariably end up with me landing on my face? Shaking my head, I got to my feet, brushing myself off, trying to convince myself that the trip to the DOTD had not been all that traumatic and that all four of us were not going to need therapy for the rest of our lives. Shaeman appeared at my side, carefully turning me away from something. I tried to look back over my shoulder. Shaeman snorted quietly as he put his hand over my eyes, preventing me from seeing anything.

'I wouldn't do that if I were you. You really don't want to see this.' He was right. From the glimpse I saw, I really didn't want to know about or see Vrael sucking at Amarath's neck. It was an image I was sure I would carry for the rest of my life, and not one I really wanted to. I squeezed my eyes shut, trying not to think about it. Shaeman chuckled under his breath.

'Not particularly nice, is it? But then again, Vrael has to get the venom out of Amarath's system before it starts converting her into a vampire like him.'

'Vrael's a vampire?'

'They don't call it the dimension of the dead for nothing. They're all vampires there. Well, Vrael wasn't when he was sent there, but they fixed that for him.'

'But he's out in sunlight… I thought vampires couldn't do

that.'

'Full bloods can't. Vrael's only a half. His demonic blood wouldn't allow vampirism to take over any more than that. He can go out in sunlight, cast a reflection and eat garlic. I'm not sure I'll let him do that last one though. I don't think I could stand the smell of it hanging around.'

'It is done. You may now look,' came Vrael's velvet tones. Amarath was getting to her feet, one hand on her neck, wobbling somewhat but intact. That's what counts.

Over the next month, we built our house. It should have taken longer than that, and would have if the construction workers had been human. But we weren't human. We had magic and strength on our side. We built it in that clearing, using wood from the trees, occasionally pulled through the forest by Merlas if we couldn't do it ourselves and stone drawn out by magic from the deep undergrowth. Shaeman even figured out how to make serviceable cement from the river, with water, sand and silt, (I suspect heavy amounts of magic). We even managed a full round of vulnerable periods. Unfortunately, that turned Vrael into a full vampire. We ended up burying him for the duration of the vulnerable period to prevent him from turning into a pile of ash. I learnt a lot about my siblings in that time spent working with them, building a sort of family dynamic between us. A strange one certainly, but it was ours. We were putting the finishing touches to the structure of the house when he started to look at me strangely. I have to admit, I was a little nervous. I didn't really fancy becoming a vampire's chew toy, even if he was my brother (okay, half brother). Shaeman noticed it and threw him a vial of blood from the collection we had all chipped in to create. Vrael shook his head, throwing it back at him, Shaeman catching it in a coordination born of throwing things at each other over the last month.

'What's up, Vrae?' Amarath asked, walking over, wiping her

hands on her cloak.

Vrael gestured towards me with one hand. 'She's pregnant.'

'I'm *what*?!'

'Pregnant,' Vrael repeated, 'I can smell the shift in your hormones.'

'But...how?'

Amarath whacked her head off her palm. 'Oh, I'm such an idiot. Karthragan punched you in the stomach. That would have been enough if you weren't blocking it.'

'Whoa, slow down here, will someone explain, please?' I pleaded.

Vrael and Amarath glanced at each other before Amarath sighed heavily, rolling her eyes at the two boys. 'All right, so it's a girl topic. Wusses! Shad, in a magical sense, a child is a bonding of the essences of the parents. In creatures such as ourselves, who can use magic to bend the rules of solidity, putting any part of your body *through* the other person's body constitutes a melding of the essences. The only way our bodies can cope with this is by focusing this on creating a child. You should have been taught to be able to counteract this, block it so that he couldn't put his fist right through you. Unfortunately, you haven't, and now you're carrying Karthragan's kid, which is wrong on so many levels.'

'Not only that, but for demonesses, the pregnancy is swift, lasting five months at most. Judging by the smell of you, you have perhaps three, three and a half months to go,' Vrael added.

I ran a hand through my hair. 'There wouldn't happen to be some big book on 'everything you need to know about being a demon', would there?'

'Nope, sorry,' Amarath said cheerily. 'Just us.'

We managed to finish the house completely by the end of two more months. After a couple of disastrous attempts, we decided to rely on magic and not on electricity in the house. The smell of fried vampire is particularly insulting to keen noses. Unfortunately, I now resembled a beached whale. Vrael had started to get together various medical supplies, pinching what he needed from a nearby city as we had done to help us build the house. What we couldn't make ourselves, we had to steal, doing so at night, teleporting into the shops so as not to set off any alarms. Most of my teleportation training was done on such outings. It also came to general consensus that once the twins were born, I would go into the city and try to find a job. After all, I was the only one with any kind of qualification that might be recognised in this dimension.

I spent more and more time with Merlas, talking to her and occasionally flying. Vrael's constant checks on me were starting to get on my nerves. Although he had studied medicine, (turns out even demons get ill, which is a little odd), he had never really had to apply it. He had learnt a lot of his healing knowledge from an old vampire in the Dimension of the Dead, and he had said himself that injuries and illness were, in a somewhat expected manner since they were all dead, rare. Somehow, I think he was more nervous about the whole thing than I was. At least until I went into labour. I was leaning against Merlas's side when the contractions started. I hissed in pain, doubling over. Merlas nickered in concern before letting loose with an ear shattering neigh. Amarath popped her head out of a window to tell the doe to shut up when she noticed that I was curled up in the grass, sheltered under Merlas's protective wing. All three of my siblings rushed out to help me back into the house.

I don't remember much of the birth. Vrael had me on a series of painkillers to help me get through. Merlas still grumbles that when she stuck her head through the window of the ground-floor room we had designated as a medical centre, I had grabbed onto her mane and refused to let go. I suppose it would explain why I had a handful of coarse black hair in my hand. Either way, thankfully, the birth went without a hitch. I had given birth to two healthy part demon girls. I held one of them carefully, feeding her with a formula Vrael had put together. For the moment, they were identical, black haired and blue eyed. I lay back, exhausted. All I wanted to do was sleep. Amarath poked her head around the door before walking into the room and perching on the edge of the bed.

'Have you thought up names for them?' she asked, sitting next to me.

'Yeah, Archangel Holly and Onyx Natalie,' I said softly.

'You miss them, don't you?'

Miss them? An understatement. I had lost my two best friends to Karthragan in the same way I had lost my mother. Every day without them was like living without a part of me. I couldn't tell Amarath that. She didn't understand friendship. She had never been taught what friends were. I needed to grieve for my friends, but I couldn't allow myself to mourn them in the same way I had mourned Arellan. The clan was relying on me for some reason, believing that I was going to be able to defeat our father. To allow myself such grief would be to destroy what faith they had in me. But I couldn't expect her to understand that. She understood duty, but not emotion. So to answer her question, I simply said, 'Yeah, I miss them.'

To her credit, she didn't say anything else. We sat in silence for a moment before Amarath got to her feet, leaving in silence with the strangely fluid pace she used to compensate for her leg. I had once asked her what had happened to cause the constant pain she seemed to suffer, but her only response had been 'something that happened a long time ago and far away'. I looked down at the two tiny bodies sleeping curled up next to me, smiling slightly before joining them in slumber.

As agreed, a week after the birth of Archangel and Onyx, I was in the city, looking for a job. I managed to find something pretty quickly, thank the goddess. A small, struggling florist shop. They dismissed my lack of qualification in the face of being able to communicate with people and arrange flowers into something pretty. I could do that. I even had the nose to be able to put together smells that complimented each other. I worked alongside a teenager, a girl who looked to be the same age as I appeared to be. She smelled a little strange though. Not quite human. She hid her strangeness well though, with a passion for flora so strong that the owner of the shop often deferred to her when it came to ordering the flowers. After a few days, I managed to feel enough at ease in the shop to ask her name. She smiled at me, and said her name was Alba Manticora.

Archangel and Onyx were growing quickly and had thirst for knowledge that superseded my own and taking very much after their namesakes. Onyx had a passion for reading the dictionary and any other informative book she could find. Amarath often grumbled, as she dismantled prank after prank, what had possessed me to name a certain child 'Archangel'. Thankfully, I escaped each day to go work, leaving them in Vrael's care. This bewildered the part vampire. He had no idea how to handle children and often found that he had to call in backup from Amarath in order to control them. Each night, I came home to find Vrael in his animal form of a panther, submitting to having his ears and tail pulled by the over-inquisitive twins. His tail now has a permanent kink in it from being pulled out of shape, but he considers it to be minor compared to having no tail what so ever. Strangely enough, they behaved around Merlas. They never put a toe out of line. Soon, she became their primary babysitter, much to her dismay, to the point where she disappeared for the best part of three months. I wasn't worried about her though. Merlas could fend for herself. Three years later, when the girls' magic manifested a dark green, I started to see myself mirrored in them, in Archangel's appearance, which mimicked mine almost perfectly, and Onyx's joking despair on her sister's part, not unlike the attitude I used to have with Holly. The only way to train them was to play, and I found myself playing games of tag in the forest to train them to teleport, always ending up breathless from laughter. It was as if I had found my best friends again.

I often escaped from my family in the forest, to reminisce. I thought about Holly and Natalie, the shenanigans we had managed to get up to at the Academy and in its grounds. Somewhere in the forest of the Academy, there was a tree with the letters HB, NP, SR. Holly Bristol, Natalie Patterson and Shadow Roth, the trio that had sparked fear in the hearts of the most experienced of teachers. It was difficult letting them go. I wandered further into the forest than I usually did, lost in thought. Something rustled on the edge of the path. I stopped, looking around, trying to see what had moved. A twig snapped. I put a hand on the hilt of the sword Amarath had taught me to use. Crouching, half hidden by a tree, I watched as a creature of fantasy crept along the path. A manticore, if I remembered my mythological creatures class properly. I sniffed the air. The scent of the manticore was familiar. I nearly whacked my head off the tree. I must be stupid. Alba *Manticora*.

'Alba?' I asked softly, stepping towards the creature. It jumped, morphing back into a rather bewildered looking teenage girl. I smiled slightly. 'I thought you smelled a little odd.'

'Shadow? What're you doin' out here?' she asked warily. I could sense her kicking herself mentally. I made a guess that it was because I'd spotted her. A lot of being a non-human rested on not being found out. It was the only way to stay alive, in one piece and preferably not in a cage.

'I live around here,' I said vaguely, holding out a hand to help her get to her feet. She coughed nervously, brushing herself off.

'I guess you, uh, saw my transformation there, huh…'

'Yeah, no worries though. I'm not going to rat on you.' I felt relief coming off her in waves before she tensed, looking back the way she had come. Grabbing my hand, she started to sprint through the undergrowth, pulling me along behind her with surprising ease and strength. She didn't answer when I asked her what the matter was until we had gone another mile into the forest where she stopped, breathing hard.

'There are...people after me,' she started to explain. I raised an eyebrow, prompting her to go on. 'I sensed someone following me out of the city, but they didn't reveal themselves until after I changed. I don't know who they are.'

Frowning, I scanned the forest around us, looking for any traces of these people. I couldn't see anything, but that didn't mean they weren't there. I turned back to Alba, pointing east.

'Look, if you go far enough that way, you'll come across a house. Tell Amarath I sent you. Get out of the forest. I'll follow behind masking our tracks.'

Alba nodded, looking nervous, but followed my orders. I glanced over my shoulder one last time, looking for any movement. Nothing. I started to walk after Alba, taking care to hide any signs of our passing. I stopped as I heard something. Something thudded against my skull. I don't remember even hitting the ground.

When I came around again, my entire body throbbed as if I had been through a power surge. Fleeting memories were quickly banished from my mind, giving me no recollections whatsoever of what had happened since I had been knocked out. Looking around, I realised I was in the hospital room of our house. Amarath, Vrael and Alba were watching me with worried expressions. However, their expressions weren't the things concerning me. I was more concerned at the fact that Vrael had his arms around Alba protectively and was holding her close. Vrael and Alba? Okay, weird pairing there. I wondered how that had happened.

'Shad?' Amarath asked. 'You back with us?'

'Yeah,' I grumbled, trying to sit up despite having the mother of all headaches. 'Anyone care to enlighten me as to what the hell happened to make me feel like someone ran over me with a bus and then reversed again to make sure they did it right?'

The trio glanced at each other. Amarath sighed irritably. 'You're such a coward, Vrael. How come I always get stuck with the task of explaining things?' She turned back to me with her best 'you're really not going to like this' face on. I cringed. Whatever had happened, it wasn't likely to be good.

'Long story short, you had a run in with the Milita.'

'The Milita?' I asked.

'A group of soldiers-come-scientists who study mythological creatures. We're prime targets for them, since they don't wait for people to volunteer...' Alba answered quietly, her head resting on Vrael's chest. I tried not to let the images of them getting together into my head. I'd never get rid of them if I did.

'The Milita tried to split your demonic side from your human,' Amarath said bluntly.

'I'm guessing it didn't work...'

'No, duh,' Amarath snorted, 'if they had managed, you'd be dead. We're parts, more specifically, halves. Every single part demon ever born has been a half, regardless of parentage. The non demonic and demonic sides can then exist in a vaguely harmonious state. If we weren't halves, our bodies would tear themselves apart in the battle between our sides. Being without your demonic side would be like living with only half of your vital organs.'

'Bloody hell, you demons are complicated,' Alba muttered. A slight smile grew on Vrael's face as he ruffled her hair affectionately. I averted my eyes. Yeesh, lovebirds.

'Anyway,' Amarath's voice broke into my thoughts. 'Since you're obviously so uneducated in the ways of demons, Vrael,

Shaeman and I have recorded everything we know for your listening pleasure.' She held up a portable CD player, a slightly evil grin on her face. 'Enjoy.'

Left alone to recuperate, I put the headphones over my ears and pressed play. There were so many things about part demons that I hadn't read in the Scriptures. Then again, there had been no way of telling if the Scriptures had been intact. I closed my eyes, settling back to listen to my siblings' voices:

Amarath: *Right, Shadow, since your ignorance is going to get you killed one day, Shaeman, Vrael and I have recorded most of what we know about half demons in order to give you a crash course in how to be a demon. Goddess knows, Arias stunted your knowledge in that area. First on your list, physical form. Vrael, you're the medic, I do believe that's one of your areas of expertise. Take it away!*

Vrael: *The physical form of a half-demon in his or her natural state is remarkably similar to that of a human, although there are several key changes. Because of these elements, it is imperative that you do not approach a human doctor who is ignorant of us.*

The first difference lies mainly in out internal arrangements, notably in our cardio-vascular system—

Amarath: *In English, that would be?*

Vrael: *Patience Amarath. As I was saying, one of the most notable differences is that we have two hearts. The primary heart, located in the same place as a human's, takes the major effort of running the body. The secondary heart, which is half the size of the primary, is located in the lower right hand-side of the chest, only intervenes to aid in funnelling the energy required for the use of magic and in the case of injury to the primary heart, can sustain the body. However, you must still be very careful of injury to the primary heart. The secondary can only run the body for a certain amount of time, normally two to three weeks. However, any stress placed on the heart, more than usual, can dramatically reduce the time it is capable of running the body. Other differences include a reinforced digestive tract—*

Amarath: *So if you throw up, there's something really wrong with you!*

Vrael: Thank you, *Amarath, although that is essentially true. Now, if I may continue without any further interruption…*

Amarath: *I'm not making any promises.*

Vrael: *Amarath!*

Amarath: *Fine! Sheesh, you're really touchy today!*

Shaeman: *Uh, guys? We don't really have all that long before someone figures out we're here…*

Vrael: *I will make this as rapid as possible. Demons and demonic hybrids also have a third hemisphere within the cranium that allows our use of magic and the cohabitation of the demon within a hybrid's mind, but I believe that Shaeman will be able to tell you more about the demonic influence on one's life and actions. Also, we are stronger and more endurant that regular humans, but once more, I believe that Shaeman knows more about our abilities than I am capable of explaining.*

Amarath: *And, of course, Vrael has given me the task of explaining the reproductive system. Coward. Okay, I'm going to make this as short as I can. Demons and half demons are hyperfertile. If you're not really, really careful, you can end up pregnant, but you already know about that bit. And because we're magical beings, we don't even need to have sex to get pregnant!*

Vrael: *What our dear sister is attempting and failing to explain is this: in a philosophical sense, a child is a blending of the essences of the parents. For magical beings such as us, the essence of a person can be found in anything deeply personal to the one in question. Handwriting, a hairbrush, a much-loved necklace and so on. When Karthragan's hand traversed you, it cause an onslaught of his essence that your body knew not how to deal with, or rather knew how to deal with in only one manner: by creating a child.*

Amarath: *Which is way wrong since Kar's our dad. I mean… Eww! But yeah, that's basically the 'how baby's are made' speech, demonic edition. The human method works just as well, by the way.*

Now a quick summary of everything else in our reproductive cycle: we're always ready to reproduce, we don't get the human 'time of the month', we always bear twins, our pregnancy period is 'round about five months. I think that's pretty much everything you need to know on that front. Shaeman? You want to tell our Shad about our demonic powers?

Shaeman: *Our powers are pretty varied. You know about the magic, about manipulating it into shields and bolts, etcetera. You have to remember though that every demon, full- or half-blooded, had a unique signature, a feeling, that other demons can sense every time you use your magic, so you need to be careful about that. Anyway, we can teleport, as you also know. Uhm, some demons can heal others. Vrael can.*

Vrael: *In truth, any demon is capable of using their magic to heal others. What makes the difference is that many do not wish to spend the time to learn to do so. However, no demon can heal his own injuries.*

Shaeman: *Anyway, as Vrael said earlier, we are physically stronger and more endurant than humans, although not as much as a full-blooded demon. We're kinda stuck in the middle. We're also immortal, to an extent. Time can't kill us, but illness, injury and all that can. The reason we're immortal to time is because demons stop ageing at a certain, random point in their lives. I believe that all four of us have reached our point, and that this is the physical age that we will retain for the rest of our existence.*

Another one of our powers is shape-shifting, but it's limited. Very limited. Every half demon has five different shapes. Normally at least. As with every species, you always have a couple of oddballs thrown in by the gods for giggles. Your everyday form, the half demon one; your human form, the one you revert to when your vulnerable period comes 'round; and the animal form, you know, wolf for you, lycorn for Amarath, panther for Vrael and a pegasus for me. Those forms you've already come across. There are two others, one of which you may have already found. There's your demon form, which is basically what you look like when you lose control of your demonic side. It's usually pretty close to your half demon form. And finally, there's your true form. Full-blooded demons know their true forms from birth, but hybrids don't. It's dangerous, Shadow, really dangerous. A hybrid who shifts into their true form very rarely come back from it. I don't know much more than that, I'm afraid. Apart from that, I don't think there's much else you need to know.

Vrael: *We may wish to inform Shadow of the basic hierarchy of Aspheri, as this is one element she may be mixing with in later life.*

Shaeman: *And I guess that's my job as well. Great. Okay, Aspheri is very simple when it comes to politics. The big chief is known as the Prince or Princess of Darkness. It used to be the strongest demon in the dimension who took control, but now it's mainly hereditary. There is a system of marking an heir to the throne, but I've never figured it out. No one really knows what it is or how it works. Anyway, under the Prince comes the Council of Elders, who are basically glorified advisors who keep an eye on the two smaller cities in Aspheri. Anything else we need to tell Shadow?*

Amarath: *Oh! Did you know that demons aren't evil? They're actually just really volatile and give in to every single emotion that crosses their mind. It was just luck of the draw that Karthragan was such an evil bastard.*

Vrael: *We must leave! I sense someone coming!*

Amarath: *Well, hope you enjoyed it, Shad!*

—Click—

Once I had recovered enough, I made up my mind. I had to go and see Karthragan. I couldn't bear to lose anyone else to his power, especially since I now had Archangel and Onyx to think about. I had to make sure they were going to be safe once I was gone. I poked my head around the door, listening out for the sounds of my siblings. The faint screams of terror coming from outside told me everything I needed to know: Shaeman and Vrael were trying to teach Amarath to fly a pegasus again. Closing my eyes and focusing my thoughts as Amarath had taught me to do, I teleported.

I appeared in Aspheri, under the scarlet sky. The perpetual sun hung low in the sky, flaming like a giant torch. Dust rose from the black, baked ground as I walked towards the palace where I knew I'd find him. The ruler of Aspheri was considered almost a god. For as long as records had been kept, Aspheri had been ruled by a Prince of Darkness, a title and power that descended through the male line. Until the prophecy. Until Arellan. Until me.

Lesser demons scattered left and right as I strode through the maze-like corridors of the palace for the first time without a guide. Any other day, I would have gotten lost or had to stop and ask directions, but Karthragan's power suffused the black marble walls. All I had to do was track the highest concentration. The closer I got to the throne room, the less scared of me the demons became. That didn't bother me though. They couldn't hurt me. They knew that only Karthragan was allowed to kill me, thanks to the prophecy. The door guards let me pass without a trace of hesitation.

Karthragan sat on his throne, glaring down at me though his red eyes, but made no move to attack me. I suppose I had to be thankful for that at least. I stopped in front of him, bowing sarcastically, returning his glare.

'Hello, *Father*.'

He looked as if he was considering ignoring the prophecy and killing me there and then, but he wouldn't. Then again, he didn't have to. He knew perfectly well how to get to me without touching me. That's what I was here to put an end to.

'I'm here to make you a deal,' I continued, folding my arms. As much as he tried to hide it, I could sense a spark of interest. I smirked slightly. Demons were demons. They couldn't resist a bargain, preferably for your soul. 'You don't hurt any of my friends, human, demon or otherwise, and I won't run from you on the night of the prophecy.'

Karthragan's rumbling laugh echoed through the dark corners of the chamber. 'You dared to present yourself before me, mere weeks before the prophecy, to bargain with me for the pitiful lives of a handful of hybrids!'

'Humour me,' I growled. 'I could run. You know I could run, faster than you could keep up with me. You spare their lives, I won't run from you.'

'You could never run fast enough.'

'Oh, I could. I would. You know it as well as I do. I could shield myself from you so thoroughly that you could walk straight past me. You could send all the demons you wanted after me, but you know I could fight them.' At least, that's what I was telling myself. It was basically all talk. I was relying heavily enough as it was on Amarath being able to train me to be able to fight and I still had a lot to learn in that respect.

Karthragan grunted. I had him there. He believed me, which was all I needed. He waved a hand irritably. 'I will grant your request, as trivial as it may be.'

I allowed triumph to twist one corner of my mouth upwards. With another sarcastic bow, I teleported myself back to the cottage.

Time passed slowly, lazily. Alba and I still worked in the flower shop and Shaeman and Vrael had found out how to play the stock markets and investments to keep our income growing and taught me more about magic in our spare time. Amarath had wandered off somewhere, no one really knew where, but nor were we particularly bothered. Amarath could handle herself perfectly well. Unfortunately, Karthragan was moving on the offensive again, probably angered by my insubordination. He often tried to break into my mind, to kill me from the inside out. This often led to my demonic side taking the chance to break free and take over. Slowly, over the course of three weeks, the attacks became less and less frequent. I started venturing in back into the city again, although under the constant escort of either Vrael or Shaeman.

I wandered around the city one night in wolf form, closely followed by Vrael's sleek panther form. He was seriously getting on my nerves though. I trotted into a square lit only by a couple of street lamps nearing the end of their life. Morphing back into human form, I put my hands on my hips, glaring at him.

'Vrael, if you keep watching me like that, I swear I'm going to spontaneously combust!'

From the other side of a broken fountain, a voice called out. 'Vrael, is that you? What are you doing here?' I whipped my head round to glare at a teenage boy, younger than me. He looked a little scruffy, and smelled a little odd, sort of like a shape-shifter, but not quite.

'Shadow wished to leave the house for a few moments, and I volunteered for the guard duty. It was only chance that lead us here.' Vrael replied calmly. He obviously knew this boy. I relaxed fractionally.

'Who are you?' I asked. He narrowed his eyes at me. I sensed apprehension radiating off him.

'Name's Bart. That's all you need to know.' I raised an eyebrow at his abrupt answer. 'I met Vrael by pure coincidence a couple of weeks ago.' He pulled a dog-eared piece of paper from a pocket of his baggy white trousers, studying it closely. He glanced at his watch, apparently waiting for something. I rounded on Vrael, arms folded. He raised his hands in a gesture of surrender.

'I was with Alba. There is no harm in that, I presume? Bart met she and I there, when you were…not quite with us.'

'You mean when I was going mad?'

'Yes.' I rolled my eyes, turning back to Bart.

'So what are you doing here? You're waiting for something, that much is obvious.'

Bart looked as if he wasn't going to talk, but ceded. 'I'm a sort of chosen one from a race called the Kraferrs. I doubt you've heard of them. Well, we've got this kind of relic, a necklace, the All-Teller necklace. There are thirteen 'One' Kraferrs, humans given the powers of a Kraferr so they can try and find it. I'm one of them, but I have to wait for a shaman Kraferr to create a replica of me so my parents don't panic.' Understanding I nodded and watched from a distance as what looked like a further evolved monkey appeared. I guessed that he was the shaman Bart was looking for since the boy walked over to greet him. Vrael and I stayed at a distance, feeling that this was perhaps not something to be observed closely. I could hear them talking, but couldn't make out any individual words. I felt Vrael stiffen beside me, putting a hand on my shoulder and clenching it hard. Glancing up at him, I saw his gaze riveted on the proceedings between Bart and the shaman. A split second later, I realised why. There was blood involved. I could smell it. I guessed that the blood-lust was starting to descend on Vrael, but he was making a valiant effort to fight it. I put one hand on his, squeezing it slightly. He looked down at me, his features rigid, but managed a tense smile. Looking back over at the Kraferrs, the shaman had vanished, leaving Bart standing over his clone. Bart lifted his wrist to his face, his features bathed in a blue light as I guessed he checked his watch. Surreptitiously, I slid a vial of blood from my belt and pulled out a wind-up mouse I had enchanted to never stop once started. I had to spend some time alone before I went nuts. Making sure Vrael's eyes were still fixed on Bart, I tipped a few drops of blood on the mouse, enough to give it the scent. Vrael's head whipped round, the hunger clear in his eyes. I felt a little ashamed about using his weakness against him, but turned the key on the mouse, sending it scurrying away into the night. Vrael shot after it in a heartbeat. Breathing a sigh of relief, I walked over to Bart.

'I should be able to disappear for a couple of months with this replica,' he said, his mind obviously a long way away.

'Why isn't it moving?' I asked. I couldn't fathom how this replica thing worked if the clone didn't move. Was it supposed to make him appear to be dead or something? In a coma?

'Won't activate until ten o'clock.' He pressed the button on his watch again, the faint blue light illuminating the planes of his face. I tilted my head to one side. He didn't look particularly comfortable in the presence of his clone. I dismissed those thoughts. Of course it was strange if you didn't happen to have an identical twin. I still got a bit unnerved when I looked at Amarath and realised that I wasn't looking into a mirror. Lost in my thoughts, I jumped when the replica sat up. It nodded at Bart before calmly sauntering off to do whatever it is that clones do when they're impersonating their originals. He looked a little lost, as if he was watching a large part of his life walking away with his clone. I felt quite sorry for him, standing in the cold winter winds, now homeless while another person took his place in his family.

'Need any help chasing that relic of yours?' I asked quietly. He glanced at me before looking up at the moon.

'I dunno,' he said, looking a little guilty. 'Someone said that you were kinda dangerous right now. I just don't know if I can trust you...'

I won't say that didn't hurt, because it did. I bit the inside of my cheek, trying not to come back with a Holly-style sarcastic quip. 'Well, I guess you met my family before you met me then, huh?' I pulled the hood of my cloak over my head, hiding my expression in shadow so he couldn't read the thoughts on my face.

'Sorry,' he said quickly, his emotions telling me that he was aware that he had made a mistake. 'I don't really want people I don't know joining me on this. It's too dangerous. It's too easy to get hurt, and I don't know what to do if anyone does get hurt.'

'Fair enough,' I answered neutrally, walking over to the

fountain and dipping my hand into its frigid waters, the cold searing my skin as I flicked the drops from my fingers. I could sense his confusion.

'Where are you going?'

'Nowhere in particular,' I murmured, 'I just need to get away from my family.'

'I need to get away from mine too, but I guess for different reasons than yours.' I turned to look at him. Instead of the human I had seen before, this humanoid was covered in brown fur, his eyes turned red, his hands clawed and a monkey's tail slicing at the air. He tilted his head to the side as he watched me. 'You're leaving your family to save yourself, but I'm guessing that there's another reason behind that one.'

I turned back to the fountain, looking down at my reflection, at the damning evidence of the prophecy in the scar around my eye. 'They're trying to protect me, to keep me away from something very dangerous, but it won't work for long. I just don't want to see them hurt…'

'I like that. You're trying to protect your loved ones even though it puts you in danger.' I felt his hand gingerly touch my shoulder, as if he was unsure of what to do. 'I guess you could come with me, if you still want to. I'll try to protect you too, but I'm not really good at medical things. I know the basic human anatomy and that's about it, and even then it's only approximately.'

'Don't worry about healing,' I replied, turning to him. 'Vrael's taught me a few bits about medicine. So, where do we start?'

'The relic's last known position was in a mountain range north-west from here, so I guess we start moving. There's something you should know about where it's kept though.' I glanced at him, wondering what it was as he took a deep breath. 'They say that the walls move. No one's ever come back from trying to find it.'

I smiled slightly. 'Sounds like a challenge.'

We moved out, starting the journey to the outskirts of the city. If this All Teller necklace had been made by the Kraferrs, then their scent should still linger on it. I sniffed at Bart as discreetly as I could. Yep, there was a scent here that was definitely not human, and not like anything I had ever come across. Taking that as the scent of the Kraferrs, I kept my nose on alert for anything close to it. There were several living scents in the city, but this one shouldn't be moving. I stopped. There was something wrong here. A smell that didn't belong. A smell that *couldn't* belong. Bart stopped as well, glancing back at me with a worried expression. I listened carefully, putting a hand on the hilt of one of the two swords strapped permanently to my side. There's one thing about walking down a deserted street with another person. There should only be two patterns of footsteps. Not three. Someone was following us.

'Shadow?' Bart asked.

'There's someone there,' I replied quickly, in a low voice. I unsheathed one sword. He readied his claws, looking around for the unknown stalker. I took on my battle stance, breathing deeply, eyes searching the dark streets. Something whistled through the air. Ducking quickly, I watched as a lock of purple hair drifted to the ground and an arrow quivered in the wall behind me.

'That was too close for comfort,' I muttered. I drew my other sword, taking comfort in the twin weights in my hands. I was good with these weapons. I could defend myself and Bart if necessary. Memories of Amarath's words started to murmur in the back of my mind, reminders of how to handle an opponent. I scanned the shadows, looking for anything out of place. I spotted the assailant, a black clothed man standing in an alleyway, bow in his hands. Another arrow only just missed Bart. The Kraferr darted towards the man, zigzagging to make a projectile attack more difficult. Obviously panicked, the attacker drew a sword, holding it at the ready. A scream caught in my throat as I watched

Bart launch himself at the person, too fast to stop his attack. The man lunged at the Kraferr with the sword, piercing Bart's arm then his chest. Bart seemed to laugh, raking at the assailant's eyes with his claws. The attacker ripped his sword out of Bart as I ran to help the Kraferr, throwing it towards me before he fled. My eyes widened as the sword headed straight for me. It was too late to dodge. Too late to slow down. Too late to do anything. The metal buried itself in my chest, straight through my heart. Gasping, I fell to the ground. I lay there on my side, trying to think of what to do. Nothing came to mind, just the pain of the blade skewering me like a particularly morbid kebab. The smell of Bart's blood came closer to me, his breathing ragged and panicked.

'Shadow, can you hear me? I need to call Vrael, but how?'

'I can hear…' I managed to get out. Goddess, breathing hurt. How was Bart holding up? I knew that demons had a secondary heart. I would be okay as long as I didn't bleed to death. But Kraferrs? I was fairly sure they weren't as resilient as the supposed spawn of evil. 'Don't call…Vrael. They…can't know.' I had to get this sword out of my chest before it caused any more damage. Grasping the hilt, slippery with Bart's and my blood, I wrenched it out, letting it clatter onto the concrete. Given the amounts of blood pouring out of the wound, I was starting to doubt my survival. Gritting my teeth, I pushed those thoughts away. The consequences were too dire to contemplate. 'I won't die,' I muttered to myself. I WILL NOT DIE!' I pushed myself up on my elbows, then my knees, then my feet, grabbing onto a nearby lamppost to keep myself upright. I felt Bart grab my arm, pulling it over his shoulders before he picked me up with an ease that betrayed his injuries. I cringed as the pain he felt flooded my mind. My own pain was too great for me to keep up my usual defences. Reaching up a hand to his temple, I let my magic flow into him, to lessen some of his wounds. I couldn't heal myself. No demon could. But I could help him. He pulled his head away from my touch.

'Keep your energy, Shad, you need it more than I do.' he murmured. We reached a doctor's surgery a few streets over. Carefully sitting me on the ground, he set about picking the locks with a claw. I put my hand against the wall, sending a magical pulse through the electric system to disable the alarms. I gasp as the energy left me, leaving me dizzy and barely conscious. He swore, picking me up again and bundling me into one of the treatment rooms. I vaguely heard him muttering to himself as he searched for the necessary materials. A syringe pierced the skin close to the wound, but I barely felt a pinprick. It was surpassed by the gash left by the sword. I was dimly aware of the needle passing back and forth, closing the wound. Slowly, I became more and more aware of the things around me, coming further and further away from unconsciousness.

'I'm sorry,' he was saying quietly. 'I'm so sorry. I couldn't protect you. This was the first time we were attacked and I still couldn't protect you.'

'It's okay,' I murmured, reaching out to squeeze his hand. 'There wasn't much you could have done.' I sat up slowly, grimacing as I pulled the sutures slightly. They were going to be a pain in the backside, especially since they would have to be renewed at some point, probably by Vrael if he didn't kill me first. With demonic blood being slightly more acidic than human, most stitches didn't last long. 'We should get moving before they attack again.' Hearing no answer, I glanced at Bart. His body was sprawled on the ground, his breathing shallow. All around the room were pools of red blood. His blood. Swearing in every language I knew, I knelt next to him, placing my hands over his wounds. Focusing my magic, I concentrated on repairing at least some of the damage. It wasn't enough. I grabbed the things I needed from the shelves, ignoring the pain in both my hearts. It didn't matter. I was going to live, but he wasn't if I didn't do something fast. I crouched next to him again, prepping a needle and thread. His hand reached out to grip mine.

'Don't let me die here.'

'I won't. I promise I won't let you die.' After disinfecting the wound, I snatched a compression pad from my pile of supplies, applying it to the wounds, trying to staunch the bleeding. He had lost so much blood. Too much blood. I narrowed my eyes, grabbing an empty syringe. I stuck it into my arm, drawing blood into it. I knew that there would be a few side effects over from of the demonic part to my blood, but it would help. It was against so many rules that I couldn't count them all, but I didn't care. He had saved me. I had to do everything I could to save him. I injected it straight into his heart, followed by two more. My head began to feel light, but I forced myself to concentrate. I continued to apply pressure to Bart's wounds, praying that my blood would help him. The bleeding was slowing, and I started to stitch the wounds after injecting some local anaesthetic around them. Once I had tied off the final stitch, I placed a finger on his forehead, murmuring a spell that would hopefully bring him back from unconsciousness. He awoke with a gasp of pain. He tried to speak, his eyes wide in panic. I bit my lip, bowing my head.

'You…you…you…'

'I had to inject some of my blood into your system,' I said quietly. 'You had lost so much…'

'What'll happen to me?' he asked, his voice sounding stronger as the demonic blood running through his veins started to take hold.

'I'm only half demon, so my blood isn't as potent as full-bloods.' I took a deep breath. 'Actually, I have no idea… Uh, from what I know, it's kinda, uh, probable that you'll convert into a part demon…'

For a moment he said nothing, processing the information. I mentally kicked myself for not looking for some human blood to give him. He reached up a hand, touching my neck. I almost flinched away, but he touched the pulse point next to my throat. 'Your main heart isn't working yet...' I moved away slightly, dislodging his hand from my neck. I didn't want to answer that question.

'We should get moving before someone finds us here.' I declared, holding out a hand to help him to his feet. I grabbed some of the medical supplies, slipping them into my pockets in case we needed them later.

As we walked down the street, I watched Bart carefully. He seemed to be holding up well given the havoc the demonic blood must be wreaking on his body. We walked in silence, the furrow of concentration on the Kraferr's forehead deepening as he tried to keep walking in a straight line. I glanced away, guilt clouding my mind. He stopped, crouching and placing one fur-covered hand on the ground.

'Strange...'

I sniffed the air, but couldn't identify the smell. It was damp, mouldy and animalistic, dangerous and threatening. A part of me wondered if Karthragan had been out in the rain in his wolf form, looking for me, hunting me down.

'We need to get out of here. Now!' Bart ordered. The edge of panic in his voice put me on edge. My already difficult concentration scattered completely. My mind froze as I tried to think of a way out, some way to escape.

'I can't teleport us,' I said, not even willing to attempt it. There was no telling where we'd end up. Bart answered the problem at hand in his own way, seizing me around the stomach with one arm, scaling the side of the building next to us with an ease that I found hard to believe. We surfaced on the rooftop where Bart staggered, clutching at his wound. I felt his pain and grimaced.

'Come here, let me heal that,' I said in a tone that implied that I wasn't going to take no for an answer. I didn't care that I was tired, or hurt, or that we were trying to hide from something I didn't know. He didn't put up a protest as I gently laid a hand on the wound on his chest, concentrating on helping the minuscule fibres reconnect and heal. Once I had done as much as I could, I sat back, discreetly raising a finger to the pulse point on my neck. Still twice as fast as it needed to be. Although I had a secondary heart, it was smaller than the primary. It had to work harder to keep my body functioning. I let my hand fall, looking out over the city once more.

'Who were they?' I asked.

'The Ku'Rutiek. They're Kraferric outlaws who believe that the necklace should remain undiscovered, that it isn't the answer to our survival.' He turned to look at me through the red eyes of his were-monkey form. 'They are the reason so many Kraferr Ones have failed.' I nodded silently, pondering. 'Shad?'

'Hm?'

'You said you were trying to get away from your family, to keep them safe. You never said why.'

I sighed, shifting into a more comfortable position, looking out over the city with its pinpricks of street lights. Leaning on my hands, I thought carefully about my words. After all, he was one of us now. He might as well know how we work. 'A part demon's life is ruled by prophecy. The more important the demon parent is, the more the prophecy impacts your life. I drew the short sword in that my father is the ruler of all demons. I'm supposed to fight him to the death for control over the demons.'

'When?'

'In a month…'

'And you agreed to help me? Shouldn't you be training to fight?'

'We're both going to die. It was in the prophecy. We both have to die, so what's the point? We should start moving again before they catch our scent.' I stepped over the edge of the building, to freefall to the ground. Normally it wouldn't be a problem. A storey or two won't do anything to a demon. Any more than that, however, and you're looking at scraping bits of demon off the pavement. As I landed, I staggered, grabbing onto a lamppost to regain my balance. The sword wound was throbbing again, my heartbeat almost a hum as it raced to keep up with everything I was putting my body through. I nodded once at Bart, signalling that everything was fine to continue the quest.

We walked in silence for another couple of streets before Bart started to have problems. The blood was starting to take effect. He stopped, collapsing onto a nearby bench, breathing ragged as his body tried to fight the onslaught of demonic transformation. I sat next to him, guilt consuming my mind again.

'I'm sorry, I need to take a break,' he said, leaning his head back to ease his breathing.

'I shouldn't have given you my blood.' I looked down at my hands folded in my lap. 'You have no reason to be sorry.'

'You did what you had to in order to save my life. I'm grateful for that.'

'There's always an alternative...'

'Shadow, what's done is done, there's nothing you can do about it.'

I said nothing, leaning my head back against the bench, closing my eyes. It was comforting to just stare at the inside of my eyelids. Nothing complicated, no prophecies, nothing to run from.

'Hey, Shad, with the blood transfer, what'll I be able to do?'

'Magic mainly. It should manifest soon, give or take a couple of hours,' I said without looking up at him. 'You'll be able to use it like mine. It requires concentration, and an ability to visualise what you want it to do. For example,' I raised a hand to chest height, palm facing upwards. 'Within my mind, I can see a small orb of magic above my hand.' After a few moments of concentration, it slowly appeared. 'You could imagine it attacking something or someone, or seeking something and bringing it to you.'

'Cool.'

'So, what's our next move?' I was starting to get restless. Staying in one place for too long when there were people looking for us was a recipe for disaster, especially since neither of us were in any state to fight, especially not if Bart was going to undergo a rather fast demonic transformation soon.

'We continue going north-west, towards the mountains. When we get there, we should be able to get up to the cave easily,' Bart said, starting to walk along the street. I followed him like a kitten on a string. 'By the way, did you recognise our mysterious assailant?'

I gritted my teeth. Yes, I knew who he was or rather, what group he belonged to. I wasn't sure Bart really wanted or needed to know though. 'Yes, I did recognise him.'

He suddenly became worried. 'Who was it?'

'No one you want to know.'

'Shad… Can you at least tell me why he was after us then?' He was starting to get a little irritated, that much I could tell. I started to chew on my lip, looking at the Kraferr out of the corner of my eye.

'He was a Demon Hunter.' I conceded.

'Like a vampire hunter?'

'No,' I had to take a deep breath. 'The Demon Hunters are a cult of humans who worship my father and do his dirty work in this realm.'

'So his coming after us had nothing to do with the fact that you were with me?'

'No. If it was, I would have to remove his head personally and spit down his neck. They're only supposed to be after me.'

I couldn't help but notice the silence Bart was keeping up as we continued our trek in silence. I pulled the hood of my cloak over my face as I glared at the ground, cursing myself in every single language I knew. I placed a hand on the hilt of my sword, keeping an ear out for anything unusual. Bart stopped again, sniffing the air. I paused, watching him carefully for any tell-tale signs that meant we had to make a rapid exit.

'Smell something?'

'No, nothing. I can't see, smell or hear anything. That's not normal.' I closed my eyes, reaching out with my mind to try to pick up any other forms of consciousness. I came up with a couple of lizards and a stray cat. Nothing of any note. But there was something else there. Something doing its damnest to hide from me, slipping out of my grasp every time I tried to get a hold on it.

A figure dropped down from the rooftop. I jumped, drawing my sword. Bart stood slightly in front of me, claws at the ready. The figure held up his hands in a peaceful, not quite surrendering gesture. A young man, perhaps only a couple of years older than me. He smelled a little strange, not unlike Bart, but a scent all his own.

'I'm not here to fight you,' he said, 'I am Sither. Sither Moonspike, last Shapeshifter standing of the Yul tribe. I was just passing by and I overheard that you were embarking on some sort of...journey.'

Bart relaxed enough to put his claws away. 'I'm Bart, this is Shadow.' Sither inclined his head gracefully towards me. I returned the gesture, sheathing my sword again but keeping my hand on its hilt. I couldn't sense anything hostile coming from the newcomer, but that didn't mean that he couldn't turn evil.

'I have a few talents in warfare that may be useful to you both, if you will allow me to accompany you.'

'Shadow?' Bart asked in an undertone.

'I can't sense anything bad coming off him. Chances are he'll be harmless enough towards us.' I took care to keep my voice low, unsure of how good Sither's hearing was.

Bart nodded and started walking again, Sither and I following quietly.

Concrete pavements soon gave way to dense woodland as we approached the foot of the mountain. We continued onwards, a strange trio of a shape shifter-turned-demon, a demon and an unknown. Bart stopped, listening carefully. I cast a glance at him, sensing worry cascading off him in waves.

'Shadow, Sither...I think we have company.'

I drew both my swords, brow furrowed in concentration and concern. I knew I was in no state to fight. Nor was Bart. I couldn't even morph! Sither was the only chance we had of getting out of the fight alive. I closed my eyes, trying to sense our attackers. All I heard was the blood pounding in my ears. All I smelled was earth, blood and shifter. All I could feel was Bart's agitation and worry. The wind ruffled the Kraferr's fur, bringing with it the sharp tang that promised rain. I tightened my grip on my sword, ignoring the pain that lanced through my damaged heart. Nature settled. Not a leaf rustled. I slashed at something not more than a shadow. Claws ripped at my arm. Shallow gashes leaked tiny droplets if blood. I strained my ears to hear more, hear better, hear past the unnatural silence.

There!

I swung my sword at neck height. It met with a satisfying flesh-and-bone resistance. A body thudded to the ground. I threw my sword at another attacker, listening out for the crunch as it hit its target, drawing my other blade and preparing myself.

'Slay the One and his allies!'

My temper snapped. Anger boiled through my mind. Magic surged through my muscles, begging to be used. I shouted out in Demonic. Black energy poured from my hands. I didn't care about losing control now. Not while Bart was in mortal danger. Sither could handle himself. Bart was still injured. He had been injured while defending me.

A handful of heartbeats later, the Outlaw Kraferrs lay dead in pools of blood around us. I fell to one knee, my arms around my ribs. Goddess, it hurt to breathe. My secondary heart was beating so fast. Bart crouched next to me.

'Shadow, you shouldn't have done that. You need to rest!'

I gritted my teeth. Rest? Now? Forget it! The monkey boys might have back up. 'I'm fine,' I muttered, pushing myself to my feet. The sudden movement proved to be too much. I collapsed onto the ground again. I couldn't hear anything through the frantic beating of my secondary heart. The magical wave had taken more energy than I had realised. A secondary heart is just that – secondary. It could run my body for a matter of about two weeks, as long as the demon doesn't do anything too strenuous, ample time for the primary heart to recover and take over full duty once more. After the exertion of the battle, I guessed I had a handful of days at most.

I expected to hit hard, unforgiving ground. Instead, someone caught me before I could, cradling me carefully in their arms.

'I told you, you need rest. So just relax,' ordered Bart. I felt like arguing back, but didn't. He was trying to help. I felt his claw rest on the pulse point on my neck. His hand then moved close to my wounded heart. I hissed in pain, pushing his hand away. He wasn't trained! He didn't know what to do! But he maintained his hand close to the injury.

'Let me try, Shad.'

Grudgingly, I let him.

When Vrael and I heal someone, we use magic to fuse together the fibres of the muscle and reconnect the cells. This becomes harder and harder the deeper we go into an organism, and becomes more difficult the older the wound gets as the magic has to interfere with the natural healing process. Bart was finding this out the hard way. Slowly, the depths of the wound began to close enough to staunch the bleeding before he was forced to stop by the toll the magic was taking on his strength.

'Thank you,' I murmured. He smiled slightly, standing up and holding out his hand. I took it, letting him help me to my feet. We looked out over the battlefield. Bart gagged, I guess disgusted by the sight of the remnants of the fight. I was used to the smells of battle. The sight of blood didn't turn my stomach. Don't get me wrong though. It's not that death and killing don't bother me, it's that this was an exception. The outlaws wouldn't have hesitated to kill us. We should not have had to hesitate to kill them. All that was left was for me to convince myself that it was self-defence.

'Why were they after us? You said that they believe the necklace should remain undiscovered, but why the violence?'

'The Outlaws used to be a group of Kraferrs who protected the Ones on their quest. But the Outlaws got scared that the Ones would ask a wrong question, which leads to the One's death and moves the Kraferrs one step closer to extinction. Well, the idea of 'protect by force' kinda turned into 'kill'.

'I see.' My eyes wandered over the corpses. I spotted my second sword embedded in the chest of a dead Kraferr. I pulled it out, trying to ignore the sound of shattered bone against the metal. I wiped the blade on the grass in an attempt to clean as much of the gore from it as possible. 'It looks like the Kraferrs are another few specimens short then.' My mind, unbidden, turned to my own species. The part demons. How we had been every-where, in almost every dimension. Now only the Roth-Mercian clan was left. My clan. And it looked like the Kraferrs were going to follow the same path.

'Yes,' Bart spoke again, shaking me from my dark thoughts. 'But it's done now. Not much we can do about it.'

'Hm.'

I listened to Bart gagging again as he looked out over the bloodstained, corpse-strewn ground. I rolled my eyes, trying to block out the sound. But there was something more behind it. There was something else coming off him. I whipped around to face him as he fell to his knees, his hands around his ribs. I knelt next to him, holding his shoulders straight to try to alleviate his breathing.

'What's wrong?'

'The…blood…' He managed to gasp. 'It's interfering…with everything!' He tried to get up again, but his legs gave way beneath him. I gritted my teeth. All the signs pointed to an imminent demonic possession. Not a good thing. I wracked my mind for a possible solution, for anything that could help him. The bracers! Digging into my pockets, I pulled out two long bracelets of metal. Shaeman had crafted them, working a length of thin, silver wire into the steel. I slid one over Bart's wrist, pulling at the lacing to keep them tight against his fur.

'I don't normally use these,' I explained, slipping the other one into place, 'but I think this qualifies as an emergency. They have silver in them. It'll help control the demon blood.'

'Shadow,' he started to say, lying back on the ground with a groan. 'Thanks.'

I sensed despair starting to well up inside him and swallowed hard. 'It's one of the few things I can do. After all, it's my fault you've got this problem.'

'Shad…' His voice held a hint of a warning. I tensed, throwing all my senses onto high alert. 'There was nothing else you could have done.' Realising we weren't going to be attacked, I relaxed slightly, keeping my head bowed. He started to try to get to his feet, but I pushed him back down again, one hand on his shoulder.

'Calm down and relax for a bit. The silver should take effect soon, but you need to let it work, not get yourself all worked up.'

Bart fell back again, grimacing slightly. I rolled my eyes discreetly, shifting my limbs into a more comfortable position. He turned his head to look at me.

'Shad, does demonic magic cause any interference with other kinds? Like, will it change or block my Kraferric powers?'

I looked down at my hands, which were absent-mindedly shredding blades of grass. 'I don't know, really. I don't think there are any specific changes. I'm going on Vrael, though. He still needs blood, but sunlight won't kill him, so I guess there are small changes that will happen. Shouldn't be too drastic though.'

He didn't reply, seemingly lost in thought. I continued to

shred the grass, trying to get my nose to focus on something other than the cloying smell of the Outlaw bodies starting to decompose. I could smell something, a scent that gradually grew stronger and stronger. The smell of vampire. And if my empathy wasn't deceiving me, which it rarely does, a very pissed off vampire. I chewed my lip nervously. Yes, the trick with the mouse had been a very low blow and incredibly dishonourable thing to do, taking advantage of his blood-lust. Not only that, but he was going to blow a fuse over the fact that I had jeopardised my safety by playing him. That, and the heart injury. I didn't know if vampires could have heart attacks, but he was certainly going to have kittens when he found out that I was hurt by a demon hunter on his watch.

True to my sense of smell, the silver-haired vampire strode across the grass with fury written all over his face, his bow and quiver slung across his back. I quickly dropped my gaze. Initiating a confrontation was not going to make this any easier.

'Shadow Wolf Alexai Roth…' he started, but I interrupted him before he could continue.

'I know, it was really dirty trick to play on you and I'm really sorry I did it. I just had to get away from the clan for a while.' Vrael's expression softened slightly, but it didn't last.

'Why can I smell your blood?'

Oh goddess… 'We, uh, ran into a demon hunter…' Vrael was instantly next to me, his silver eyes boring into mine.

'Are you hurt? Where?'

I pushed him away gently. 'I took a sword through my primary heart, but I'm fine as long as I don't stress myself. Bart's the one with the real problems, not me.' Vrael turned to look at the Kraferr, who was starting to look a little unsettled under the vampire's unwavering, scrutinising silver gaze. Vrael sniffed the air.

'By all the gods above and below, Shadow, please tell me you did not…'

'I wasn't thinking.' I muttered, looking down at my shoes. 'He was so close to dying from blood loss…'

Vrael sighed, rubbing his temples as if he was starting to get a headache. 'This breaches so many of the ancient protocols that it aches my mind to contemplate them.'

'I know! I already said, I wasn't thinking about protocol…'

'What is done is done. Although I cannot understand one more thing. With your heart so grievously injured and Bart's current conversion, who slew so many?'

'We picked up a helper along the way,' Bart chipped in. All three of us turned to look at Sither, who was roosting up in a tree. He looked, given the circumstances, impeccable. If I hadn't known, I wouldn't have thought that he had just fought such a bloody battle. I wondered how he had done it. I had been so focused on the Outlaws, I hadn't even noticed how he fought. I don't think I was even aware that he was there. Bart scratched the back of his neck.

'Well, we should probably be getting on with the quest before the Outlaws send another party to attack us.'

'No, Bart,' Vrael snapped. 'You require complete rest until your demonic conversion has had time to complete. Shadow and I must return home before word gets to the demon hunters that she is out and not heavily defended.'

'Vrael,' I growled before Bart could respond. 'I said I'd help him in this quest. You know as well as I do that I need something to occupy my mind, or else I'll go mad and surrender myself to Karthragan.'

For a moment, I thought the vampire was going to argue back, but he sighed and shook his head. Defeat radiated off him, defeat and worry. He knew well enough that once I had set my mind firmly to something, it was easier to move a mountain than it was to make me change my mind.

'As you wish, Shadow, although I will insist that you at least take the remainder of the night to rest yourselves before undertaking the next leg of your journey.'

I glanced at Bart. 'Sounds like a fair enough compromise to me.' Bart nodded, lying back on the grass once more and staring at the stars. Vrael folded his long legs to sit down, pulling his longbow and quiver from his back. He took wooden shafts, arrow heads and black and red feathers from the quiver, setting about fletching his own arrows. I smiled faintly. Shaeman and Merlas both gave Vrael their moulted feathers for his fletching. It was a comforting thought, thinking about how well the clan worked together despite our demon sides. I gathered some wood, lighting a small fire to ward away the chill of the night. I curled up next to it, closing my eyes to rest, but sleep refused to come. I sighed irritably. My mind was too awake for anything more than waking nightmares as I imagined the horrors waiting for me in the darkness of the city streets and the future. I sat up, rubbing my eyes. I glanced at Bart, making sure he was okay, then at Vrael. The vampire smiled slightly at me, pulling something from his quiver and tossing it to me. I caught it with an ease born of building our house as a team. In my hand was a sharpening stone. I nodded gratefully at my half-brother, pulling out one sword and running the stone along the edges of the blade. Sharpening a sword, practising my moves, target practice with a bow, grooming Merlas, all repetitive actions that helped me calm myself.

'Alexai, I do not believe that it is safe for us to remain here.' Vrael spoke in demonic.

I had to hold back a growl. Vrael knew perfectly well that I couldn't stand being called by that name, which meant that he used it to make sure that he had my full attention. Glaring openly at my brother, I snapped back at him in the same language: 'Don't ever call me that!'

'Alexai…'

I snarled, leaping to my feet. Vrael mirrored my actions. From within my mind, the tendrils of the demon's influence grew and took hold as I struggled to keep on top of it. In front of me, Vrael's eyes had turned red, splitting into four. Demonic possession. Now it was a show of strength. My vision became tinted by crimson. The smell of blood and death became as pleasing a smell as that of fresh air and mountain wind had been. I released my iron control over my magic, allowing it to erupt into a flaming aura. Vrael copied, his red magic bursting forth in what could have been considered an impressive show of pyrotechnics. Here and now, all that mattered was showing how strong we were. It was a fight. Anger began to consume me. Until I heard Bart's voice calling my name.

My magic flickered. I stamped down on my demon side, trying to regain control, to force its influence down. I gasped aloud with the effort. Vrael seized the opportunity. He leapt at me, attempting to make the first strike. I kicked out, managing to force him to divert his course briefly. His strength bolstered by his magic, his fist struck my chest. I felt my ribs crack. I fell back with a shout of pain. Bart jumped towards Vrael.

'What the hell do you think you're doing?' The Kraferr snarled. I gasped for breath. Vrael closed his eyes. I felt his anger ebb away as he calmed himself. I glanced over at the pair. Bart stood behind my brother, one arm round his neck, the other wielding its claws as if to gouge out Vrael's eyes. I sat up slowly, cradling my ribs with one arm. Bart released Vrael, still watching him warily out of the corner of his eye as he crouched next to me.

'He missed my heart,' I assured him, sensing the concern radiating from him. 'He must have broken a rib or two, that's all.'

'Yeah, but it's still a broken rib. Come on,' he gently pulled my arms away, laying his hand lightly over my splintered bones. I threw my head back and snarled silently to the moon as they snapped back into place. Bart leant back on his heels. 'You okay now?'

'Yeah,' I replied. 'Yeah, I'm all right now. Thanks.' I lay back, rolling onto my side so that my back was facing Bart. A hint of confusion wafted from him, but he didn't ask. I was glad about that. I was so tired, so sore. All I wanted to do was sleep.

I didn't even notice that Vrael had gone. A wave of anger and confusion hit me like a herd of galloping pegusi. I bolted upright with a gasp. Vrael never felt emotions with such power, but they had undoubtedly come from him. Something was very, very wrong. I grabbed my swords, scrambling to my feet and running back towards the city, towards the epicentre of the emotions, trying to ignore the pain lancing through my chest with every breath I took. I arrived in a back alley on the outskirts of the city.

'Vrael, take high ground!' I shouted. The vampire, bow in hand, swung himself up onto a fire escape. I drew both my swords, preparing to fight. I faced my opponent. Sither and another, cloaked, figure. I sniffed the air. Kraferr. A female Kraferr whose smell was somewhat close to Bart's. But now was not the time to ponder over the Kraferr's scent. The emotions I was sensing from Sither were not good.

'Why were you really with us, Sither?' I growled, my eyes narrowed. I heard the subtle creaking of Vrael's bow as he drew back the string. I barely noticed the Kraferr female slip away. Sither grinned at me. I didn't like that. It didn't bode well at all. Only an enemy who knew how to win would smile like that. My chest throbbed painfully as it reminded me that I was living on borrowed time until my heart healed. I couldn't afford another injury!

My fears were confirmed when Sither morphed. I cursed under my breath. I had forgotten he was a shifter. Shapeshifter were an increasingly rare shifter race, and damned strong in their 'true' forms. I had read scrolls about them back in Synairn. And Sither's form did nothing to inspire confidence within my mind. A two metre tall Praying Mantis was not what I wanted to see. I tightened my grip on my swords, highly conscious that the hilts were starting to feel a little slippery. One of Vrael's arrows appeared out of the corner of my eye. It broke in half as if hit one of the interlocking pieces of armour that formed the Praying Mantis's exoskeleton. I brought both blades up to parry a blow from the giant bug's bladed arms. The impact shook my arms down to the very bone. Goddess, he was strong. I ducked under another attack, swinging my sword in a short arc. I barely scratched his exoskeleton. Growling in frustration, I reluctantly gave ground, concentrating on keeping all my limbs attached to my body. I couldn't see any weak points in his armour plating, nothing I could take advantage of. Another arrow narrowly missed me.

'Watch where you're aiming!' I yelled without taking my eyes off Sither.

'Shad?' called out Bart's voice. I half turned to tell him to get the hell out of here. One of Amarath's combat rules floated through my head: Never turn your back on an enemy. I jumped out of the way just too late. Sither's bladed arms ripped through my calf. I fell hard onto the unforgiving ground. Pain stabbed through my shoulder, blinding as the impact hit my chest. I could only lie in shock as the agony froze every thought in my mind. For a moment, I prayed for the fatal blow I knew was going to come. I prayed for it to kill me, to save me from the prophecy. But the blow never came. I glanced up. Bart stood over me, his arms crossed in front of him as he held off Sither's attack. I rolled out of the way. Sither screeched in agony. Blood rained down. I scrambled to my feet, almost falling again as my injured leg gave way beneath me. I grabbed onto a drain pipe. Bart was ripping at Sither's face with his claws as he hung down the Praying Mantis's back. Sither screamed once more, throwing Bart to the ground and fleeing. The Kraferr sprang back to his feet as Vrael swung down from the fire escape. He slung his bow over his back and pulled my arm around his shoulders so he could help support my weight. I leant against him, relief and gratitude flooding through me.

'It is unwise for us to linger here, we should… Bart?' We both turned to look for the Kraferr, who had lapsed into unnerving silence. He lay on the ground. His agony surged through my mind with such an unexpected force it almost blinded me. I pressed the heel of my palm against my eye as I knelt next to him, trying to relieve the pain building up in my head as I felt his pain combined with my own, blinding in its agony. Vrael was trying to pin the Kraferr to the ground to limit his thrashing. Violet fur swept over the brown. Not far off, the silver bracers lay in pieces.

'Bart, come on, let go of your emotions,' I tried to urge him, but he was too far gone for us to bring him back with words. His claws lengthened, digging deep grooves into the concrete. His eyes, already red with his Kraferric transformation, split into four. A double row of bone spikes erupted from his back.

'Vrael! The Salent!' Calmly but quickly, the vampire handed me a slim vial of silvery liquid. Pulling out the stopper with my teeth, I grimaced as the smell hit me. Salent was a particularly nasty concoction the part demons used in extreme cases to control their brethren. It removed all emotions from the mind for a few moments to a few hours, effectively trapping the demon, which used the emotions to free itself. I grabbed Bart's jaw, trying to ignore the fearsome fangs he now sported, tipping a couple of drops into his mouth. The effect was immediate. He stopped struggling, instead lying on the road much like a limp sock. Slowly, he began to change again. The spikes receded, his claws shortened, his fur turning brown once more. Vrael and I sat in almost identical positions, watching the Kraferr change back into himself. His red eyes, now only two, were still dull. I closed my eyes, focusing on his emotions, blocking out all else. I could feel the faint stirrings of something, but not enough for Bart to pull himself out of the stupor. Not yet.

Ten minutes passed with an agonising slowness. Vrael was on

edge, waiting for another attack. I was focused on Bart, praying that he would recover from this. Stronger flickers of emotion started to spark in the weremonkey's mind. Shadow breathed a sigh of relief as Bart slowly sat up, one hand on his head.

'What happened?' he asked groggily. 'It feels like I've got a heavy metal band playing in my head...'

I bit the inside of my cheek to keep from smiling. 'You had a close run in with your demonic side. We were worried that you would not pull through as you are.' To his credit, Bart didn't ask any questions. I wasn't sure I would be able to answer them. What he had just gone through was the rough equivalent of what nearly every born part demon went through between the ages of three and five. We discovered our demonic sides, and one side would be chosen, usually because of the strength required to subdue the other side of our personalities. Bart hadn't been expecting his. It was pure luck that he came through still thinking as a human and not as a demon. For all we knew, Bart could had been overwhelmed by his demonic side. We had taken a big risk with what we had done, but the important part was that it had worked. Bart pulled his watch from his pocket, staring at it for a moment.

'We should probably be going. I don't want to have to explain this to anyone,' he reasoned. I glanced at Vrael, who nodded slightly. Getting to his feet, the vampire then helped me to stand, once more helping to support me. With Bart at our sides, we walked back towards the forest, to the mountain where the Kraferr necklace was hidden.

We walked for a few miles before Vrael suggested we break for a rest. While he was perfectly capable of continuing, the look he cast me said it all: he was worried about the physical state Bart and I were in. Grudgingly, I realised I had to agree with him. There was no point in getting there if we keeled over from pain and exhaustion so close to the end of the mission. A few hours would make very little difference. Bart looked as if he was desperate to continue, but he couldn't go against Vrael's words, not when he saw Vrael's expression, in any case. There was no way any intelligent being would contradict a grouchy vampire who had made up his mind. I was secretly glad. My leg pained me a great deal, but I didn't want either Bart or Vrael to attempt to heal it. They needed their energy to continue on the quest. I sat myself on a fallen tree trunk. The forest was quiet, a silence only broken by a distant river's thunder. I rubbed my temples. Dawn had come over the land not all that long ago, shining through the canopy of leaves to create a forest floor dappled with light. Vrael morphed into his animal form of a panther before he disappeared into the trees. I leant my head back, glaring at the sky. I didn't want to be stopped for any longer than was strictly necessary. The prophecy loomed over my head like an ominous black cloud that didn't hold a storm but a hurricane. A month. That's all I had left. Just a month. My fingers strayed down to the wound, to determine the extent of the damage Sither had managed to cause. I pressed lightly on the bone in my shin. Pain shot through the entire limb. I couldn't help but wince. The damned Praying Mantis had certainly managed to cause a lot of damage. I felt concern radiating from Bart once more. Glancing up, I saw him watching me with worry on his face.

'Look, Shad, if Vrael didn't heal that, I'm guessing I shouldn't try either. So please, please try not to worsen it?'

I twisted my mouth into a half smile. 'You don't have to worry. The injury is minimal. It's what I believe the humans refer to as a 'flesh wound'.' Who was I trying to kid? Demons, and by extension, half-demons, could normally see through lies if they were looking for them. It wasn't a difficult thing to do. Bart locked gazes with me before he spoke quietly.

'If I said I believed that, I'd be lying, Shad.'

I closed my eyes and bowed my head. I thought so. I could feel him glaring at me still. He was annoyed that I was trying to hide things from him. I turned my own glare at him out of the corner of my eye.

'You have your things to worry about. I have mine. It would be wise for you to remember that,' I growled, getting back to my feet. Knowing that my leg wouldn't hold me, I summoned my magic. Hovering above the ground I willed myself forwards. I passed Vrael slinking back towards our temporary encampment, a few rabbits in his mouth. He nodded his head once to me, his conscious brushing against mine long enough to express his concern that I keep myself safe. I inclined my head slightly, acknowledging his thoughts.

I hovered a little further into the forest before sitting down with my back against a tree trunk. Leaning my head against the bark, I closed my eyes. A month. It seemed so short. I felt tears beginning to gather, but I wiped them away angrily before they could spill over. Now was not the time to get emotional. I had to stay in control. Tendrils of someone else's thoughts gently probed mine. I lowered my barriers slightly, allowing the familiar feel of Vrael's consciousness wrap around mine in a gentle embrace.

Shadow? Are you okay?

Yeah, just...you know...prophecy getting to me again. It's...

I understand. Please return to camp, I worry about your safety.

Sighing quietly to myself, I got to my feet, grimacing as pain shot through my leg and chest. I glanced around. I couldn't afford to keep using magic to move around. It was too exhausting and I needed my energy. I had to find something. I picked up a broken branch, about as thick as my wrist and a little longer than I was tall. Stripping the off shots and leaves from it, I planted it firmly against on the ground, testing it. It held under my weight. It would serve as a staff for a while, hopefully until I got home. Using the staff to share the weight on my injured leg, I began to make my way towards the others.

Back at camp, Vrael and Bart were quietly eating the rabbits the vampire had caught, sitting around a small fire. Well, Bart was eating it. Vrael was sucking the blood out of his. Without a word, he tossed me the last of the three creatures. The smell of it turned my stomach. I felt ill. I ate a few mouthfuls for appearance, then set it aside. There were creatures in the forest who would be glad to eat it for me. Instead, I sat back against a tree. Vrael coughed politely. I glanced at him. He tapped his calf, asking for permission to see to my wound. I sighed, nodding and turning my head away. The vampire moved in, gently pulling the fabric of my trousers away from the gash and setting to work. Within a few minutes, it was cleaned out and stitched. Vrael calmly packed away his tools.

'We should get going, the cave's only a couple of hours away,' Bart suggested, getting to his feet.

We arrived in front of a cliff, where symbols had been carved into the stone in the shape of an archway. I chewed the inside of my cheek, leaning heavily on a tree branch I had found, trying to keep the weight off my injured leg. There was magic here, certainly, the same kind that I sensed around Bart. Kraferric magic. I reached out a hand to touch the stone surface, but there was some sort of magical barrier. I couldn't get closer than a couple of inches away. Bart stepped closer, unhindered by the magic, to run his fingers over the carvings. I tried to understand the runes, but without success. I had no idea where to even begin to try to read the Kraferr language. Judging by the concentrated look on Vrael's face and the confusion I was feeling coming from him, he had no idea either. Great. Even Bart seemed to be struggling to read them. I wondered if the Kraferrs even taught their Ones how to read the language.

'I've got it!' Bart called back excitedly. He laid a hand on the door, chanting something under his breath that I couldn't understand. With an ominous crack, the rock within the carvings broke away, sliding to the side. Vrael and I glanced at each other as Bart stepped inside. Warily, we followed. For a moment, there was a feeling like walking through syrup before the magic reluctantly let us pass. We were inside the cave.

The cave echoed eerily with our breathing. Bart's eyes glowed a little in the darkness. Our footsteps resonated off the stone walls. If any of the little group had been human, we wouldn't have been able to see a thing in the gloomy cavern as we crept through the maze. I sniffed the air, trying to get a lock on a possible smell of the locket. I smelt nothing, but I could smell blood. Fresh blood. I opened my mouth to warn the others, but the sound of grinding rock pushed all thoughts from my mind.

'The walls are moving!' Bart cried. The three of us huddled together, the walls shifting like liquid around us. I gritted my teeth, trying to tune out the deafening sound. Gradually, the noise abated. The walls ceased to move. The dust started to settle. We continued on as fast as we could, determined to find the necklace before the walls started to move again. Vrael's nose, more acute than mine, smelt the scent of Kraferr and metal and took the lead until we came to a small, rectangular chamber, right in what we guessed was the heart of the maze. I looked around. In the centre of the room lay an amulet.

'This is too easy. There has to be something else,' I muttered.

'There's poison,' Bart answered. 'The decorations on the walls hide poison darts.' I glanced at the walls in front of us. Carved into the stone were Kraferr faces posing with various grimaces. Sure enough, there was a faint smell of poison in the air, an overly sweet, metallic tang. I pulled a face. I hate that smell.

'Shadow? Give me your staff,' Vrael said quietly. I handed the stick over without a word, leaning against the wall for support. The vampire stepped forwards, crouching low to the ground, using the staff in an attempt to find the trigger for the darts. Without warning, darts started flying out of the walls. Bart and I, still in the corridor, were safe. Vrael dodged, back-flipped and ducked, his vampire and demonic reflexes strained almost to breaking point in his struggle to stay out of the lines of fire. The onslaught stopped. Vrael, breathing heavily, bent to pick up the necklace. In a blur of motion, two figures jumped past, us, heading for Vrael, grabbing the amulet. The smell of Shapeshifter blood went straight to my head. I clamped my cloak over my nose, trying to filter the scent. Vrael had paled, trembling. I sensed his distress as he tried to keep his hunger contained. I tried to summon my magic. It sparked feebly. I swore. The sheer weight of the Kraferric magic was interfering with mine!

'Sither,' Bart growled.

The mantis shapeshifter smirked at us, a bandage obscuring his ruined eyes. 'Who else?'

'Who's your pal?' I asked, referring to the other person who had ambushed us. The person in question lowered the hood on her cloak. That explained the smell from before. A female Kraferr.

'Name's Domina,' she said, the All Teller necklace dangling from her fist. I gritted my teeth. Vrael was crouched on the ground, glaring fixedly at the stone, trying to control himself. Domina handed Sither the necklace. Bart tensed, worry pouring off him.

'You'd better not ask it about my death,' the Kraferr growled.

'I don't have to,' Sither answered. 'You die now!' In a flash, Sither had thrown a dagger at Bart, slicing his neck. He collapsed next to me. Vrael was crouched next to Bart in an instant, tense as a coiled spring. I glanced at him worriedly, but he had his medical equipment out, not his fangs. My heart sank. I could smell poison. Anger clouded my mind. Roaring, I leapt at Sither, intent on ripping out the bastard's heart. Domina jumped in front of him, two more daggers at the ready. I dodged, trying to get around her. Stepping back into a defensive position, I watched the female Kraferr carefully. Out of the corner of my eye, I saw Sither raise the amulet to his lips, whispering to it.

'What is the meaning of human existence?'

Bart coughed out a laugh as the amulet started to glow strongly, its white light surrounding the mantis. I squeezed my eyes shut against the glare, turning my face to the wall, the light searing my eyes. By the time it had died down again, Sither was nothing more than a pile of ash. The smell of burnt flesh hung heavily in the air. Domina had disappeared. Breathing hard, I scrambled to Bart's side, checking his wound. Vrael had beaten me to it, having already administered an anti-poison. I took over pressing the sterile pad to the wound, desperately trying to stem the blood flow. We had come too far to let him die. Too much was at stake for the Kraferr race. Slowly, Bart got to his feet, one hand keeping the compress clamped to his neck. He walked unsteadily to the pile of ash that had once been Sither, touching the golden chain of the amulet.

'Keep an eye on his emotions,' Vrael said under his breath to me. I nodded discreetly. Bart wound the amulet's chain around his wrist, gazing down at the heavy gold and blue gemmed necklace. I could feel the weight of it pressing down on him, that there were unanswered questions in his mind, that he held the future of his entire race in his hand.

'Come, Shadow, Bart, I have a scent trail to the outside.'

We split up with Bart when we reached the outskirts of the city again. Vrael and I bade our goodbyes and started to walk back towards the forest to teleport out of sight of human eyes. I ran through the procedure in my mind. It shouldn't be too difficult. As soon as we were far enough out of sight, I reached out and touched his shoulder.

'Sorry, Vrael, but I've got to follow Bart and make sure he isn't going to do anything stupid.' Releasing the magic, I teleported him back to the house. I then started after the Kraferr, but the pain in my leg forced me to stop after only a couple of steps. I growled under my breath in frustration, casting a charm on the wound to block the nerve endings. I wouldn't feel anything until the magic wore off. Sniffing the air to locate the scent trail, I started to track Bart.

He was standing outside a heavy metal door in a dingy alley, back in his human form, when I found him. He was hesitating to go inside, which I understood completely. There was a feel in the air, something screaming at me to run away, that something bad had happened there. I clamped a corner of my cloak over my mouth and nose. The smell of a battlefield was heavy, all blood and rage and desperation, sickeningly sweet and bitterly sour at the same time. Bart gripped the amulet tightly, his mind made up. He pushed open the door, stepping inside what looked like an even danker and dingier corridor. I, being my usual curious self (for which I still blame Holly, since she encouraged that particular trait), followed him. I stuck to the wall, still using my cloak to filter the rank smell. Now I knew what had happened here. Death. The massacre of the few remaining Kraferrs. Who or what did it, I didn't know. Bart barrelled out of there, his emotions whirling dangerously. I couldn't leave him alone in that state, not when he was so young in demon years. It would be all too easy to let go of all control in an emotional outburst. It's okay for humans, but demons could easily level a city with our kind of power. Once outside, he leant against a wall, breathing heavily. I dropped my cloak, trying to think of something to say.

'Well, I'll happily admit that I am never going to get that smell out of my nose, ever.' Not the best of things to say, if his reaction was anything to go by. Fur erupted from his skin as he turned Kraferr, anger boiling up within him.

'You don't get it Shadow! You don't get a damned thing, do you?' Bart shouted. I gritted my teeth, stamping down on my own emotions. Boy did I 'get' it.

'You think I don't get it? Oh, I get it all right. I thought I was the only one of my species until I was eleven! My supposed guardian sent me into a war at the human age of four! I had to learn to be indifferent to these things, or else I would have destroyed the city by now! Death is an everyday occurrence. Get used to it and get on with your life.'

'Get on with your life? That's all you can say? You're telling that to a guy who just failed to save a whole goddamned race from extinction! HIS race! This stupid necklace was supposed to save us, but now they're all dead! It's OVER! I'm the last one!'

Scowling, I grabbed his hand, projecting a memory of mine into his mind, the memory of my first ever battle, of losing control, my magic not distinguishing between friend and foe, of lying surrounded by the dead, pinned to the ground by a sword through my leg. He gasped, stumbling back. I nodded curtly, retreating to the shadows of the alley to get myself back under control. Running footsteps entered the alley in a flurry of cloak. Expecting Vrael or one of my other siblings, I rolled my eyes. They were never going to leave me alone, were they? But the person who stopped in front of Bart wasn't one of the clan. She wasn't a demon. It was Domina. I heard Bart growl low in his throat.

'Why did you do it, Domina?' he snarled. I frowned slightly. It took me a moment to connect the dots in my head to figure out that he was referring to the killing of the Kraferrs, but there was something in the emotions of the female Kraferr. Something new and something missing.

'Who?' the girl asked.

'You, stupid. You killed the others! I know you did!'

'I've never killed anyone! Any my name's Dominique, not Domina!'

'I know you killed them! You're the only other person who could have known where they were!'

'I didn't! I swear! I only just woke up in a forest! I don't know what happened!'

'Bart,' I intervened quietly. 'She's telling the truth. I can feel it.' Bart sighed irritably, looking down at the amulet still in his hand. He looked defeated, his shoulders slumped, head bowed.

'Now what?' he asked softly. 'All the Kraferrs are dead and this...*thing* is now useless. So much for it being able to save us.'

'Not all the Kraferrs are dead,' I offered as consolation, 'you're still here. Welcome to feeling like the last of your species.'

'Ha, ha, very funny.'

I retreated to the shadows of the alley, watching as the two last Kraferrs in existence met each other properly. Dominique and Bart Kraferr. Two Kraferr Ones who, as Bart so vehemently put it, were definitely not going to try to recreate the Kraferr line together. I smiled slightly and teleported away, back to my family.

I had decided that I wouldn't run away from my family again, but after only a couple of days I had to. The heavy silences were too much to bear. Amarath still hadn't come home, and I was worried about her. I didn't want to lose my family ever again, not after Arellan. Merlas picked her way through the forest, playfully shying away from the woodland creatures. I sat bareback on her, not really paying attention. I trusted the doe absolutely. I sighed, playing with her mane. Both of us wanted to fly, but given the fact that hunting season had just started, I wasn't going to risk Merlas being shot by one of the humans prowling through the edges of the forest. She stopped, sniffing the air. Suddenly a gunshot shattered the air. Merlas took off at a full gallop. I came off her back almost immediately with a thud. For a moment, I lay in painful shock. Vrael may have insisted on healing my injuries once I had returned to the clan, but I still had the residual pain. Groaning, I picked myself up, heading after the pegasus. For all I knew, she was going to get herself into trouble.

I found her eyeing another being, a young man. At least, he seemed to be a young man. He smelt strange. Merlas lowered her head, having a good sniff. I copied her actions, although I did at least try to be a bit more discreet than the doe. There was blood in the air, and not from Merlas or me. I noticed that he had his hand clamped over his arm, blood welling from beneath his fingers and I could sense his pain. I eyed him warily.

'Who are you?'

'I am Ahrach, Ahrach Lusari.' I allowed my expression to soften a little as I gestured to his arm.

'Do you want me to help you with that?' I offered him a brief smile. 'I'm Shadow, by the way. Shadow Roth.' He watched me for a moment, as if gauging how much he could trust me. He took his hand off his wound, showing me. I probed it as gently as I could. The pellet was still lodged in the tissue, and he was definitely not human. For a start, his bones were hollow. 'This is going to hurt,' I warned him before using my magic to extract the fragments of metal and seal the injury into a neat scar. The drain on my energy was immediate, but not overwhelming. Ahrach jumped away with a yelp as he looked at the scar. He watched me with new wariness in his eyes.

'Who are you?'

I let one corner of my mouth tug up in a half smile. 'The question you're looking for is *what* am I. Half demon would be the answer. How come you're here?' As soon as I had told him my species, I realised that I had taken a momentous risk. What if he told someone in the Milita? I had just put my whole clan at risk! My family! Was I getting so scared of the prophecy that I cared so little for my own life? For the lives of my brothers and sister?

'I was out flying and got shot by some hunters,' Ahrach said. I felt a wave of panic surge through him. I guess he had said more than he intended to say. Then again, so had I. I have to admit that I was put on edge by his statement as well. Who was this guy, really? I rested my hand on the hilt of my sword, ready to draw if I had to. His eyes flickered to the sheathed blade. 'I'm a shapeshifter,' he admitted. 'I can change into an eagle.'

I felt happier knowing that. Okay, so the last shapeshifter had been a right dirt bag, but I couldn't expect Sither to be representative of his race. I dropped my hand from my sword, much to Ahrach's relief if his emotions were anything to go by. 'I know your race,' I answered, hoping to put him further at his ease. It unfortunately had the opposite effect. He grasped a weapon he carried strapped to his back. I cursed in my mind. I hadn't noticed that. It wasn't even a particularly friendly looking weapon; a long staff, one end topped by a curved, scythe-like blade, the other a vicious looking spike.

'My race isn't known by many others, and we've never consorted with demons.'

I raised my hands a little to show him that I wasn't a threat. Okay, so I was always going to be a threat as long as I wasn't confined to a human body, but he didn't know that. 'I met one recently.'

'What was his name?'

'Sither Moonspike.' Ahrach grunted in response, sitting down on a tree stump. I relaxed as well, leaning against Merlas's shoulder as the doe grazed quietly. She raised her head, looking out across the forest. Her ears were pricked up, listening. Her ears flicked back, lying flat along her neck. Not a good sign. I gripped the hilt of my sword again, eyes following Merlas's line of sight. Out of the corner of my eye, I could see Ahrach take on a battle-ready position, watching me.

'Peace!' Called out a woman's voice. My blood froze. That voice... No, surely she wouldn't come here. Would she? As she stepped out of the tall bushes that had concealed her, I saw that she hadn't changed at all, not in the slightest. High Priestess Arias stood there, watching me with her silver eyes. I gritted my teeth, tightening my grip on my sword. 'Alexai,' she crooned.

'Don't call me that,' I snarled in response. She had no right to come calling me that now. She was the one who took that name away from me. I glared at her through narrowed eyes, trying to keep myself under control. She sighed heavily.

'You must get over this aversion...'

'Who are you to tell me that? Oh yeah, High Priestess Arias. Well, you may rule Synairn, but you don't rule me!'

'Alexai…'

'I said DON'T!'

'Enough!' Ahrach thundered. I turned a surprised gaze to him. He looked angry enough to kill someone. I hoped he might go for Arias and get her out of my hair. 'Who are you guys? I mean, I know almost nothing about you apart from your names!'

'Arias used to be my guardian,' I explained, throwing a dirty look at her.

'I came to fetch you back.'

'Well you're barking up the wrong tree!'

'Need I find Meran?' Now that was just a low down, nasty trick. She knew that he wasn't allowed anywhere near me. But then again, she was High Priestess. I guess she was capable of rescinding the Senate's orders. I may be stronger, faster and bigger now, but the thought of him still scared the living daylights out of me.

'You wouldn't…'

Arias simply smiled at me before she vanished. I swore under my breath. I had no way of telling if she was going to make true on her threat or if it had been empty. I didn't want to think about it. I leant against a tree, trying to look as nonchalant and carefree as possible. No need for this Shapeshifter to think that there was a real danger on the way. After all, Meran wouldn't attack him. Not unless he did something to really piss the Senator off. I glanced to my left as a twig snapped, terrified that she had already come back. Relief flooded through my as I saw the familiar silver hair of Vrael coming towards me. Ahrach huffed in annoyance.

'Okay, so who are you?'

'I am Vrael Mercian.'

'This is one of my brothers.' I explained shortly.

'But,' Ahrach continued, 'there's something I don't get. How can you to be brother and sister, if you don't have the same last name? I mean, Vrael Mercian, okay, but then, wouldn't it have to be Shadow Mercian too? Instead of Shadow Roth? Or is this some kind of demonic thing?'

'We are semi siblings,' Vrael explained. 'We share the same father.'

'Yeah, 'one same father' who hates our guts.' I muttered under my breath. Vrael shot me a dirty look. I raised an eyebrow, tapping the half circle scar. He rolled his eyes in return. I turned away from the two males as Vrael made some comment on the knife Ahrach was carrying in a sheath on his belt, leading the pair off into a discussion about weaponry. Merlas's pushed her soft nose into my hands, snuffling. I rubbed her forehead absent-mindedly. Arias's threats concerned me. I didn't want her to get wind of my family, or at least the bits she didn't know about. While I was certain that she was aware of Amarath's existence, I wasn't so sure about Shaeman and Vrael, even less so about Archangel and Onyx. The thought of my twins falling into her hands terrified me. I wound my fingers into Merlas' mane, trying to calm myself. I was so concerned, I nearly believed that I could sense Arias nearby again!

'Shadow? Are you okay?' Vrael's gentle voice broke into my imaginings.

I hadn't realised that my thoughts had mirrored themselves in body language. I stood rigid, staring past the pair. Vrael glanced at me, but I took no notice. There were people moving in around us. I threw my mind out, trying to identify them. I gripped the hilt of my sword tightly. Ahrach took hold of his own weapon. Silence reigned. The bushes rustled.

'Don't think I don't make true on my threats,' Arias stepped out from the trees, accompanied by a group of soldiers. Meran stood to one side of her, but on the other side…

'Amarath!' I exclaimed, wondering what she was doing there, dressed for battle none the less. She didn't look up at me. Shame came off her in waves. Vrael froze beside me, muttering under his breath in the language of the dead that I couldn't understand. He only ever spoke that language when the situation was too grave to be expressed in Demonic or English. That did not bode well.

'Well, Shadow?' Meran asked. 'Are you going to come? In fact, your friends here can all help us too.'

'We have units from the army here. We will take you by force if necessary, along with your friends if we have no other alternative,' Arias warned.

'You're not going to take me anywhere!' Ahrach exclaimed fiercely.

I gritted my teeth, realising that they had backed me into a corner. Either I went with them willingly, or I risked being dragged back *anyway*, and the others taken as well. 'Leave them out of it,' I growled.

'I have another idea, Arias,' Vrael suggested. 'Perhaps we could agree on a different manner of settling this. A duel, perhaps? If I lose, you take us and Shadow to Synairn. If I win, though, you let us, including Shadow, depart.' His silver eyes glinted a little in the dappled forest light. 'Do you accept?' I frowned at him, trying to think of what he could be up to. This wasn't normal for Vrael. He usually stayed out of fights as much as he could. Arias considered the proposition for a moment. She nodded once to Meran, who stepped forwards. Amarath glanced at Vrael before she came forwards, her characteristic limp noticeable only to those who knew it was there, placing herself in as the designated duellist for the clan. Oh goddess, Amarath was going to be fighting Meran. I tried not to think about the outcome, but rather concentrate on not running to either side's aid. All I could hope for was that they wouldn't kill each other. Amarath stepped into position standing opposite Meran in the centre of the small clearing. She drew her two-handed sword, preparing herself to fight. Vrael stood next to me, putting a hand on my shoulder. I flashed him a brief smile, glad for his support.

It seemed as if nothing was happening, and would look that way to Ahrach, but for those with a magical inclination, the static electricity feel of magic was heavy in the air. Amarath shifted a little, as if destabilised. The leaves on the trees rustled. The wind picked up its pace, but it seemed to be focusing on creating a tornado effect around Amarath. She tensed, trying to keep her feet. Without warning, she jumped into the branches of a tree to escape the winds. Another handful of heartbeats passed before Meran roared in anger. Another blast of wind knocked the demoness from the tree, but she scrambled to her feet, jamming her sword into the ground. Her hair whipped around her head in the hurricane force winds, her cloak billowing and twisting itself tightly around her. She reached up a hand to unclasp it, letting it fly away. Her eyes narrowed, doubling in number and turning red. Amarath was unleashing her demonic side. I bit my lip, hoping for her sake that she would go too far into possession that she couldn't come back. The wind stopped. Meran, taking one of his two swords blades, drove it into the ground with such force that, aided by his own magic, it created a split in the ground aimed at Amarath. She jumped out of the way, rolling as she landed. Springing back to her feet, she summoned her magic, firing bolts at the Synari. Meran deflected them with his blades, charging towards the demoness. My heart was in my mouth as they began to clash swords, Meran attacking and Amarath remaining on the defensive. Amarath parried most of the blows with her sword, taking the others on her armour protected arms. Slowly, she began to take the offensive, attempting to strike Meran where she deemed his weak spots to be. She managed to spear him through the arm. My heart clenched. He ripped the sword from her hand. She jumped out of the way. His blade caught her leg, leaving a deep gash down the thigh. Growling, she ran towards me. I froze, not knowing what to do. She yanked my sword from its sheath before running back into the fray. She attempted to cleave the Synari's head in two with my sword and her own spare short blade, but he blocked the attack. I glanced at the people gathered round, chewing my lip. Everyone was fixated on the two combatants, following the movements. I sensed something coming from Ahrach an emotion, but I couldn't concentrate enough to interpret it.

The fight turned into a dance of death, all flashing metal and clashing swords. She kept one sword on near constant defence, horizontal across her stomach. One of Meran's blades managed to ram through Amarath's hand, forcing her to drop one sword. Magic exploded from her in her fury and pain, directed at him. The Synari managed to deflect it with his magic moments before it hit him. He lunged at Amarath with his blades, but met the demoness's shields. Dropping the barrier, Amarath made her own lunge, her one good hand still gripping a sword. She started to attack without any discernible patterns or tactics. I frowned, trying to understand what was going on. Amarath had always taught me never to do that, to always think about what I was doing. What was she trying to do? Meran blocked her attacks with apparent ease. Amarath yelled out in pain as one of his swords cut into her side. She managed to slash at his legs, drawing blood from the deep injury, but it wasn't nearly enough to incapacitate him. Sweat was starting to drip down Amarath's forehead while her opponent looked as if he could keep up the pace for days. Her injured leg was starting to tremble as exhaustion took its hold. I clenched my fists, willing Meran not to hurt her too badly. Then Amarath just stopped fighting. He slashed at her with his two blades. Amarath had a small smile on her face, seemingly relieved. Her leg gave way beneath her, and she fell onto her side, blood welling up in the two wounds to her chest and stomach. Although her eyes were half closed, as if in death, she continued to breath.

'Amarath!' Ahrach yelled. He dashed to her side, putting a hand on her neck to check her pulse before moving on to check her wounds. Vrael's hand gripping my shoulder prevented me from going to her aid as he stared at Arias, waiting for her verdict. I clenched my fists, desperate to go to my sister's aid rather than leave her in the hands of a stranger. I had to content myself with listening in on Ahrach's emotions so as to warn Vrael if Ahrach was going to hurt my sister. All I felt from him was a soft tenderness. A hint of love. Maybe she was in good hands with him. Closing my eyes briefly, I prayed that, if he did make a move on her, he wouldn't break her heart. If he did, I might have to hunt him down and kill him.

Eyes turned to Arias. The High Priestess raised one eyebrow in distain and turned her back, gesturing to her group of soldiers and Meran to follow her. Glancing back once over her shoulder, she cast an eye over the defeated demoness.

'If your best fighter cannot win against a simple Senator, then you are of no use to me." She paused for a moment before adding, "Leave Amarath. She's no use if she can't win a simple fight.' Amarath turned painfully to look at Arias, her hand stretched out to the soldiers following the High Priestess.

'Marcus...' she said hoarsely. 'Don't leave me here, Marcus...' The captain of the group glanced at Amarath, his expression dispassionate. He vanished without saying a word. Amarath uttered a quiet, strangled cry, her hand falling back to the ground. Vrael let me go. I knelt next to Amarath, murmuring words to try to comfort her as tears started to drip down her cheeks to darken the earth below. I ran my hands gently over the wounds, trying to focus my mind enough to heal her, but my thoughts were too scattered. Vrael gently touched my shoulder.

'Go back to the house. Tell them what has happened and assure them that everything is now under control and Amarath has returned to us. I will look after her. Worry not.'

I nodded, seeing sense in Vrael's words. If the others knew what had happened, they would be ready with back up if needed when Vrael brought Amarath home. I was of no use to anyone there. Saying my farewells, I concentrated on teleporting.

Something went wrong with the teleportation. I could feel it as soon as I had started it. Teleportation normally feels like jumping into cold water, just a little less wet. This felt like swimming through treacle, but it was too late. If I tried to reverse the magic now, I would end up falling into the void. I couldn't breathe. The magic was starting to drain me.

The teleportation ended suddenly, like a piece of elastic snapping. I gasped, drawing in the air I had been denied. My muscles ached. My head throbbed. And that wasn't the only thing wrong. Concrete walls. Concrete floor. This was definitely not the house the clan had built in the woods. The smell was familiar, but I couldn't place it. I couldn't remember where I had smelt it before. Slowly, I pushed myself to my feet, highly aware of the residual pain, putting most of my weight on the leg that didn't hurt so much.

'Hey! We got one!' yelled a male voice seconds before I found myself rugby tackled to the ground. The assailant twisted my arm up behind my back, sending pain shooting through my damaged heart and shoulder. He clamped handcuffs around my wrists before dragging me upright by my hair. I tried to summon my magic to fight him off. Icy fear gripped my heart. I couldn't feel my magic. They must have put silver in the handcuffs! Two men in lab coats surveyed me as if I was nothing more than a lab rat while the man who had tackled me pinned me against the wall, confiscating my swords.

'Mark it up and bring it through.' The man nodded and dragged me into a small room just off the concrete chamber. Heat suffused my body from the fire in the centre. I fought with all my strength, kicking and biting. He called for back-up. I found myself slammed to the floor, one of the men sitting on the small of my back, keeping my arms pinned to the ground. Another held my legs down. Someone ripped my shirt away from my shoulder. I tried desperately to buck my assailants off, but to no avail. Out of the corner of my eye, I watched the third man put a metal rod into the fire. A few minutes later, he pulled it out. Taking care not to touch the white-hot end, he approached me. I couldn't struggle. I had no energy to struggle as he carefully positioned the rod. With one quick gesture, he pressed the sizzling metal onto my right shoulder blade. I yelled out as it seared my skin. I could feel the flesh blistering under the metal. He lifted the metal away, dumping a cup of icy water over the branding. For the rest of my rather short life, I would bear the numbers 004-666 on my shoulder blade.

'Okay, take it to the doctors.'

I fought against the restraints in some sort of lab. I was strapped down on an examination table, spread-eagled. I growled at myself, banging my head on the metal slab underneath. They had taken every single piece of weaponry I carried, even the dagger I had up my sleeve. They had left me in my blood-encrusted tank top and trousers, without even my boots. Whoever these people were, they weren't taking any chances. I gritted my teeth. Somewhere to the left, a door opened, admitting the lab coated scientists I had seen before. They stood over me, just watching. I narrowed my eyes.

'When you pervs are done watching me, could you let me go?' I said. I thought I might as well try. You never know. They didn't answer me to begin with. They just scribbled a few notes on clipboards before talking as if I wasn't even there.

'It's not an ideal model, I'm afraid, some damage has been done to this specimen. There's a puncture wound to the left hand side of the chest.'

'It shouldn't impact the studies though. It'll also give us a chance to observe the healing process for more natural wounds.' This put me on edge. More natural wounds? More natural compared to what? I growled again, trying to pull out the straps on my arms. The physical effort sent pain lancing through my chest, but I didn't care. I just wanted out of here. They watched with the same fascination of a five year old watching an anthill.

'From what we already know, this isn't a particularly weak specimen. That means that the silver does indeed have an effect on this species of demon. We can conclude that not only does it prohibit the use of magic, but also limits physical strength. I believe additional testing is needed to prove this, but I'm guessing that the silver actually brings their strength down to the average of an ordinary human child.'

'Useful for the ground teams to know.' Oh goddess. Now it all made sense. Amarath had told me about these people, after I had a run in with them once before, of which I remember nothing. The Milita. Oh goddess, it was the Milita.! I was in even more trouble than I had realised. The more they learned from me, the easier it was for them to take down the rest of the clan. I couldn't let that happen.

I kicked out at the door of the cell, grinding my teeth. I rubbed my arm, where they had tested the effects of water, holy water and silver solution. Needless to say, I had two large burn sores on my arm. I sighed heavily. The cell wasn't big, two metres by two metres with a glass front. A concrete ledge that served as a bed took up half of the space. I sat down, putting my head in my hands. Just how had I landed myself here? By not concentrating enough to see the trap, of course, a stupid, stupid mistake. Now what was I going to do when Karthragan turned up? There was no way I could fight him on this ground. I lay back with a grimace. The Milita had only just begun with me. X-rays, scans, lots of poking and prodding had already gone on to give them an idea of how a part demon worked. I scratched at my wrists, where metal cuffs inlaid with silver had been fitted. No magic for me. I had less than a month before Karthragan would find me. I already knew that he was tracking me, keeping an eye on my every move so that when the time came, he knew exactly where I was. Not that he'd help me get out of here. The weaker I was, the easier it was for him to defeat me. *Stupid prophecy*, I thought as I curled up in a corner. *Stupid, stupid prophecy.*

* * *

I screamed as electricity spiked through my body. The scientists scribbled a few more notes down on their clipboards. Three days to go before the prophecy, and I was still in the Milita's lab, and nowhere close to being able to escape it. Don't get me wrong, I had tried. I had tried everything I could think of, and nothing had worked. If anything, it had only made things worse. I now had two guards armed with silver bullets posted outside my cell at all times. I spent most of the time outside of the lab drugged up to my eyeballs in sedatives. Inside the lab, they ran experiments on me, determining my weaknesses. My arms were already covered in sores from silver and holy water. They had even tried putting ice against my skin, which had burned without leaving a mark. Fire had invigorated me, to the point where I had almost managed to break free, but I hadn't been able to get further than the door out of the lab. Now they were trying electricity, having hooked me up to all sorts of vital sign monitors. As glad as I was to see that my primary heart was starting to function again, this was not the way I would have wanted to find out. I arched my back, trying to muffle my scream as another, stronger bolt of electricity spiked.

'That charge would have been lethal to humans.'

'I think we can count that although electricity can serve to slow a demon down, in the long run all you will do is anger it.'

'So the ground teams shouldn't rely on their tasers.'

'No, not if they want to make it out alive. We already know that it is nigh on impossible to contain an angered demon.' A needle slid into the skin of the crook of my elbow, releasing a sedative serum into my bloodstream. Waves of tiredness and nausea slid over my mind. Two guards unhooked me from the machines and dragged me back to my cell.

I lay on my side on the concrete bed, closing my eyes. Tears threatened to spill over. I reached a hand over my shoulder to touch the branding, still heavily scabbed over. I had seen the reflection in the glass front of the cell. The fourth demon they had managed to capture, six black numbers against pale skin. My hand flopped back down onto the concrete, my muscles too tired and heavy to use.

'Okay, now, how the hell do we open this thing?' muttered a voice outside the cell door. I tried to lift my head, but the sedative denied me the energy. I could barely lift a finger. My eyelids didn't want to open.

'I don't care how you do it, just get it open before they realise something's wrong!' hissed a second.

'Got it!'

'Shadow?' A finger touched the pulse point in my neck before gently pushing one eyelid up. Vrael! The vampire had never looked so good to me as he did now. Even better than that, behind him stood Amarath and Shaeman, both in total bad ass mode, armed to the teeth and expressions set to kill. Vrael pulled off his cloak, wrapping the thick red cloth around me.

'Vrae? She okay?'

'Sedated, rather heavily, weakened by the trials she has been put through, but she is still conscious. Pass me the green vial.' Vrael turned me over onto my back, raising my head slightly. As the potion trickled down my throat, I felt the life coming back into my limbs. I sat up, feeling more alive than I had done for weeks. 'Slowly, Shadow, slowly, you are not going to feel very well for the next hour or so.'

'Vrael, we don't have time to hang around and wait for her to come to her senses. You're going to have to carry her. We've got to get out of here, now!' The vampire scooped me up as if I was no more than a doll. My stomach lurched, threatening to bring up the meagre meal I had been given to eat.

'Three, two, one...'

We appeared on the edge of the forest I had crossed with Vrael and Bart not all that long ago. Amarath sagged against a tree for a moment, regaining her strength after having teleported four people. Vrael put me down, but still kept my arm around his shoulders for support, for which I was infinitely glad. My stomach was churning.

'She's gonna hurl,' Amarath warned a moment before I threw my guts up on the grass. I gasped for air, my legs shaking. It takes a lot to make a demon throw up, but the warring of the sedative and Vrael's antidote had done the trick. I groaned quietly. And of course, just to make things worse, as the first star appeared in the sky, a shiver raced through my body. I glanced at my hand. Oh great. Human again. I glanced at Vrael, who's vulnerable period coincided with mine, curious to see what he looked like. I had never really seen him in human, well, vampire form before, mainly because he always shut himself away to avoid the sunlight. With his russet brown hair, golden eyes and a slightly less pale complexion, he was, and I know this sounds wrong coming from his sister, incredibly sexy.

'Hey! Did you find her? Is she – Whoa, who's that?' Alba emerged from the trees, her eyes locked on Vrael. 'Is that… Vrael?' I smiled weakly as Vrael's girlfriend took in his appearance.

'Yes, it is me. This is my more human appearance.'

'It's the new moon,' I explained. 'For Vrael and me, that means we turn human for three days and three nights.'

'And also means we're in trouble,' Shaeman added. 'We've got three days before Karthragan turns up looking for a fight, Shadow's injured and weak and Vrael can't help her.' For a moment, there was silence, but the silence was soon broken by a thud announcing the arrival of yet another person.

'Hey every – What happened to you?' Bart said, staring at Vrael and me. I gritted my teeth.

'Yes, we're a little different. This is what we would have

looked like if we hadn't been part demon.' I snapped. 'And before you ask, three days and three nights.' In one corner of my mind, I remembered Holly teasing me about human 'time of the month', even though she knew I didn't get them. Demons don't, as a general rule. The half-demons just end up with a different 'time of the month' which was every bit as much of a pain in the arse. 'And how long until the prophecy?'

'Three days.' I closed my eyes as a wave of despair crashed over me. *In three days, I die.* I may have been mentally preparing myself for this event, but I wasn't sure if I could just walk up to Karthragan and fight him, knowing that I wasn't going to live.

'So what are we going to do?' Bart asked quietly. I glared at the ground, working hard to conceal my emotions from the rest of the group.

'I don't know,' I answered. 'I just don't know.' There was silence for a moment before Bart spoke again.

'You must be really brave, Shadow.'

I shook my head. No way was I being brave in facing this. 'I'm not brave, just scared. If I was brave, I'd be facing Karthragan now, telling him where he could stick his precious prophecy.' I paused to take a deep breath. 'But I'm not. I'm sitting here, waiting for it to happen.'

'You are brave, Shadow,' Bart insisted, 'to actually keep on going like this. Your final days have come, and you accept it. You knew all these years that this day had to come. And you lived with it. That's what I call brave.'

'Everything has its time, and everything dies.'

'Well, at least you only have to die once.'

'I'm pretty sure Karthragan's planning on killing me so I don't come back.'

Amarath coughed politely. 'We should probably get back home. I don't want to be caught out by the Milita. when they come looking for Shadow.'

Three days later, I was sitting up a tree, waiting for the sun to set and give me my demon powers back. The house had been deathly quiet over the last few days, everyone knowing that the prophecy was getting close. Even Archangel had held back on the pranks. Normally she would have been getting the best of Alba and Bart, who were staying with us. Vrael sat on a branch below me, swathed in a cloak to avoid the last of the sunlight as he waited for the transformation to be reversed. I glanced down as I heard Bart's voice mutter a hello. The whole house had been under a black cloud since this morning. No one was really talking to each other. A rush of relief flooded my heart as the first star appeared. The tremors ran through my muscles, followed by the warmth of my magic. I swung down from the tree, nodding at Bart. I touched my injured calf, wincing slightly.

'So…now what?'

'Now, we wait. He'll come to me.' I took a deep breath, calming myself. 'And I will wait for him.' I looked around the clearing, taking in everything I could. The smell of the twilight, the last rays of sunshine filtering through the leaves.

'How's the leg?' asked Alba's voice. I turned around to face my friend,

'It's getting better,' I replied, rubbing my temples. The emotions coming from Bart and Alba were starting to get to me. I tried to smile, but it turned out more as a grimace, so I wiped the look off my face. A spark of excitement came from the house. I looked up, past Alba, to see Archangel running towards us, brandishing a piece of paper. She slid to a stop, panting hard.

'We…found summat…in the prophecy!' She managed to gasp. I bit my lip, hardly daring to breathe. She took a moment to get her breathing back under control, her eyes shining brightly in her excitement. 'Remember that line that was always scratched out of the prophecy? Well, we finally found a version on the internet where it wasn't. It reads, 'When One is present, one will survive'.'

I glanced at the sky. It was rapidly darkening. It was too late. He was going to arrive soon. 'We don't have time to decrypt it fully. We should assume that everything will go as we thought it would. Now, everyone, leave. I have to do this on my own.'

The forest stilled as the others left. The leaves stopped rustling. Silence descended. I couldn't hear the stream. I swallowed hard. I tried to control my breathing, to control my fear. Then he arrived. Karthragan. Every time I saw him, someone died. The first time, Arellan, the second, I lost Holly and Natalie. This time, it was my turn. I wouldn't walk away from this, but I was going to try damn hard to make sure he wouldn't either. He would pay for what he did to my friends.

He stood at the other edge of the clearing in his more human form. Muscular torso bared, he wore only a pair of ragged, cut off trousers. His black hair flopped over his eyes. In all, the demon only appeared a couple of years older than me. It made my stomach heave to remember everything he had done to me. I raised my chin in defiance. Neither of us said anything as we approached each other, closing the distance between us to a few metres. We took up fight stances. I spied a sword on his hip and glanced down to make sure I had mine. He chose this moment to strike. I dodged as fast as I could, but his claws scraped the side of my neck. I gritted my teeth as my eyes flashed red. I couldn't afford to lose control in front of Karthragan. Not now. He launched into a series of kicks, forcing me to give ground, dodging as much as I could. My leg seared in pain as he managed to land a clawed strike, but I had to try to move past the pain. I felt my muscles starting to tire as I tried to block his attacks, each blow jarring my joints. I hadn't even tried to go on the offensive yet. What was I doing? He was a full demon, stronger, faster, more endurant than I was. There was no way I could defeat him. I tried to dodge another kick. It connected with my shin, breaking the bone. I yelled out as the pain exploded through my leg, falling to the ground. Karthragan laughed, moving in for the kill.

I squeezed my eyes shut. With the sensation of jumping into a fire, I teleported to the other side of the clearing, in the shelter of the trees. Desperate, I glanced around, trying to find something, anything I could use against the demon to give myself an edge. I clapped eyes on a surprised looking Kraferr. I narrowed my eyes, making shooing motions with my hands. He nodded reluctantly, running in the direction of the house. I took a deep breath, moving out from the shelter offered by the trees, pulling down the barriers around my magic. Time to take this battle to another level. I summoned my magic into a fire-like aura around me. Karthragan mirrored my actions with his deep crimson magic. Before long, the clearing was splattered with black blood as we threw razor sharp blades of magic at each other. Karthragan was starting to lag. That was giving me a tiny spark of hope, but I had to face the fact that I was faring far worse than he was. My limbs were trembling with exhaustion. My broken leg couldn't support even a fraction of my weight. My head felt light from the blood loss. My other leg was about to give way beneath me. Behind me, I heard something rip and a feral roar. I whipped around to see a manticore standing on the edge of the trees. Hadn't anyone listened to me? The creature lashed her tail, sending the spikes flying towards us. Karthragan used the distraction, blasting me several metres away. Blood poured from a new, deep gash across my stomach and chest. I scrambled back to my feet as fast as possible, turning to face my father. His chest and side were peppered with the spikes, but he wasn't hindered by them. He was walking towards me, pulling them out. I backed away a few paces. Another volley of spikes passed me. Karthragan grabbed one from out of the air. I swallowed hard, fear gripping my heart. I turned to run, but Karthragan lunged. I collapsed to the ground under his weight. The spike speared my arm, poison beginning to pump into my system. I gasped, trying to pull out the deeply embedded dart. Karthragan pulled his sword out. I froze. He barked out a laugh.

The sword plunged downwards, through my primary heart, then my secondary. Strangely, I couldn't feel the pain. There was no pain. Lifting my limbs seemed almost out of my capability. Karthragan started to walk away. I gritted my teeth, anger sweeping through me. He had done this to me. He had killed me, and now he was walking away from it. No. I wasn't going to let him walk away from this. I reached under my cloak. Gratitude towards Shaeman flooded through me as I pulled out the handgun he had insisted I carried through my vulnerable period, in case Karthragan decided to turn up early. The weapon felt dirty in my hand. A human weapon for mass killing without the sport and honour of combat. It disgusted me, but it was all I had. Using all my strength, I lifted my arm, sighting down the barrel. I squeezed off three shots, one through each heart, one through his head. The gun grew heavy in my hand. I let it drop to the ground, watching as Karthragan keeled over. I let my eyes close. I was so tired. I couldn't hear anything past the rushing of blood in my ears. The beating rush started to slow. My eyes drifted beneath my eyelids. I felt someone pressing on my hearts, trying to keep them going. Something on my arm burned. I flinched violently, but something held me down. Then the pressure was lifted. Someone gently kissed my forehead.

'Kraferric way of saying goodbye,' murmured Bart's voice. There was a darkness in the back of my mind, comforting, beckoning. It felt so welcoming. My body started to feel cold. The darkness felt warm. I let it engulf me, blotting out my pain.

PART 4

EARTH – NEW EYES

It was cold. I shivered slightly. My limbs felt stiff as I tried to stretch them out. What had happened to make my muscles feel so sore? I sat up, looking around. I was in a clearing that looked vaguely familiar, like an unnerving sense of déjà vu. A group of people sat not far off, linked by a silver thread of magic. I wondered what they were gathered around and why the air felt heavy with sadness. A cold nose nuzzled my hand. I smiled slightly as I saw a black she-wolf curled around me. I ruffled her ears gently. Movement from the group of people turned my attention back to them. They had disbanded a little; two silver-haired men walked a little way off and started to dig a hole. I saw what they were all gathered around. A dead girl. Disgust welled up inside me. Had they murdered her? No. That didn't make sense when you considered the sadness in the air. A strange cross between a human and a purple monkey stood up, taking the girl into his arms. I watched with a child-like curiosity as he walked over to the hole and carefully laid the body inside it. A girl with short, purple hair reached into the hole. With the sound of metal rasping against metal, she pulled out a sword, thrusting it into the earth at the head of the grave.

A girl in ragged clothes detached herself from the group, heading towards me. I tilted my head to one side as she crouched in front of me. There was something about her that I knew, that I recognised. It took her a few attempts as she tried to choke her words through her grief, but she eventually said, 'I'm Alba.'

'I know.' The words escaped from my mouth before I could stop them. Yes, I did know her, but I couldn't remember how, or why. Then again, I couldn't even remember my own name, who was I to judge?

'Shadow?' Alba asked quietly. 'Is that still you?'

Once more the name sounded familiar, but I couldn't place it. 'I...I...I don't know...' Tears welled up in Alba's eyes, spilling down her cheeks. I felt terrible. We glanced up as the purple monkey boy joined the little group.

'Do you remember anything?'

'It seems like a dream...'

'A dream... You mean your memories are vague to you?' He seemed to think for a moment. He pulled a necklace, an amulet, from his pocket, showing it to me. I frowned slightly. There was something about it that I recognised. 'Do you remember this?' I did, I remembered pain and blood. The hurt of betrayal. I squeezed my eyes shut, trying to remember through the haze of emotion.

'It seems so far away... I remember blood, and betrayal, but that's all...'

'But who are you?' Alba blurted out. I looked at her. Her bright green eyes searched mine, attempting to see something. I rubbed my temples, desperately trying to remember. My fingers brushed over a thick scar around my eye. Frowning, I tried to remember how I got it. I shook my head.

'Everything is so mixed up, so blurred,' I murmured, hugging my knees to my chest. The rest of the group gathered around me, fixing hard, distrustful gazes on me. I fixed my eyes on my knees, unwilling to look up to see their faces, faces of people I distantly recognised but couldn't place. All I knew was that I felt deep affection and love for them. Why did they hate me? Why were they asking me so many questions?

'You can't even remember Vrael? Vrael Mercian?' Bart asked quietly, pointing out one of the men in the group. I tried to swallow my rising panic as I glanced up and saw the barely concealed anger on the man's face.

'No! I can't remember anything!' Bart gently laid a hand on my shoulder, bringing my attention back to him. I calmed down a little, but I couldn't tear my gaze away from the silver-haired man's. I slowly got to my feet, keeping a wary eye on everyone. I backed away a couple of paces before turning tail and running as fast as I could. I had to get away from them. I didn't even know who these people were! I found myself crashing to the ground. The other silver-haired man had me pinned to the ground, snarling. The rest of the mistrustful group gathered in a circle around me, surrounding me so that I couldn't escape.

'Shaeman!' Bart said, arriving alongside us. 'She's scared, that's all! Just let me and Alba talk to her. We might be able to get something out of her.'

'We can't trust her,' Shaeman spat.

'We don't know if she's Shadow. She doesn't know if she's Shadow. We don't know anything about her. The only way we can is if we get her to think calmly.' Shaeman shifted, releasing his hold on me. I sat up slowly, rolling my shoulders. The wolf slunk alongside me, curling around me and licking my cheek. I buried my hand in the thick fur around her neck. Bart put a hand on my shoulder again, looking into my eyes.

'Think carefully,' he began. 'Try to remember your name. Search deep into your memories, or else I'll have to use magic and search the deepest of your thoughts.' I could feel his unease as he spoke, as if he really didn't want to. I swallowed hard, trying to get a grip on my emotions long enough to form a coherent thought.

'I remember lots of names...' I murmured. 'Wolf... Roth...'

'Well, uh, I guess we could call you Roth for now...'

'No,' Shaeman interrupted. 'She bears no relation to our clan, and therefore has no right to bear the name. Call her wolf, if she is so attached to the creature beside her.'

Bart shot a glare at Shaeman before turning his gaze back to me, encouraging me to keep going.

'I remember a library with lots of books... I can remember a kind, black haired woman singing to me... I remember,' I paused, opening my eyes wide, 'I remember killing people...

standing on a battlefield and killing people...' Bart clamped a hand over my mouth. I pulled away, burying my face in the wolf's fur. I tried to bite back my sobs as memories assailed my mind. So many memories of blood. I tried to think through them. I saw a man with four red eyes standing over me with a sword. Of Bart's voice as he kissed my forehead.

'I...I remember...I remember that my name is Shadow.'

'That's what we were supposing before...' he said, but he seemed to be more interested now. 'Do you remember anything else that might be good for our ears to hear?'

'I can remember everything...' I murmured, looking down at my hands. 'But I can't believe that I'm still here...' Alba was watching me with a confused and curious look on her face. I shifted uncomfortably. 'Alba, can you stop looking at me like that? I know I just died, but still...'

'Sorry,' she murmured, looking away. I glanced up at the ring of demons still surrounding me. My family. My clan. The distrustful look on their faces made my heart ache. Amarath looked down at me. She looked at me with a look of such furious disbelief that it shattered my heart. My sister... My twin... Surely she should recognise me? Her glare broke the fragile assumptions I was desperately clinging onto. She didn't know me. The sister she knew was dead. Dead and not coming back. For them, there was nothing left to do. They had buried their sister and that was the end of the matter. Amarath glared down at me, one hand resting on the hilt of her sword, threatening to draw the weapon.

'Run, Wolf, run as fast as you can and never look back.'

What else could I do? I ran.

For two weeks, I sat in a cave, keeping a low profile. The wolf that had appeared during my reincarnation curled herself around me. I had decided to name her Wraith. I don't know why. It just seemed to suit the black wolf. She started up her strange, canine version of a purr as I rubbed the diamond patch of white fur between her eyes. I had managed to pinch a few pieces of clothing from washing lines in the city. A hooded sweatshirt and jeans several sizes too big for me, but they were good enough. My eyes were rimmed red from crying. I had lost everything. Everything I had held close. All because of that stupid prophecy. It made me want to scream, but my throat was already raw from screaming in rage. I tugged on my hair, remembering the reflection I had seen in a window in the city. I hadn't even recognised myself. My eyes were still purple, but more angular, my ears more pointed. My hair was still waist-length, but black, with two white streaks on one side. I looked as if I was fifteen. No wonder the clan had chased me away. No wonder they hadn't recognised me. I rested my head against the stone wall, trying to figure out what I was going to do. I had never thought about what I would do with my life. I had never had reason to think that I was going to live very long. Now I had the whole of eternity stretching out before me as long as I kept away from fatal diseases and people who generally wanted to kill me. I sighed heavily. My mind wandered back to my family as it had done so often since my death. What was Amarath doing? Were Archangel and Onyx okay? I knew that the clan would look after them, but that didn't stop me worrying. A small part of me wondered if this was what Arellan had felt after Amarath and I had been taken away, a deep-seated ache somewhere in my heart. I rested my head back against the stone wall, closing my eyes as I let despair wash over me once more.

'Shadow?' called a voice. I cracked open one eye. Wraith's plumy tail beat out a rapid rhythm as she wagged it. Bart Kraferr stood at the mouth of the cave, looking a little sheepish, his tail wrapped around his leg. He stepped a little warily into the cave before gathering up his courage and sitting next to me. 'How're you holding up?'

'Bart, I killed my dad, got killed myself, reincarnated and then got rejected by my own family. How do you think I'm holding up?' I replied bitterly. Bart grimaced, the tip of his tail flicking as if it just couldn't keep still.

'Well...uh...I...' Bart trailed off, looking towards the mouth of the cave. I followed his line of sight. At the mouth of the cave stood the other Kraferr One, Dominique. She hovered there, unsure, before stepping forwards to stand close to Bart. They glanced at each other. I didn't need empathy to see what was happening between them. Fate and the death of the Kraferrs may have thrown them together, but they had chosen to stay that way. Somewhere in the back of my mind, I wondered what Kraferric children were like. If they were anything like demonic children, I didn't want to know. But above all, I silently wished them every happiness possible. Sighing quietly, I looked out past them, to the forest the cave looked out onto. The tops of the trees were waving in a peculiar pattern, almost circular.

'Bart...' I said quietly, warningly. Wraith barked in warning, jumping to her paws.

A helicopter swung into view. I charged at Bart, knocking him and Dominique into the shadows at the back of the cave, Wraith following close behind. They had to stay hidden! They wouldn't be taken! I wouldn't allow it! The Milita. swarmed into the cave, weapons at the ready. I drew a knife I had managed to steal, preparing myself to fight once more. I glared at them, trying to seem as menacing as possible, to keep their attention on me and not on searching the rest of the cave. From out of nowhere, a rifle butt collided with my temple. In a shower of stars, I went down.

The thing with the Milita. is that they learn from their mistakes. Although they didn't know that I had actually had help to escape from the cell the last time, they had taken extra care in shackling one arm to the wall and fixing bands of silver around my wrists and ankles. I sat rigid in the cell, trying not to move so as not to aggravate the burns and sores opening beneath the silver. I had already gouged deep scratches in my skin around the metal in an attempt to get them off, the effort and pain proving futile. A pair of guards arrived to take me to what I guessed was going to be a round of torture disguised as experimentation. Whoopee! I couldn't wait.

Instead of being taken to the lab, however, the guards escorted me down a different corridor of the underground base to a concrete bunker-type room. This was odd. I hadn't seen this part of their base during my previous visit. Two scientists were already standing there, waiting. I watched them with what I hoped was a look of bored annoyance on my face. They didn't react to it, instead looking down at their clipboards.

'Despite a different look, this is specimen 004-666. The mark is still on its shoulder and the blood tests came up exactly the same. Do we assume that they can actually change their physical appearance?'

'We can't be sure for now. In any case, let us test that device before the demon gets any funny ideas.' The soldiers gripped my arms firmly as the scientists took a loop of metal out of a box. As they came closer, I noticed various wires and circuit boards in the metal, giving the whole thing an appearance of a computer gone wrong. Whatever this thing was, I was pretty sure I didn't want it anywhere near me. Everything about it seemed wrong. Unfortunately, I didn't have much of a choice. The strange thing was fixed around my neck. As soon as the two ends joined, the little switch in my head that controlled my transformations flipped.

Normally, my transition between humanoid and wolf is smooth, the joints, muscles and fur acting as if a well greased machine. This transformation was all wrong. Every inch of my skin burned as fur pushed its way to the surface. My bones snapped to fuse themselves in different positions. Pain ripped through my spine as the extra vertebrae of my tail formed. My hands and feet folded up on themselves to make paws. My screams of agony turned to howl of pain as my face elongated and vocal chords rearranged themselves. My entire body ached as I lay, panting hard, on my side on the cold floor. The scientists chattered excitedly to each other. I twitched my ears feebly to try and catch their words, but my muscles were too exhausted to move anything else. Anger started to blossom in my chest. They had put me through all that agony and all they could think to do was to stand there and make stupid notes on their goddamned clipboards! A growl rose from deep within my belly. Gathering every possible scrap of courage to withstand the chorus of aches in my body, I launched myself at them, teeth bared in a snarl. Grim satisfaction flooded through me as I felt my mouth lock around soft flesh. Blood spurted into my mouth. Muscle tore beneath my claws as I gouged at the scientist screaming beneath me. The rich feeling of vindication surged through me. Even as blows rained down on me from the other scientist, I didn't care. The guards pulled me off by the scruff of my neck, clamping my jaws shut. The scientist I hadn't attacked jumped forwards to take the collar off my neck. I collapsed to the floor as the transformation once more wreaked havoc through my body until I lay, once more, as a humanoid. I couldn't help it as a bubble of laughter floated up from my aching chest. I had attacked one of them. I had attacked one of them! It felt so good, like I had finally done something I had needed to do for a long time. They deserved it. They deserved everything I dished out to them for everything they had done to me! I was still laughing when a needle slid into my skin, releasing a sedative into my system.

The feeling of vindication and fulfilment had gone by the time the sedative had started to wear off. Instead, it was replaced by the feeling that I was in for it now. I sighed heavily, rolling over, the clinking of the chain tying me to the wall the only sound to echo in the tiny cell. I glared at the wall, cursing myself for getting into this mess in the first place. It wasn't like Amarath was going to come dashing to the rescue this time. Not while she thought her sister was now lying six feet under in a clearing next to the house. I sighed again, scratching at the silver bands. Blood started to clot under my claws as I did, but I wasn't paying attention. Somewhere on the floor, a piece of paper fluttered. I frowned. That wasn't normal. I wasn't allowed anything in the cell. The scientists were too scared that I'd find out a way to escape. I glanced at the floor. Sure enough, there was a piece of paper there. I reached down to pick it up, straining slightly against the chain in order to reach it. Two words had been scribbled on the scrap.

Hey there.

I glanced at outside the cell, at the two guards who stood in front as an extra precaution. One of them turned his head slightly. Hope flared up in my heart. Bart! He smiled a little, turning around and reaching for the keys on the belt of the uniform I guessed he'd nicked. The other guard turned as well, showing Dominique's serious, I'm-trying-not-to-smile face. I had never been so glad to see the pair of them. The door swung open. Dominique pulled a pair of handcuffs from her belt, clamping them over my wrists as Bart unlocked the chain. Neither of them spoke, but I knew that they were trying to simulate what the real guards would have done.

Bart teleported us away as soon as we had lost sight of the Milita's headquarters, landing back in the cave. Well, I say he teleported us. If he hadn't had help, we would have ended up in the North Pole. Tiredly, I made a mental note to teach him how to teleport properly without Dominique having to navigate for him. I leant against the wall, trying not to throw up. Bart really hadn't got the hang of teleporting. Waiting until the wave of nausea passed, I closed my eyes. Every single part of my body ached from the forced morph. Dominique stepped up to my side silently, putting her hands over each of the silver bands in turn. With a murmured word, they cracked and dropped from my limbs. I nearly cried in relief. The skin where the metal had touched had been burnt black, angry red sores weeping clear fluid breaking the dark colour. Wraith crept out from her hiding place, nosing my hands in gentle concern. I laid my hand on her head, taking comfort in the feel of her soft fur.

'Bart, can you heal those?' Dominique asked quietly as I sank to the ground. My skin crawled and itched as he touched the wounds, concentrating on healing them. When only faint scars remained, he sat back, sweat beading his brow.

'Thank you,' I said to the pair of them, knowing that the simple words didn't express the extent of my gratitude towards them. Bart smiled weakly, getting to his feet to go and curl up at the back of a cave. His light snoring soon began to echo off the walls. I sympathised with him. Healing took a lot of energy. Dominique sat and watched him quietly. I closed my eyes, hoping to get some sleep myself. It would seem that fate was not on my side.

It didn't take long for us to realise something was wrong with Bart. His breathing became hoarse. He twitched as if he was fighting someone in his dreams. In the gloomy light, I spied the bony spines of his part demon form protruding from his back. Shit. The static feel of magic filled the air as he began to lose control. Pulling Dominique back, I tried to think of something, anything I could do. Only one thing came to mind. I had to fight him, try to bring him back that way. I summoned my magic, issuing a challenge. Four red eyes illuminated the darkness near Bart's head.

'Dominique, you've got to try and stay out of this fight,' I warned the Kraferrin. I didn't want her getting hurt. This was going to be an intense enough fight without me worrying about trying to pull my shots in case they hit her.

'Shadow, you know that Bart's a Kraferr. I know more things about Kraferrs than you do, like their weak points and reflexes. You need my help!' Bart leapt forwards, trying to land a punch. I bared my teeth at him as I jumped away, throwing up my mental defences. The battle had begun.

'He's also a demon! You have no idea how much that changes things!' Bart tried to attack again, magic strengthening the blow. I closed my eyes, letting my own demon side burst forth. It flooded through my muscles, taking control. My vision turned red. I brought my arms up to cross them in front of my head and chest, strengthening a shield I had created from my magic. Bart crashed into it with astonishing force. Despite the shield, I staggered back. Bart retreated a few paces, planning his next move. I took a deep breath, trying to get my demon side back under control. He drew one hand back. I braced myself. He threw a bolt of magic. It passed through my shields easily, striking my shoulder. Snarling in pain, I started to launch my own magical attacks at him. I managed to get his right knee, weakening him considerably and hampering his movement. I had to try to bring him down. I threw another bolt at his knee, trying to destabilise him enough to make him fall. As soon as he started to wobble, I curved another blast round his back, knocking him onto his stomach. I manipulated a net of magic to pin him down, muttering a string of spells under my breath in an attempt to keep him there. He struggled madly, forcing me to double my efforts to keep him down. Slowly, he started to calm.

'Bart?' I asked quietly, wondering who was going to answer me. The Kraferr or the demon? The being under the net of magic started to laugh. It wasn't in mirth. It was high and mocking. It chilled my bones to hear it. I wanted to clamp my hands over my ears just to keep it out. 'Who are you?' I snarled, feeling the deep vibrations in the ground that told me I was using my demon voice. 'Identify yourself!'

The laugh faded away much to my relief. 'You've changed a

lot, I see, ever since my death. If I told you the truth of who I really was, you wouldn't believe a word I say.'

I ground my teeth. This was definitely a demon presence. I decided to pull the power card. 'I am Shadow Roth, heir to Karthragan, Prince of Darkness. I demand to know your identity!'

'I am what you were in the past. Shadow Roth – before the prophecy. I am what you would call – yourself.'

'You are not me. I was in control of my other side. It posed no threat!' I snarled, but in the back of my mind, I wished that I could believe my own words. With a near deafening crack, Bart broke free of the net of magic, aiming a kick at my chest. It connected, sending me flying back. Shaking my head to clear the daze, I started to get angry. If this really was the demon side he had inherited through my blood, I should have no qualms about bringing him down as efficiently as possible. Taking three running steps, I executed a manoeuvre Amarath had spent hours upon hours teaching me. Using my magic to help me, I jumped over Bart, turning on myself to land facing his back. As soon as my feet touched the ground I dropped a little to turn a round-house kick. Bart ducked to try to avoid the attack. My foot struck his neck with a sickening crack. He lay sprawled on the ground. Seeing him there broke every hold my demon side hand on me. I crouched next to the Kraferr, running a light hand over the damage I had inflicted.

'What did you do to him?' Dominique screeched, reminding me of her presence.

'Broke his neck by the looks of it,' I said. I moved his head as gently as possible, realigning the bones the best I could before my magic healed the injury. I sat back, exhausted. I struggled to keep my eyes open. Without the adrenaline rush of the fight, I could barely stay awake. Dominique knelt by Bart's side, stroking his hair. I let my head fall back as I tried to think about the chances of Bart reawakening as the demon. From what I could determine, they were pretty slim. That was comforting at least.

'Shadow?' Dominique sounded nervous. I opened one eye I hadn't even realised I had closed.

'Hmm?'

'Do you know how to tell if someone's sterile?' I had to think about that one for a few moments, coaxing my tired mind to give me thoughts that were at least vaguely coordinated. It was pretty much like trying to get Amarath to stop sleeping with every single sword she owned. Unlike that venture, I did manage to remember a spell from the book Armen had given me. It wasn't specifically for testing someone's fertility, but it was close enough. I nodded to the Kraferrin.

'Could... Could you perform it?' She asked. With a heavy sigh, I moved to sit closer to her. Taking her hands, I pressed them together between mine, focusing on the spell I needed. It was pretty long and not one I had ever used before. Had it been anyone else but one of the people who had rescued me from the Milita., I would have said no. But I owed Dominique a favour. I pushed my exhaustion to one side, concentrating hard. I watched our joined hands carefully. Dominique was staring at them with a single-minded determination I hadn't seen since I hid the dictionary from Onyx and she had all but torn the house apart in search of it. My magic started to spark above our joined hands, like tiny droplets of fire. They took the form of a triangle with the single summit facing upwards. Dominique looked at me.

'Well? What does that mean?' I had to take a moment to try and best phrase the spell's findings.

'I'm sorry Dominique, it's not possible for you to bear a child.' Not knowing what to do, I got to my feet, moving to the back of the cave where I curled up, closing my eyes.

When I woke, the cave was silent. Bart and Dominique were nowhere to be seen. Bright daylight spilled through the mouth of the cave, lighting up the interior better than a light bulb ever could. I yawned, stretching before running a hand through my unruly hair. You could say that I was really not a morning person. The only time I had ever vaguely resembled a morning person was the time Archangel had rigged a trick over my bed so that as soon as I got up, I would simultaneously be doused in icy water and hauled upside down by a snare. Let's just say I was awake and ready to do some damage. Or I would have been if I hadn't caught a cold from it. Melancholy flooded my mind as I started to think about the clan. Someone coughed politely from the mouth of the cave, raising me from my thoughts. I leapt to my feet, drawing my dagger. A young woman stood there, no, not a woman, a demoness, about the same height as me. She had small, pointed horns poking out from her bright red hair, her equally red eyes averted. For a moment, I tensed, ready to fight, sizing her up, but she felt and looked nervous as she bowed to me, one hand fisted over her heart.

'Please excuse me for this intrusion, Princess,' she said, 'My name is Aleth. The Council of Aspheri wishes to know if you intend to step up to take the throne? If so, I have been instructed to escort you to the dimension and serve as your lady's maid.'

Princess? I had to sit down again. The demoness gasped, rushing to my side, fussing over me. I pushed her away with assurances that I was fine, just a little shocked. She nodded primly, stepping back. I took a deep breath. Of course, the prophecy said that the victor of the fight was to take over rule of the dimension. I had nothing left here. Not now that my clan had rejected me. I looked up at the other demoness. Getting to my feet, I raised my chin, standing tall. It was time to take control of my own life, now that I had one to live. The prophecy was over and I was free to do what I wanted.

'Yes, I will take over rule of Aspheri in my father's stead.'

The demoness squealed in delight, clapping her hands. I couldn't help but smile. Her joy was infectious. But my smile faded a little as I remembered Bart and everything he had done.

I couldn't leave the dimension without saying goodbye.

The demoness agreed to let me have a little more time to myself, to say goodbye to the Kraferr, while she took Wraith to Aspheri. I tracked Bart's signature, teleporting to a small lake not far away. Well, his final teleportation ended up at the lake, or rather in it. In the last ten minutes, he had made at least five attempts. One of them landed him in Antarctica. I crouched on a boulder on the shore of the water, watching as the Kraferr pulled himself out, soaking wet.

'Well, I have to say it, apart from Archangel and Onyx's failed attempts at navigation during their teleportation, you have got to be one of the worst cases I've seen.' I tilted my head to one side as I watched him. 'Most demons actually manage to get within one kilometre of their target on the third attempt. I think you broke the record.'

'Shadow!' he protested. 'I'm trying! Not my fault I can't get it right! I'm used to just being a Kraferr. Demons have magic throughout their whole lives. I've only used magic occasionally up to now... And I'm still worried about submitting to my demonic side. If ever that happens again, and you aren't there, you can say bye-bye to most of people on the face of the earth...'

I chewed the inside of my cheek, wondering if I should tell him now that I wasn't going to be around any more. I opted not to. Not yet. 'Part demons only have their magic from around their third year of life. Other than that, welcome to the life of every part demon that has ever existed. You're lucky. You're not alone.'

'I'm going to get this teleportation thing sooner or later. Just watch me,' Bart said. There was a hint of boastfulness in his voice. I tried hard not to laugh. 'I'll get it in no time. I think I got the knack now...'

'Yeah...we'll see about that...' I walked a little closer to the Kraferr before pushing him back into the lake and teleporting to the other side of the water, yelling out, 'Tag!'

Bart broke the surface, spluttering in confusion. Seeing the smile creeping over my face, he concentrated hard for a moment, vanishing from the lake, appearing a couple of metres away from me. Trying to hold back my laughter, I teleported away again as he lunged for me. The game turned into a lightening quick battle of wits, trying to outsmart each other. It was a case of trying to get to grip on your new surroundings before the other cottoned on to the fact that you were there. We both ended up in the water more than once when we forgot to be precise in our coordinates. Bart managed to tag me once, but I got him back. Before long, we were breathless from laughing, sitting on the banks of the lake, wringing out hair and fur. I wiped the tears of laughter from my cheeks, turning to look at Bart. Movement out of the corner of my eye caught my attention. Oh goddess. I got to my feet, facing Vrael, Shaeman and Amarath. Bart scrambled up to stand next to me.

'Don't come any closer!' he warned. The demons didn't move, staring at me. I gritted my teeth. They were testing their dominance over me. Okay, so I had decided to take my father's place, but this was really not the time to bring that up. I broke eye contact with them, lowering my gaze, admitting that they were stronger than me. In pretty much every sense, they were. Three on two. More specifically three trained warriors against one warrior and a half-trained Kraferr. Not great odds. Vrael pulled an arrow from his quiver, nocking it onto his bow. I kept an eye on that. It didn't bode well, especially not at this range. If he had his bow out, I would rather be on the other side of the lake to him. Vrael's natural talent with a bow had been honed over years and turned his muscles into steel. From this range, his arrow could easily go straight through me. Shaeman and Amarath pulled out their own weapons, Shaeman his throwing stars and Amarath her sword. I drew my dagger, but placed it on the ground, signalling to them that I was not a threat to them. I was never unarmed while I had my magic, but it was the symbolism of the act that counted. I dropped slowly to one knee, fisting a hand over my heart in a manner that felt right for the situation, even though I had no idea why. I glanced up at them before getting back to my feet. Vrael was scowling, an expression I had rarely seen on his face before. He was always so calm, so rational. To see a look of such open hatred and anger on his face was terrifying. He raised his bow in warning, pulling back the string.

'What are you doing here?' Shaeman demanded.

'Training. I was helping Bart with his teleportation,' I answered calmly, trying not to think of the drawn weapons on front of me. If I thought about them, I'd break down. I was sure of it.

'Leave, now,' Vrael ordered. I raised my head so as to stand tall. With hindsight, I would realise just how stupid a move this was at that stage.

'This isn't clan territory. We have a right to train here as long as we don't attract attention to the clan, which we haven't.' Vrael's arrow buried itself in my shoulder. I didn't react, as hard as it was not to flinch. Hoping my voice didn't shake, I spoke again. 'Have you got that out of your system now?' Vrael didn't answer, taking another arrow from his quiver. I raised an eyebrow, but I didn't want to start a full on fight. Touching Bart's shoulder, I turned my back on them and started to walk away from the three demons, my three siblings. I steeled my mind, trying to escape the emotions that wanted to run riot through my mind. The hurt of being rejected by my own family, the denial that Vrael had hurt me of his own free will, the disbelief of their coldness. I reached up to my shoulder, pulling the arrow from my flesh and throwing it to the ground. Once we were out of sight of the other demons, Bart turned to me, laying a hand on my injured shoulder. I felt the skin crawling as if swarmed by insects as it healed over beneath his hand.

'Thanks,' I said, flopping down against a tree. He watched me for a moment before sitting down.

'What are you going to do now?' he asked. I turned to look at him. Time to let loose the news.

'I'm going to Aspheri, the demon's dimension, to take over Karthragan's place.' For a moment, he said nothing, but then he nodded.

'You're going to finish the prophecy.' He looked at me with a sadness in his eyes that I could feel, but couldn't find the cause of. 'I wish you good luck with that.'

I smiled at him a little sadly before kissing him on the forehead. 'Kraferric way of saying goodbye,' I murmured, echoing the words he had spoken to me the night I died. Before he could answer, I teleported away, back to my cave where the demoness was waiting for me, to take me to Aspheri.

PART 5

ASPHERI

We appeared in a chamber I recognised to be the throne room of Aspheri. It seemed like a very long time since I had stood there as a scared child. Now I had returned as a woman, ready to take over from my father. A group of black robed demons had gathered in the chamber as a welcoming party, a group I guessed to be the Council. They stood in two lines with a passage down the centre so I could walk past them towards the black throne. I glanced down at my oversized, baggy clothes and thought of my unkempt hair. Next in line to the throne. Yeah, more like a scrap picked up off the street which, I realised after a moment's thought, I was. I faltered for a moment, realising how monumental a decision this was. Was I really ready to take on ruling a dimension? I looked at the expectant faces of the council and remembered that I wouldn't be alone. Squaring my shoulders, I stepped along the line, walking towards the throne. The demons bowed, one hand fisted over their main hearts as I passed them. When I eventually read the books on demonic decorum, I learnt that the salute was one of utmost respect to the receiver, showing you the location of their primary heart before it became normal for it to sit in the left hand side of the chest. Case in point for the phrase: 'old habits die hard'. It felt strange, this new behaviour. They were treating me with respect, not hatred or fear. I turned to face them again, taking a moment to look at the council before I sat on the throne. Applause rang through the room. The eldest member of the council stepped forwards with some sort of delicate crown cradled in his battle scarred hands and spoke in demonic.

'There will be an official coronation soon, but to set things in motion...' He lifted the piece so I could get a good look at it. It was a piece of craftsmanship I would have thought beyond the demons I had seen here before. Delicate strands of a silvery white metal had been intricately wound together in a circle, dipping into a point that would come down to rest between my eyebrows. A trio of black gemstones had been worked into the design around the point, gleaming red in the torchlight. The council member bowed slightly to me before placing the circlet on my head. It was lighter than I had expected, but it fitted perfectly. I reached up a hand to touch it, barely able to believe that I had just been crowned as a ruler. The metal was warm to the touch, the design intricate beneath my fingers. A smile crept over my face as I thanked him and the council as a whole in the demonic language that every demon knew instinctively from the cradle, the language I would be speaking for years to come. The council erupted in cheers.

'All hail Shadow, Princess of Darkness!'

Several hours passed before I was left on my own again. Well, I say left on my own. For the next however many years I would rule over this dimension, I would never be completely alone. Aleth was still at my side. I rubbed my eyes, trying to shake off the tiredness of the last few days. A lot had happened since the prophecy and I was still getting used to the idea that I actually had a life of my own to live as I pleased again. And there was still a lot more I had to do just to begin my life here in Aspheri.

I stood opposite a trainer in a hall designed for arms practise, breathing heavily. I wielded two elaborate short swords. Over the last three days, I had undergone rigorous testing to determine my levels of competence in battle, from magic to hand-to-hand to weapons. I had never been drilled so hard, not even with Amarath! I had been assured that it was simply to know whether or not I required further training. For the moment, I had been able to hold my own against the trainers. I had retained a high degree of control over my magic in this incarnation, thank the goddess, as that could have been a very big problem. I wiped the sweat from my brow, rolling my sore shoulders. This trainer wasn't mincing his blows against a young girl. Every strike from his two-handed sword that I blocked had reverberated through my arms and spine. He bowed respectfully to me as we finished the final bout of sparring.

'I apologise, Princess, for the rough play...'

'Don't,' I interrupted. 'It's what you're supposed to do.'

'Well, you may rest assured that although you could perhaps be a little finer in your swordplay, you are a proficient fighter. You require little more training.' He bowed once more before leaving the training hall. I carefully sheathed my swords, trying to ignore the symphony of aches running through my body.

'My Lady?' asked a timid voice. I smiled slightly to myself. Aleth, the demoness who had come to Earth to find me and who was now my lady's maid, had never really gotten over her shyness around me. I could understand the sentiment, although I was sorry that she felt the need to be nervous around me. 'My Lady, you must prepare yourself for your coronation. It is getting late...'

'Thank you, Aleth,' I said, turning to face her. 'Perhaps you could help me? I don't really know my way around the temple, or a wardrobe for that matter.'

The demoness's face lit up in a smile as she nodded enthusiastically. I knew that she enjoyed picking out things for me to wear, that she felt proud when I sat with the council, dressed by her care. I allowed her to lead me from the training hall along a further maze of corridors I was sure I was never going to remember the layout of, towards my personal quarters.

My quarters were comprised of three rooms: a bedroom, a bathroom and a receiving/living room kind of thing. Aleth ushered me through to the bathroom where I was delighted to see that the pond-like indentation in the floor had been filled with hot water. She took charge, now in her element, telling me to strip off and get clean while she rooted through the mounds of clothes, some made especially for me, others left by previous female rulers. I gladly wriggled out of the skin-tight clothes I wore while training, slipping into the water and ducking my head under to get my long hair wet. The pool was deep enough in the centre for me to stand on the bottom and be completely submerged, but I stayed on the outer edge, where the water reached my midriff while I was standing. I picked up a bottle of soap, lathering myself up before ducking back underwater. I held my breath, enjoying the serene, silent realm below the surface before I had to come up for air. Aleth had found a mass of black fabric, which I guessed was what I was going to be wearing, but first she had me climb out of the pool so she could dry me off with magic.

Clicking her tongue, she dashed around, fetching this and that before handing me the first garment to put on: a pair of skin-tight trousers. She then helped me struggle into a dress, lacing up the back of it as tightly as she could. After that came a sort of corset-style bodice that forced me to stand up straight. I glanced at the silver glass propped up on the wall. I couldn't believe my eyes. The sleeves of the dress hugged my arms like a second skin, leaving only my shoulders bare. The bodice emphasised my curves to a degree I didn't think was possible, ending just above my hips to taper into a central point. The skirt was slit up one side to the hip, showing my black clad leg. Around my waist went an intricate belt holding a double-handed sword I would be required to carry at all ceremonies as well as a dagger concealed under my skirt. I pulled on a pair of heeled, knee-length boots, wondering how on earth I was going to walk in them. Aleth then clasped a light cloak around my shoulders, finishing off the outfit. I stared at myself in the mirror. I looked like some strange warrior queen. At the time, it seemed alien, but it would grow to be the norm. Aleth fussed around me, brushing my hair until it fell in a soft curtain down my back. I stared into my own violet eyes, trying to prepare myself to do this, to seal my new status as a princess.

The coronation was being held in the town so that everyone could see. I was escorted by several heavily armed soldiers down through the main street, at the end of which stood the council. A hush fell over the crowd as I walked past them. I sneaked several discreet glances as my soon-to-be subjects, noting with a hint of amusement that they had all preferred their more human appearances. I vaguely wondered why: was it because of me or because they enjoyed having opposable thumbs? The council stood in a semi circle, in the centre of which I knelt. The eldest member of the council lifted the circlet so that everyone could see it. I bowed my head, listening to him intone in demonic the proper rites and blessings that accompanied the coronation of a new ruler. The static feeling of magic flowed through the air, binding me to the dimension as its ruler as well as its servant. I held my breath as he lowered the circlet onto my head and bade me to rise. I did so as gracefully as I could, allowing myself to be turned around to face my people.

'Look well upon our princess's face, for it is the last time we will during her reign!'

I sat on the throne only an hour or so after the coronation, listening to the last of dozens of ambassadors who had come to present their congratulations upon my 'ascension' to the throne. I inclined my head in Graceful Gratitude as instructed by Aleth. He had no sooner left when Aleth stepped forwards from her place concealed behind the banner of the dimension that hung behind the throne.

'Oh, you're a goddess, I swear,' I said as I noticed the cup of tea in her hands. She blushed slightly, stepping forwards onto the raised dais the throne sat on. I tugged on the knot of the black ribbon that held a mask over my face. I glanced down at it The black face stared back at me. It was one of the laws of the dimension. The face of a female ruler may not be seen by anyone other than their lady's maid and their husband if they are married. It was supposed to protect me from unwelcome suitors and guard my appearance of innocence yet still tough enough to charge into battle at the head of their army. This particular mask had been made to measure for me. The black face covered mine completely with only one eyehole for my right eye. A concealed slit allowed my voice to be heard clearly. It disgusted me to have to wear it, but it went with the position. Aleth passed me the cup of tea, taking the mask from my hands and putting it on a small table beside me. I took a sip of the strong, sweet tea. It invigorated me again as the warmth spread in a pool in my stomach. I leant my head back against the throne. One of the good things about the mask was that I was free to look bored without anyone realising. I carefully set the delicate cup down on the table.

'So, Aleth, what's next today?' Aleth started braiding my hair back as she replied.

'You will be introduced to your guard units, after which a meal will be laid out in your private chambers. The rest of the evening will be yours, although I recommend that you try to sleep.'

'Okay, will do.' Aleth tied off the plait, picking up the mask and securing it back over my face. I touched her handiwork, glad of the tight weave that kept my hair from getting too tangled and being near impossible to brush. A foot soldier stepped into the throne room, his eyes averted until he realised that I was masked. He bowed low, announcing the arrival of my guard unit. I inclined my head in acceptance, shifting on the throne into a more comfortable position. I guessed that I had a long wait ahead of me before being left alone, so might as well sit it out as comfortable as possible. A group of five demons filed through the door, lining up in front of me. I will admit that I was interested by the uniforms chosen. I already knew that my guard was to be composed of the most elite of the dimension's warriors. To put not-too-fine a point on it, these guys were *fine*. They wore the traditional male dress of the dimension, also known as nothing but a pair of loose trousers and a cloak. They carried long broadswords across their backs, a shorter sword on their hip and an expression of 'tangle with me and your great grandchildren will feel the blow I will deal you'. These were people that not even the bravest of demons tangled with. The most suicidal perhaps, but not the bravest, nor even the stupidest. I ran an admiring eye over their musculature, similar to humans, but divine in mass. These were lean, mean fighting machines. I listened distractedly as the captain, Nergal, introduced them to me: Aym, Vetis, Ose and Furfur. I did manage to commit their names to memory, but telling who was who was another kettle of fish altogether.

'And finally, my Lady, the guards who will remain at your sides at all time: Phantom and Wraith.' I couldn't stop a look of delight flash across my face as Wraith sat at the end of the line, tongue lolling and tail wagging. Phantom was another wolf, who I guessed was the same as Wraith was, graced with a human intelligence. He, however, sat ramrod straight with an expression of seriousness on his canine face.

'Thank you, Captain Nergal,' I said, inclining my head to him. He bowed gracefully in return. All of the guards except my new wolf companions filed out of the room. Wraith and Phantom took up positions on either side of me, lying down like sphinxes on the dais. I rubbed the silky fur on Wraith's head, smiling slightly to myself. Maybe ruling wasn't going to be so hard after all.

* * *

I take that last statement back. Three years on, I knew that ruling a dimension was not as easy as it first looked. For a start, the council argued with each other about the most trivial of things until I told them to shut up and made the decision for them. There were ambassadors constantly clamouring for my attention, invitations to dine with heads of state, my people needing my attention to solve their problems. The list was never-ending. If it hadn't been for Aleth, I would have gone crazy within the first few weeks. She schooled me in the appropriate ways to evade the ambassadors, how to behave at important events and dinners and taught me to limit the things I was taking on. She was always there every few hours with a cup of tea or a piece of helpful advice. She even had an indoor garden created for me, where I could go and no one was allowed to disturb me unless whatever the problem was vitally important and could only be solved by me. My guard was, thankfully, understanding of the fact that I was having difficulty adjusting to the new lifestyle required of me. If they had to follow me when I would rather be alone, they shadowed me as discreetly as possible. It wasn't ideal, but it was as close to it as I was going to get.

I lay back gratefully on the bench thoughtfully placed in my little garden and gazing up through the leafy canopies, my mask left at the door. Most of the plants were a sort of greyish green, the flowers all red, purple or black, but I didn't mind. Aleth had tried her best to instruct the demons on how a garden was supposed to look from pictures in books brought from Earth, but they didn't have a lot of imagination. They had tried their hardest, even creating a pond with a small waterfall feeding into it, filled with fish. Fish the same colours as the flowers, but I wasn't complaining. It added soothing, unobtrusive sound to the otherwise silent room. There was a knock on the door. I opened one eye irritably as Aleth stepped inside, looking very nervous about something.

'My Lady, there is a demon here who insists on seeing you straight away... He won't tell us his business, although he has told us that his name is Teran Dementius.'

I sighed, getting up and taking my mask from her trembling hands. 'I'll deal with it. Better hope he has a good excuse for this.' I muttered, tying the mask over my face. I swept out of the room, lifting my skirts with one hand. I no longer wobbled in the high-heeled boots Aleth made me wear so that I stood equal in height with the majority of demons (because my 'diminutive' height of one metre eighty was small for a demon). Phantom and Wraith, who had been patiently sitting outside the garden room as always, fell into step with me.

I swept into the throne room and sat myself on the throne, casting an eye over this Teran Dementius. The surname rang a bell. I remembered it from somewhere, but I pushed those thoughts from my mind. Now was not the time. I had to admit that he was a handsome demon. His hair and eyes were a golden colour that reflected the red of the torches illuminating the room. His face was all planes and angles, his body lean muscle and a stance that told the world that he may not look like much, but he could probably best any opponent. Most young demonesses would be panting after this specimen of demonhood. I would have joined those ranks had it not been for the look of extreme arrogance on his face. He knew how he looked and he knew that he could use those charms to beguile any female into doing his bidding. The part of my mind that still retained Holly-like characteristics didn't mind about that though. In fact, the exact words going through my head were 'oh, I would'. I mentally shook myself, trying to bring my head back into the present. Whoever this guy was, he was trouble and I couldn't afford to lose face. For the sake of my dimension, I had to keep a clear mind to deal with whatever it was he wanted.

'What urgency that couldn't wait has brought you here?' I asked.

'My Lady,' he said, a hint of mocking in his tone as he bowed in supposed respect. 'I know that you have probably not had time to review the traditions of succession, especially since you have only recently come to us, but I wish to inform you that you are, in fact, not the true successor to Karthragan the Destructor.'

Behind the mask, I frowned. What was Teran up to? It was true that, age wise, I wasn't the direct successor. Vrael and Shaeman were. But the prophecy had named me. Karthragan himself had marked me. I raised my chin a little in defiance, determined not to let this demon think that he could intimidate me. 'Who else would take the throne?'

Teran didn't answer me directly. Instead, he turned his head slightly so that his left eye caught the light. A scar that mirrored the one I bore curved around his left eye. I clenched my teeth. He smirked a little. 'He marked me as his first heir. That you bear a similar scar around your right eye means that he marked you as his second.'

I raised an eyebrow. That didn't make sense. If he was truly the first heir, then why would Aleth have come to find me on Earth when he resided in Aspheri, ready to take over from Karthragan? But if he was lying, then why had Karthragan marked him like that? Why did I have the scar around my right eye when it was common knowledge that the devil was always on the left? I softly called my lady's maid's name. Aleth was by my side in an instant, looking a little worried. Of course she did. I never called for her during an audience.

'My Lady?' she inquired.

'Could you please summon the council? I need to speak to them.'

Within moments of Aleth's departure, the council congregated in my throne room. A collective scowl appeared on their faces as they clapped eyes on the golden haired demon who was obviously the reason they had been summoned from their other duties.

'Lucas,' I said, addressing the highest demon of the council, 'could you tell me about the marking done by scarring? More specifically, that done by Karthragan to mark his succession?'

'My Lady, the crescent scar that you bear marks you as the first successor.'

'And if it were to be around my left eye?'

'Then it signifies that you are second in line for the throne.'

I leant back in my throne. 'Lucas, what would happen if I died without marking an heir?'

'We would seek the demon with the left scar.'

'Thank you, Lucas, you have been most helpful and given me much to ponder. You may depart, and please take Teran with you.'

Aleth appeared as soon as the council had filed out, having a quick word with the guard on duty outside the chamber before returning to my side. I glanced up at her before taking my mask off. Goddess, I was tired. I had my first major rival. I wasn't sure, but I got the feeling that he wouldn't hesitate to stoop to the lowest available means to gain the throne. I would have to be prepared.

'Aleth, could you bring me a sword, by any chance?'

'Of course, my Lady.' A few moments later, I belted a short sword around my waist, concealed a dagger within my bodice and a second up my sleeve. No way was I going to let Teran get the better of me. I hadn't spent the best part of three years trying to repair the dimension left to ruin under my father's reign just to let someone, who was likely to undo all that work, take the throne. I leant back against the elegant chair, rubbing my temples. My vulnerable period was coming up. It always gave me a massive headache and I had a tendency to get rather irritable. Holly used to call it 'PMS', and joked that although he was a guy, Jamie suffered from it permanently. Sighing heavily, I dropped a hand to scratch Wraith's head. She thumped her tail happily. Suddenly, she pricked up her ears, sitting bolt upright. Her nose quivered. She seemed ready to bolt after whatever it was that had caught her attention, but her sense of duty forced her to stay. I grabbed my mask, tying it over my face once more.

'Okay, Wraith, let's go see.'

Still quivering with anticipation, Wraith set off at a controlled trot. I strode after her, wondering what had excited the wolf so much. When she darted down a dimly-lit passage, I hesitated slightly. For all I knew, Teran was waiting for me down there. On the other hand, I was probably just being paranoid. I had to start being more like Amarath, sticking my hand into the box even though I didn't know if the contents would be friendly or whether it would bite me. Squaring my shoulders and straightening my spine, I followed Wraith.

My eyes quickly adjusted to the gloom. Being a part demon thankfully brought good low-light vision. A dull torch flickered, throwing dancing shadows across the black walls. A new smell wafted past my nose. A familiar smell. One I hadn't smelt in so long. Just over three years, in fact. It couldn't be…he would have to had really screwed up. Purple fur glinted a little in the firelight. Red eyes gleamed from the shadows. Wraith barked.

'You!' I spoke the single word, the English sticking a little in my throat after years of only speaking demonic. An air of slight confusion emanated from the figure in the shadows.

'I don't think we've been introduced,' growled Bart's voice. I couldn't help but smile. Of course he wouldn't remember me like this. Last time I had seen him, I hadn't made the transition to ruler.

'No, you wouldn't remember me. I shall introduce myself. I am Princess Shadow Wolf Alexai Roth.'

The red eyes widened in the gloom. He tried to speak, tripping over the word 'princess'. After a moment, he sank into a deep bow. Resisting the urge to roll my eyes, I placed two fingers under his chin, lifting him out of the position of subordination. For a handful of heartbeats, I studied his face, smiling a little behind my mask.

'You really messed up this time, didn't you?'

'Yeah, I really screwed up. I don't even know how I managed

to change dimensions, Your Highness!'

'Not 'Your Highness',' I corrected, 'Shadow.'

'My Lady?' called Aleth's voice. I turned to see my lady's maid hurrying towards me. She looked flustered. That wasn't normal for her. She was usually so calm and composed.

'What has happened?' I asked, switching back to Demonic.

'An ambassador from Alena has arrived, my Lady. Alena is an ice dimension close to ours and he suffers here. It is most urgent that you receive him immediately!'

I sighed, a little irritated. 'Okay, Aleth. Could you take Bart to the garden hall? I will receive the ambassador in my private reception chamber. It's cooler in there.' I smiled briefly at Bart, but then remembered that he wouldn't be able to see it through the mask. I glanced down at Wraith, motioning for her to follow Bart. Her tail drooped a little, but she obeyed, trotting reluctantly after the Kraferr. An ambassador from Alena couldn't be bringing good news. Relations between our dimensions weren't hostile, but they were far from friendly. Gritting my teeth and preparing myself for the worst, I strode towards my private chambers, Phantom following close behind me.

I paused at the door, letting my eyes adjust to the dimmer light. The usual torches had been replaced by orbs of magic that gave off light, but not heat. I gazed at the ambassador, catching my first glimpse of an Alenan. I had never even heard of them, let alone seen one. He stood on two bird-like legs, the knee joints facing the opposite way to a human's, with four toes apiece, each one tipped with fearsome talons. His upper body and head were human enough, although his hair was composed of long feathers, the back of his arms also lined with softer looking plumage. A pair of wings was folded neatly against his back. His skin shone a little with sweat despite his only clothing being a knee-length skirt that resembled human kilts. What struck me the most, however, was his pallor. His skin was only a couple of shades darker than his white feathers and, when he turned to face me, eyes that were such a pale green that they were hardly distinguishable from the white. He bowed low to me.

'Princess Shadow,' he murmured respectfully.

'Ambassador,' I replied, inclining my head and gesturing for him to take a seat. 'I believe that we should dispense with the usual formalities. It must be most uncomfortable to be in this dimension.'

'Thank you, Your Highness.' The Alenan seemed somewhat relieved as he folded his awkward limbs to sit down. 'My Lord and Master, Prince Melek of Alena wishes to mend the bridges that he burned with your predecessor and hopes to build new, more intimate bridges with you.'

I had to process that information for a moment, but still had to ask for clarification. I had an idea about what he was saying, but you can never be too careful when it comes to diplomacy. That and, if I was right, I really didn't like the idea of what he was proposing. The Alenan ambassador laughed coldly.

'Why, he means to unite our dimension through marriage.'

Damn, just what I didn't want to hear. Now I had to tread really carefully for fear of starting the war Karthragan had nearly managed to begin. Marriage between dimension rulers was a finicky subject at best, and this was definitely not 'at best'. 'Hypothetically, and this is by no means my answer, what would happen should I decide that it was within the best interests of my people to decline his most generous offer?'

The ambassador seemed aghast. 'No female could refuse my Lord and Master! His wings are strong, his talons sharp and his eyes bright! He is the perfect male! But he has told me, and I shall relate to you his exact words: 'Should she decide to refuse me, I will raze Aspheri to the ground'.'

I dismissed the Alenan as quickly as the rules of diplomacy allowed. I tried to calm myself, but I couldn't stop my hands from shaking. Aleth poked her head around the door. She gasped as she saw my state and rushed to my side, grabbing a goblet of *Stykka*. I gulped the sweet, spiced juice as she waited patiently for me to tell her what had happened. She could wait a little longer.

'Prepare a small bag for me. I will accompany Bart back to Earth and remain there for a couple of days. *On my own.*'

'But my Lady...'

'Now, Aleth!' I felt my voice take on the deep rumbling of my demonic side. Aleth squeaked and darted away. I listened to her rummaging through my clothes for a good few minutes before she returned with a satchel, looking distinctly unhappy. I took the bag, apologising for my outburst before setting off for the garden.

Another messenger intercepted me, looking harried. I ground my teeth. I had to get away and deal with getting Bart back to Dominique before he managed to get himself into even more trouble. Deciphering the babbled message about an uninvited warrior appearing in the main courtyard, I fought down my anger and turned around, heading towards the doors that would lead onto the courtyard.

What I saw there made me realise exactly why the messenger had been in such a state of panic. The being in front of my eyes certainly looked humanoid enough, but surrounding him was an air of evil so potent I could almost see the darkness around him. Drawing myself up to my full height in an attempt to look in charge, I strode towards the creature, passing through the ring of guards.

'Who are you, stranger to my realm?'

The being looked down at me through strange turquoise eyes. And when I say 'looked down', I mean that this creature stood at about my height and half again, a giant, even by the terms of the demons who more often than not stood a good head and shoulders over me. His pale skin seemed all the more pale because of the spiked, black armour that covered the majority of his skin. A helmet had been tucked under his arm. Dark hair had been left loose to fall to brush his shoulders and, when he spoke, he showed two rows of teeth sharpened to points.

'I am Kaleb of the Dead.' Although he spoke in a quiet voice, it seemed all the louder and more powerful by his presence and what his name meant.

'The Would-be King…' I murmured. That's what legend called this creature. The Would-be King of the Dead Dimensions. Named so since he ruled over everything dead and dying, but it was considered that, since the dead were the dead, he ruled over nothing. For species such as demons, who knew about the legends of the great legions of the undead who resided in other dimensions, this was untrue. So he was named the Would-be King. Many religions paid tribute to him to watch over their ill and deceased. Yet, here he stood, in my dimension. He chuckled deep in his chest, his eyes fixed on my mask.

'I believe that it what they call me.' His eyes fell to Phantom. Unsure of his intentions, I laid a hand on the wolf's head, unnerved. 'May I become acquainted with your wolf friends, my Lady?'

'I have only one of my guards at my side for the moment,' I explained. 'His name is Phantom.' The wolf curled one lip back, showing his teeth. Phantom's usual way of greeting people.

'I am gifted with Truesight. I am able to see your other companion inside the palace, as well as the Kraferr. I see things as they really are. No amount of magic can disguise anything. Your mask, for example, provides no challenge for me. You are quite lovely, if I may say so without meaning any disrespect, My Lady. I know it is by law that you wear it.'

My hand flew to my mask, my eyes widening. The guards had raised their weapons, but I motioned for them to stand down. There was no need to antagonise the Would-Be King. If legend was accurate, he could obliterate the dimension in the blink of an eye. I closed my eyes briefly, regaining my composure. I had to try to find a way around this.

'Why have you come here, Kaleb of the Dead?'

'I seek companionship, my Lady, a place to stay where the inhabitants will not be put off by my presence.'

I nodded once, turning to one of the guards nearby, instructing him to find suitable quarters for the Would-Be King. Turning back to Kaleb, I inclined my head. 'You will be given a place to stay here for as long as you wish, Would-be King. Should you allow me to excuse myself, I have affairs that require my attention.'

Bart was sitting on the bench, waiting patiently. He jumped as I walked in. His eyes dropped to my shaking hands, but to his credit, didn't comment. Instead, he enquired about the bag across my shoulders.

'I'll be taking you back to Earth and staying there for a couple of days,' I explained. 'I don't want you messing up again and ending up in yet another dimension.' Without another word, I held out my hand for him to take. He took it immediately. Smiling slightly, I focused my mind, and teleported.

PART 6

EARTH – THE KRAFERR TIME

Earth was colder than I remembered. I pulled my cloak closer around me, shivering briefly while I got used to the smells again. Oh, the joys of polluted air. It stinks. It made me glad that the demons had no use for industrialisation, not while we had magic in its place. We had landed on the roof of an apartment building where I guessed Bart lived with Dominique. Both the Kraferrs' essences were infused into it. Bart lead the way down a few flights of stairs, taking a set of keys from his belt to open a heavy front door. He gestured to me to pass, closing and locking the door behind him. I leapt back as a homicidal hurricane streaked past me in a flash of fur and metal, pinning Bart to the door with a formidable growl and a knife at his neck.

'Where the HELL have you been?!' Dominique snarled. The knife clattered to the ground as the Kraferrin crushed his ribs with a hug. Bart looked completely bewildered by Dominique's violent mood swing, wearing an expression that made me wish I had brought a camera.

'Dominique?' the Kraferr gasped, 'Dominique, we have a guest...' The Kraferrin released Bart, but the glare she dealt him declared that she wasn't finished. She straightened her clothes, turning to run a critical eye over me for a heartbeat before her face took on an expression of forced welcome.

'Sorry about that. I'm Dominique...'

'I know,' I replied. She looked a little confused by my answer. I reached up to pull off the mask. A look of delight crossed her face before she nearly bowled me over with a hug. I patted her back, trying to draw breath under the affectionate attack. It was almost a relief when she let me go.

'I can't believe you're back! Bart told me that you had to go and take over from your dad!' She glanced over her shoulder at the Kraferr in question. She wrinkled her nose slightly. 'Bart, why don't you go and take a shower while Shad and I catch up?' She turned back to me. 'I'm guessing you're going to be here for a couple of days at least if you've crossed dimensions. You can stay with us.' I opened my mouth to argue, but Dominique shot me a silencing glare. I shut my mouth again. I may rule a dimension, but I wasn't going to argue with a Kraferrin on her home turf. I kinda liked having all my limbs attached to my body, thanks.

Dominique showed me to a small guest room. I thanked her and put my satchel down. I held my mask a little longer before placing it on the bed along with the circlet that told the world who I was; It felt a little odd to take it off. I had been wearing it for so long that I barely felt its weight any more. Now my head felt strangely light.

'What brought you back to Earth? I mean, Bart told me you weren't planning on coming back, that you were an important figure over there.'

'I rule the dimension,' I admitted. 'I took over from my father.'

'And you just left? Surely that's not a very, uh, royal thing to do?'

I sighed heavily, sitting down. 'I had to get away from Aspheri. I've got to make a really difficult decision.' I rubbed my temples in an attempt to alleviate my headache. 'To make a long story short, I either marry the prince of another dimension, or go to war and see Aspheri destroyed.'

'So there's a man who thinks he can bully you into marrying him because he can't get a girl any other way,' Dominique clarified. 'Do you want to marry him?'

I snorted in laughter. 'Alena's an ice dimension. Aspheri's fire. Even if I did love this guy, there's no way I am going to share a bed with an ice cube in human form!'

Dominique smiled at that. 'But you can't refuse him or you'll lose your dimension…'

I shook my head. 'I'd lose Aspheri no matter which option I chose. I guess I'm just going to have to do a little diplomatic stalling until I can ally with a few more dimensions.' Dominique looked down at her hands, blushing a little. I could tell that there was something she wanted to talk about. Pushing my own problems to the back of my mind, I waited patiently for her to speak.

'Shad, is there any record of a part-demon becoming a full demon?' She looked up at me, worry written on her face. I tilted my head to one side, inviting her to elaborate. 'Well, there have been times when Bart's turned demonic and struggled to come back. I want to know if…if there's any chance he won't be able to come back.'

I leant back on my hands, trying to put my thoughts into words. 'Part-demon minds are complex,' I began. 'We have our non-demonic sides, but there's also the demon. We can't survive without it. The two sides of us are constantly fighting for control, and only one can be in command at any one time. Bart was raised as a human. That part of him will always be stronger, but it also means that when he does submit to demonic possession, the demon will hang onto control with everything it has. There are ways to help someone come back, as well as training yourself to fight it, but it's a lot of work, especially for an Unborn like Bart. You have to help them focus on something very human to get them back from a demonic possession. The clan used pain, for example.'

Dominique left me to change out of my dress, leaving with a thoughtful but slightly puzzled look on her face. I rummaged through my bag, pulling out the clothes Aleth had packed for me. I made a mental note to grant whatever favour she next asked of me. She had packed a pair of trousers, a hooded sweatshirt and my favourite pair of low-heeled boots. The demoness definitely knew me. I pulled my hair into a high ponytail, a style Aleth would never let me wear on the account that she had enough trouble trying to make me look like an adult, a complaint I always answered with: 'It's not my fault I got stuck with a fifteen-year-old body!' A bit childish of me, perhaps, but one of the perks of being a ruler is that you can get away with it.

Within a few minutes of me changing, Dominique called me though with a cry of 'Dinner's nearly ready!' I have to admit that I had smelt the food cooking and realised how much I missed earth food. More than that, I missed regular meals! I may have been Princess of Darkness, but that didn't mean I had the time to eat as much as people think I did. I was just too busy most of the time. Seriously, there's a lot any ruler has to do in one day. I laid the table, revelling in the normality of everything. My mouth was watering with the smell of the seasoned steak and potatoes. Dominique brought the food to the table, looking a little embarrassed.

'I know it's probably not what you're used to…'

I stopped her there. 'It smells great.' Looking a little happier, she set the food on the table, and we began to eat. I watched Bart out of the corner of my eye. He ate little, a dark expression clouding his face. That troubled me greatly. What troubled me even more was the fact that he was playing with a bread knife. He held it in a way that was definitely not suitable for cutting bread. Throats, perhaps, but not bread.

'Get down!' he yelled a split second before a window shattered. A human, a man, grabbed Bart from behind. The Kraferr head-butted him, breaking the human's nose in a spray of blood, sending him staggering back while Bart dived for the knife he had dropped. I allowed my seething magic explode from my hands, pushing the would-be assassin up against the wall while wrapping tendrils around Bart to pin his arms to his sides, flicking the knife out of reach of either the Kraferrs or the human.

'Useless slab of human flesh!' Bart snarled, struggling against my hold. 'Every week you try again! Do I have to kill you all?!'

'Bart,' I growled in warning. 'Emotions in check, please.' The Kraferr glared at me, but fell silent. Dominique stepped forwards.

'Listen, you! You can tell your employers that if they don't start leaving us alone, the next soldier sent here will find himself sent back to base in a matchbox while he's still alive, got it?'

'Okay, Dominique, I think you can stop threatening him now. He looks scared enough and we don't want to have to clean up the puddle.' Casting a final murderous glance at the assassin, she stood down. I released the magic, letting the human fall unceremoniously to the ground. With a look of absolute terror, he scrambled for the door, running away as fast as possible.

'Well, uh, I think I'll just, uh, go to bed,' Dominique said shortly before dashing into her room and slamming the door. Bart shot me a dark look, moving to stand by the window, looking out over the dark city. I stood next to him, my hands in the pocket of my hoody.

'If you're going to tell me off, Shadow, get it over with.'

I leant against the wall, running a hand though my hair. 'Bart, you have to learn to control yourself. You're a danger not only to yourself, but to others as well.'

'I know, you keep telling me.'

I had to grit my teeth and count to ten before answering the Kraferr. 'You're not some low level demon with all the inherent magical ability of a wet paper bag! There's a reason Karthragan's line is the royal line! If you don't start stamping down on your emotions, you are going to turn this city and everyone in it to dust!'

'The demon's going to take over sooner or later. Why bother fighting it?'

I suppressed the urge to hit my head off the wall with some difficulty. 'Welcome to the life of every part demon who had ever lived! You have another being in your head trying to take control! Most of the time, you can ignore it, but for the rest, you have to actively suppress it with the sheer force of your will!' I paused and softened my tone. 'I care about you too much to see you become a rogue demon the clan has no choice but to put down.'

Bart grunted in response, glaring out over the sleeping city.

I sighed heavily. 'I will be paying a visit to the clan tomorrow. I would appreciate it if you would come with me.' Without waiting for an answer, I turned away and shut myself in my borrowed room for the night.

I stood a little way off from the clearing where the clan had made their home. I tried not to think of them as my family now. Every time I did, the scar from Vrael's arrow ached. I glanced back at Bart, who gazed at the house with mixed emotions on his face. Tearing my gaze away, I spotted my old sword, still planted upright in the ground, marking the head of my grave. Moving to stand next to it, I touched the blade Shaeman had forged for me, which Amarath had taught me to wield. The long sword I carried on my hip was perhaps a finer blade, but it still paled in comparison to the one now rusting in the ground. Dropping my hand to my side, I turned back to Bart and then looked up at the trees.

'Okay, you can come down now. I know you're there.'

With a couple of muffled curses, my guard unit dropped from the trees. The captain of the unit, Nergal, looked particularly uncomfortable.

'My Lady, you were not supposed to be aware of us.'

'Captain, since you and your demons follow me everywhere you can get a trace on my magical signature and that I know you post a guard in my room while I sleep and carry more weapons than my sister whether you're on duty or not, it was safe to assume you had followed me here.'

The captain turned an interesting shade of grey which, given that our blood is black, equated to him blushing. I guessed that it was because, as new as he was to being in charge of a guard squad, he wasn't used to people noticing his tactics. Smiling slightly to myself, I headed towards the clan's home.

As soon as we got within smelling range of the cottage, an earth-shaking, braying neigh shattered the air. I shook my head to clear the ringing noise from my ears. At least Merlas was still around, acting as a smell activated doorbell. Within moments, Amarath, Shaeman and Vrael stood outside the house, armed to the teeth, but thankfully adopting defensive stances. Vrael and Shaeman were the first to realise that they were facing the ruler of Aspheri, dropping immediately into a bow, Shaeman's hand dragging Amarath down with them. We came to a stop a few metres away from the trio, my guards fanning out around me to take their positions. In a flurry of thundering hooves, Merlas came charging out from behind the cottage. The guards raised their weapons. Their intent towards the doe was clear.

'Stand down!' I commanded. Merlas snorted at them as they lowered their weapons. She stepped past them, lifting her hooves high, ears pinned back and baring her teeth. She came to stand in front of me, head turned to one side to get a better look. Her ears flicked back and forth, as if trying to work something out. She had a sniff at my hair. The tension was tangible. The trio of part-demons needed to know what Merlas was up to. My guards had no idea what a pegasus was, let alone whether or not it was dangerous. None of that mattered to me somehow. All that mattered was if Merlas recognised me as the same Shadow that lay six feet beneath a sword gravestone. I had never thought about how much I had been changed by the reincarnation. The clan had rejected me vehemently. Would Merlas? She had been away during the prophecy. She hadn't seen me die. Maybe... Maybe she would know who I was... I prayed that she would accept me. The doe lifted her left hind leg, watching me with a critical eye. She pawed the air a little. Memories of Synairn surfaced in my mind, of Merlas and me by the little stream in the mountains, of learning to walk on four legs. I raised my left leg, mimicking her movements. She squealed, almost barrelling me over as she charged at me, thrusting her head into my hands. I laughed aloud, throwing my arms around her neck. After allowing myself a few moments to be deliriously happy about being reunited with my first ever friend, I came down from that high. Amarath, Shaeman and Vrael looked highly confused. My guards doubly so. I turned my strictest gaze on them.

'You will not speak of this,' I warned. Realising what I was about to do, they averted their eyes, finding somewhere to look that was most determinedly not at my face. As I pulled my mask off, Vrael growled and raised his bow. Shaeman ripped the weapon from his grasp.

'First of all,' Shaeman growled to his brother, 'if you so much as draw that string back, those guards with tear you apart. Secondly, if you want to argue with Merlas, be my guest. I wouldn't, and definitely not just after she finds the rider she thought was dead.'

Amarath just watched me, as if trying to convince herself that Merlas was right. I wound my fingers into the doe's mane. For a few moments, we simply stared at each other. Amarath shook her head.

'Who am I to argue with Merlas about her bonded rider?' I stepped forwards to hug her tightly. After a moment's hesitation, she hugged me back. 'Goddess, my sister's still alive!' The sisterly affection turned into a group hug as Vrael and Shaeman joined in. When we eventually let each other go, Shaeman gestured towards the house.

'I guess you should meet the latest additions to the clan.' His eyes drifted over to the guard unit. Captain Nergal raised to hand to ward off the forthcoming question.

'We will keep eyes on the perimeter.'

The house hadn't changed much. A few more painted-over scorch marks on the walls. A little more clutter. New teeth marks on the furniture. But it was still the same. I could still see old, familiar marks: patches of not-quite-concealed black from Vrael's experiments with electricity, a line of claw marks on the door from a frustrated babysitter, a slightly green ceiling from a failed attempt to teach Amarath how to brew a decent painkiller. I ducked as a hawk came swooping down the staircase, straining its wings to keep ahead of a determined looking dove. Amarath sighed, shaking her head before calling out to the two birds.

'Keegal! Archangel! Fall in and leave each other alone for once!' The two birds stopped mid-flight, dropping back to solid ground and morphing back into their human forms. One young boy I didn't recognise, the other was my Archangel, who narrowed her eyes as she caught sight of me.

'What's Wolf doing here? You banished her!'

Amarath glowered at the young part-demon. 'If you want to argue with Merlas as well as an entire dimension of demons about your mother being reincarnated, be my guest.' To her credit, Archangel didn't look too happy about that prospect. I made a mental note to ask Merlas exactly how much she had terrorized the clan to make them that afraid of her reactions. Archangel gazed at me critically, as if trying to spot all the tiny indicators that I wasn't actually Shadow. After a few tense moments her gaze softened.

'You really are Shadow, aren't you?'

I smiled a little, ruffling her hair in the way I distinctly remember her detesting, which was why I used to do it. It was hard not to get on each other's nerves when your family was basically comprised of your siblings.'I should hope so,' I replied. 'Otherwise, these memories I have of giving birth to you are false.' I turned to look at the boy who she had been chasing through the air. 'And who's this lad? Karthragan manage to spawn another kid before I put an end to that?'

Strangely, Amarath blushed deeply. 'Keegal? Uh, he's your nephew.'

I stared at her. 'Are you serious? Who're the parents?' I glanced at Archangel. She snorted, raising an eyebrow and putting her hands up in a surrendering gesture.

'Don't look at me, I'm your daughter, despite the fact that we have the same dad, which is just *wrong*.'

I turned my gaze back to Amarath, who was fidgeting with the hem of her cloak. I waited patiently for her to explain.

'When I was back in Synairn, before the fight with the Redeemer, I fell in love with a captain of the city guard. He was a part demon as well, but one who had never developed the use of magic. A non-manifested part demon. He claimed he loved me back.' She gritted her teeth, anger flashing briefly across her face.

'He lied?'

'Yes, got me pregnant and left. I could have killed the…idiot.'

'Mum usually uses words a lot ruder than that when she talks about Captain Dementius. She just tries not to say them in front of me or Draconiss,' Keegal added.

'Dementius?' I clarified. Same last name as Teran as well as being a part demon. I made a mental note to look up the bloodlines when I got back to Aspheri. There might be some kind of connection.

Amarath looked at me a little strangely. 'Yes, Marcus Dementius.' She shook her head a little. 'In any case, that's over and done with. There are still three more new kids for you to meet.' She took one look at my expression of shock and laughed. 'Keegal's twin and two more of Karthragan's offspring Shaeman and Vrael adopted, don't worry.'

Amarath called the other three demon children, each one standing next to their twin. I should have recognised Keegal and his twin as Amarath's children. They looked very much like her, especially Draconiss. The other two, Cika and Mairae, looked very uncomfortable, holding on to each other for support. They didn't look like twins. Cika didn't even look like a part demon. I reasoned that it was possible that he was on his vulnerable period. The pair scarpered as soon as Amarath said they could, disappearing back up the stairs. I glanced at my sister for an explanation. She ran a hand though her short bob, sending her hair sticking up in all directions.

'Cika's a non-manifested. He's finding it a little hard to adapt to being with us. Shaeman found him in a children's home trying to figure out what was different about him. We found his twin a couple of months later, a manifested demon dying of cancer in an alley. Vrael had to bite her to save her life, so she has to learn to deal with the whole vampire thing. They refuse to be separated.' She shrugged. 'It's easier just to leave them alone. Anyway, was there a particular reason you came all this way to visit?'

I took a deep breath. 'I came to mark you as my heir. I'm running into problems on Aspheri that made me realise that if I don't mark an heir now, should I die, the dimension would fall into hands would rather it didn't.' I met her gaze fully. 'It means I have to give you a scar around your eye, if you decide to accept the position. Karthragan didn't give me a choice, but you do. You can choose to refuse or accept.'

Amarath watched me for a few moments before reaching up her sleeve and pulling out a dagger. She handed it to me, hilt first. 'Do it. Give me the scar.'

I took the blade. Summoning up every scrap of courage, I raised it against my sister. I rested it against her skin, next to her eyebrow. Her eyes bored into mine. A bead of blood dripped from under the blade, testament to how sharp she kept it.

'I'm really sorry,' I murmured, 'but this is going to hurt.' With one quick swipe, the knife parted the flesh. Blood poured down Amarath's face as she jerked away. The dagger clattered to the ground. Vrael burst into the room, closely followed by Shaeman and my guards not far behind.

'What the hell did you do to Amarath?' Shaeman thundered.

'I told you we could not trust her!' Vrael muttered as he escorted my sister towards the treatment room. Shaeman stopped me from following, his throwing knives at the ready. The captain of my guard placed himself in front of me.

'The princess has granted her sister a high honour by scarring her in such a way.'

'Honour?' Shaeman spat, glaring at me. 'What honour is there in blood or betrayal or pain?'

'Honour because I marked her as the first in line for the throne!' I snapped back. How easy it was to change anyone's mind if they didn't know all the pieces to the puzzle. Shaeman stared at me as if I had announced to him that he had just turned into a fish.

'Your heir?'

'In order for Amarath to take over from me when I die, I had to give her the same scar Karthragan gave me all those years ago,' I touched the pale scar-tissue that proclaimed my rank. Even though it had been so long ago, it still pained me to feel it. To feel what my father had done to me, to remember everything he had taken from me.' Without it, she won't be recognised as my next-in-line. You have on good authority that I am still Shadow, the sibling you buried a long time ago. Think about that. Since when would I ever, willingly, raise a weapon against my sister unless there was a very, very good reason behind it?'

Shaeman's mouth flopped open for a brief moment before he managed to come to his senses and claw back some modicum of composure, stowing his knives away with a look of deep embarrassment.

'Princess,' a guard stooped to murmur in my ear. 'We should be returning to Aspheri. You have been absent long enough.'

I apologised once more to Amarath, explained myself to Vrael and made my farewells. I knew that they could easily find me if they needed me, and the clan had agreed to help Bart get to grips with his demonic side and powers. That was at least something off my mind, and knowing that Amarath was going to take over from me instead of Teran was a relief in itself. Now, if only the Alena problem was as easy to solve. Tying my mask over my face, I let the captain teleport me back to Aspheri.

As soon as my feet touched the ground back in Aspheri, a tremor of ice flashed through my muscles. As predicted, my vulnerable period was starting. In the way that had been drilled into them over the years of practise, my guards surrounded me and escorted me to the safe room.

I don't normally mind the safe room. It was the Aspherin's way of trying to keep their ruler safe while I was unable to defend myself. As soon as they had found out that I was only half demon, and therefore had periods of time where I was forced into a form that was no stronger than a human and certainly magicless, they did what seemed to be the best option. They built a safe room. The black stone room was sparsely furnished: a bed, a table and two chairs, with a small alcove furnished as a bathroom, separated from the rest of the chamber by a curtain. There was a gun concealed within the masonry, a habit from my days on Earth that was hard to kick. The strongest spellweavers in the dimension had placed magic around the walls that prevented anyone, save myself and Aleth, using their powers. Aleth was only allowed to teleport in once a day to bring me food. No one was allowed in and I wasn't allowed out. Bolts both inside and outside of the door ensured that. The only way for me to get out was to teleport. If I could teleport, then there was no point in me being in there.

Someone had thoughtfully left a couple of books on the table, but I ignored them. They couldn't be dangerous. The guards would have inspected them thoroughly. Instead, I paced the length of the room. I was no further forward with the Alena situation. I rubbed my temples, my mask abandoned on the table. I still didn't know whether or not to go to war or to marry this guy. It was a lose-lose situation for me. I couldn't risk a war. The dimension's army had largely been left to ruin under Karthragan's reign and was nowhere near ready to confront an army like Alena's. We wouldn't be ready for another few years by the time we managed to make all the weapons and train enough soldiers. On the other hand, I couldn't marry the prince. Being in the presence of such a powerful ice mage for the length of time required in a marriage would weaken me to the point of death. Fire and ice don't mix, and I couldn't leave Aspheri in Prince Melek's hands if I died. That would end in disaster. I sighed, turning on my heel and throwing myself into another frantic bout of pacing. I ran my hands through my hair, trying to think of a way out of the situation. I needed advice, but there was no one who had enough experience of being a ruler without having political ties to the dimension. I could have hit my head off a wall. It was staring myself in the face. Kaleb. Of course. The refugee king from another dimension. I stopped pacing, and tried to concentrate.

My powers as a Synari had never properly developed, mainly because of the demonic magic overtaking it and superseding it. I couldn't manipulate Synari magic the way they could. I couldn't even summon the stuff more than a spark, not even good enough to light a fire. Nor could I speak freely with my mind, nor determine the cause of emotions. All I could do was sense the emotions and touch another's mind to convey a vague idea. I prayed it would be enough, and that his magic was different enough to bypass the protective wards. I reached out with my mind as best I could, seeking his alien consciousness. Within a handful of heartbeats, he was standing in front of me.

'My Lady, you have summoned me?'

'Kaleb, yes, I did summon you,' I replied, turning back into the room and taking one of the two chairs. The very fact that I had turned my back on Kaleb meant not only that I trusted him not to try to kill me, but also that my intentions were non violent. It was a point I considered rather important since I didn't know the extent of his powers. 'Please, sit.'

'I will stand, my Lady, it would appear you have been left unguarded. That was a relatively foolish decision. I offer you my protection, so you may be safe in these times.'

I nodded once to acknowledge Kaleb's decision to stand. 'I am not completely unguarded, as I am not unlearned with sword. In usual times, no one may enter this room during the short time I am rendered no more than a normal mortal, but these are not usual times. I call you here on graver matters, and I am in need of advice from one who has no political ties to this dimension. It would seem that, using an Earthen expression, 'we are caught between a rock and a hard place', and you were the first person that came to my mind who could give me such advice, as you are not blinded by the needs of nor by love for the people who reside here.

'My father left this dimension's army in ruins and on the brink of a war with another warrior dimension known as Alena, a world of ice. An ambassador arrived in this dimension a not long ago, and he brought a choice with him from the ruler of his dimension. In shorter terms than the ambassador's speech, I must either endanger the lives of everyone in this dimension by entering a war, or I cede and bind this dimension with his by the joining of the rulers, which would also endanger the people and myself.'

'I could kill him for you.'

As amused as I was by this, rather direct, statement, I shook my head. 'I think that would be unwise from a diplomatic point of view.'

'Then perhaps I could help you give the Prince a war he cannot win?' I tilted my head to once side, intrigued by his statement, inviting him to continue. 'I can combine my army to yours. It will be a battle they will not forget in a hurry.'

'No,' I answered, getting to my feet in order to pace again. Kaleb's eyes followed me as I walked back and forth. At this rate, I was going to wear a hole in the floor. 'I cannot allow you to put your people and your dimension at risk in order to save mine.'

Kaleb let out a hollow bark of laughter. 'If anyone is at risk in this alliance, it would be Alena. My people are the undead nations. They fear no death for they are already dead. They hunger for a use.'

I sighed, running a hand through my hair. 'In any case, you suggest we engage in warfare?'

'I wish you to know that you will not be alone in waging war against this tyrant.' He paused for a moment, thinking. 'When will you be delivering your choice?'

'In three days.'

'Is it agreeable to you if I accompany you? To keep you safe?'

'Yes, I think that would be a good idea.'

* * *

Three days later, I stood in front of the mirror in my private chambers, shaking off the last fingers of cabin fever from the safe room. Aleth was fussing around me, putting the finishing touches to the dress I was wearing. I swirled a thick, heavy cloak around my shoulders. I would need it to ward off the chill of the ice dimension. I carefully tied my mask over my face, setting the circlet over it. Looking myself in the eye, I tried to steel myself towards going to Alena and telling Prince Melek to, in much more diplomatic language, stick his proposal of marriage where the sun doesn't shine.

PART 7

ALENA

As I've said before, Alena is an ice dimension, one of the many city-dimensions grouped together through alliance to create what is known as the Snow Kingdoms. Normally, I would avoid them like the plague, but I'd found that normality had decided to bow out of my life. The only way to describe Alena would be to call it a snowscape. Even the sun, hanging frozen in the sky, cast a light that was faintly blue. The buildings had all been carved from ice, the architecture and designs growing more and more intricate the more important the structure. Now imagine coming from a dimension whose main element is fire, to arrive in the centre of the palace in an ice dimension. I shivered, clenching my teeth to keep them from chattering, pulling my cloak further around my shoulders. Kaleb stood at my shoulder, towering above me, wearing nothing more than a pair of loose trousers and the scabbard of his enchanted sword slung across his bare back. Shaking my head in wonder at how he had yet to turn into a large icicle, I turned to face the group of nervous-looking Alenan guards. One stepped forwards to salute me.

'Princess Shadow, Prince Melek awaits your arrival with impatience.' I glanced at Kaleb, who inclined his head slightly. Nodding once, I let the Alenan guards escort us to the Prince.

Prince Melek was sitting on his throne, reading from a pile of paper when a footman announced my arrival. He got to his feet, bowing low to me and running a critical eye over Kaleb. I ran a critical eye of my own over him. Unlike most of the Alenans I had seen, his plumage was darker, a pale brown rather than white. His eyes were equally darker, his hands and bird feet tipped with talons I would not like to be on the receiving end of. His muscles were well defined, especially those required for flight. For an Alenan woman, he would no doubt be a fine catch. For me, however, he was simply a nuisance. A good-looking nuisance perhaps, but a nuisance none the less.

'One would have thought that the ruler of such a warrior dimension as Aspheri would have brought an entire battalion of guards, not just one…being.'

'I can assure you that Kaleb is perfectly capable of performing his duty.'

'Hmm…' Prince Melek mused. I didn't like the look on his face. It looked as if he was sizing Kaleb up for a fight. Taking his eyes off the Would-Be King, he gestured to the elevated platform where his throne of ice stood. I was glad for my heavy cloak that managed to ward off a little of the chill as I spotted what Prince Melek had gestured towards. Beside his throne, someone had formed a chaise longue and covered the ice with thick pelts. I gritted my teeth. As a princess, most humans would imagine that I spend most of my royal life lounging and reclining on such furniture. Chance would be a fine thing. I spend most of my time sitting on the throne trying to sort out the dimension's problems or in the library trying to catch up on a lifetime's worth of Demonic history and lore. In any case, I don't like reclining. No sensible warrior does. It exposes the stomach to attack and is a difficult position to spring out of in a hurry. Unfortunately, as a visiting ruler, I wasn't really allowed to stand in order to talk to him, so I compromised, sitting upright on the chaise. Prince Melek turned a worryingly flirtatious smile to me.

'Princess Shadow, I believe you have come to deliver your choice. As I remember, I proposed that you choose between uniting our dimensions or angering Alena, which would, I'm afraid to say, end up in Aspherin blood being shed.' The tone of the Prince's voice suggested that he wasn't actually sorry to say those words. I felt my fists clench.

'Yes, I remember your proposal,' I began, but I couldn't bring myself to say anything else. I couldn't phrase it in a way that wouldn't offend the Prince. I inwardly cursed the need for diplomacy, glad of the mask that hid my expression of disgust. I would have loved to spit at him, to tell him to get stuffed and leave Aspheri alone, but the laws of courtesy I was subject to wouldn't allow it. In a quiet rustling of feathers, he moved down to sit next to me. The cold radiating from him froze my breath in my throat, but I denied him the satisfaction of seeing me shiver.

'Now, I'm sure that you don't wish war to be declared on your dimension, so I shall assume that you would prefer the union of our dimensions…' he said softly. A muscle jumped in my jaw as I desperately tried to think of a way out. I cast a desperate glance at Kaleb. The Would-Be King stepped forwards calmly, drawing his sword and using the flat of it to keep the Prince back.

'Do not press the Princess,' he growled. Melek pushed the sword away coolly. He stood up, sweeping back to his throne where he used his fingers to comb a few feathers back into place. He turned his gaze back to me.

'Your decision, Princess Shadow?'

I raised my chin, my defiance fortified by Kaleb's powerful presence behind me. 'I will not consent to marry you.'

Melek leapt out of his throne with a growl, tearing his sword from its sheath, slashing at my throat. I raised my arms in defence, the blade glancing off the metal bracers, leaving a deep dent and a rip in the metal. He drew his arm back to strike again. The smell of damp earth assailed my nose. Metal ripped through flesh. But not mine. A young man stood in front of me with Melek's sword buried in his side. His old suit, torn and muddied, smelt of earth. He turned to look at me with eyes so pale they were almost white. One of The Would-Be King's subjects, one of the dead.

'We have eternal life to lay down for you, Princess of Darkness,' he said. Melek growled, pulling the sword from the undead man's side then neatly severing my protector's head from his shoulders. The young man crumbled to dust before he even hit the ground. I sensed a spike of anger from behind me. Within a heartbeat, Kaleb's sword was resting on Melek's throat. Melek smirked, turning aside Kaleb's claymore with his own, blood-stained sword. I used their distraction to scramble off the chaise, drawing my own blade. Melek snapped his head round to look at me. Our eyes locked gazes. Ice spread down my spine, freezing me into place. I struggled to breathe. I couldn't look away. All I could do was defend my mind as Melek tried to break into it. Sweat began to slide down my forehead from the effort. The claws of Melek's mind scrabbled for any gap. It found one. My defences were ripped down, Melek's talons beginning to tear through my subconscious. I struggled to push him away as memories clouded my thoughts. Ruling Aspheri, talking to the Kraferrs, living in the home, Holly and Natalie, Meran and Armen. And my mother. Arellan's death. With a yell, I broke Melek's spell, panting, doubled over, tears streaming down my face as my demon side begged for a taste of Melek's blood. The memory of Arellan's death, even after so many years of being buried, were still raw and painful. The Alenan prince stepped forwards, taking my chin in his hand, lifting my head to look at him. His touch froze my skin, thousands of tiny, icy needles digging into me, spreading out from his hand over my jaw and neck, burning in a way I thought impossible for ice. He raised a hand in warning to Kaleb.

'Try to interfere, *boy*, and I will freeze your princess where she stands,' he growled, not turning his gaze away from me. 'You're such a naughty little girl, aren't you? You killed your mother. If it wasn't for you, she'd still be alive now, living a happy life. Tsk, tsk. And I thought that the ruler of a dimension such as Aspheri would have been stronger. Your father certainly was. Are you still adamant that you will not consent to becoming my wife?'

I couldn't wield my sword at such close quarters. He was pressed almost intimately against me. Clearly, he had never heard about personal space! Gritting my teeth, I borrowed a move from the *Holly Bristol Manual of Defence Against Overbearing*

Males and prayed that Alenan anatomy was somewhat close to human. It was. Melek doubled over, cupping himself with a high-pitched howl of pain. Kaleb's arms wrapped around me, cradling me to his chest as he teleported us away.

Kaleb took control as soon as our feet touched the black stone floor of the throne room in Aspheri, setting me on the throne and calling for a healer. He crouched in front of me, examining the ice burn that had spread out from my cheek down to my neck. A healer was ushered through the arch into the throne room, where he bowed nervously, stammering a request for permission to treat me. Kaleb answered before I could, in a voice that could have easily turned an army to jelly in the space of five seconds. I gingerly pulled my mask off, hearing the ice on it crackle as it started to melt. Later on, when I looked in the mirror, I would see a pale blue mark that stretched from my ear to the hollow of my throat, covering the entire expanse of skin in between. I rested my head on the back of the throne. I felt weak and ill, as if someone had drained all the strength from me, no doubt an effect from the cold. I'd never realised just how much of a weakness cold could be to me. Aleth arrived with a pile of blankets, clucking at the healer and forcing a quilt on Kaleb, sure that he must have felt the cold as well. I hissed, biting back a snarl as the healer prodded the ice burn. Once he had examined it thoroughly, he began to prepare something with various ingredients from his bag that I didn't recognise, his hands flying as he worked. Within a few moments, he spread a balm across the burn. I tried hard not to flinch as the salve stung my skin but it started to thaw the damage that had been done. After placing strips of cloth over the balm to protect it, he stammered his farewells, escaping from the room and Kaleb's gaze as fast as he could. I sighed, tying my mask back on as gently as I could. The burn was going to ache for a good while yet.

Kaleb faded back out of the shadows as I pulled the blankets further around my shoulders, desperate for warmth after Alena. Aleth had thoughtfully left a steaming cup of tea waiting for me, which I sipped from gratefully, feeling the heat pool in my stomach.

'My Lady, it would be wise to start amassing the troops. Alena will soon be marching to war in order to soothe their ruler's wounded pride.'

'It's going to take more than a war to repair what I did to him,' I muttered into my tea. In a louder voice, I added. 'Would you please ask the Council to congregate in this room with whatever captains remain in the army as well as an interdimensional messenger.'

Within an hour of my informing the council and captains of the impending battle, the dimension rang with the sound of metal being hammered back into shape. Shouts of encouragement and rallying echoed through the streets. Aleth was helping me to strap on battle armour, still warm from the forge, while I listened to the captains and Kaleb discussing tactics. One of the main problems, however, was that I was missing several captains, which meant that many of the battalions who had gathered were without leaders. I prayed that the messenger would soon return. They were my only hope.

My prayer was answered. The captains looked up in surprise as three more demons appeared in the middle of the throne room. Armed to the teeth, armour buffed to a shine, expressions ready to kill, but still one of the best sights I had seen in a long time. The messenger, looking terrified, peeked out from behind the trio. Amarath strode forwards, wrapping me in a boa constrictor's hug accompanied by a loud clattering of armour.

'Thank the goddess,' I said as we broke apart. 'I was terrified that you were going to turn your backs on me.'

Amarath laughed, pulling her helmet off. My eyes flickered to the half-healed cut next to her eye, the scar tissue still an angry red. 'You thought I was going to pass up on the chance to march to war alongside my princess of a sister? Not a chance!' Another figure appeared in the hall, cutting off my response and filling the space with her huge presence. Her own battle armour gleamed in the torchlight. Merlas butted my shoulder with her head, as if telling me off for not visiting.

'My Lady?' Kaleb asked. 'You are planning to march out with us? Will you not keep yourself away from harm in your safe room?'

I turned to the Would-Be King, raising an eyebrow. 'And what would that do to the moral of my troops? It would demoralise an already shaky army. No, I will ride out with Merlas at the head of the troops. You can trust her completely to keep me away from harm.'

Kaleb looked ready to argue, but his eyes flickered to Merlas, examining her critically for a moment before nodding reluctantly. I introduced Amarath, Shaeman and Vrael to the captains, and settled down to plan how we were going to do this.

I sat with a hand on Merlas's guidance strap, looking out over the army. My eyes scanned the ranks, spotting my siblings at the head of their assigned units. Kaleb, despite my protests, stood as captain over a rabble of the undead. With a dimension roughly the size of America and Canada put together, I had a population of two or three hundred million. Compared to modern day earth, that wasn't much, but to me, it looked like the entire dimension had turned up to war alongside several hundred thousand undead. I just had to hope it was going to be enough. I checked my belt for the umpteenth time, making sure that I had my longsword as well as two more short swords strapped in a cross on my back, backed up by a further three knives. I wasn't taking any chances.

They announced their arrival with a wave of cold. Every demon in the regiments shivered, but held their ground. Merlas danced on the spot, tossing her head. I kept one hand on the hilt of my sword. Behind me, on a small hillock, I could hear the nervous plucking of bowstrings. The Alenans burst out from the air itself as they teleported into Aspheri. A single winged figure took to the sky. I couldn't help but feel a small twang of satisfaction as I heard the Prince's voice, a little higher than what had been given to him naturally.

'Come and play, little princess! Show your people how you fight on your own!' Without any command from me, Merlas bellowed a wordless reply into the air, a fearsome war cry for anyone not acquainted with the pegusi. She leapt into the air, her powerful hindquarters kicking off from the ground before her great wings took over the labour, her hooves cutting easily into the turf. I ripped my sword from its sheath, shouting my own wordless war cry. The Aspherins surged forwards, engaging the enemy in a thirst for their blood. Melek sneered at me as Merlas drew even with him, hovering out of range of him, her wings beating steadily to maintain height. I scowled back. He would expect me to play clean and fair, very much like a girl, like a *princess*. In most cases, I would fight with as much honour as I could. But I couldn't afford to let him predict my moves. Amarath had taught me to fight dirty. It was time to use it. And the first thing to do was rile up the enemy. An angry enemy didn't think. An angry enemy didn't plan. An angry enemy made mistakes.

'Have they managed to remove your genitals from your head yet?' I asked innocently. 'You know, just in case you might actually want to start thinking with your brain instead of your balls for once?'

'Ha! What kind of effeminate ruler of a warriors' dimension chooses to fight with words?'

'A girl!' Below me, the sounds of the battle filtered upwards. The clashing of swords, the ringing of armour, the screams of the dying and the silence of the dead. I heard Kaleb's voice yell up at me.

'My Lady! Behind you!' Hands grabbed hold of my armour, dragging me from Merlas's back, blades slicing through the ties that kept me bound to the saddle. Merlas screamed as another sword slashed at her wings, raining blood down onto the battle-field. For a moment, Melek's guard held me suspended in the air. The prince himself turned a malefic smirk to me.

'How well do demons fly?'

I can't remember if I screamed or not as the hands let me go and I began to plummet towards earth. I tried to focus my mind enough to use magic to slow my descent. The whistling sound of the wind past my helmet gave me a distressing, constant reminder of my situation. Merlas neighed in desperation, trying to get to me, her one good wing labouring, the injured one next to useless. I tried to grab a hold of her saddle, but my hand slipped, the straps slippery with her blood. One of her flailing hooves struck my arm. Agony ripped through me as the bone shattered under her iron shod hoof. My dented armour pressed against the break. The ground was approaching fast. I closed my eyes, waiting for the impact. Arms encircled me. My descent slowed rapidly. From high above, Melek bellowed his rage.

'I've got you, My Lady,' Kaleb's voice murmured in my ear. 'Fight on the ground a little longer. I will take care of Melek, and then I will take you to safety. You have fought with the troops. No need to take it to extremes.'

I wasn't about to argue with him at that point. He left me within a ring of his soldiers, his undead warriors, before regaining the sky on skeletal wings. I vaguely wondered where the wings had come from, but dismissed the thought. The Would-Be King had many powers I didn't know about, but I couldn't afford to let myself worry about that now. I drew my long sword, wielding the hand-and-a-half blade clumsily in one hand. Its blade sliced through the enemy with ease, splitting skin and severing muscle. The undead laughed alongside me, revelling in their role, in their usefulness. Their battered, rusted and chipped blades cut through the swathes of enemy with the same ease as mine. Several foes managed to wet their blades with my blood before I dispatched them to the next world, the black liquid running freely down my armour, tarnishing the bright metal. I started to feel light headed. My movements became jerky and slow. Kaleb's soldiers closed in around me, trying to keep me safe, to defend me as I tried not to collapse from exhaustion. I planted the tip of my sword in the blood-soaked ground. The fog of unconsciousness hovered dangerously on the horizon. An arrow landed close to me. One of Vrael's. I recognised the red and black fletching that he used on all of his arrows, feathers taken from both Shaeman and Merlas. I knew what it meant. He was telling me to get out of there, to get the hell off the battle-field. No. I wouldn't. I couldn't afford to run. I had to prove to my dimension, to myself, that I was neither weak nor a coward. I had to prove that I was good enough to rule over them. Summoning the last dregs of my energy, I raised my sword again, separating a foe's head from his shoulders before the ground rushed up to meet me.

'My Lady?' A distant voice decided to irritate me. I didn't deign to answer it. I was too tired. Whatever I was lying on was soft and warm. 'My Lady? Why will you not wake?'

'Did she not have her vulnerable period recently? Did she not rest then?'

'She frets during her three days. She paces her safe room and will not rest nor sleep enough.' My fingers twitched, sending spasms of pain through my arm, in turn setting off every single ache in my body. I groaned. Surely one battle couldn't have made me hurt this much! I opened my eyes to see the worried faces of Aleth, Kaleb and Vrael. My muscles complained bitterly as I pushed myself into a sitting position, noting that I was still in my muddied, bloodied leather top and trousers, although I was glad to see that someone had thought to remove the metal armour plates. Vrael handed me a vial of some sort of painkiller, which I downed without a second thought. Sighing happily as the comforting numbness soothed all the aches, I leant back against the pillows. Vrael put on his best you're-not-going-to-like-this-but-you're-going-to-do-it-anyway face. My heart sank a little. I hated that face. It always ended up in an argument and I still had to do whatever it was he was going to tell me to do.

'Shadow, you're going to have to take a break or at least take thing a little more slowly,' he warned, sorting through some medical supplies that I guessed a healer had passed on to him. I turned a cool glare to my brother.

'Have you ever *tried* running a dimension? I can guarantee you that it's not something you can pick up and drop on a whim!'

'Calm yourself, Shadow,' he replied in that infuriatingly level voice that he always used when the argument was just starting. 'I am merely suggesting that there is perhaps a way of ruling that would be more accommodating to your health. A manner of delegation, perhaps?'

I sighed heavily. There was no getting out of this now, not by a long shot. 'Okay, once everything with Alena settles down I'll take a break as long as there are no more crises to deal with.'

Vrael didn't look particularly enthused by my answer, but as far as I was concerned, he could stuff it. It was the only compromise he was going to get. 'I have healed most of your wounds, including the ice burn Kaleb informed me you received from the prince. However, there were two I was unwilling to touch: a stab wound from an ice dagger and the break to your arm. Both are injuries I am not confident enough in my abilities to touch. It will be better for them to heal naturally.'

'Merlas's hoof,' I explained. 'She was trying to catch me when I was falling but she didn't...' I sat bolt upright. I had completely forgotten the doe! 'Merlas! Is she okay? Did someone...'

'Peace, Shadow,' Vrael reassured me. 'Shaeman's with her now. We considered it best that he take care of her wing as he had more intimate knowledge of how the muscles are put together. He believes that she will make a full recovery.'

'And Amarath?'

'Out with your troops to make sure that all the Alenans have retreated. It would appear that we halved their army's numbers.' I allowed myself to relax again. Everyone seemed to be safe and sound. At least, I relaxed until Vrael cleared his throat. 'A messenger from Alena arrived for you during your unconsciousness. We managed to pass Amarath off as you in order to give the impression that you were unharmed and, please excuse the term, fighting-fit.' He must have read the expression of panic on my face like an open book. Amarath was not the kind of person that you sit on a throne without having words with her beforehand, and especially not without putting in place a list of words that were forbidden in diplomatic language. 'Worry not, little one, she impersonated you rather well and kept her tongue in check. With that, the mask and a little illusionary magic to change her hair, it would have been difficult to tell you apart.'

'So what was the message?'

'He is reproposing marriage and begs you to consider it seriously.'

'My Lady, if I may,' Kaleb interjected. 'Prince Melek seems to be desperate. He has played all his aces. He cannot defeat Aspheri by the strength of his arm alone, not while you have alliances with the dead dimensions, but his ultimatum has been issued and he is unable to deliver on one of his options.'

I opened my mouth to speak, but I was interrupted by Vrael.

'Before you start thinking of ways to wheedle out of that one,' he said with a slightly malevolent twinkle in his eye, 'a prospective suitor has arrived. I believe he wishes to court you.' I groaned, burrowing under the blankets. I did not want to have to deal with this right now. I wasn't ready for it.

Aleth patted my shoulder a little awkwardly as I resurfaced, running a hand through my hair. 'Worry not, My Lady, he is quite the gentleman, and a crystal demon! They are rare now since the wars that raged between their clans.'

'It would help your cause, My Lady. If you are being courted by a male, then you cannot accept to be courted by the Alenan Prince, and he has yet to issue an official request. However, a courting does not obligatorily lead to marriage. You could, in short, accept the courting of this demon in order to gain more time during which to think about what to do about Alena. It will delay your decision in a more diplomatic manner.' Kaleb spoke in a careful, measured tone, as if trying to convey how this idea would slow down the proceedings with Alena from their current rapid-fire state. I had to admit that it was certainly a good idea.

'Aleth, I'm going to need your help to get ready to meet this guy.'

Aleth did her best. The dress, cut in the usual style she had picked out for me that clung to my body, leaving only my shoulders bare, was a deep purple, darker than my eyes in order to bring them out. Touches of silvery thread and a black bodice complemented the look. She styled my hair in an intricate knot of tiny plaits, weaving a few bloodstones into the design. A belt held my more ceremonial sword to my hip, and a shimmering cloak swirled around my shoulders. I looked into the mirror as she tied my mask over my face. I barely recognised myself. My eyes flashed red briefly. Who was I becoming?

Four guards escorted me to the throne room, not only to give the air of a ruler of a warrior dimension, but also because Kaleb had reasoned that Melek wasn't going to give up that easily. He was likely to attempt less open methods of trying to get rid of me. Phantom and Wraith trotted alongside me, claws clicking on the black stone floors. One or two steps behind me, Kaleb and Captain Nergal strode side by side.

I settled on my throne, resisting the urge to run a hand

through my hair. For all the effort put into making me look my best and reassure me, I was still terrified of what was going to come. All I knew was that this suitor was a demon from a rare sub-species. For all I knew of him, he could be another Karthragan, or possibly some relation of Teran's.

The man who walked through the doorway of at the footman's announcement was certainly a handsome demon, although I had yet to meet a demon who was ugly in his human form. His silver hair glinted gold and red in the torchlight, my heart skipping a beat as I took him for a Dementius. But his expression was open and honest. He was definitely not a relation of Teran's. His face sparked some sort of recognition in my mind, but I couldn't place it. He bowed low to me, one hand fisted over his heart.

'I thank you for setting aside the time to meet with me, My Lady.' He spoke in a strange lilting accent alien to this dimension yet he spoke like a native, which was probably not something to go on since every demon instinctively understood demonic. 'My name is Ilrune of the Wingless.'

I froze. Ilrune? The wingless Careen I had met at the Academy? He wasn't a demon, I would have sensed it. 'My lord Ilrune,' I said respectfully, 'your presence here brings back many memories of my time spent on Earth. However, you were not always a demon, I believe…'

'An accurate observation, my Lady, I am a converted demon. An Unborn. To save my life, the decision was taken to put the blood of demons in my veins in order to assure my survival. I stand before you today, despite the turmoil, to ask you permission to court you.'

I took a moment to observe Ilrune. At the Academy, he had still been very young, still a little wet behind the ears and unsure of the world. But that child was not the creature that stood in front of me now. Now, he was a man of impeccable form, a man who could easily have risen through the ranks of my army to become an officer. From what I knew of the Careen, they would have raised Ilrune to the best of their ideals: kindness, respect, etiquette and honesty. He would make a good king for the people of Aspheri without trying to usurp me or take my decisions for me. The people would accept him with ease. Perhaps this courting would end in a marriage. Only time would tell.

'My Lord Ilrune, I grant you the right of courting.'

Aleth squealed in delight when I told her of my decision. I lay back in the bathing pool, careful not to let the splint on my arm get wet, daydreaming a little as my Lady's maid untied the mess of plaits. I'm still young by demonic standards. I'm allowed to daydream about love. Aleth chatted happily about all the positive attributes Ilrune had, from his species to the length of his claws. I half listened to her, but my mind was elsewhere. Well, my mind was with a certain crystal demon.

Ilrune courted me over the next month in the traditional Careen fashion. At every meeting, he brought me gifts, the meaning in Careen society being to show off your wealth and knowledge of your lady's tastes while attempting to buy her favour by offering things that she would appreciate. The first thing he brought me was a ring, which showed that the female was favouring a male. And he definitely proved his wealth with it: A band of white gold inlaid with three gems, a bloodstone, the stone favoured by the Aspherin royal line, flanked by an amethyst and a diamond. I wore it on a chain around my neck at his suggestion to avoid it getting in the way of my sword play. Diplomatic courtesy had obliged me to tell Prince Melek of my courtship with Ilrune, and his answer had been only slightly short of furious. Kaleb and Captain Nergal were increasingly worried about an assassination attempt, especially since I 'insisted on gallivanting off with that Unborn' and leaving my guards behind. Although, once or twice, I did spot one of them following us, trying to remain unseen.

At the end of the month, I strode through the corridors of the palace, eager to get to the courtyard, where Ilrune was apparently waiting for me. I wasn't just excited to see him though. The courting law for the Careen states that a courtship must last only a month. Today was the last day of that month. One month was perhaps not a long time to have known someone, but over the time I had spent with him, I had started to see that he was, for all the stigma attached to his rank, a man with a heart, who treated me not as a princess, not as a ruler of a dimension, but as a girl who still dreamed of love.

Ilrune was indeed waiting for me in the courtyard, astride a fiery red pegasus, another one standing beside him. I stroked the doe's silvery coat, admiring her build. Ilrune, ever the gentleman, swung himself off his stag in order to help me to mount.

'A final gift, My Lady,' he said formally. 'Not as fine as the doe bonded to you, but one of the finest of our herds.'

'She is wondrous,' I breathed, running my fingers through her silken mane. From what I knew of the pegusi, she was a carnivore, a heavier build compared to the herbivores, like the Earthen draft horses. I touched the plate on her collar, reading her name: Moonmaiden.

We flew out over the walls of the palace, leaning low over our mount's necks. My hair streamed out beside me as I raced Ilrune, not even knowing where we were racing to. He smiled at me as we flew side by side for a moment before he pulled ahead, starting to angle for a descent. I straightened up, leaning backwards a little to aid my doe in her landing. I pulled Moonmaiden up next to Ilrune's stag, looking out over the villages. Demons moved in the streets, oblivious to us watching them, finishing the repairs from the bloody battle fought against Alena. The red sun cast its warmth over the black ground, bringing out the crimson flecks in the palace stone. Pride swelled my heart as I looked out over it. There was no way I could let this fall into the hands of Teran or Melek. These demons, these people needed better than that. Ilrune turned his gaze to me, swinging himself off his mount's back. Standing next to me, he cleared his throat.

'My Lady, we have been courting for a month now, and it is traditional in Careen circles for each side to state their feelings following the courtship. What I wish to say, My Lady, Shadow, is that I would be honoured if you would consent to allow me your hand in marriage.'

In true girly fashion, I flung myself off Moonmaiden, into Ilrune's arms.

'Yes, goddess, yes!'

We set the date for another month's time, as I was scheduled to visit another dimension in order to secure a trading deal. Ilrune took to disguising himself as one of my guard, with permission from Captain Nergal, in order to stay close to me as for the moment, he had no need to be at my side, and it was not 'proper' for him to get involved with the affairs of state before the marriage. The one place Captain Nergal refused to let him accompany me to were other dimensions. That job mainly fell to Kaleb and a few others. It was considered that my guard was composed of the finest warriors of my army and the captain didn't want an amateur making a rookie mistake to jeopardise that image. He knew that the weaker my guards appeared, the more danger I was in. What they hadn't counted on was how much danger I could put myself in.

Spending several days in another dimension to secure a trading deal was not my idea of a riveting activity, not even with the amusement of watching Kaleb trying to hide his boredom. Although my mask hid a lot of my own boredom with the proceedings, it did nothing for my irritability. My vulnerable period was fast approaching and the long, roundabout diplomatic language was definitely not helping my headache since I had to be on alert for every single tiny detail that could be seen as ambiguous. Not to mention that my broken arm had yet to finish healing and it was very much taking its own sweet time about it, much to the healer's annoyance. I absent-mindedly scratched at the splint discreetly hidden by my sleeve. I froze. I was getting better at predicting the exact strikes of my vulnerable period, and this one was imminent. I tugged on Kaleb's cloak as inconspicuously as I could. Sensing the urgency in my actions, he nodded once. He knew the score and would take care of excuses. Desperate to get back to Aspheri before losing my magic, I teleported.

I vanished not a second too late. I materialised a little high and fell the remaining few feet to the ground as I felt the change come over me. I pushed myself to my feet, staggering a little, grabbing onto the wall to steady myself. I closed my eyes, fighting down the feeling of nausea.

'Oh sh—' This wasn't Aspheri. I was back on Earth! And even worse than that was the all-too familiar figure someone I really didn't want to see leaning against the wall a couple of metres away from me.

'Well, well, well, the little princess is a little lost. It would seem that you are without your guards as well. This is not a good situation for you, is it?'

'Teran Dementius,' I growled, glaring at the demon who seemed to be determined to take the throne from me as I reached for the sword at my hip. 'Just because I seem to have teleported at the wrong moment doesn't mean I still can't take you down!' Even thought I knew that, in human form, I held no threat against the powerful demon. A blade already glinted in his hand. I scrabbled desperately in my mind for an idea to get away from him, to escape from this situation. Late night reading came to the rescue. 'Law dictates that in order to fight for leadership, the duellers must be on equal footing. I'm in human form, so that would invalidate your claim.'

Teran growled low in his throat, obviously not pleased that I had found the time to look up the old laws of the dimension (all seventeen volumes of the damn thing. Took me near enough a year to get through them).

'Shadow?' called a voice. I cursed in my mind. Now was not the time for Bart to turn up. As much as I loved the demon Kraferr hybrid, he had yet to grasp a better sense of timing. 'Is everything okay?'

'Who's that?' Teran snarled. 'Yet another hybrid that you've added to your clan! How many hybrids are you planning to accept? All you're doing is diluting our blood. I would have thought better of the supposed princess of our kind. What would your father have said? Then again, your father sired hybrids left and right. What an example to give. But a three-way hybrid? That's just senseless.'

'Don't worry, Bart,' I called to him, my gaze not shifting from the demon in front of me. 'Teran was just leaving. He won't attack me until we're on equal ground.'

'What're you doin' here in the first place?!' Bart hissed at Teran, his eyes glowing red in the gloom of the alley.

'I had come to confront Shadow,' Teran drawled. 'But it would seem that she's human. As she cleverly stated, I can't challenge her now.'

'And thank the goddess for that.' I muttered under my breath before addressing the demon. 'So you can shift! Go on! Scoot!' Teran mockingly bowed to me before vanishing from sight. 'I have never been more glad for that rule,' I added to myself. A few moments later, Bart relaxed, the bolts of magic disappearing from his palms as he straightened up, staring at the place where, a few seconds ago, Teran had stood. He sighed, grabbing two silver bracelets from his pockets and clasping them around his wrists. A wave of brown streaked over his fur, transforming it back to his Kraferric pelt, before he twisted his head to look at me. I leant against the wall again, pulling my mask off and running a hand though my hair. What a fine mess I had managed to get myself into now. Human and no guards with Teran on my tail. Just brilliant.

'What happened, Shad? Who was that guy? Why're you here instead of Aspheri?'

'Can you slow down on the questions please?' I asked, rubbing my temples. Boy, did I have one hell of a headache. 'I was visiting another dimension, sensed my human period coming on and tried to teleport back to Aspheri. Unfortunately, I screwed it up and landed here.'

'And human.'

'And human, yes.'

Bart sighed heavily, rubbing the back of his neck. 'As far as I'm concerned,' he said, 'you can't go back to Aspheri or Synairn for quite a while now. I think the more wise decision would be to take you to where Dominique and I live. It'll give you shelter while you're…vulnerable.' He held out a hand to me. I grasped it gently, bracing myself for the teleportation.

Bart's teleportation may have improved in the way that it only took him two attempts to land in the right place, but his method still left you with the unpleasant feeling that you had just been pulled through a cheese grater. I had to close my eyes and force down the feeling of nausea for the second time that night as we landed. Goddess, how much trouble was I in now? There was no way Teran was going to let me get away. He'd be on my trail for the next three days just waiting for me to get my magic back. The only way I would be able to fight him now would be to get angry enough to discover my true form. A demon or half-demon had an extra morph known as their 'true form'. The picture I had seen of Karthragan in the Book of Demons, the flaming wolf that was his true form. A full-blooded demon knows their true form from birth. A half demon only discovers theirs if they get angry enough to approach what is called the 'point of no return', the point where the demonic possession is so strong that it overlaps the other side of a half-demon's blood. It was the only power a half demon had up his or her sleeve during their vulnerable period, but it was a difficult power to control and not one ever taken lightly. In fact, there were only six documented instances where a part demon had done so, and five of them hadn't come back. Bart touched my shoulder lightly. Nodding to him, I dragged a sleeve across my eyes, following him down into the flat.

I braced myself for the onslaught of homicidal fur, but the absence of such a phenomenon told me that Dominique was probably out. I stood in the hallway, unsure of myself or what to do. This wasn't my land to rule. This was Bart's territory and I was trespassing once again. The fingers of my broken arm twitched as the old injury throbbed. I followed Bart through to the living room, taking up a post by the window, looking out over the city where rain had just begun to fall. I watched Bart in the reflection of the glass. He had changed a lot since I had first met the Kraferr. He had been younger than me in physical years at that point, ageing as a normal human despite being a Kraferr hybrid. He used to have a kind of naïve optimism with the enthusiasm of a young person embarking on their first adventure in the footsteps of his Kraferr One predecessors. Now he was several years older, surpassing me in physical years as I had stopped, with a maturity superseding his age. I was, in no minor part, to blame for that. I had burdened him with demonic blood. If I could take it back, I would. It wasn't fair on him, already one of the last Kraferrs, to have to deal with the rapidly expanding, precarious world of part demons. As I watched him from my discreet positioning, his face was set in an expression of neutral seriousness that I knew all too well as one favoured by my siblings when sorting through their emotions from an objective point of view.

The front door opened again to admit one very wet Kraferrin, who walked into the living room with her head down and, ignoring his protests, hugged Bart tightly. The Kraferr pushed her away, playfully grumbling about how she was getting him wet. I stood still, waiting patiently for her to figure out why there was something not quite right with her living room.

'Shadow!' You're back!' she exclaimed. I smiled at her, unclasping my cloak and draping it around her shoulders as I realised that she was shivering. Dominique wrapped her arms around herself under the cloak before speaking again. 'We haven't seen you for quite a while now... What brings you here?' she asked, lifting her head, her eyes glinting in interest.

'I'm sorry about dropping in on you like this,' I apologised, 'I had a little trouble with my magic.'

'Basically, she's human right now and pretty much defenceless while also having an insanely evil demon chasing her,' Bart added.

'Yeah, that just about sums up why I'm here.' I said before sighing. 'Teran's father was Karthragan's right hand demon. Had Karthragan died first, then Teran's father would have made sure that Teran got the throne. As you can tell, he's a little sore. The whole Dementius clan now bears a grudge against the Roths and, by extension, the Mercians. That's the long story short.'

The door was thrown off its hinges as a blast of nearly white magic blasted it out of the way. Ilrune strode into the flat, sword drawn, confronting the two Kraferrs after pushing me to the side. He growled a challenge in demonic, glaring at Bart and Dominique. The Kraferr swept Dominique behind him, skipping backwards and turning the table onto its side. He bared his fangs, his eyes flickering red.

'Stop!' I shouted, grabbing Ilrune's arm, trying to get his attention before he could hurt either of the Kraferrs. 'They're friends, Ilrune! Friends!'

Ilrune's magic faded slowly as he pushed down his emotions. Closing his eyes briefly, he grabbed me in a hug, as if trying to reassure himself that I was okay. I pressed my face into his chest, breathing in his smell. I hadn't realised how much I had needed the comfort after my run in with Teran. The two Kraferrs slowly emerged from behind the table, watching the crystal demon warily. As Ilrune let me go, I coughed nervously. I guessed that introductions were up to me.

'Ilrune, this is Dominique and Bart, the last of the Kraferr race. Bart's also an Unborn of the Roth-Mercian clan. Bart, Dominique, this is Ilrune of the Wingless, part-demon and soon to be Prince of Aspheri.'

Bart choked on something unknown, spluttering and coughing. Dominique just stared. After a few moments, Bart began to recover a modicum of composure. 'What do you mean 'soon to be Prince of Aspheri'?'

'In the way that we are engaged to be married.'

'You're getting married?!'

'Bart, shut up,' Dominique muttered before adding in a louder voice. 'Congrats Shadow!'

Ilrune bowed to the two Kraferrs, speaking up in his deep voice. 'I apologise for the sudden attack. Shadow warned me of the threat posed by Teran, and I was not sure of your intentions.' Bart was glaring at Ilrune, but the Wingless was returning the look in none too friendly a fashion. I stamped on my fiancé's foot as inconspicuously as I could. He glanced down at me, taking in my expression. Sighing, he turned to look at the door, which lay barely hanging off its hinges from his exuberant entry. He cast an eye over the damage before holding his hand towards the wood, letting his whitish magic seep into the wood, reconnecting fibres in shattered wood and reshaping bent metal. Bart looked at me.

'I take it that now that he's here, you'll be going back to Aspheri,' he said flatly.

I shook my head. 'That would throw up a magical signature strong enough for Teran to trace without very much difficulty at all. Ilrune wouldn't teleport me for fear of messing up and being followed by Teran without any back up on our side.'

Bart said nothing but glanced at Ilrune before walking out of the newly repaired door. Ilrune cast a look at me before following the Kraferr. I sincerely hoped that Ilrune wasn't about to go and cause any trouble. That was the last thing we needed at the moment. Careen were known to be highly protective of their females. I knew that Ilrune was about as pacifist as a demon could get, unwilling to shed the blood of another if there was any other way, but Bart didn't know that. Bart was more likely to let his anger get in the way of anything that even sniffed of a challenge. Dominique ignored the goings on, walking into the kitchen and making a start on the washing up as if there was nothing amiss whatsoever. I grabbed a cloth and stood silently next to Dominique, drying the dishes as she washed them. We continued in a companionable silence until Dominique suddenly gasped. The glass she had been holding fell, shattering on the floor as she doubled over in pain, tears starting to stream down her face.

'Oh god,' she gasped. 'Bart's turning demonic!'

I didn't ask how she knew. Dominique was a Kraferr. Sometimes they just knew things or had ways of knowing with their own kind of magic. She had probably placed wards or something around the Kraferr. Instead, I asked, 'Where is he?'

'On the roof, with Ilrune!' I grabbed her arm, pulling it around my shoulders in order to help her remain upright as we ran for the stairs to the roof. I reached the door, gently propping Dominique against the wall before trying to open it. It was locked, sealed with magic. I growled in frustration, slamming my shoulder against it.

'Curse this human body!' I snarled at myself, trying once again with brute force. I hated being human. I had no strength, no magic, no way of fighting. Not unless...

'Dominique, can you link to Bart's mind and transfer the link to me? I need his anger!' For a moment, she simply stared at me.

I must have looked a sight. Not many people ever saw me angry. It was dangerous in demonic form. Now that I was human, I could cut loose. She nodded briefly, starting to mutter under her breath, weaving the spells through the air.

Bart's anger hit me like a slap to the face. I struggled with my ingrained training, forcing myself to accept the emotion, to take it as my own. It flooded through my mind, crushing the dams built around my demonic side. There was no going back now.

Cold air. Don't like cold air. Little creature beside me. Strange smell. Not a target. Not a threat. Ignore it. Find target. Find three-way-hybrid. Three-way-hybrid in Desert Dimension. Teleport.

Badlands warm. Badlands good. Magic strong. Three-way-hybrid here with Crystal hybrid. Must take down three-way-hybrid. Lunge. Bite. Scratch. Pain of magic. Stinging. Anger. Snarl. Flesh beneath my claws. Smell of blood. Good smell. Falling back. Crystal demon fighting me. Magic around my muzzle. Must get it off. Must get it off! Growl. Snarl. More magic around my paws. Can't stand. Crystal demon next to me. Warning growl. Get away. Magic still binding. Singing. Crystal demon singing. Familiar song. Soothing. Growing weaker. Can't hold on to form.

Someone's voice softly crooned to me. A song I knew from so long ago. The Awakening of Worlds, an old Synari lullaby.
   'Run through the forest chasing the wolf's tail, Know that in the awakening of the worlds, in the end of dreams, I will forever be here to comfort you.' I let my mind wander back to Synairn, to the last month I spent there. Of the nightmares that would wake me up at night with screams of terror. Of Arellan's arms holding me close, her fingers gently combing my hair as she sang to me, as she sang me back to sleep. For a moment, I lost myself in memory. The loss of Arellan ached deep in my heart, a pain long ago buried

returning to rip its way through my mind. I longed to stay in this world of fantasy, where she was still alive, but the singing voice wasn't hers. The singing voice was quietly begging me to wake up. My arm was screaming in agony when I finally opened my eyes on reality. Ilrune looked down at me with concern burning in his eyes. His hand gently brushed against my cheek.

'Are you all right?' he asked quietly. I ignored that question as I started to remember what had landed me here, lying on the couch in the Kraferr's flat

'How's Bart? I didn't hurt him, did I?'

Ilrune scowled at the mention of the Kraferr's name. 'He has yet to awaken. The fight between you was rather violent. I do not believe you have caused him any lasting damage.'

'I need to see him.' I attempted to stand, grabbing my cloak, but someone seemed to have replaced my legs with wet noodles. Growling in frustration, I grabbed onto a nearby table, trying to support myself. Ilrune sighed heavily, wrapping one arm around my waist and helping me to walk over to Bart's room.

Dominique sat alone in the gloomy room, sitting on the edge of the bed, holding Bart's hand as he lay, unconscious. She glanced up as I pushed open the door, her eyes, wet with tears, gleaming in the light.

'He's...he's not awake yet,' she murmured. She dragged a sleeve over her eyes, sniffing before looking back at me. 'He will wake up, won't he?'

I looked at the floor, unable to look at the Kraferrin. I had no idea what I had even done to Bart, or what had happened during the fight. Dominique hiccupped a sob, looking back at Bart. I chewed my lip, trying to think of anything to say.

'Dominique, I'm...'

'Sorry? Possibly. I know you probably did what you had to do in order to break up the fight. I just wish I knew he was okay.'

'Well, isn't this an interesting situation?' A figure detached itself from the deep shadows of the room. Golden hair glinted in what little light there was. Teran barked out a single burst of harsh laughter. Dominique shot to her feet, her eyes flashing in anger. She pulled a knife from her belt, growling.

'Don't you dare come any closer!'

' How…cute. The Kraferrin standing up for her friends even though she knows that she has no hope in defeating me. The Kraferr, the great protector, unconscious and unable to defend his loved ones. This would simply kill him to know that he could do nothing. The princess, so weak in her human form, powerless, incapable of protecting her friends. And the crystal demon who would do anything to protect the princess, but even he knows that he's no match for me.'

I reached a hand up my sleeve to draw my dagger but snarled in pain, the blade clattering to the ground as pain shot through my arm. Ilrune's arms grabbed me, pressing me to his chest in an attempt to protect me.

'Leave here, Dementius,' Ilrune growled.

'Come, come, Wingless, the Kraferrs are well known for their hospitality. 'My dear Dominique, how trying this must be for you. The only unblooded demon in this room. I know that you asked your little friend on the bed to blood you, but he refused… Such a selfish thing for him to have done, wasn't it?' He took a step closer, holding out one hand to the Kraferrin. 'I am willing to blood you, if you are willing to accept…'

'No!' Dominique snarled, baring her teeth at the demon.

'Such a gift as demonic blood could give you what you most desire.'

'Shut up,' Dominique said quietly, her rage echoing through her voice.

'Are you sure? No one from Shadow's clan will accept to blood you, and your little friend has already denied you. Why remain weak when you could be strong, strong enough to protect your loved ones?'

'Shut up.'

'Strong enough to bear a child?'

'Shut up!' Dominique's claws were millimetres away from Teran's throat. They trembled slightly.

'I have no qualms about giving you what you want.' Her hand shook, then folded into a fist and dropped back down to her side. She picked up the knife she had dropped, holding it tightly as if in reassurance.

'Don't!' I shouted in warning. He mustn't blood her. He must not! It was against every protocol in the book! It was not something to be taken lightly. He would want something in return, that was almost certain, and you couldn't accept gifts from a snake like him!

'Do it,' Dominique murmured. 'Give me the blood.'

Teran smirked at me, defenceless, imprisoned in Ilrune's arms. He knew exactly how much I treasured my friends, how I wanted to please them, but I had never even considered what he was planning to do to Dominique. It was barbaric, crude and painful. Turning his gaze to Dominique, he rolled back his sleeve, using a claw to draw a neat gash down his forearm. At his prompting, the Kraferrin copied his gesture. I struggled against Ilrune's hold but, as a human, I had more chance of head butting my way through a brick wall than I had of breaking free, and he wasn't about to let me go running into danger. Curse this half-blood status! All I could do was watch in horror as the demon and the Kraferrin pressed their wounds together, demonic blood starting to flow into Dominique's veins. She collapsed to the ground in agony, clutching her arm. Teran wiped the blood from his own wound on his sleeve, looking down at the Kraferrin.

'I will return when she has converted,' he vowed before vanishing. Ilrune let me go. I fell to my knees, using my cloak in attempt to stem the blood flow. The scarlet was turning dark. Black veins stood out around the wound, starting to travel up her arm. By the time they reached her heart, she would be in pure, burning agony. Already, her eyes were wide, staring at the ceiling, her claws starting to gouge grooves into the floor. I chewed my lip, applying more pressure to the wound. There was nothing to do but wait for the conversion to finish.

'Ilrune, try to wake Bart up. He's going to be pissed off enough without delaying things.' Ilrune did nothing, simply glaring at the Kraferrin. 'Ilrune!' Still, he didn't more.

'They're consorting with Teran, Shadow. They deserve everything they get. We should get back to Aspheri and get you to safety before Teran returns with no qualms about the law.'

I growled low in my throat. 'You're such a pain!' I snarled, grabbing a scarf from the top of the dresser, binding it tightly around the wound. Casting a glare at my fiancé, I started shaking Bart's shoulder. Getting no response, I started to grow desperate. Tears began to prick the back of my eyes as I begged the Kraferr to wake up.

'Oh, Goddess, Bart, please wake up! I need you to wake up! Dominique's in danger! Teran's given her demonic blood! Goddess, I don't know what to do! Please, Bart, please wake up!'

Something in my plea must have gotten through to the Kraferr's subconscious. His eyes snapped open as he sat bolt upright. He snarled at Ilrune and me, dropping down next to Dominique.

'What the hell did you do to her?!'

'I didn't do anything!' I pleaded with him to understand. 'I couldn't do anything!'

'That's just it, isn't it?' he growled. 'You didn't do anything and now she's going to end up as a part-demon as well! She was the last pure Kraferrin! You've ruined everything!'

My tears began to run down my face. I couldn't have done anything to save her. There was nothing I could have done! I was only human. I had no strength, no magic, no way to hold a blade in order to fight. Bart had been unconscious at the time. How could he blame me? I couldn't have done anything to stop Teran. Nothing!

'You don't get it, do you?' I screamed at the Kraferr. 'I'm human! Human! I have nothing to fight with!' Dragging my sleeve across my eyes, turning on my heel and leaving the room, I closed the door behind me without waiting for an answer.

I sagged against the window, trying to regain some semblance of dignity and composure. I wiped my eyes again, sniffing hard in an attempt to stop crying.

'Aw, has the little princess had an argument and come out here to cry?' asked a mocking voice. I didn't have to think very long to guess who owned it. And what was it with me being called the 'little princess' by everyone? Okay, I was short for a demon, but that didn't mean anything! I rounded on Teran, who was leaning nonchalantly against the wall, intending to yell at him. It didn't really turn out as I expected it to. In a single heartbeat, my back was against the wall, standing on my toes with Teran's hand at my throat. I scrabbled at his hand, trying to relieve the pressure on my windpipe, unable to draw breath, starting to become light-headed. Teran released his hold a slight degree. I gulped down air desperately.

'Weak little human,' he crooned. 'I'm not even close to being finished with you. I may not be able to challenge you for a while, but I can certainly make your life hell until I do.'

Ilrune burst out from the bedroom like an enraged bull. I half expected him to grow horns. Bart wasn't far behind him, a look of anger personified on his face. Teran let me go, turning to face the two Unborns.

'How sweet, it would seem that the Kraferr protector and the crystal demon have formed a rescue party. I didn't think they would be able to work together without ripping each other's throats out.' Teran commented conversationally. Bart pulled back a fist to punch Teran. A ball of fur erupted from the bedroom, knocking the Kraferr back.

'Leave him alone,' Dominique growled.

'Are you feeling better, my dear Dominique?' Teran asked.

'Dominique... What has he done to you?!' Bart growled.

'The worst is going to come soon, Bart,' she answered quietly, 'After this...we'll be able to save our race.'

'Are you fr—'

'Quiet!' she snapped, frowning slightly at Bart before softening her voice slightly. 'Quiet, please. I want to be able to do this alone for once.' Teran smirked a little. Ilrune was speechless. I wheezed quietly, still feeling Teran's hands at my throat.

'I would guess that you are better, Dominique,' Teran said, smiling. 'We can move on to the next stage. Bart and Ilrune, you will stay here.'

'Yes, she murmured under her breath, 'let's go. You can finish whatever you have to do and then get the hell out of my home.' Glowering at Bart and Ilrune, Dominique swept back into the bedroom. Teran smirked at the two Unborns, seized my arm and followed the Kraferrin, but not without a parting threat.

'If you wish no harm to come to your loved ones, I suggest strongly that you stay out here and keep quiet.'

There was no way I could have fought against Teran with any hope of winning, so I didn't. It would only have make things worse, for either Dominique or for me. Instead, I curled up quietly where he had left me. My broken arm ached. I wanted to go home. I wanted to get away from Teran. I wanted my family. Teran got Dominique to lie down on the bed, telling her to relax before he turned back to me. I knew what he wanted, and tried not to resist. He rested his hand on my stomach, careful not to allow his hand to pass through my skin. He drew out a tiny white orb, carefully suspended over his palm. A tiny fragment of my essence of who I was. An orb of magic that could grow into a whole new being. My coding would be overrun by Dominique's, all it needed to become a child was a piece of Bart's essence. Teran leant over Dominique for a moment, speaking softly to her in a voice too quiet for my human ears to hear Whatever it was, she agreed to it, and Teran pressed the tiny orb of magic into her belly. Dominique gasped in pain, her hands fisting in the sheets beneath her. Teran straightened up, staring to search the room. From a small, journal-like book, he drew a second orb of magic, which he carried to Dominique. Bart must have kept a diary or something. That's all I would think of that could give Teran enough of his essence to satisfy his needs. Physical form wasn't the only thing that could be used to house a person's essence. It was anything and everything personal and unique to a single person, and handwriting was one of the most personal and unique non physical things a person had.

'Congratulations, my dear Dominique, you will bear twins in approximately five months.' Bowing low to the Kraferrin, he took hold of my arm once more, teleporting out of the flat.

Wherever he took us, at least it was warm. I knew that it was still Earth. Teleporting between dimensions left a strange feeling of having jumped into a bucket of cold water for a few moments. Teleporting within a dimension left only a brief sensation of pins and needles. As soon as I could, I scrambled away from Teran. I had no intention of joining Kaleb's ranks any time soon. This bastard of a demon wasn't about to change that. I bared my teeth, feeling the acute lack of fangs to scare him with. No fangs, no claws, no strength and no magic, what a fine state I was in now.

Teran cornered me easily, a manic grin fixed on his face. He took hold of my broken arm in a parody of gentleness, prodding the break with a light touch. I gritted my teeth. I wanted to pull away, but it would only make matters worse. With one quick movement, he twisted my arm, snapping the healing bone easily. I couldn't stop the scream from escaping my throat. Teran barked a laugh, still holding my arm in his hand, grinding the broken bone beneath his fingers.

'Teran!' bellowed a, unfamiliar, female voice. An angry looking woman who looked very similar to Teran strode towards us, closely followed by Ilrune and Bart. The relief on Ilrune's face was obvious, as if he hadn't expected to find me at all. He darted to my side, carefully cradling me in his arms. I buried my face in his chest, desperately needing his support. My arm was in agony as I held it against me, my tears beginning to seep into Ilrune's shirt.

'Elva,' Teran growled in response. The woman tossed her hair out of her eyes glaring at what I guessed was her twin.

'I'm only doing this because I need a favour from the Roth-Mercians and Shadow is technically the head of it,' she said before turning her yellow gaze to me. 'I saved your ass. In return, you tell Vrael that Elva's back in town. Now get the hell out of here.'

Ilrune held me for a moment longer as we arrived in Bart's flat. I squirmed a little in his grip, but he refused to let me go. He rested his forehead on my head, murmuring quietly to me.

'Gods, next time, please scream or something so I will know that things are not right.' Only then did he let me go. With tender care, he touched my broken arm, wincing as I hissed in pain. Murmuring something under his breath, he let his magic flow, putting the bone back together with crystal. I flexed my hand gingerly, expecting the usual flash of pain. Nothing. Healed. I flung my arms around his neck, pulling the taller demon down to hug him tightly. Summoning my courage, I let him go and turned to check on Dominique.

The Kraferrin was huddled in a corner of the room as if terrified. As soon as she realised who had walked in, she refused to look up at me. Carefully arranging my skirts, I sat, cross-legged, opposite her, close enough to comfort, far away enough not to threaten.

'I'm sorry,' she murmured. I could see the tracks from her tears, still fresh, gleaming in the room's low light.

'It's okay, Dominique. No one was badly hurt apart from you.'

'It's not okay, I sold you out to that bastard!'

'Then I forgive you.'

'No! There are some things that are unforgivable!'

'I choose who I forgive and, right now, I forgive you, Dominique Kraferr. There are far worse things that could have happened, but they didn't, and for that I am grateful.'

For a moment, Dominique remained silent. Behind me, I heard the door creak open. Ilrune, standing silhouetted against the light, glared at Dominique. I glowered back, causing him to back up a couple of steps. I pointed a finger at him. The crystal demon quickly made himself scarce, disappearing back into the living room. For all I had been complaining about him for the past while, he was still intelligent enough to know not to cross me. I turned my attention back to Dominique, rubbing her arm in an attempt to comfort her.

'Hey, it's okay, he was just annoyed earlier because Teran was being a bum. He won't be hurting you any time soon if he values his crown jewels.'

Then, for the first time, she looked up at me. 'Am I really pregnant?'

I took a moment to think carefully through my answer. 'Demonesses are quite a bit different to humans in that respect. I'm not sure about Kraferrs though. Basically, we don't have periods, we're always ready to reproduce, there's a high chance of becoming pregnant when we have intercourse, we never miscarry and we always give birth to twins. In short, yes, you are pregnant.'

'Two children...' Dominique repeated, lowering her head, 'Am I really sure of what I'm about to get into?' she asked herself, 'I mean, two lives to take care of... I've already seen Kraferric mothers give birth and I have already seen how newlings are treated. Physically, I'm able to do that, but will I be able to keep up? I don't want to screw anything up by doing this...' Dominique let her hair fall over her face as she spoke. 'I'm willing to be hurt for them, I'm willing to do anything for them.

I just don't want to make any mistakes.'

'And you won't,' intervened Bart's voice. I glanced over my shoulder to see the Kraferr leaning against the door jamb. I briefly wondered how long he'd been there. He gazed down at Dominique. 'Sure, you made a big mistake by risking all of our lives with this,' he continued, crossing his arms, 'but something tells me that what you're doing is right. You always wanted to save the Kraferrs, and even though they will never be what others call 'pure' Kraferrs, they will still be descendants. By doing this, maybe you're braver than most. Maybe now you'll achieve your goal. And I respect that. The ends don't justify the means to me, but hey, I'm pretty happy that we won't be the only Kraferrs on this planet.'

'But you won't be alone in this,' I added. 'You can call me any time and I'll be back as soon as I can.' I stood up, pushing my hair off my face. 'Ilrune had better get me back to Aspheri. They need me there.' I smiled slightly at Dominique. 'Get Bart to call me whenever you need me here or when you go into labour. I'll help you through it.' Before walking out to the living room, I paused by Bart, talking to him under my breath so that only he could hear.

'You'd better look after her. Pregnancy isn't easy at the best of times, and demonic pregnancies have a tendency to be worse.' Ilrune stepped forwards to take my hand, preparing for the teleportation. I cast one last look at the Kraferrs, my mask in hand. 'I guess I'll be seeing you. Thanks for putting up with us and all the crap we've put you through.'

PART 8

ASPHERI – MARRIAGE

Ilrune and I landed slap-bang in the middle of a heated argument between my guards. Well, we landed off to the side, hidden a little by the shadows of the room. Kaleb seemed to be doing most of the shouting which, if the faces of the rest of the guard unit was anything to go by, was one of the scariest things they had ever seen. Then again, if I was the one being shouted at by the Would-Be King, a creature powerful enough to destroy an entire dimension in the blink of an eye, I would be close to wetting myself as well.

'For the love of the gods, does no one plan anything using a calendar? It should have been obvious that her trip to Rathol coincided with her vulnerable period! On top of that, no one has been able to find her! Has no one ever thought to try and memorise her human energy signature? Don't look at me like that, I know you're capable of doing it, even if I can't!' He started pacing the line of demons. 'How would you lot like to have to tell the people that we *lost* the *princess* when she was defenceless!? I can tell you now that it would *not* be a fun job! Just be glad that I haven't had any messengers coming here and asking me why the hell the Princess of Darkness turned up in one of my realms! Not only that, but we lost the demon *engaged* to the princess! And do any of you know how to find or contact the first in line?'

Just to toy with the Would-Be King, I spoke up. 'I do.'

'Well thank the gods that…Princess!' It took Kaleb a couple of seconds to retrieve his jaw from the ground and regain his composure. 'Where have you been? We have been scouring Aspheri, Rathol and were about to try Alena, searching for you!'

'I misdirected myself to Earth. Friends of mine there found me and kept me safe until Ilrune managed to track me. Worry not, Would-Be King. There has been no harm done. Now, if you don't mind, I think I should retire to the safe room and wait until I turn back into a demon again.'

Two days later, I teleported out of the safe room, relishing the feeling of the warmth of my magic coursing through my veins once more. It felt good to be back in control, back in power. Nodding to my guards, I wove my way through the corridors, heading for my private chambers. With less than a month to go before my wedding to Ilrune, there was still so much to do. A small part of me wriggled in joy. I never thought I was ever going to be married. When the prophecy came into my life, it pretty much ended all thoughts I ever had of spending the rest of my life with anyone. Not much point when you knew exactly when and how you were going to die. Now that it was actually happening, I wanted to squirm in happiness like a hyper puppy.

Ilrune kept very quiet unless asked for his opinion, happy to let Aleth and I talk about colour schemes and invitation lists and how to go about organising the ball traditionally held one week before the marriage. Aleth, ever the prepared one, had already sketches several possible designs for a dress, nattering on about colour and fabric. I kept glancing at Ilrune, as if I was scared that if I just blinked, everything would simply vanish. How did I become so lucky?

I might have recalled that statement two weeks later, when I found myself standing in my dressing room with a fretting Aleth, trying to get ready for the ball. Aleth slapped my hands down as I tried, once more, to help her fix blood-stones into my black hair. Despite her angry wielding of hairpins, the stones did not want to sit properly, or what Aleth deemed to be properly. The stiff, formal dress was already beginning to get uncomfortable as I tried to sit as still as possible, listening to my lady's maid swear in all manner of demonic dialects that were definitely not suited to her station and sounded very odd coming out of her mouth. Throwing her hands up, she abandoned the gems, her eyes flickering red. I patted her hand, grabbing a brush and a comb inlaid with the dark red bloodstones. I dragged the brush through my hair, attempting to get it to lie flat before sweeping a section of it up to secure with the comb. I glanced at Aleth for approval. She looked relieved certainly. Setting my circlet on my head, I stood up. Time for Cinderdemon to go to the ball.

By the time I got to the double doors, Ilrune was already there, waiting. He jokingly shook his head, tapping his wrist in the universal gesture for 'what happened to you to be so late?'. I felt a blush creep over my cheeks, thankfully hidden by my mask. I shrugged at him, linking my arm through his. It was time to meet and entertain several hundred high class demons and dignitaries from other dimensions for an entire evening. Whoopee.

'Having second thoughts?' Ilrune asked jokingly.

'Only about the ball. Nothing's going to stop me marrying you.'

'Then let's get this over with.' Ilrune squeezed my arm gently as the doors opened before us, and a footman announced our arrival. I knew that there were only about a couple of hundred people in there, but it looked more like a thousand. My courage suddenly decided to turn tail and run screaming for the hills. Only Ilrune's arm through mine kept me on the course, sweeping into the ballroom that hadn't been used for years. I fixed a smile on my face and began to greet my guests. In the centre of the room, three demons played drums accompanied by a lone demon with what sounded like a flute crossed with bagpipes. Despite the image, it wasn't unpleasant to listen to. A voice suddenly spoke in my ear: 'I hope you realise just how much I am not enjoying this, Shad.'

I smiled at that. There was only one person I knew who would say that to my face. 'Hello, Amarath,' I said, turning to her. 'Glad you could make it.'

My sister glowered at me. Her short purple bob had sections of it braided with sparkling red gems, matching the deep red dress she was wearing. I couldn't help but smile. Amarath was definitely one of the tomboys, but there was no way she could have gotten away with the demonic male formal dress, which was composed of a pair of loose trousers, a sword and a cloak. Although, knowing Amarath, she was probably carrying more weapons than Captain Nergal.

'At least you don't have to put up with the mask, Amarath,' I countered. She rolled her eyes at me, shaking her head.

'Yeah, well, don't expect me to dance with anyone. Vrael's already threatened me with pretty much everything possible to have at least one. Seriously, is there anyone here under the age of a hundred?'

'How can you tell? Most of them stopped ageing between twenty and thirty. I'm the youngest looking person here! I mean, you look twenty, I'm your twin and I look fifteen! By the way,' I dropped my voice, 'I think you'd get on really well with the captain of my guards. Demon called Captain Nergal. He'll be around here somewhere. Listen out for the clanking of his weaponry.'

Amarath sniffed in disapproval, but given the glint in her eye and the careful positioning of her head to listen more carefully, she was actually going to track this guy down, perhaps for nothing more than comparing notes on swords. I shrugged mentally. She might as well have a go with him. They'd get on like a house on fire.

Ilrune lead me to the centre of the dance floor, taking my hands in his. I prayed that I would remember the dance steps Aleth had painstakingly rehearsed with me over the last two weeks, and not stand on his toes. Out of the corner of my eye, I spotted both my brothers with demonesses, and a flash of red dress approaching a trying-to-look-as-if-not-on-duty Nergal. I grinned to myself. The poor captain wouldn't know what hit him.

The evening flowed as easily as the *Styan*, an alcoholic version of *Stykka*. *Styan* was similar to wine, but it was still something I avoided. I may be part demon, but that didn't mean I could handle their alcohol. It was about ten times as potent as human wine. I wasn't going to touch the stuff for fear of what it would do to me, both in appearance and in terms of a hangover the next morning. Instead, I spent most of the night dancing, with Ilrune, with Shaeman, Vrael, even Kaleb at one point. In a week, I would be happily married. Tonight, I would enjoy myself. Amarath seemed to be hitting it off with Nergal. Vrael was dancing with a pretty, golden-haired demoness with a look of longing on his face. Shaeman was sitting at the side, talking to ademoness, who was flirting with all she had. Yes, things were good.

* * *

When I opened my eyes the next morning, I couldn't remember why today was so important. There was something really big happening. The guard in the corner shifted slightly. Daylight was beginning to seep around the curtains, taunting me with the knowledge that I should be getting up and beginning the usual morning duty of hearing the problems of my people and proposing solutions, followed by a tactical debriefing with the army captains about the state of my army. I seriously considered sticking my head under the pillow and going back to sleep. Aleth burst into the room, caught up in a hurricane of excitement, tearing open the curtains to let the red sunlight suffuse the room and ripping back the blankets.

'My Lady, you must rise and begin to prepare for your wedding!' I shot bolt upright. My wedding! Leaping out of bed, I shook off the last fingers of sleep, darting for my bathroom with Aleth close behind.

I don't really know when Aleth stopped being my lady's maid in her attitude towards me, becoming instead my best friend and one of my most trusted confidantes. On the morning of such an important day, I was infinitely glad for her company and expertise. I shed my nightclothes, diving into the bathing pool, already filled with scalding hot water. I surfaced, shaking out my hair. Aleth paused in her flitting around long enough to throw me a glass bottle of shampoo. Only once I smelled of my favourite pomegranate soap and had washed my hair into submission did I emerge from the pool, grabbing the towel left out for me. Aleth sat me down on a stool, running a critical eye over me. I tried to sit as still as possible. This was her territory, not mine. She nodded once, scurrying off. She returned with what I guessed were the underlayers of my wedding dress: a pair of dark grey leggings and the length of soft, white cloth that was usually wrapped around my midriff and chest to protect me from the sharp edges of my armour. Once they were in place, Aleth began attacking my hair with a ferocity I had only ever seen on the battlefield, drying it with her magic as she worked, fixing a couple of black feathers donated by Merlas into the locks as an acknowledgement to Ilrune's Careen origins. I tried very hard not to squirm under Aleth's attentions. With my wedding being one of the few occasions where I wasn't required to wear my mask, Aleth wanted to take full advantage of it, applying a black paint to outline my eyes and a deep red on my lips My lady's maid was having the time of her life, preparing me for this ceremony. For her, it was a case of showing off what she could do, the importance of her position. She darted away again, returning with my dress, which I was seeing for the first time. I slipped into the pale grey fabric, softer than those of my usual dresses, but cut in the same style, designed to flow rather than to protect, for beauty rather than utility. Aleth pulled at the lacing at the back of the dress, tying it off neatly before handing me my boots. I wrapped an intricately tooled sword belt around my waist, twice round, as was the Aspherin custom, one loop high on the waist, crossed on the left hip so that the second loop, holding the sword, rested just below the right hip. Aleth brought me the final piece of my dress, a cloak. She brushed the light grey fabric over my shoulders to drape down my back. I touched the clasp holding it up. Arellan's brooch. I hadn't worn it since I had taken over in Aspheri, but kept it safe in a small box in my bed chamber along with other objects of value from my time on Earth and in Synairn. I wanted my mother to be present for my wedding, to be proud of what I had become and pleased with my choice of husband. This was the only way I could pretend that she was here with me. I took one last look at myself in the silver glass. Every piece of metal gleamed, the delicate beadwork on the dress sparkled, my hair shone. Aleth clapped her hands, chattering excitedly. She darted away once more, returning this time with the circlet. I crouched down slightly for her to place it on my head. She took my hands in hers, smiling openly.

'You're ready, my Lady.'

I couldn't believe how nervous I felt as I walked, alone, towards the hall where the wedding was being held. Well, I say alone. Two guards were discreetly following me as always. A demoness was always supposed to walk alone to her wedding, supposedly to give her a last chance to run away if she didn't want to go through with it. But I did. I wanted this marriage. I wanted a chance at being willingly and happily married to a demon of my choice for the rest of what I hoped was going to be a very long life.

According to Careen custom, a trusted member of the bride's family would wait outside the hall of the ceremony in order to reassure a nervous bride if necessary and escort her inside. Aleth had refused to let me have any say in the wedding outside of a preferred colour scheme and the guest list. All I knew was that they had blended demonic and Careen traditions. I had no idea of what to expect. I had never realised before how much my footsteps echoed in the empty halls. The sound had always been hidden by other demons rushing around, going about their duty. Even the guards made little noise today.

Vrael stood waiting for me outside the hall, resplendent in his deep red demonic formal dress, his bow and quiver strapped across his back. Even for something as supposedly peaceful as a wedding, demons went in armed. He bowed deeply to me, one hand fisted over his heart as was the custom for a demon to his ruler. As he straightened up, he spoke to me, not as the Princess of Darkness, but as his sister.

'Are you prepared for this commitment?' he asked, his face and tone soft. I offered him a shaky smile.

'As ready as I'll ever be.'

'You do not wish to marry him?'

'Yes! I'm going to marry Ilrune, no matter what. No, facing a hall full of people I don't or barely know is what worries me.'

Vrael's faint expression of alarm faded. Taking my hand and raising it to shoulder height, he said, 'Then let us proceed without further delay. He is anxiously awaiting you.'

We turned to face the doors into the hall. Vrael used his magic to push them open. Inside, the fruits of Aleth's secretive labour beckoned.

I had to admit that Aleth had done well. The hall looked splendid. She had hung pennants of violet and pale grey from the walls and ceiling and liberally strewn *kai*, a flower of Aspheri resembling an Earthen lily, over the black, polished stone floor along with the occasional feather. Vrael lead me forwards, slowly walking towards the raised circular dais where Ilrune and Lucas were waiting for us. Vrael helped me to step up onto the dais before melting back into the crowd. I scanned the beings gathered there, dignitaries from allied dimensions intermingled with nobles from my own dimension as well as many of the winged Careen Ilrune had invited. I turned my eyes to my soon-to-be-husband, smiling at him. He smiled back with an expression of love in his eyes that, as clichéd as it sounds, made both my hearts skip a beat. He stepped behind me, taking my hands in his and folding them over my stomach. Silence fell over the hall. Lucas began reciting the marriage spells, weaving magic between Ilrune and I to unite us completely, our minds and our hearts locked together. For as long as we both lived, we would be more in tune with each other than with other demons, able to hear each other's thoughts even over long distances, able to feel every tiny emotion in each other's soul. The spells had been written long ago, when the position of Aspheri within the other demonic dimensions was precarious. A spellweaver of that era, many thousands of years ago, had realised that many of the fighting demons were distracted from the tasks at hand; worrying about and missing their mates. To remedy the situation, he had written the marriage spells, allowing the demons to know if their demonesses were safe and giving them the ability to communicate. Now, the threat from the other dimensions wasn't as great, but the spells had remained. I could already feel Ilrune's consciousness, a warm, comforting glow close to mine, growing ever closer as Lucas's spell came to its conclusion. Joy surged through my heart. Ilrune was now officially my husband, my companion, my mate. I turned to face him as Aleth stepped forward, holding the circlet of the Prince of Darkness. I took it from her, gazing at it for a moment. It was of a similar design to mine, but a thicker band of metal in the place of three braided strands and a single, larger bloodstone instead of three smaller ones. I touched the bloodstone briefly before reaching up to place the circlet on Ilrune's brow. It fitted him perfectly. He caught my hand, kissing my fingertips then moving to capture my lips. I was dimly aware of the hall cheering and applauding, but my mind was more engaged in Ilrune's kiss.

Reluctantly breaking away, he touched my cheek softly.

'I present to you Shadow of Aspheri and Ilrune of the Wingless, Princess and Prince of Darkness!' Lucas announced.

I found myself under attack as soon as I stepped off the dais. Amarath came at me with a flying leap and an ear-splitting screech, closely followed by Aleth. Vrael and Shaeman stood a little way off with the young of the clan, watching me with what seemed to be a glimmer of pride in their silver eyes. Even Vrael wore an uncharacteristic but welcome expression of warmth on his face as he stepped forwards to congratulate Ilrune in a somewhat quieter manner. I hugged Aleth and Amarath tightly before moving onto Archangel and Onyx. Ilrune came to stand next to me, looking down at them with a smile. I leant against him gently, glad of his easy acceptance of my twins. I had told him all about the pair, but they had never met. I held my breath for a moment, praying that the twins would accept him as easily as he had them. I needn't have worried. Archangel's face split into a wide grin as she charged at him with a fierce hug, followed closely by Onyx.

Although the ceremony may have lasted an hour, having to sit through the congratulations of the guests took quite a while longer. Thankfully, it was over dinner. I laughed alongside my family for the first time in years, teasing Amarath about her apparent affections for the captain of my guards. Vrael turned a delicate shade of grey when asked about his continuing relationship with Alba, with most of the questions being answered by Shaeman, much to the vampire's horror. Ilrune and I exchanged glances frequently, smiling at each other, barely able to believe the fortune that had befallen us.

Eventually, the party ended and the guests took their leave. I yawned as discreetly as I could, tired from the day's events. Ilrune leant down to rest his chin on my shoulder.

'The party may be ending, my dear Shadow, but the night is

far from over.' I smiled a little to myself, turning my head to look at him out of the corner of my eye.

'Why, Ilrune, I believe that is the kind of remark made before the dashing hero makes off with his girl.' Ilrune didn't respond to that, verbally at least. He swept me off my feet, into his arms. I gasped in surprise. He smiled, carrying me to what was now *our* private quarters.

He didn't put me down again until we stood in our bedroom, where he took my hands, holding them in the small of my back. I could feel my limbs trembling, although whether in anticipation or apprehension I couldn't tell. Despite having brothers and kids, I had never actually seen a naked man, let alone had proper intercourse. What strange creatures demons be. Ilrune must have sensed my worries and started to murmur reassuring words in my ear.

Well, I think you can guess what we did all night, I needn't go into detail. All I knew was that there were two satisfied part demons that night, and two more on the way.

PART 9

SYNAIRN – THE RETURN

Ilrune had been asking for a while if he could take me back to Synairn to present me to his people and, perhaps more importantly, to meet his parents. I have to admit, I guess I sort of looked for excuses not to go back. I would busy myself with the affairs of the dimension every time the topic came up. Now that I had been told by the council to take two weeks off to enjoy my marriage, I couldn't really refuse. Ilrune was delighted.

I hadn't been back for so long. Ilrune and I stood on a small hillock outside of the city, between it and the surrounding forests where the Careen lived. Merlas dropped her head, starting to graze quietly. Ilrune took my hand, squeezing it gently. Last time I had come back, it had been because of Arias and I had been too angry to really think. Now there was nothing to be angry about, nothing to distract me. Now all my thoughts were filled with that dark night that Armen had carried me though, bundling me onto Merlas's back and sending me on my way to a new life on Earth. The night Karthragan had killed Arellan.

'Worry not, Shadow, there is nothing here to harm you any more,' Ilrune assured me. I smiled faintly at him, squeezing his hand back.

The Careen villages were places that the Synari rarely ventured into. It was difficult to negotiate your way through the woodlands unless you either knew you way very well or had wings. However, the Careen also preferred to keep to themselves. Many did go to the city and were always very hospitable to the Synari who did make the effort to come to them. They were excellent healers and craftsmen, constructing their homes in the lofty treetops of the forest, accessible only by wing or magic. When Ilrune and I rode into the main village known as Kaliah, or 'home' in the language the Careen used before adopting Synari. Many of the winged people flew down from their homes, calling out to Ilrune, welcoming him home, saluting him and cracking jokes only they understood. I found myself under heavy scrutiny from them as well, mainly by the female population, as if they were trying to decide whether or not I was worthy of Ilrune's time. Without my mask to hide my face, I had to make an attempt to seem friendly, so I tried to smile as I listened to them murmuring amongst themselves. I wound my fingers into Merlas's mane, listening to her familiar snort as she judged my fears of rejection as silly. The Careen began to line the forest paths, watching and cheering their Wingless on. As we reached a particularly old and wide tree that I guessed had some symbolic meaning in their culture, Ilrune turned his pegasus round to face the crowd that had followed us. Taking my hand, he raised it above our heads.

'I present to you Shadow Roth of Aspheri, Princess of Darkness and my mate! Pray welcome her into the warmth of your hearts!'

I felt the blood rushing to my cheeks as the people loudly shouted their approval before they started to disperse. I breathed a quiet sigh of relief. At least for now, there hadn't been any outraged cries of 'half blood'.

'They will love you, worry not,' Ilrune said, glancing at me. I snorted softly, shaking my head.

'I'm fine,' I assured him. 'Simply readjusting to being in a dimension which has previously scorned me. It will take a little time for me to be at ease again. I'm still waiting for someone to twig who I am and start cursing me.'

Ilrune reached over to plant a kiss on my forehead with a smile. 'If anyone should do that to you, they would earn themselves the wrath of the Wingless. Now, I believe that there is a feast waiting for us at my home here.'

That evening, I lay curled up against Ilrune's side, my head resting on his stomach as he gently stroked my hair. It seemed that the Careen preferred to have blankets piled into a depression in the floor for their bed. Ilrune had explained that it was easier to lie comfortably in them with wings. I sighed contentedly, a sound that was echoed by Ilrune. We had eaten our fill of an amazing meal with the upper echelons of Careen society, we had no duties to worry about, just the sounds of the forest at night and each other. At least, until someone started banging on the tree the house was built in. I cast a puzzled look at Ilrune, wondering who could be calling at this time.

'Open up! City Guard!' called a voice from below. Ilrune pressed a finger to his lips, listening carefully as one of his servants jumped down from the tree to confront the Synari.

'Please keep your voice down sir. There are many children in this village who are asleep at this time. What urgency brings you to call here?'

'I have an arrest warrant for Shadow Roth. It has come to the attention of the High Priestess Arias that she has somehow escaped her prophesied death. If she is in the dimension, we are under orders to arrest her and take her to the city!' Ilrune pulled me to my feet as silently as he could, terror in his eyes that I was sure was echoed in mine. If Arias was looking for me, it did not bode well at all. I wouldn't be able to escape if the City Guard caught me. Arias would make sure of that. He ushered me to a window, grabbing a knife from a drawer and handing it to me. I slid it into the empty sheath on my forearm, looking cautiously out of the window.

'Shadow,' Ilrune said in a low, urgent tone, 'I will divert the guards. Flee into the forest and wait for me. Do not use your magic, not even to contact me. They will be able to track you if you do.' Looking down at the tree, I felt infinitely glad that I had elected to wear leggings under my dress. A mass of vines clung to the trunk which would make it easier to climb down. After hugging Ilrune tightly, I turned away, straddling the window ledge, planning the jump I needed to grab hold of the vines. If I missed, I would definitely be noticed by the City Guard. I had to be as discreet as possible. Taking a deep breath, I brought my legs up so that I was crouched on the ledge and jumped.

I leapt with a little more force than I needed. I collided with the tree trunk hard, my fingers scrabbling for a purchase on the thick vines, the toes of my boots scraping against the wood. For a few heart-stopping seconds, I thought I was going to fall. My fingers were starting to scream at me to get a move on. Slowly, hand below hand, foot below foot, I began to make my way slowly down the tree.

At long last, my boots touched the forest floor. I didn't hang around as I heard Ilrune's polite tones contrasting with the City Guard's harsh demands. I had to get out of here. Ilrune was safe. Ilrune would be okay. They wouldn't dare arrest him for fear of outraging the Careen. The Careen would be outraged on my behalf as well, although whether it was enough to make Arias release me would be another thing.

I started to run uphill, towards the top of the Deas mountains, where Ilrune would be able to come and find me later, when the City Guard had gone. There was no point in me trying to teleport away. Arias would have closed the dimensional barriers as soon as she realised that I had returned. Why she was so determined on catching me, I had no idea. In the one evening I had been here, I was fairly sure I hadn't broken any of the laws. Oh wait, there was always that bee in her bonnet she had about me still being alive, despite the best efforts of Karthragan and Meran. That was probably enough of an offence to her, the fact that I was still breathing. Unfortunately for her, I intended to keep on breathing.

'There! Get her!' came a cry from somewhere far enough behind me. Panic surged through my mind. I started to run as fast as I could. I had to get away from them. I couldn't let them catch me!

Stones scattered under my feet as I scrambled up the mountain. They were getting closer now, closer than ever. Their mount's hooves clattered on the rocky surface as they leapt after me. My skirt tangled around my legs, slowing me down. I tore the material with my claws, tossing it to the side, running in the leggings I wore underneath. My breath came in ragged pants and no matter how fast I ran, the City Guards were gaining on me. I took a sharp turn, hoping to throw them off. No such luck!

I broke out of the forest onto the summit of the mountain itself, skidding to a halt on the edge of the cliff, looking down. The edge of the dimension. The only thing down there was the void. An expanse of nothing that claimed the souls of the dead, isolating them for eternity. Not even Kaleb ruled over that domain. Arellan was down there somewhere. I could only hope that Karthragan was there as well. Glancing back over my shoulder, I could see the City Guard getting closer, their mounts slowing a little to negotiate the tricky terrain, stopping just on the edge of the trees.

'Halt there, Shadow! You are under arrest!' called out one of the guards.

'Not in your life,' I muttered, taking another step towards the edge of the cliff. They wouldn't come this far out to get me, no matter how much High Priestess Arias wanted me caught. The fragile ground beneath my feet began to crumble a little. I narrowed my eyes at the guards. Would they attempt to catch me if I decided to jump? If I let them catch me, what would my future hold? Either way, I lost. Either I died, or I died. Well, screw that! Closing my eyes, I took another step back, a step into nothingness, and started falling.

* * *

My head ached as I woke up. For a moment, disorientation

claimed me. Piece by piece, the fog started to lift over the last few conscious moments I had experienced. My head was spinning wildly as I sat up, my stomach lurched. Fighting to keep from throwing up, I looked around the room with apprehension. I shouldn't be alive. I jumped into the void. I should be dead, yet another soul lamenting in the endless dark. Instead, I was... Oh Goddess, I was in a cell! The stupid City Guard must have caught me! I pushed my hair back off my face, trying to think of some way to escape from this place. A flash of metal caught my eye. Around my arm, a thick bracelet had been clasped. Reaching out a hand to touch it, I hissed, pulling back sharply. Looking a little more closely, I could see a thin line of metal just a slightly different shade worked into it. Silver. Nice one. Now I was definitely not getting out of here. I had more chances going head to head against Teran while in human form.

The door creaked open to show four City Guards, their expressions set in stony glares. Returning the look, I got to my feet, making a show of dusting off what was left of my dress. The captain of the squad made an impatient noise in the back of his throat.

'Come on, half-blood, we haven't got all day. Get a move on!'

I treated him to another cool glare as I stepped out of the cell, allowing two of the guards to take my arms, leading me out into the city itself, where the Synari waited expectantly. I looked down at them, raising an eyebrow. What were they all gathered for? High Priestess Arias stood in front of them, saying something I couldn't hear. The High Priestess Arias, beneficent ruler of Synairn. Yeah, right. No one in the crowd moved. No one spoke. Her silver hair glinted like a thousand daggers in the biting wind, despite the darkness. The towers loomed above the people, casting bitter shadows as they blocked out the despairing warmth of the sun struggling to heat the streets.

The High Priestess led the procession, with me escorted behind her, to the temple of the goddess. A statue of a woman with her arms outstretched in benefaction stood at the top of a sweeping flight of stairs. As Arias strode up the stairs, the cracks of age in the temple's impassive face seemed to deepen. The dark oak doors lost their warm look, turning to a glaring hole in the face of the pallid stone. The loving face of the statue turned to the empty look of a mother holding an unwanted child before her family. Arias was the high priestess. She was the Goddess's representative in Synairn, the benevolent ruler. But I knew who she really was. She wanted power, nothing more, and I was a threat to that power. It didn't matter that I didn't want her place. She saw me as competition for the top seat and that was enough. The altar in front of the statue loomed above the crowd. The susurration of Arias's voice passed over my head. I couldn't be bothered to listen to her. At least, until the final sentence.

'And to appease our beloved Goddess, who has seen fit to plague our lives with misery these past many years, I offer to sacrifice the cause to our Goddess! The half-blood Arellan brought into this world!'

Whoa, sacrifice? Forget it! I had died once already, and I wasn't planning on doing it again any time soon! I started to pull against the guards holding me, determined to escape, but the silver was doing its job. I was no stronger than a human. All I could do was make it as hard as possible for them to drag me towards the altar. Digging my heels in, biting at them, head-butting one of them, I tried every single dirty trick I knew, but they had armour in all the appropriate places. The only piece of grim satisfaction I could draw from my fight was that it took four guards to drag me to the stone table, and a further two to make sure I stayed down as they threaded ropes through convenient little notches to keep me in place. Arias stood by the table, looking down at me.

'You have had this coming for a long time, demoness.'

I didn't deign to answer than with anything more than to spit in her eye. She wanted to kill me, fine. Don't think I was going to respect her for it. She growled in anger, wiping her eyes with her hand before raising a long, ceremonial knife. I glared at her, daring her to do it. The knife plunged twice, through both my hearts. Pain lanced through me briefly as blood began to spill from the wounds. Somewhere in the back of my mind, I began thinking about the life I had lived. About my family. For a cursed half blood born into a world that didn't want it, I had done well. In my mind, I could see Amarath, who had taught me how to really fight, who had saved my backside more than once, with her limp, her sarcastic quips and sharp tongue. The blood was starting to run down the sides of my chest, dripping down onto the stone. I could see Shaeman, the big brother, who tried in vain to teach Amarath how to ride a pegasus, his strong bond with his brother, his coffee strong enough to keep you up for a week. The blood outlined grooves carved into the altar's surface, starting to trickle down to the ground, staining the white stone black. Vrael, with his quiet disposition, his vulnerable periods spent shut away in his room with nothing more than three vials of blood and a book, his measured tones and his determination to help creatures, from nursing back a bird that had crashed into a window to helping Amarath and I deliver children. I could barely feel the pain now. I stared at the sky, my breath rasping in my chest. From somewhere close by, I could hear Ilrune's voice screaming my name. Ilrune's voice, Kaleb's voice, Amarath's, Vrael's, Shaeman's. I didn't turn my head. Then Arellan's voice.

'Take my hand, Alexai, it is over. It is all over. No one can hurt you now. Take my hand.'

**OUR STREET
BOOKS**

Our Street Books for children of all ages, deliver a potent mix of
fantastic, rip-roaring adventure and fantasy stories to excite the
imagination; spiritual fiction to help the mind and the heart
grow; humorous stories to make the funny bone grow; historical
tales to evolve interest; and all manner of subjects that stretch
imagination, grab attention, inform, inspire and keep the pages
turning. Our subjects include Non-fiction and Fiction, Fantasy
and Science Fiction, Religious, Spiritual, Historical, Adventure,
Social Issues, Humour, Folk Tales and more.